THE

MERMAID MADONNA

*'The isles of Greece,
the isles of Greece!
Where burning Sappho
loved and sung.'*

The Mermaid Madonna

Stratis Myrivilis

Stratis Myrivilis, born in 1892 on the Isle of Mytilene in the Aegean Sea, is today the most highly respected and foremost literary figure in Greece, and occupies an assured place in the world of letters.

Myrivilis studied philosophy and law at the University of Athens. From 1912 to 1922 he was a volunteer in the service of his country, participating in the Greco-Turkish and Greco-Bulgarian wars and in World War I. Twice wounded, Myrivilis received many medals and citations. During World War II he was active in the Greek underground.

By profession Stratis Myrivilis is an author and journalist. He has written numerous successful novels *(The Life in Tomb, The Schoolmistress with the Golden Eyes, The Mermaid Madonna, The Argonautes, Vassilis Arvanitis, The Goblins, Pan)*, short stories *(Stories, Red Stories, The Green Book, The Blue Book, The Red Book, The Vermilion Book)*, essays *(Man and Art, Lonliness and Art, Woman and Art, The High Peak, Byzantine Music, Thought and Heart, The Law of the Heart)* and poems *(The Song of the Earth, The Small Flames)* and has published newspapers and literary journals. His works have been translated into many foreign languages, and as author and scholar he has won the plaudits of critics throughout Europe.

Originally published in Greek under the title

Η ΠΑΝΑΓΙΑ Η ΓΟΡΓΟΝΑ

Stratis Myrivilis

THE

MERMAID MADONNA

Translated from the Greek by Abbott Rick

EFSTATHIADIS GROUP

Greek edition ©1955 Stratis Myrivilis, Athens
English translation ©1959 Hutchinson & Company (Publishers) Ltd.

First published in Great Britain
by Hutchinson & Company (Publishers) Ltd., 1959

First published in Greece
by Efstathiadis Group 1981

ΕΥΣΤΑΘΙΑΔΗΣ GROUP A.E.
ΕΚΔΟΣΕΙΣ, ΕΙΣΑΓΩΓΕΣ & ΕΜΠΟΡΙΑ ΒΙΒΛΙΩΝ
ΚΕΝΤΡ.: ΔΡΑΚΟΝΤΟΣ 88 - ΑΘΗΝΑ ΤΚ 104 42
ΤΗΛ. 210 5195800 - FAX: 210 5195900

ISBN 960 226 087 4

© ΕΥΣΤΑΘΙΑΔΗΣ GROUP A.E. 2007

Printed and bound in Greece

1

D I R E C T L Y in front of the fishing port, and looking the west wind straight in the eye, stands the Chapel of the Madonna, on the crest of a huge sea rock which the villagers call the Mount of the Madonna. Anchored firmly to the bottom, this massive rock tosses its mane like some monster of the deep that had turned to stone as it lunged halfway above the water. By building out to meet the rock, the villagers have easily constructed the harbour breakwater, which also serves as a bulwark against the wild gales from Anatolia.

In the afternoon when shadows darken the water, the Mount takes on the colour of old rose in the sunlight. At night its bulk rises above the shoreline, bleak and sombre, like a sentinel watching over the few houses and shops of Skala. Transient fishermen, overtaken by darkness, climb to the top and cook their food over fires that they kindle in the hollows. As they move about, their elongated shadows flicker across the white-washed walls of the chapel and vanish.

The chapel in no way resembles the small architectural gems which the Byzantine masters planted all over Greece. Solid and four-square, it was erected less than a century ago with more devoutness than taste by a few God-fearing sailors and stone-masons.

With the contractor they were passing by in a small sailing ship on their way to a town on the north side of the island where they had been engaged to build a soap factory. Suddenly they were caught in a violent squall. Just as the ship was about to capsize off Cape Korakas, the Mount of the Madonna loomed up before them. 'Save us, Holy Virgin,' implored the contractor, 'and we will build you a chapel.'

The sqall immediately subsided. Workmen and crew made straight for the harbour of Panayia. There they moored the ship and hastened to fulfil their vow. This is why the chapel, the work of humble artisans, looks like an oil shop.

A bell hangs from a plain iron arch. Also of iron is the cross on the roof. Behind the apse, a tall ship's mast embedded in the rock with molten lead originally served for a flagstaff. The relic of some Greek naval battle, it had somehow drifted into these waters. The islanders salvaged it and after the liberation from the Turks they planted it up there. Every Sunday they raised a blue and white Greek flag for all to admire as it rippled joyously in the breeze.

Then came years of hardship. War, poverty, political unrest lrained the people's vitality. The flag gradually was tattered by the winds, bit no one was interested enough to replace it. So the mast was abandoned to bleach and warp in sun and weather.

Formerly, before the wars began, a silver vigil lamp burned perpetually before the icon screen inside the chapel. Every night its tiny flame lit up the blue pane of the high round window. It was like an eye watching tenderly through the night over the uniform lapping of the waves, the slumbering boats and houses, and the endless olive forest which swayed and whispered beeath the stars with thousands of infinitesimal, mysterious rustlings.

This lasted as long as Captain Lias occupied the chapel. He was nicknamed the *dedes* (the hermit) because he lived there in solitude like a Moslem ascetic in his cell. He made it his business to see that everything was kept clean and bright—the floor stones, the window-panes and the brass—and that the tiny beacon never lacked oil or a fresh wick.

Nobody knew where this man had come from. Among the old residents of Mouria who got to know him, some said he was from Tchesme but others said he was from Alatsata. He himself never spoke of his life. Once when someone thoughtlessly asked him about his origin, he was silent for a moment and then, looking off into the distance replied: 'I am of this world like you, my son. So, you see, we are fellow countrymen.' Years have passed since he picked up and went away (no one ever learned where he went or when he died), but his reply still passes from mouth to mouth like a proverb or the tag of a tale. 'I am of this world like you. We are fellow countrymen, my son.'

In the chapel was a small, wooden locker in which he stored his tools, brushes, and cans of oil paint and water colours, as well as a mallet, a wedge, tow, pitch and everything necessary for caulking and repairing a hull. But his chief delight and enthusiasm lay in painting mermaids and flowers on the bows of caïques which their owners entrusted to him for refurbishing. All his mermaids had the archaic smile of ancient statues, the same smile that was on his own face. His flowers were done in unnatural colours. He painted roses blue, green, and silver, and the leaves, purple or blue, according to the hue that pleased his fancy at the moment.

The seamen said to him: 'Roses, you know, are red, Captain Lias. Why is it yours have the colour of unripe almonds?'

'This is the way mine are', the captain would reply with a smile but without raising his head. 'You can find red and white roses in any garden, my son, but these are the only blue and green roses in the whole world.'

From his bearing the villagers concluded that Captain Lias had been, not a monk, but a skipper who had come down in the world, a disinherited son of the sea, one of those weather-beaten derelicts cast up from time to time like uprooted, polished tree trunks which the gales of Asia Minor drive to our shores from no one knows where.

Then one morning Captain Lias vanished from the Mount of the Madonna. It was in the midsummer of 1914, the day before the first refugees arrived. It was never learned where the *dedes* went or why he so abruptly forsook his lodging, but it was rumoured that possibly there was some person in Anatolia whom in no circumstances did he wish to meet again.

After the war of 1912-13, when it was reported that the Turks were going to drive the Christians out of Anatolia, Captain Lias said to the panicking villagers, 'Don't behave like that. Wherever we go, we are only sojourners. Let us be sure that our bundle is tied and ready for departure at any minute and that we have a knife to cut the mooring quickly.'

So had it been in his own case.

When his time to leave came, he set his box of tools on his back, unflinchingly severed the cable of his mooring and disappeared. But his name stayed with us and—most important of all—a strange painting on a wall of the chapel, where it can still be seen, partially effaced by the salt sea air, the most remarkable Madonna in Greece and in the whole of Christendom.

Her head is done in the familiar, conventional Byzantine style—a dark-complexioned face, sensitively drawn, with an expression of reserve, rounded chin, almond eyes, and a small mouth. A purple pallium surronds the upper part of her body and covers her head down to her eyebrows. There is also the golden halo, as in all the icons. Her eyes are extraordinarily wide and green in colour. But from the waist down, she is a fish with blue scales; and in one hand she holds a ship and in the other a trident like that of the ancient sea god, Poseidon.

When the fishermen and the villagers first saw this painting, they stood in wonder before it, but it did not seem odd to them. The women said their prayers to it and offered it incense as they did to the other icons.

It was called the Mermaid Madonna, as it is to this day, and from it the chapel and the port took their names. No one stopped to reflect that, on the day when this Madonna was conceived in the mind of the old hermit, there sprang as from the head of Zeus and established herself on this unique sea rock near an Aegean island a new Greek divinity, who in a miraculous manner united all the epochs and all the meaning of the race—a race that struggles with the elements and tempests of the world, half on land and half on the sea, with the ploughshare and the keel, always subject to a warlike divinity, female and virgin.

The villagers, the fishermen, the skippers and transient captains regarded the Mermaid Madonna without suprise, for she already dwelt in their souls where Captain Lias had dived and brought her up, and thus they had known her long before he gave her to them on the chapel wall.

2

T H E natural beauty of the countryside here is something to see. This Aeolian landscape loses none of its charm whether it is scorched by the heat of August or battered by the winter. The mountains descend in graceful lines to the coast, the land gaily rises and falls like the sea, and everywhere there are trees, coloured rocks, and the eager wash of the surf on the beach.

The valleys are adorned with vertical poplars rising like rows of candles from Skala up to the village of Mouria. They are dainty trees, with leaves that quiver incessantly even when no wind is blowing. When autumn turns them yellow, their silver boughs catch fire and blaze with golden flames.

The sky is liquid; and the sea, ebbing and flowing, glitters on all sides through the trees. Its water is as clear as holy water and on the studded bottom are stones, shells and marine flowers of every conceivable hue.

High up on the mountainside lies the village of Mouria. The whitewashed houses have been built helter-skelter among the olive and almond trees and look like a flock of sheep scattering in panic. From there the descent to Skala is easy. But the climb is such rough going that it takes three times as long even by the steep mule path from Skala.

The factory, a large olive mill with four presses, is in Skala. When the olives are ripe, and harvesters from Mouria pour down, company after company, decked out in all their finery and swinging huge baskets. The mill is filled with workers, and the fields and roads with pickers.

This is the olive season, for which all ninety-eight villages of the island wait each year, since the entire population of 150,000 poor folk and well-to-do, depends on the olive branch for its livelihood.

The fishermen are poorer but more secure. The sea, however much it is harvested, is never exhausted. It knows only the ploughing of the keel. In winter, the sea turns dark as vinegar. Many of the boats are drawn up on land where they rest on blocks until the weather becomes milder, for the north wind gives this harbour a severe punishment.

It is a fine spectacle to watch the Mount of the Madonna ride the tempest when a blustery norther from the Gulf of Adramytti throws the world into chaos, and Cape Babas, opposite, deflects the currents from the straits of Constaninople to send our way the mighty floods from Mount Athos.

The Mount of the Madonna has waged battle from the beginning of the world. It is covered with ancient wounds and pocked with scars. Its stone is saturated with brine; the pounding of the surf has pitted its breast.

The waves leap out of the murk. Towering like dragons, they descend savagely, thrusting forward their bulging, tiger-streaked chests and toss their foamy manes in the gale. Driven by titanic fury, they sweep in with a roar and in a final burst rise, howling, and crash down on the Mount. Enormous masses of water grind their teeth and bellow as they strike and try to undermine, pulverize, and consume it.

During the onslaught the foundations of the Mount shudder to their roots. But the Mount does not give way a step. It plants its rocky feet in the black depths and its whole mass smokes with rage. The contest fills it with the power and fury of a wild animal. It groans and trembles. From its bared jaws it spews foam into the face of the sea. The more furiously the tempest belabours it, the more savagely it rears itself. The rock knows that it alone is the defence of the caïques, the fishing boats, and the light craft behind its broad shoulders. They shrink back in fright between their double moorings and pull at the cables like strong, simple beasts overwhelmed by terror while tied to their halters.

The storm demon wears himself out during the night. He whistles through his fingers above the mastheads and down the chimneys. He stands astride the arch that holds the bell of the Madonna, hangs from its iron tongue and clangs it with crazy irregularity.

The fishermen hear the mad tolling in their sleep; the Mouriotes hear it up on the heights. The sailors open their eyes worriedly under their quilts and curse. The women softly leave their beds, offer incense to the icons and cross themselves.

'May the Mermaid Madonna defend the world!'

Then the sky breaks through the tempest and each gust of wind is seen driving the shredded water over the surface of the waves and blowing it into the air. The salt spray rises in clouds and dusts the roofs until the tiles become encrusted with white crystals. At last the water elementals become exhausted, the sea abates, and the waves subside.

The sun bursts out gloriously above the crest of Vigla and the olive trees drip with peace. Once more the rock laughs in the golden light. Still drenched and battered, it pants wearily and glitters with diamonds, but it stands solid and unshaken. On its summit it wears like a battlement the Chapel of the Madonna with its bell and crooked, flagless mast. It also wears a clump of wild fig trees that have drunk the brine of the sea and remain unwithered, as a dandy puts a spring of basil behind his ear when he has given a good account of himself in a brawl. At such times the rock is as debonair as a pallikari (brave youth).

When the weather turns mild and begins to smell of spring, nothing is more attractive that the Mount of the Madonna. The rock glows in the sun like warm flesh. The fishermen, after furling their sails, go up and hang their dripping nets on the chapel wall, on crossed oars set upright and from the iron bell arch. The wind blows them out like veils. They have been dyed in boiled poplar bark and are the colour of rust. Often there are so many that they completely envelop the chapel. No other Madonna in Christendom except the Mermaid Madonna wears such veils.

3

U N T I L the Anatolian disaster, Captain Lias, the *dedes*, was the only foreigner among the few inhabitants of Skala. The ones who now swarm over the waterfront with their families and boats and have so greatly increased the population of Skala, all came from Anatolia, only a short distance away by ship, at the time of the persecutions.

They arrived here one dismal day. Destitute and harassed, they came with their hearts in their mouths. In their frantic eyes remained the reflected flames of unlicensed pillage. Their breeches were rolled up to their broad, woollen cummerbunds. On their heads they wore caps of frayed velvet.

The afternoon was overcast and the leaden waves were swelling without breaking when the boats suddenly appeared through the mist. Soon the sea was covered with caïques huddled together and approaching laboriously on the heaving billows.

There were fishing boats and old rowboats, some with a bedsheet or a woman's dress for a sail. They entered the harbour by short tacks. The Skaliotes thronged the breakwater, watching and waiting to seize ropes and lend a hand. A shocked, subdued murmur rose from the crowd:

'The refugees. . . .! The refugees. . . .!'

The flotilla drew nearer. Loaded to the gunwales and weighed down with a silence that was even heavier, one after another entered the port, hauled sail, and threw out ropes which the villagers looped around the stanchions to bring them alongside the breakwater.

Most of the boats were decrepit vessels with weathered timbers and faded paint, but a few, here and there, were new. Their red and blue paint was mirrored even in the grey water.

This incongruous brightness as well as the names ornamented with flowers and scrolls on the sides contrasted dissonantly with the horror and misery aboard.

The refugees disembarked pell-mell—men, women, and children. Their faces were grimy and copper-green; their teeth were clenched. Their staring eyes were inflamed and swollen from lack of sleep. They had brought their wounded with them and some of their dead, among whom was a youthful, fair-haired woman. Her cheek was gashed, her chin was bound with a white cloth, and her eyes were fixed wide open on the sky. They were jet black eyes.

The corpses were rigid and were taken off in old army blankets. There was no weeping, just the words 'Easy now.Take it by the armpits. Throw the rope', as if they were unloading freight. They put ashore an old man who had been blinded in both eyes. He stood on land, crossed himdelf, and started for the sea, holding his arms in front of him. A woman took him by the arm and pulled him back saying: 'This way, you poor devil!'

The man turned back. His eyes had been gouged out with a knife and were red, gaping sores.

There was a young mother who held in her arms a very thin little boy wrapped in a red-fringed blanket. His skinny legs dangled back and forth. His pale right arm hung over his mother's back and his head rested motionlessly on her shoulder.

Those who ran to assist her thought he was sick. But he was dead. He had died only a short while ago.The young women held him as if he were merely ill. She refused to let his head be uncovered lest he should take cold, but she knew he was dead.

Her husband leaped off the boat to give her his hand. He was a short, sturdy man, bare-headed, with curly hair. He noticed that his wife had trouble in leaning against him, since in her left hand, which was not occupied with the child, she clutched something wrapped in a blue tablecloth. She gave him the bundle to hold for her.

He took it and unwrapped the cloth. When he saw it was only an icon, he ground his teeth. Without a word he stuffed the cloth in his belt and broke the icon across his knee. It snapped in two and he threw the pieces one at a time into the sea.

'Come. Get out,' he said brusquely to the woman.

She glanced frightenedly at the two pieces of floating wood. Then she crossed herself and silently went ashore with the child in her arms, her thin, dark face grimly set. The blue glass bracelets tinkled on her arms as she stepped on land. She looked back at the broken icon and crossed herself.

One old woman, as soon as she placed her feet on the breakwater, fell to her knees and prostrated herself. She fondled the earth in her withered hands, kissed it, and wailed loudly, like a lost bird. Then others around her began to weep.

Now that the silence had been broken, the little square of harbour was loud with the tumult of noisy voices. The islanders were making a great stir in their eagerness to help the distressed. They seemed more upset than the refugees. Somehow, weeping and sobbing, they managed to lodge these homeless people in old houses and shops and in huts in the fields nearby. Some were even put in the warehouses where the factory owners stored olives for pressing. The island women brought them food, raki and coffee to revive them.

Dr. Platanas came down from Mouria with his medicine bag. He was fat, ruddy and stocky with fierce, bushy eyebrows like misplaced moustaches. He puffed out his cheeks and said: 'My, my, my,' and with his pudgy, hairy hands sterilized wounds and bound them with gauze bandages.

The dead they buried up in Aya Sotira, the cemetery of Mouria. An old church is there outside the village, surrounded by a grove of venerable evergreen oaks, sombre trees with a dense foliage of dark green, metallic leaves with sharp barbs. Near the graves are wild rose-bushes and clumps of yellow daisies which riot in the spring as they draw nourishment from the dead.

The whole village went to the funeral and wept. They were quick to comfort those who had been bereaved by ill-fortune, for in their troubled souls they knew their duty and responsibility to the race. Here the island women who had lost sons in the war and in the prison camp renewed their grief. Around the family graves they mourned loudly for the unburied dead who had loyally remained in Anatolia.

4

T H E refugees at first kept strictly to themselves like hunted animals safe for the time in a hollow tree from which they peer furtively and suspiciously at the outside world. Their sombre, desperate eyes smouldered with hostility and distrust. They cast oblique glances, lowered their heads and spoke in hushed voices. They were wary about answering questions. After measuring the inquirer from head to foot, they refused to reply or lied with childlike artlessness.

Then all of a sudden the women with their scarred heels and gnarled hands started boasting to the islanders about the fine two- and three-storeyed houses they had been forced to abandon.

They described gardens and olive plantations where the music of running streams and singing birds caused the heart to bloom like a rose. They spoke of estates that would never again be theirs, and they kept their haggard eyes fixed on Anatolia as if they could still see all this luxury and magnificence.

It was not mere boasting for effect. It was the anguish of nostalgia, the flaming love for their wretched, miserable hovels which thus transfigured these abandoned dwellings in their over stimulated fantasy. It was this that transformed into gardens with running streams the courtyard plots with tiny bitter almond trees and the pots of basil and other commonplace house-plants.

The islanders listened patiently to all these silly fabrications. They nodded their heads and exchanged glances with each other, for they knew that the really wealthy landowners over there had vanished into the 'work battalions' and had perished in the flames or by the sword. Those who had escaped were the rabble, a nondescript spawn of beggarly fishermen who lived from hand to mouth. Some of them even engaged in smuggling and illegal dynamite fishing and barely managed to keep one jump ahead of the police or the Turkish revenue officers.

The odd thing, however, was that for all the readiness with which they described the blessings they had left behind, it was difficult to get anything out of them about the atrocities they had survived. When they undertook to relate such things, their eyes became veiled and their tongues twisted into knots. If one asked them, for example, why such and such a person, whom everybody in Mouria knew, had not come with them, they shrugged their shoulders and said curtly, 'They took him away.'

'Away where?'

'Oh, away.'

'And Manolis Mitsaphis, the baker, what happened to him?'

'Oh, they captured him, tied him up with his wife and son, lighted a fire in the oven, and threw them into it. They tied them up with wire.'

The refugees skimmed rapidly over details of this kind, and refused to say another word.

But as the days went by, the pain of exile diminished and the refugees became more at ease. The new Skaliotes slowly realized that fate had dealt most generously with them in the circumstances. Here were excellent fishing grounds, virgin territory that had not been worked for many years, since before the war, the Mouriotes were so prosperous from their trade with Turkey that they had no need of fishing with its labour and hardships. So the refugees accepted their lot, pulled themselves together, and went to work.

They overhauled and caulked the boats. There was the smell of paint and boiling pitch everywhere. The cliffs echoed with the blows of mallets and clubs crushing the bark to make dye for the new nets.

Thus the harbour of Panayia resounded with the din of industry, and the shore was lined with nets. The government provided some assistance, and the islanders voluntarily imposed a heavy tax on oil and created an ample fund for the relief of the refugees in their emergency.

The fishing grounds of Panayia were just what these people needed. It was not long before they felt themselves once more in a position to resume the struggle for a livelihood. They fished, cursed, drank raki, danced under the vine trellises of the coffee-houses and begot children one after the other.

The women, worn by care and trouble, were not beautiful, but most of them had the lovely dark eyes of their race, which sparkled with cleverness and flashed with passion. No sooner had they recovered their spirits and established themselves under a roof than they married and bore offspring. It was the talk of the village. One never saw a refugee woman in Skala who was not either pregnant or with a child at the breast.

They brought forth their children in hovels and huts, behind the sacking curtains that permitted two families to live in one room. They even gave birth on boats under lowered sails, without a doctor and without fuss and bother. One child was not placed at the breast before another was on the way.

Within a few years the shore of Skala, the cliffs of Panayia and Vigla, the beach of Kaya, and the square were loud with the shouting of youngsters. The country was fertile and the climate was favourable. Like all sturdy weeds, these people eagerly rooted themselves in the new soil, clung to the rocks and crannies, and prolifically put forth lusty shoots for future seeding.

One day the Housing Commission paid a visit. They saw the refugees packed together like sardines and they saw the wretched shanties they had for dwellings, the families lumped together, young and old, men and women, sleeping side by side at night. These cramped conditions created a serious problem.

There was constant quarrelling among the women of the families that were separated by curtains of sacking. They would strike each other, pull their hair, scream unrepeatable obscenities until their husbands came home at night from fishing or from the taverns and beat them into silence. When they wearied of this pastime, each man would take his wife into his arms on the pallet and caress her until her moans fell into the rhythm of love. The small boys and girls, wide awake, observed and heard all this and became thoroughly educated far in advance of their years.

5

T H E Bishop of Hora learned of this predicament and persuaded the Commission to alleviate it. A native of Moschonisi in Aivali, he was a fellow countryman of the refugees, and before he became a 'fisher of men' he had been himself a fisher lad and many times had helped his father with nets. He understood these people and was filled with compassion for them. But these riff-raff responded to his good offices quite unexpectedly.

When the Commission called a meeting of the fishermen to inform them of the plan to build homes for them, houses of their very own which they could occupy for life, they received the news ungraciously with sour grimaces, and glanced suspiciously at each other. Afterwards they gathered at the coffee-houses and heatedly discussed the news. Why, to put it bluntly, should the Commission bestow an entire house on each family of barefoot, destitute folk like themselves as casually as if it were just a box of cigarettes? What was behind this sudden generosity and what did the Commission hope to get in return?

'Not a thing,' said the Commission. The idea was merely to rescue the refugees from their wretched living conditions.

That was difficult for the fishermen to believe.

'Free, did they say? Whom do they think they're hoodwinking?'

'Politics!' said the cleverer ones and put their fingers to their temples. 'It's politics. Athens is trying to force us to stay here so they can use our property in Anatolia for bargaining with the Turks. Let's watch our step!'

Old Avgustis, the schoolmaster, fired them with his fanatical rhetoric.

'We're all right the way we are. And when the time comes for us to have houses again, they will be our own, our ancestral homes!'

While the refugees were working and multiplying here on the island, their minds were obsessed with the dream of going back to Anatolia. 'When the time comes,' they would say. They meant when arrangements would be made for their return. They would climb the Mount of the Madonna to gaze at their homeland, almost so close that if you cast a spear it would impale itself in the threshold of one of the ruined houses. They would gaze, sigh nostalgically, and work themselves up emotionally.

'No houses. We don't want any houses.'

In Athens, meanwhile, each political party tried to attract the immense refugee population which poured into the land and was a solid bloc of potential votes for whoever could herd them to the ballot boxes.

So unscrupulous political leaders arose who played on the homesickness of the refugee bloc. 'Don't worry,' they said. 'We'll get you back at the point of the sword, if necessary.'

It is a tradition in Greece for generals to turn to politics when they have no war on their hands. One of them, the most ambitious and the most unscrupulous, had formed an impressive party dedicated to the return of the refugees. He published a newspaper in Athens for which he wrote editorials filled with demagogic bombast. He signed himself: The Thunderbolt.

Avgustis, the schoolmaster, kept a copy of this newspaper in his pocket like a sacred talisman. He was a poor man with a puny, shrivelled body, but his eyes burned with unquenchable fire. For forty-five years he had taught in the Anatolian schools and all this time he had inspired faith in the rebirth of Great Greece in the hearts of his pupils.

The race, so he preached, will recover its ancient heritage. It will return to the fathermost places of which it has been despoiled as soon as it has expiated its sins against the Lord. 'Once again when the time comes. . . . '

The rehabilitation of the refugees which Greece of the mainland was trying to effect on her own soil he regarded as the ultimate betrayal. Should he, a teacher, remain aloof from his gullible people at a time when their historic destiny was at stake? Could he, with folded hands, watch the fires die out, the fires which for a score of years he had kept alive in the youth entrusted to him by the stricken race? What now should be his mission in the face of the new calamity which friends and enemies alike were preparing for the Greece of the Diaspora?

The fishermen listened to him passionately. He was educated and also one of themselves. Resistance to the housing project gathered force. The Bishop, nevertheless, stubbornly insisted on decent quarters for these toughened vagabonds of the sea.

He called them together, spoke to them in the language they understood, and showed them the shortsightedness of those who were influencing them against their best interests. The Commission, furthermore, was disgusted and ready to throw the handle after the axe and leave them to the mercy of the Lord.

A severe winter came to the aid of the Bishop. The miserable lodgings of the refugees were no defence ? ıst the cold. Children died of pneumonia. At last the Bishop prevailed. He ordered the fishermen to organize themselves into a corporation and elect a committee.

After endless bickering and quarrelling, they elected Varouhos president. He was not only the best qualified and the most level-headed among them, but he also had a certain kinship with the Bishop through his wife, Nerandji, as she divulged. This relationship was rather tenuous, a matter of the Bishop's father being Nerandji's godfather, but it lent great prestige to Varouhos in the eyes of the refugees.

Nerandji was not a typical fisherman's wife. She alone among the women was not at her husband's beck and call. Her mind was keener than Varouhos's, and she controlled her husband's views on all matters as firmly as she governed the household. He respected her intelligence and did as she told him. So although Varouhos was held in high regard by all, it was his wife who sustained him with her canny advice.

As president of the corporation, Varouhos had to make frequent visits to Hora on the housing business, which now was progressing smoothly. Every time Nerandji saw him off at the breakwater, she waited till the boat was so far away that she had to shout. Then she would cup her hands to her mouth and admonish him solemnly:

'And don't forget to stop at the Cathedral and present our reverences to the holy Bishop!'

6

T H E fishermen were in the habit of meeting outside Fortis's coffee-house, the Mulberry Tree, to discuss—sensibly now—the housing project. The coffee-house took its name from a huge mulberry tree which spread its branches nearby. It bore no fruit but it provided deep shade for the wide, level garden patch in front of the coffee-house.

In the evening a flock of birds would roost in the dense foliage and make a fearful racket with their chattering. Fortis was fond of them, but the fishermen had no such affection, for they soiled caps and fouled the coffee-tray with their droppings. 'Tsk! Again?' they grumbled as they wiped themselves and went so far as to threaten not to come there any more. Fortis would smile reproachfully at the birds and then say to the fishermen:

'I'd be sorry if you stayed away, but they came here before you did. It wouldn't be fair to drive them away.'

He couldn't very well drive them away, for he practically lived with them. His rooms, of course, were on the second floor of the coffee-house, but all summer, noon and night, he would climb a ladder into the tree and sleep in a small wooden chamber he had built among the brances. He drew the ladder up after him so as not to be disturbed. While is wife was alive, she, too, would follow him up into this airy bower on balmy summer nights when the cicadas sang incessantly and the sky and sea were a-glitter with stars.

One day when he was tossing his little son, Lambis, in his arms, he pointed out to him the high wooden nest.

'Do you see that, you? That's where you came down into this world. Just like the birds.'

His wife looked at him reprovingly, then lowered her eyes and blushed.

She was dead now. She died during her second confinement and left him with Lambis, his only child.

There were other coffee-houses in Skala, but the better class of Mouriotes went to Fortis's when they came down to buy fish. They preferred Fortis because the credits he chalked on the wall behind the door were honest, and his coffee was not adulterated by so much as a grain of barley, and his raki was double- or triple-distilled. But, more than all, they enjoyed his marvellous stories which for as many times as they were retold never lost their flavour and were never discouraged.

Fortis was a legendary figure. Like another Sindbad the Sailor, he regaled his patrons tirelessly with accounts of his travels, particularly in America, and these were so remarkable that they utterly dumbfounded his listeners, who often wondered if such things were really true or if Fortis had confused fantasy and odds and ends he picked up in the glossy magazines which arrived monthly in bulky packages from New York.

The fact that Fortis had crossed the Atlantic four or five times was in itself enough to make the fishermen listen to him with attention. For six years he had been employed in the Ford plant. He pronounced the name 'Fortis' and spoke it so frequently, that at last it became his permanent nickname.

His job had consisted entirely of standing in front of a bench and tapping the heads of screws as they passed before him in a row on a belt. One day a screw flew up and struck him in the eye. He was taken to the factory infirmary for treatment. Then they paid him five hundred dollars as compensation for the injured eye and discharged him.

Fortis took the money, withdrew his savings from the bank, put on a pair of powerful spectacles with American gold frames, and returned to his native land to settle down and enjoy his wealth. He built a house, bought the coffee-house and some small farms, and married a beautiful girl. She blushed like a May rose and had dimples in her cheeks when she laughed, but Fortis was not destined to have her long.

For years he had described all the wonders of America to the villagers from Mouria and now he repeated them for the benefit of the refugees, who clicked their tongues in amazement at the customs in that other world where they gave a whole fortune to a man for one eye, and that not completely ruined.

Inside the shop, beside the counter, Fortis had three photographs in a single frame. On one side was Venizelos, on the other was the Patriarch Joachim and between them was Henry Ford, his face wrinkled like a raisin. Fortis called them his Holy Trinity.

Although the fishermen would gather at the coffee-house to talk about the housing project, the conversation inevitably turned to America. This was natural, because the money for rehabilitation came from there and the heads of the Commission, Morgenthau, for example, were Americans.

So they would put Fortis's chair in their midst and he would begin his tales. As he spoke, the others would catch his enthusiasm and listen open-mouthed and enthralled. If anyone wondered why for six whole years a man was given nothing to do but strike a small screw on the head, it was enough to remember that over there was a different world.

To make them understand, Fortis explained it was the 'system', and he solemnly raised a finger. The word acted on the fishermen like a spell and they looked in awe. But when he went on to say how in this way workmen did the work more quickly, more easily, and more efficiently, the word lost its magic.

'No,' said the fishermen, 'it isn't that. It must be something else that Fortis couldn't see.'

This contrary view was first stated by old Perthikis who had listened with bowed head, scratching the ground with his big toe and holding to his own ideas on the matter.

Fortis regarded him indulgently from under his spectacles, wagging his head. 'Then you tell us what is behind it, you who have learned so much in your boat!'

Perthikis raised his head and rubbed is unshaven chin. 'Politics!' he said gravely and widened his eyes for emphasis.

'Politics! What kind of politics, for instance?'

'It's plain as daylight,' said the old man. 'They tell you about the system and all that so you won't catch on. As for their reason for setting you to strike screws for life, that's something else.'

'What?'

'It's so that nobody will learn the secrets of the whole business. There, that's it. With us, an apprentice works with a mechanic, a blacksmith, or a shoemaker and in two or three years, if he has any brains, he becomes a master and opens his own shop. But these people don't want this. That's why they don't let the worker gradually learn the construction of the whole automobile from A to Z. One man works by himself making screws. Another makes only tyres. Always this, until he dies. . . it's politics, I tell you, Comninos! Politics! Because if they taught everybody the 'how' of the business, the world would be full of Fords and he would lose his living. There, that's it.'

They all turnea and looked at Perthikis. They understood well what he said about the 'how' of the work. There was no doubt that this was the motive and Fortis, because of his honest heart, hadn't caught on. So now the whole 'system' was explained.

Fortis smiled condescendingly, took out of his pocket a large blue handkerchief, and slowly and with dignity wiped his spectacles. Then he got up to welcome Ramona and Garbo, the two goats which Alekos Tsalekos, his odd-job boy, was bringing in from pasture.

Tsalekos said good evening and dropped from his shoulders a great load of tender shoots of white poplar and turpentine trees. Then he went into the coffee-house and washed the tumblers and raki glasses while Fortis talked affectionately to the goats as he milked them.

7

T H E fishermen began wrangling again about the houses and Varouhos, as president, tried to answer their foolish objections. Fortis, bent over Garbo, soliloquized just loudly enough for the men to hear him, 'A peasant was given a donkey and he examined its teeth.'

While they were arguing, a little girl came and stood in front of Varouhos.

Varouhos was alarmed. 'Zena?' he asked. The little girl nodded emphatically.

'It's nothing. She's been eating green fruit,' said Fortis, stripping the goat's udder. 'I'll send her a glass of fresh milk to straighten her out.'

Varouhos paid for his drinks and left. When he was gone, Lathios, who was drinking his raki apart from the others, said, shaking his head, 'That's the way it is when you have only one child. All worry and fear. "One child, no child".'

Panayis Lathios, tall thin, and the best fisherman among them, could speak with authority on this subject. Every year he acquired another baby. First there had been a daughter, then a son, next the twins and now his wife was pregnant again.

The daughter had married a young fellow, now only twenty years old, a sailor in the Greek Royal Navy. Once a year he came home on leave, begot a new infant and tossed in his arms the one he had fathered on his previous visit. Thus it was that mother and daughter gave birth side by side in the hovel which the Ministry of Housing had assigned to them.

There was Lathios's whole clan gathered at night, the only time when they were all together, his wife Maria, his four children and the daughter's three, who often got mixed up with his own. The two mothers never bothered to sort them out and even exchanged them at the breast.

With them also was Aunt Permahoula, Lathios's mother-in-law, a scrawny old crone of unnumbered years, all skin and bone but as strong and active as a girl. She had nothing to do but chase after the gang of young ones. At nightfall she would go out and call them, until all Skala rang with her shrill voice. None of them would answer until finally she promised to tell them her best fairy tales. Then the loitering grandchildren and great-grandchildren would sweep down from the cliffs, the trees, the boats, and other refugee houses, far and near.

'We're coming, Granny!'

All this was more than Panayis Lathios could endure. When he was not away fishing, he would spend every evening drinking raki at Fortis's.

In the same house among this mob of children was Zenovia, Varouhos's only child. She was quite different from the others and was lavishly pampered with an affection unknown to fishermen's children. She had been born when her parents had given up expecting a child and the couple had made her the centre of their life.

Her glossy black hair was combed regularly and tied with a red ribbon. She wore shoes every day, like the well-to-do children in Mouria, and her feet were bathed every night. One day when her father went to Hora, he brought her a little frock of pure red silk and black patent leather shoes to wear on the next fifteenth of August when the festival of the Madonna is held on the Mount.

On the day Varouhos was called home, he found Zena burning with fever on her pallet, which was filled with rustling seaweed. Her dark eyes were dull with suffering. Nerandji was sitting beside her with a crockery cup filled with diluted rose-vinegar. From time to time she changed the damp compresses on the girl's hands and forehead.

'Well, what's the matter with out little lady that made you send for me?' he asked with a smile.

Nerandji looked up at him, her great dark eyes fill of anxiety. She said nothing. Varouhos laid his hand on the little girl's hot face and promptly withdrew it in alarm at the fever. Lathios' wife and daughter were standing in a corner waiting to help if they were needed. Varouhos looked at them worriedly.

'What has she got?' he asked.

'I don't know . . . she has a high fever,' said Maria.

The fisherman looked from one to another of the three women. Then he looked in bewilderment at the child, who was breathing rapidly. Suddenly, as if seized with terror, he dashed out of the house. In the street he met Tsalekos, who was coming with a cup of fresh mild from Fortis.

'Run as fast as you can and find a mule,' said Varouhos to him, 'and go up to the village and bring the doctor at once. Look! I spit. By the time my saliva has dried, I want you back with the doctor. Now run. I'll tell your master that I sent you.'

The sun was setting when Alekos and the doctor arrived. Varouhos was waiting gloomily for them at Fortis's, since the road passed the shop. He leaped to his feet to greet the doctor and in spite of his heartache induced him to sit down and have a coffee. Dr. Platanas savoured the coffee in small sips and smoked a large cigarette which he unhurriedly rolled from a box with a picture of Venizelos on the cover and carefully moistened the paper. Varouhos watched him on pins and needles. When he saw the doctor swallow the dregs of his coffee, he stood up.

'Come now, doctor. The child is very sick.'

They found Nerandji at her post. Maria and her daughter were washing sheets and clothes in a wooden rub. The child was whispering and moaning and struggling for breath, which came in short gasps with a dry, whistling sound. Sometimes she would stop. Then her face would darken and she would open her eyes in fright and look from side to side without seeing anyone.

When the doctor entered, old Permahoula darted from under the carpet that separated the two families and stood beside the patient. The other women stood aside with folded arms. Platanas sat down on a stool that was placed for him and administered the thermometer to the girl.

'What are those coloured things you've stuffed into the youngster's nostrils?' he asked in his deep voice. 'Are you trying to suffocate her?'

'It's a bit of indigo,' said Nerandji timidly. 'Aunt Permahoula said it would be good for her.'

The doctor laughed loudly. 'Since when, Aunt Permahoula, have you been a doctor? I've heard of you only as a tippler! Do you still guzzle brandy, eh? Does your heart still long for it?'

'She can't leave it alone,' said Lathios's wife.

The women thought they ought to smile at the doctor's raillery. Platanas looked at them genially.

'Come, come!' he said. 'It's nothing. These small fry of yours are completely immunized. They've been infected with every kind of microbe from the filth they roll in day and night and they get rid of them by themselves.'

He removed the thermometer and went to the window to look at it in the light on account of his farsightedness. 'Aha!' he said and glanced about the shabby room until his eyes fell on the tub of washing.

'Take those things out,' he ordered. 'Heat some water and give her a bath.'

The women made themselves busy while the doctor uncovered the little girl, listened to her with his stethoscope, and pressed her stomach here and there. Varouhos heard Zena's soft weeping and his heart trembled with unknown fear. He tried to read the diagnosis in Platanas' face.

'What has she got?' he asked in a low voice.

'Quite obvious. It's a case of pulmonary congestion,' the doctor said as if to himself. 'What is the little one's name?'

'Zenovia,' said Nerandji as she covered the child.

The doctor caressed with his heavy hand the black curls which lay damp and tangled on the pillow and gazed thoughtfully at the ceiling.

'Ze-no-vi-a!' he whispered, dividing the name into syllables. 'Ze-no-vi-a!'

Then, as if he suddenly had found what he was searching for, he closed his bag, stood up, ready to leave.

'Don't go, doctor,' pleaded Nerandji, her eyes reddened with anxiety.

He smiled at her tenderly. 'It's not necessary for me to stay. Don't worry. You will give her a bath now. As hot as your elbow can stand it. The child will revive after the bath. I'll come back tomorrow to have a look at her. Send Tsalekos for me about nine in the morning.'

'What about medicine? Aren't you going to give us any medicine?' Varouhos asked humbly.

'I'll send it to you tonight with Tsalekos as soon as I get back. It will be in a small bottle. You will give the child a soupspoonful every half-hour.'

Platanas stopped at Fortis's coffee-house again and waited for Tsalekos to bring the mule. Fortis asked him softly, 'How's the little one, doctor? Is she really as bad as they say?'

The doctor looked at him without replying. Then he smiled with satisfaction. He touched Fortis lightly on the elbow with his finger. 'Comninos, you can read,' he said.

He took a cheap notepad out of his pocket and wrote something on it, folded the sheet four times and put it into Fortis's hand. He lifted his finger to his lips to signify silence, mounted his mule and rode away.

Fortis went to the lamp in the coffee-house, pushed his spectacles back on his forehead and read:

> *Small you were, Zenovia*
> *And you left us all too soon*

Platanas' weakness was writing verses which he read in church at the funerals of villagers who had died. They were usually composed in couplets which he would declaim with rolling eyes and the full diapason of his deep voice that echoed to the cupolas.

After the bath, Zenovia seemed to improve a trifle. Her distress abated and her eyes cleared up. She smiled wearily at her mother, but only with her lips.

The agony, however, returned before dawn. The women and children on Lathios's side of the curtain made as little noise as possible. They spoke in whispers and walked on tiptoe lest the aged stairs and floorboards should creak.

Varouhos went out very early to Fortis's and drank coffee while he waited till it would be time to send for the doctor.

As soon as Varouhos was out of the house, old Permahoula raised the curtain, nodded mysteriously and allowed three women to enter. Nerandji turned her weary head and stared at them.

'What is it?' she asked uncomprehendingly.

The old woman made a sign of silence with her fingers. The visitors were Maria, Lathios's wife, and two other girls: Maria Lamaras and Maria Baras. Each held a china incense burner. With downcast eyes and without saying a word, they approached the child. The old crone touched Nerandji on the shoulder and said softly, 'The child is sick, my daughter. Don't you understand what it is? Somebody has put the evil eye on the poor girl. What can doctors know about such things? I've brought three Marys to cense her. Let me perform the exorcism as we learned it from our forefathers. Only by divine means can this evil be driven out.'

Nerandji made way. One after another, the three Marys knelt and censed the child three times, first in circles around her and then crosswise. Meanwhile the old woman muttered exorcisms over the girl. When the magic rite was finished, Permahoula put into a saucer a glowing coal from each censer. Then she threw a clove on them and blew gently.

She watched the wisp of smoke rise and waited until the clove was consumed. Then she turned to the three Marys in distress. This meant: 'The clove didn't leap in the fire; likewise the sick one will not leap.' She took a glass of water and quenched the coals. Zenovia was given a spoonful of this mixture of water, ashes and burnt incense to swallow. She resisted and tried to avoid it.

'Come, my little lady! Drink it darling, to get well! Drink it, my love!'

In the meantime, Fortis at the coffee-house was watching Varouhos's impatience. He was stongly tempted to tell him what the doctor had decided about Zena, for he had immediately understood the oracular verses on the piece of paper. While he was seeking a tactful way of preparing the fisherman for what was to come, he went in and out of the coffee-house and scolded Lambis for teasing the goats. Far inside the shop could be heard the rhythmic pounding of Tsalekos, who was pulverizing coffee in a huge mortar with an iron pestle. This sound shattered the silence into fragments. Flies buzzed about brightly in the golden air.

Fortis started to speak, putting a finger on the bald spot on the crown of his head, as he invariably did when he was nervous. For no reason at all, he pushed back his spectacles, circled around Varouhos, and belched. Then with sudden decisiveness he brought up a chair beside the fisherman. Clearing his throat, he handed Varouhos the folded paper.

'Listen to me,' he said unsteadily. 'I talked with Platanas yesteray before he went home. The child, you know, is in a very bad way. . .

He broke off and waited for Varouhos to react, but he merely looked composedly at Fortis and sighed, as if to lighten what had been kept from him, a truth which he had suppressed because he had been unable to admit it to himself.

'I knew it from the start,' he said. 'I shall lose the child. She's not going to live.'

Both were silent for a while. Then Varouhos said hesitantly, 'But he said for us to call him again. . . .'

'To send Tsalekos if you needed him. But see? The doctor won't come back. It's the way he does when he makes up his mind about a patient. It was the same way in my wife's case.'

And so it proved to be.

Tsalekos went with the mule up to the village, but the doctor said there was no need for him to come. They were to give the girl the medicine he had sent them and await what would happen.

Towards evening, Zena revived a little, but later she was seized with a violent paroxysm which interfered with her breathing. The fever increased so that the cold compresses steamed as soon as they were applied. Then she went into a crisis accompanied by convulsions. Presently the death struggle began. She died at dawn.

Nerandji dressed her in her little red frock and patent leather shoes. She combed her hair and tied it with the red ribbon so that the bow rested on her curls like a large, crimson butterfly. On her breast they laid the icon of the Madonna which till then had lain on her pillow. In her hands Maria, Lathios's wife, put three cherry-red carnations. When they were finished, Nerandji, plunged into an abyss of grief, sat down and wept.

As Maria watched Nerandji's grief, she thought to herself, 'Let God send Zena back and take another child.' She was on the point of saying 'one of mine' but she couldn't agree to that, so she said, 'Let him take the one I carry in my womb, now while I still don't know it.' At that moment she felt the unborn child kick within her. She interrupted this line of thought in alarm and furtively made the sign of the cross on her belly with the palm of her hand.

The children crowded around and watched the goings-on with interest and perplexity. It was the first time they had seen a dead person; and Zenovia, lying there quietly, beautiful in her best clothes with the three carnations in her hands and all this strange festivity being held just for her, suddenly seemed to occupy a wondrous, enviable position and they were jealous of her.

8

A D I S P U T E arose with the refugees over the building site. The Community of Mouria offered them gratis an attractive level area between the village and Skala. The refugees objected that it was too far for fishing people to travel. If they were to build, the site must be closer to their nets and boats. Then the community offered them another tract just above Skala. The refugees turned this down also. They wanted to be in Skala. The Mouriotes became weary and resentful. Then the State complicated matters by distributing among the refugees the farms and olive plantations which had been left behind by the Turks after the exchange of populations.

The distribution was administered in a most impractical manner. Men who knew nothing but the use of boats and tackle awoke one morning to find themselves the managers of huge olive estates. The 'benefactors' had carefully seen to it that these plantations were often hours of travel away from their new owners. So the refugees left it to agents to harvest the crops, from which they themselves received only a pittance of revenue.

When the cold of winter arrived, the refugees remembered that these olive trees were their property. Whereupon they took axes and proceeded to fell the venerable, century-old giants to make charcoal for their stoves. The villagers who for time out of mind had cherished these trees with religious reverence, since they were the one resource of the island, rose up in revolt against such vandalism. They even accused the fishermen of coming up to the gardens by night to steal fruit, dig potatoes, and trample the vegetables.

Antagonisms multiplied day by day. Sensible, reasonable folk on both sides had all they could do to prevent the infuriated parties from attacking each other with weapons, like enemies. The village youngsters made up satirical verses about the refugee children, which they chanted as they clapped their hands to the rhythm.

The village women invented a scathing name for the newcomers. They called them 'the spoils of war'. This enraged the victims. The men gathered separately at the native and refugee coffee-houses.

Avgustis, the schoolmaster, pleaded with them, 'Children, we are all Greeks. In the name of God, don't give the enemy cause for rejoicing!'

'If you want to build houses for us,' said the fishermen, 'you'll have to build them near the sea. Otherwise we don't want them, and good day to you!'

A year passed in this way with no progress in building the houses. The committee of the building corporation remained deadlocked and the fishermen asked tauntingly: 'When are they going to lay the foundations, Varouhos?'

One person, however, did not weary of this project as it dragged on tiresomely. This was the Bishop. He made trips to Athens, conferred with Greeks and Americans, interviewed bankers, and finally won. A piece of 'exchanged' land near the shore was allocated as a building site. It was a fine, level strip with large olive and fig trees. Then one day the surveyors arrived from Hora to lay out the lots. The fishermen were unable to believe their eyes, and Varouhos again became the active president of the housing corporation.

Avgustis, more and more disturbed, walked among the engineers in his shirt sleeves, his hands in his pockets. He watched the felling of the trees and with bowed head he strolled between the red lines which were marked on the ground to indicate the streets of the future village. The odious spectre was taking on substance and becoming a reality.

'Well, it seems there's to be a housing project after all, thanks to the Bishop,' Fortis said to Avgustis one day.

The dejected schoolmaster replied heatedly, 'If our clergy are possessed of demons . . . how can you talk to these numbskulls? Their heads are filled with fish brains.'

'And the Bishop?'

'He's the son of a fisherman. What can you expect? These people see only as far as the ends of their moustaches. All they want is to lie down under a roof. Besides, it's free!'

To needle him still further, Fortis innocently remarked: 'The consecration will take place in a week, so they can start laying the foundations.'

'Let them. Why not? It was thus they laid the foundations of the Tower of Babel . . . and here is the tower of impiousness. From underground the blood of Asia Minor some day will cry out. You'll hear it. They will delve with the mattock for water and blood will gush forth. Then we'll see who will survive the curse.'

The Bishop sent word to the fishermen that they were to help as much as possible with the construction so that the project might be finished forthwith and they might have a roof over their heads before winter and that the labour costs should be kept within bounds. This was to their interest, because later—when they had sufficient income —the Ministry of Housing would ask them to pay for their homes a little at a time. The chief engineer explained the matter to them at the coffee-house.

'Over beyond the hill of Vigla,' he pointed out, 'is the beach of Kaya. From there the islanders haul sand for their own homes, which often are three or four hours away by road, and they pay the tax imposed by law. The government has granted you permission to take the sand tax-free. Most of you have boats. Few of you have much to do. I watch you dragging your feet from coffee-house to coffee-house. So I ask you to organize a work force of two or three boats every day. They will go to Kaya, it's only a cigarette smoke away by sea, and they will haul the sand. I reckon that in a week you can get all I'll need without adding a lepton to the cost. This will reduce expenses as much as fifteen or twenty thousand drachmas. I leave it to you to decide.'

He swallowed his coffee and left. The fishermen at once erupted in a stormy argument. Varouhos and those who found the engineer's suggestion reasonable were drowned out by the others. The schoolmaster said nothing and held himself disdainfully aloof. Fortis smiled and maintained the strict neutrality of a host.

At last the matter was put to vote. Varouhos, as president, took Octapodomatis, the secretary, with him to call on the engineer and report on the decision of the majority.

'They refuse to do a thing, Mr. Pistatis. Nobody is willing to work for nothing.'

The engineer was astonished. 'What do you mean "nothing"? Each of you will work only two or three hours on the building of your own homes. They are for your children, your wives, and your sick who now have to sleep in shanties!'

'You're right,' said Varouhos. 'My wife says the same thing.'

The engineer lost his temper and told them to go away. Never had he dreamed there could be such a lack of self-respect. He would report it to the Rehabilitation Commission. He would write to the Bishop. His reverence would be given to understand the kind of people he was dealing with.

At that moment Lathios appeared. Swarthy, diffident, and reserved, he greeted them and said: 'Excuse me for breaking into your conversation. I've come, Mr. Pistatis, to tell you this. When my boat isn't out fishing, I and my sons are at your service for the sand. Without pay. This is what I had to tell you. Excuse me for interrupting your conversation.'

The engineer crossed himself.

'Now there's a man at last,' he said.

9

T H E engineer was not mistaken. Panayis Lathios was 'a man.' Poorest and hardest worker of all, he avoided the tribe of wrangling, brawling fishermen. He spoke seldom and then softly. His saintly face almost never smiled and he invariably drank his carafe of raki by himself along with pickled damsons and salted sardines.

With his nets and lines—he had been the best fisherman in Aivali—and with his clandestine fishing raids on Anatolian waters with his depth charges, he managed to make both ends meet. His breadboard was never empty or his kettle off the fire. His one desire was raki. As soon as he moored his boat and disposed of his fish in the shops, he made straight for Fortis's and started drinking leisurely and systematically. Silent, withdrawn and solitary, he found distraction and relaxation in this manner. But for all his drinking, he never got drunk, never spoke irritably or became abusive.

Time would pass thus until the stars appeared above Fortis's mulberry tree and the noises of day were stilled. The hour arrived when he must go home. Then the old grandmother's troubles would begin. After Aunt Permahoula had corralled the children and told them fairy tales, it was her next duty to go out once more and summon Panayis. Her bare feet made no sound as she walked through the darkness. Suddenly her aged face popped from behind the massive mulberry tree like a phantom from inside its trunk.

Patiently and insistently she would plead: 'Come now, Panayis. Get up. The children want to eat.'

She would get no answer. Lathios would remain seated at the end of the bench with a carafe of raki before him. At long intervals he would take a sip or eat an olive; he would say nothing. Again Aunt Permahoula would poke her head out of the darkness and repeat in the same quiet, insistent voice: 'Come now, Panayis. Get up. The little ones are hungry.'

Sometimes Lathios turned to the old woman as if he had heard her for the first time and would say indifferently: 'Tell her to feed the children.'

But he knew that even should the world come to an end, Maria would not set the table till he arrived. At times he grumbled about it but deep in his heart he was filled with pride. Finally he would feel sorry for the fasting children and weary of the crone's nagging, he would drain his carafe, pay his bill, say good night and leave.

On the other hand, if he felt inclined to linger a bit, he knew how to bribe the old woman. 'Give her a dram to keep her quiet,' he would say to Fortis. 'She annoys me.'

Tsalekos would take her a glass of strong, cheap brandy, which was her passion. Curled up on the ground behind the tree, she would seize the glass and sip it lovingly. Her eyes glowed in the darkness and she smacked her lips while her soul was comforted. 'My blessing on you from my twenty nails,' she would say. But, even so, she allowed Panayis only a quarter of an hour's grace. Then she resumed: 'Come now, Panayis!'

Finally he would get up and leave. Then Fortis, his last customer gone, listened in solitude to the bubbling of his elegant Turkish *nargileh* filled with Persian tobacco and to the voices of the sea. And the summer night listened also in all its glory, its constellations wheeling above the trips of the mulberry tree and drowsing above the gleaming masts, above the Mount of the Madonna and above the shabby hovels of the fishermen where, one by one, the little lamps would be extinguished.

Lathios would follow the old woman into the house and latch the door. Then the meal would begin. The low table extended from one end of the room to the other. The horde of children, sitting crossed-legged, would dig in enthusiastically with their spoons and eat greedily from large earthen porringers.

On the other side of the carpet which divided the room sat Varouhos and Nerandji, alone and childless, whose grief for Zena had not been tempered by the passing of time. Stretched out on the divan, Varouhos rolled and smoked thick cigarettes one after the other. Nerandji knitted woollen stockings near the lamp and sighed. Her pitiful dark face, wrapped in a black headcloth, was etched with suffering.

Grief for Zena spread inkily from her heart and stained everything around her. She had dyed her clothes black, her husband's shirts, her head- and chin-cloths, even the table napkins and the apron of the Madonna on the icon. She deliberately plunged herself into a bitter orgy of remorse which was gradually turned in savage revenge on herself. It was her own unworthiness that had permitted Death to snatch the child from her arms.

All day she sat shut-up indoors to avoid seeing the sunlight and flagellated herself with the thought of how great a sinner she must be for the Lord to have punished her thus. Every Saturday evening she would climb the Mount of the Madonna and visit the church to tend the tiny lamp and burn incense. On the wall at the right of the door as one entered was the Mermaid Madonna, her colours faded and the plaster fallen in places where the human and fish bodies met.

Nerandji would prostrate herself, burn incense and say her penitential prayers. Then she would lift her eyes to the face of the Madonna, who stared back at her with her own unnaturally wide and terrifying eyes as she held the trident upright in one hand and the ship in the other and curled her monstrous tail with blue fish scales. Nerandji would remain thus, gazing awe-stricken into the eyes of the dreadful divinity until darkness obliterated everything in the church. To her lips would rush with a sob the plaintive question for which she received no answer:

'Why did you take her from me, Mermaid Madonna? Why?'

The Madonna stared back at her in intolerable silence until, little by little, her form was swallowed up in the dusk. Her wide green eyes were the last to disappear. Then Nerandji would say three prayers and leave the chapel. For a short while she would stand on the Mount, outlined against the red-gold sky, her spectral frame erect and motionless.

From the lichen-covered base of the rock rose the vast incessant murmur of the sea, now pleading and now comforting. Far off, from the open sea which was growing dim, from the olive grove, and from the mountains of Anatolia, two eyes still looked into her heart where a festering wound oozed dark blood. They were the almond-green eyes of the Mermaid Madonna. Invisible beneath the roots of the rock, tiny waves spoke words of solace in the language of the deep, meaningless to the mind but grateful to the soul. From the sky with its subdued tints there dropped into her heart the 'oil of peace'. Only two drops. A mere nothing, yet a healing balm.

'It is the relief that comes from telling my grief to Her Grace,' Nerandji would sigh.

Then she would wrap her kerchief tightly around her chin and descend the stone stairway, slowly, one step at a time.

The women, the children, and the fishermen whom she met in the street would break off their conversation and silently move aside to allow this night-wandering spectre to pass.

T H E construction engineer provided Varouhos with a copy of the plans and explained it to him in detail so that he might arouse the interest of the other fishermen. The sheet was posted on a wall in Fortis's coffee-house, where in no time they were peering at it and discussing it. Varouhos explained the red and blue lines as the engineers had interpreted their significance to him. Each building plot was indicated with its own number.

The fishermen gabbled noisily around the paper with the unreasonable egotism of little children. Each one declared where he wanted his lot and shouted to the president to record it before any-one else could make the same choice.

The dispute over the lots increased until the men split into two factions. They placed their stools at separate tables, put their heads together and talked excitedly. Each group glanced sourly at the other, uttered scornful 'pshaws,' and shrugged their shoulders. Finally one party deserted Fortis's coffee-house and drank their brandy at another, which was actually a tavern. Fortis stretched his long neck and watched them in dismay from under his spectacles. What a people!

Avgustis put a drachma piece on his saucer, lifted his finger and said triumphantly: 'What did I tell you?'

'About what?' asked Fortis.

'About the Tower of Babel! Look in front of you. The hour has come and God has confused their tongues so that one cannot agree with the other. Now do you understand? Babel!'

The engineer at first was alarmed by all this angry shouting. Then he laughed at them, grown men with bushy moustaches under their noses giving themselves up to childish wrangling. He informed the fishermen immediately that all assignments and selections made so far meant nothing. The houses would be assigned by the Bishop and the Commission, by lot, and families with the greatest need would have first choice. Then he brought up again the matter of the sand. He tried to appeal to their pride. It was wasted breath.

The engineer refused to back down. He wrote a frank account of the impasse to the Bishop. The latter wired to Mouria that Varouhos was to get into his boat without delay and come to Hora, where he, the Bishop, would have a few things to say to him.

The president was frightened. The Bishop was not joking and his orders had to be obeyed to the letter. The other fishermen shared this fear which a bishop, as their natural leader, inspires among the Anatolians. They put their tails between their legs when Varouhos told them he was leaving at dawn the next day. He knew he was going to have a bad time, but he must go.

All that evening he spent at home talking with Lathios and Nerandji about the forthcoming interview. Nerandji briefed him for hours on what to say and how to conduct himself. 'Agree with him, do you hear? Make a note of everything he says and don't pay attention to what these barefoot numbskulls tell you to say.'

Varouhos had a sleepless night, sighing and writhing like a snake on his pallet. Towards dawn, when it began to grow light, he dressed himself in his best breeches and his black velvet waistcoat. Wearing shoes and his velvet cap, he set out, tall, fat, solemn and complacent. Behind him went Nerandji with a red portmanteau in which were provisions for the journey and a gift of fine lobsters for the Bishop. Scores of prematurely awakened fishermen were waiting to see him off. It was a real ceremony. Varouhos acted his distasteful role with a dignity that befitted him as president and envoy. Everybody gave him orders for fish-hooks and lines and various other things which he was not to forget. When he went aboard his boat, he felt broken by the weight and responsibility of his mission. He nodded his head, said, 'yes, yes' and listened to no one.

When the boat had moved off a little, Nerandji, who had not spoken all this time, shouted the final admonition, which was merely for the benefit of the others.

'And kiss the hand of the godfather and give him my reverences. Tell him it's from his god-daughter, Nerandji Hadjidiamandi!'

Gaunt, austere, enveloped in black, she returned home, proudly aware of the distinction which this title gave her.

Varouhos entered the Bishop's palace laden with gloomy forebodings and the gifts of seafood. The latter he got rid of hastily, handing them over to a deacon who told him to wait on a divan in the corridor until he was called. His premonitions grew more sombre. A little more and he would have sprung up and burst out of that long corridor with the narrow red and black carpet which seemed to extend for a whole kilometre. His heart was thumping as if clubs were beating under his velvet vest. Then the trap was sprung. Through the half open door he heard the growling voice of the Bishop, which foretold no good.

'Bring him in!'

'You may enter,' said the deacon with a bland smile.

Varouhos cleared his throat, took his cap in his hand, smoothed his moustache and entered.

The Bishop kept him at least half an hour and all that time his voice boomed like distant thunder as far as the innermost recesses of the cathedral. Finally Varouhos was permitted to leave. He backed out with his hand respectfully on his chest and made awkward bows which were intended to be obeisances.

When he found himself in the street, his ears were still burning from the episcopal scolding. He was so bewildered that he walked in a daze among the cars and pushcarts of the main thoroughfare. The din of horns and of people shouting 'Watch where you're going!' was so unsettling that he thought he would never escape.

At last he managed it and pushed on, depressed, disconsolate, and shaken by the Bishop's harsh words. He plodded towards the waterfront, where his boat was moored, to lie down awhile under the awning and put in order the thoughts that were buzzing in his skull like a swarm of irritated wasps. For the Bishop had berated him so unmercifully that Varouhos had been unable to give him Nerandji's greetings, however much she was descended from the Hadjidiamandes. Nor had he been able to mention the lobsters and red mullet which he had intended to temper the severity of his reception. Once or twice, it is true, he had tried to get a word in about the gifts, but the Bishop interrupted him with his booming voice.

'Sh! Not a word! I don't want to listen to the idiotic excuses of stupid people! . . . Silence, I say, donkey!'

He stamped his foot to emphasize the word 'donkey,' and the wooden floor trembled and his blue eyes flashed sternly.

11

W H I L E Varouhos was ambling slowly with his heavy cap pulled over his forehead, his mind preoccupied with all that had happened, he heard his name called.

'Hey, Uncle Varouhos! Uncle Varouhos!'

He looked up and in the doorway of a small tavern saw Zafirakis, the son of his old friend, Markos Mermingas. Varouhos's features cleared immediately. He embraced Zafirakis and grasped his hand like a drowning sailor.

'Well, Zafirakis! So you keep a tavern, eh?'

'As you see. "Take the wind as you find it," my late father used to say.'

'Captain Markos stayed behind, then!'

The young man shrugged his shoulders and sighed.

'Yes. Now I'm on my own with my mother and three sisters on my back . . . right? May good times return for our fellow countrymen. They keep the shop in business and I make a go of it. Right?'

He used the expression 'Right?' quite liberally. It was a sign that he was now a city man and had learned sophisticated manners.

The two of them entered the tavern. Varouhos seated himself on a bare wooden bench. A carafe of raki was placed before him as an *apéritif.* Then Zafirakis brought him the remains of a mutton stew and some salt mackerel. A delicious fragrance filled the shop when a cucumber-tomato salad also arrived with an oil and vinegar dressing and fat, ripe olives.

With his first mouthful, the fisherman realized how hungry he was. He remembered that he had gone with only a coffee since the night before. After the appetizers he turned to a beautiful dark wine and exchanged treats with the other customers while they related their misfortunes and recalled the frightful days and endless nights of the Anatolian disaster.

Thus the afternoon passed, and when the shops began to empty, the little tavern was crowded with Moschonisi and Aivaliote refugees. Zafirakis left the table to wait on customers. Varouhos, however, was not left alone. There were greeting from all sides, handshaking and treating. The Anatolians sat down beside him and asked for news of Panayia.

'Is it true they're building houses for you at the port? You fishermen are certainly lucky. You ought to light a candle to the Bishop.'

'Enough of gloom! Enough of this depressing talk!' shouted a curly-haired Aivaliote, staring at his glass in a melancholy that reached to his fingertips.

'Watch this miracle!' called Zafirakis from the counter and they all turned to look. With a sudden flick of the switch he lit all the lights in the shop. Then he held up a sparkling glass and filled it with wine. In the brightness the liquid glowed like blood and threw off crimson glints.

'To your god!' said Zafirakis, the rogue. 'Never can gloomy hearts and thoughts survive in this! You dip them once, you dip them twice, and *whoop!* out they come like carnations! No matter how black they were! Right?'

The little Aivaliote with the curly hair put his elbow on the table and rested his cheek in his hand.

'Some hearts are so black,' he said, 'that they never become carnations, not even in wine!'

'Fotis is in good form!' cried the guests, looking expectantly at the melancholy youth. Zafirakis realized that the climax of the evening was about to be reached and sent a waiter to fetch some musicians.

'Sing, Fotis, so we can remember our Aivali!' cried the customers. The youth continued to brood dejectedly without lifting his head from his hand. The instruments pleaded with him with tremolos. They laid siege to him and nagged at him, the lute and zither lightly sketching the rhythm of the song that would presently rest upon it.

When at last Fotis began to sing, all conversation ceased as in church. His voice rose softly and earnestly, a manly voice, capable of supporting the vaults of the weightiest melody. It rose, step by step, and hesitated uncertainly. Then it moved forward in its deliberate, studied ascent until it seemed to reach the pinnacle of grief. There he paused, borne aloft on a single note like an eagle soaring with outspread wings. From there he looked down upon humanity, plodding along, bowed with suffering, while he released slender silken ribbons of tone, light, gossamer strands of green, gold and rose, which undulated slowly and sadly in the sighs of the whole world.

It was not song. It was the spell of heartache driving outward in unfolding waves to the sky, the sea and the forests, sometimes retarded, languid and plaintive, at other times swift and seething like a waterfall from a high cliff. At the end, when the capping rhyme was fitted, it was like hope coming to rest on a firm foundation, an unburdening of the heart which was left lightened and tranquil. Then in a triumphant outburst, the musicians picked up the refrain with a joyous lilt and the guests all joined in, clapping their hands loudly.

44

The night was far advanced when Varouhos got up to leave. His spirits were at high peak and he had delayed his departure again and again. But now he would hear no more of procrastination. In the first place, he had spent all his money on food and drink and secondly, there now would be a good wind which would bring him to the port of Panayia in three hours. If he missed the wind he would have to row all night and till noon next day in the morning calm.

Zafirakis detained him at the counter to drink 'one for the voyage'. When he saw that Varouhos was having difficulties with his legs, he tried to persuade him to remain a little longer.

'Sit down, Uncle Antoni, and sleep here tonight. I see your legs don't obey you very well!'

From the door Varouhos replied quite logically, 'Do you think, my boy, I'm going to walk to Panayia?' A guffaw of laughter applauded this retort.

Varouhos went aboard his boat, smiling radiantly and humming over and over the refrain of Fotis's song which kept going around in his fuzzy mind. But this fuzziness was no longer the mist of fear. It was now a rosy vapour which agreeably numbed the brain and gladdened all the thoughts and half-thoughts that formed in it.

He untied the stern hawser, hoisted the anchor, and rowed till he passed the harbour lights into the open sea. There he raised the sail, took his seat at the tiller, and steered along the shore. His heart was as gay as that of a child released from school. His thoughts continued to float without logical connexion on a rosy sea of wine. They were like the red sailboats of pine chips that the fishermen's children toss into the water and which sail aimlessly here and there as the wind blows their rectangular sails made from cigarette boxes.

The sea was lovely, as only the Aegean can be on summer nights when a light north wind is blowing. On the shore the outlines of white cliffs with grassy summits swept past him in violet luminousness. Little whitewashed churches stood up to look and then sank back again. Sandy coves opened under the starlight that made the water glitter with fire. The sea murmured voluptuously in its sleep. Hours passed.

When Cape Korakas, with its lighthouse and its pointed nose of rock, appeared in the distance, a thin streak of soft light was brightening the mountain tops in Anatolia. But the morning star still shone overhead, a splendid, wonderful star that illuminated the open sea like a small but powerful moon.

As he left Cape Korakas behind, he heard from the shore the bells of a flock of sheep. The tiny, tranquil sounds penetrated his drowsy brain like a shower of happy, celestial drops of music.

Varouhos felt more irresistibly than ever the call to slumber which, up to this time, he had driven from him with sheer effort of will. Now his eyelids felt as heavy as lead. Once more he stubbornly shook off the torpor which threatened to overcome him just as his voyage was about to end.

'Ahaayayaa!'

He yawned and stretched his arms and legs. The cliffs on the shore sent back his yawn as if they, too, were joining him from all their caverns.

'Ahaayayaa!'

Simultaneously, as if waiting for this signal, a wailing cry replied from under the forward deck where he stowed rags and a wooden bucket.

'Oowaah! Oo-oowaah!'

Varouhos came to himself with a start and rubbed his eyes. 'Hey! What's that? A car or a dog?' he said out loud.

Again he rubbed his bleary eyes with his fist. 'Bah! It's the wine and sleepiness. It would do that. It's noth . . .'

'Oowaah!'

This loud yell, as shrill as the scream of a hungry seagull, cut short the word he was about to speak. The clear wail of an infant echoed as far as the top of Vigla. The fisherman remembered Aunt Permahoula's fairy tales and crossed himself.

'Come, Holy Madonna,' he said. 'Let it not be some goblin that will lay a spell on me. May Jesus Christ conquer and disperse all evil things!'

He got up, lowered the sail and went to the prow. Bending down, he drew out the basket of fishlines. In it he found a wriggling, crying baby, waving its arms wildly in the first light of dawn. As he knelt in consternation to see better, the baby became quiet and, putting its finger into its mouth, tried to extract nourishment from it.

Varouhos was open-mouthed in amazement. His first impulse was to turn back to Hora and hand the foundling over to the police. But he looked up and saw the Mount of the Madonna right upon him; and his boat, left to herself, was veering dangerously towards the cliffs of Vigla. He put the oars in the rowlocks and made directly for the harbour with the basket and the child between his legs.

All this while the infant was nursing at its finger and fretting because nothing came from it. From time to time it impatiently beat the air with the free arm and cast reproachful glances at the fisherman as if he were responsible for the frustrating predicament. Varouhos could not help smiling.

'Ah, you little bastard, what trouble you're letting me in for!'

12

V A R O U H O S moored his boat, took the basket with the child in it, and hurried home with long strides to avoid greetings and explanations.

'How is Nerandji going to take this?' he wondered apprehensively. 'What's going to happen now?'

His worst fears were realized. There was a regular reception waiting for him. How such a crowd had got wind of something so unforeseeable was a mystery.

All of Lathios's tribe gathered around the basket. They were joined by a number of neighbour women and the schoolmaster, who had heard the commotion and wanted to see what was going on. Even Fortis came. He had sighted the boat from his crow's nest as soon as it rounded the point of Cape Korakas. They all exclaimed at the infant's expensive clothes and fingered the daintily embroidered blankets that formed a warm nest in the basket. Everything was immaculately white and contrasted vividly with this house of mourning.

'Man, what a catch you made!' said Lathios, rubbing his drowsy eyes.

The baby stirred, whimpered fretfully, and tossed its arms as if it were testing little wings. It looked up peevishly at the dark faces and tried to kick free of its wrappings. It had slept well in the rocking boat and now was ready to be fed.

Varouhos told in a word or two all he knew about the child. Nerandji, meanwhile, stood at his side with her arms folded, severely silent. In the grim expression on her face, the fisherman sensed the question: 'Were you sent to Hora to bring back foundlings or to see the Bishop on business? Why didn't you turn the child over to the authorities?'

To the unspoken words he replied: 'Because, I tell you, I didn't find it till I reached Cape Korakas. The rascal hadn't made a peep the whole trip!'

'And now?' asked Nerandji. 'What are we going to do with it? Dry it in the sun like an octopus?'

Varouhos shuffled his huge head. At last he blurted defiantly, like a culprit: 'Whatever you say, woman! What do I know about such things? It's the first time small fry of this kind got tangled in my net.'

In the meantime, Lathios's Maria knelt down, tenderly lifted the baby into her arms and, withdrawing to a corner of the room, gave her breast to the child. It was a large, full breast which one would not have expected from such a scantling of a woman.

'Now there's a holy act,' said Fortis. 'This is what's necessary for the present. We'll see about the rest later.'

The infant eagerly seized the bursting nipple and squealed greedily. Then it moaned with delight and blinked its eyes at Maria as she bent maternally over it.

When the child had appeased its hunger, Nerandji took it from the other woman's arms, laid it on the divan and unwrapped it. The baby kicked its freed legs gaily. It was beautiful with a lively, rosy body, very blonde hair and seagreen eyes.

'What a happy little devil he is,' said Varouhos.

Without looking up, Nerandji replied scornfully, 'This little devil, as you call it, for your information, is a girl!'

She replaced the baby's wet clothes with dry ones and then with her hand made the sign of the cross on the little one's head. The baby smiled at her cherubically.

'Now that you've come to us uninvited,' Nerandji said to her, 'what are we going to do with you, my lady? We can't throw you behind the Mount of the Madonna.'

Fortis, who had slipped away briefly, returned with a jar of fresh milk. 'Garbo sends this,' he announced and set the jar on the floor.

Nerandji gave the schoolmaster a piece of paper which she had found pinned to the child's coverings.

'You read what it says here.'

The paper was the size of a visiting card but had no writing on it except one word inscribed in a broad, firm hand: 'Unbaptized.'

'It's a woman's handwriting,' declared Fortis, looking at the paper over the old man's shoulder.

'Yes, a woman's hand. It says the child is unchristened.'

'That's the way of these city women,' scolded Lathios's wife. 'They bring children into the world secretly, pin a paper to them and toss them into fishing boats.'

'When they find some poor fool of a fisherman befuddled with drink,' added Nerandji.

Varouhos, the culprit, said nothing.

'Now we must decide what we're going to do with this poor child,' said Fortis tactfully. He was kneeling by the baby and making funny faces at her. 'Eh, Smaragthi? I'm going to call you Smaragthi on account of those strange, emerald eyes of yours!'

'Let's christen her Aphrodite, since she came out of the sea,' the schoolmaster suggested.

'What do you think we ought to do with her?' Varouhos asked Fortis.

'The legal thing is to report it,' he replied officially. 'There is an orphanage in Hora. That's the proper thing to do.'

Then Lathios's wife spoke up. She looked at the child and said quite matter-of-factly: 'Christ and the Madonna, what are you talking about? I'll take the poor little thing. She won't know luxury but she'll never have an empty stomach. Not with me and my daughter . . . eh?'

The question was directed at her husband.

Lathios smiled good-naturedly and shrugged his shoulders. 'Why not? I've lost count of my youngsters. One more or less, what does it matter?'

'He's right,' interjected Aunt Permahoula, the grandmother, who saw another recruit among the flock of children she herded. 'The baby needs the breast.'

Then Nerandji interrupted abruptly from the window where she was spreading the baby's wet covers on the sill to dry.

'I say not to bother people who didn't beget it. I don't think I've asked anybody what I should do with the child. She came to us from the sea and she is welcome. The Mermaid Madonna, who sent her, will take care of her. She who brought her to a childless home understands better than Uncle Fortis and my neighbour Maria and old Permahoula and all of you. This is what I say!'

'And that's what I say,' cried Varouhos from his corner, where till now he hadn't dared to speak a word.

But Nerandji had no mercy on him.

'It's best you keep your mouth shut. And the next time you go to Hora on business, don't leave your boat and get drunk!'

13

N E I T H E R the threats nor the counsel of the Bishop had any effect on the fishermen. Only Lathios and Varouhos volunteered their co-operation in hauling sand or in anything else the engineer ordered. Lathios did it for the sake of his family and his daughter's family, and Varouhos, now that he had a daughter to look out for, for the same reason.

The others refused to lift so much as a little finger without pay. Avgustis the schoolmaster never relaxed his efforts to foment resistance through his inspired fanaticism.

'Cursed are these homes they want to build for you,' he said. 'In them you will bury all your stength and your faith in the great return!'

To Fortis, who scolded him for this, he replied passionately:

'My dear Comninos, nobody understands this barefoot people! All the difficulties they create come from the same sacred source, even though they may not understand it clearly themselves. It is because their hearts cannot tolerate their betrayal of Greeks in Asia Minor. This is the reason, if you want to know it. You islanders must not concern yourselves about them; you have no idea of what it means to be uprooted from your soil, from your church and from the cemetery where your forefathers lie. All the trouble that you see results from this ardent longing. It is no easy matter for any brain, Comninos, and you are not to blame for not understanding it.'

Fortis sat down beside the schoolmaster and asked in a low but agitated voice: 'And their putting the axe to the olive trees of the island and their picking the unripe fruit that belonged to others!'

'And that, too,' said Avgustis soberly.

'And the women making their washing-lye by burning the shutters and stairs of the houses we gave them?'

'That, too,' said the schoolmaster. 'All these things are done so that the people won't betray their own Madonna, their church, their soil. They detest all your houses, trees, churches and icons, because they are not theirs. They want to maintain without compromise the feeling that they are unfurled for departure at any time. They entered this port because they were beset by a great calamity. We shall remain until the evil passes and then we will hoist sail and go back to our own land.'

Rapt by the vision which his imagination evoked, he repeated for the sheer joy of hearing it again: 'Then we will go back to our own land. . . .'

Fortis, stubbornly unconvinced, said nothing.

In the silence was heard the dragging, stumbling footsteps of old Vastagos. The blind man groped his way with his cane. The schoolmaster took him by the arm and helped him to sit down.

'Isn't it so, Uncle Vastagos?' he asked.

The blind man smiled patiently.

'I don't know what you were talking about, my son.'

'About our Anatolia. We will go back, isn't that so?'

'We shall go back, my son when our sins have been forgiven. Why not?'

The schoolmaster turned exultantly to Fortis.

'Do you hear? This is *faith*. As Christ said, "If you have so much as a mustard seed of faith, you can tell a mountain to come here and the mountain will come." We don't ask that much. It's enough that we go to the mountain . . .that mountain.'

He pointed the mountains of Anatolia which were smoking with mist on the horizon, towering serenely above the tranquil sea.

'Do you see them, Uncle? Don't you see them?' he asked the blind man excitedly.

'Of course, I see them, my son. Having left my eyes there, I can see with no others.'

Nevertheless, nothing prevented the building project from going forward. The engineer, cursing, in the end was forced to pay the fishermen for the sand. He did it, however, as a matter of conscience, since the labour would have cost ten times as much if he had ordered it hauled by land. With the arrival of cement from Hora, the construction started. Wells were drilled in the centre of what was to be the new village and the carpenters made wooden forms for the concrete.

The work advanced briskly. Where till then had spread a great coastal olive grove, was planted, day by day, a village with attractive, well founded houses which extended in straight orderly rows from the shore up to the olive forest. They were all alike, with two rooms, a kitchen, and a courtyard for the hen coop and ornamental plants. After the labourers finished a day's work and withdrew, the fishermen would stroll through the new streets, which already were clearly discernible, to familiarize themselves with this prodigious undertaking.

'Here there will be a square,' they would say, pointing to a clump of trees which the engineer had left unmolested in the centre of the village.

Avgustis became less talkative as the days passed. He went to Fortis's and slumped dejectedly on a chair away from the others. He listened to the fishermen excitedly discussing the new village and was furious at the wrong that was being done. He regarded them sadly and ached to warn them. Then he shook his head, gnawed his moustache, and began to drink.

'It's not good for you to start this,' Fortis admonished him when he saw the schoolmaster drinking to excess.

Avgustis merely raised his head, sighed and spread out his hands in hopeless futility.

'What else is there?'

The happiest of all was Varouhos. He would settle his immense bulk on Fortis' bench until it creaked from end to end. He smoothed his drooping moustache, ordered a coffee, and drummed a tattoo on his tobacco box before opening it to roll a fat cigarette.

'How could I have known, godfather, that I was bringing joy to my house in the basket of fish-lines that night.'

Fortis had been chosen godfather for the baby, whose christening would take place in a month or two, since Nerandji wanted to complete two years of mourning for Zena. The first thing every morning Fortis sent a big jug of fresh milk by Tsalekos to his prospective godchild.

He would say in his courteously formal manner, 'Before I give the oil, I give the milk. May God bless both to our long life and may I later give also the wine at the wedding. . . .'

14

V A R O U H O S spoke truly. With this baby girl, joy had once more entered his house. The miracle began with Nerandji. This woman for two years had drunk the poison of her grief with a strange voluptuousness and now was beginning to hate herself as she became aware that time was gradually effacing her vivid image of the dead child.

This she fought as a new disaster, the prospect of losing her grief, the one treasure her heart possessed, and she condemned it also as a sin, a betrayal of the child she had lost.

Up to the present, Zena had relived within her all the days, hours and minutes of her brief life. One by one Nerandji stored away the smiles and words of the lost daughter. She ransacked her memories frantically so as not to overlook any action, any utterance, any facial expression and she felt a mingling of joy and pain whenever she salvaged some new bit for her collection. Forgetting even one thing would be for her a thrusting away of the girl's idolized figure.

Nerandji felt that such an action could never be forgiven, as if she were a humble nun, living in the world to serve Zena's memory, veiled in black from head to foot, shut off from the sunlight, the sea and every happiness.

One night, a month or so before her husband's trip to Hora, she had awakened in icy terror. In her sleep she had seen Zena coming from the seashore. She was holding her apron with her hands. It was probably filled with shells. She held it so high that her thighs and red underdrawers were exposed. As she looked at the child, Nerandji felt her hair stand on end in horror. Zena had no face! There were the familiar black curls and the red ribbon but no face. 'Oh!' she cried and sat up in bed, shaking all over, her heart pounding. She crossed herself and drew a deep breath. 'It was only a dream, thank God!' she said and lay down again to sleep. Still obsessed with the dream, she closed her eyes and struggled to recall Zena's face in order to fill in the horrible blankness of the dream. 'Oh, my God,' she thought, 'I'm going to lose my mind!'

She struggled and fought until in despair she realized that she was unable to recover the features of her beloved daughter. Finally she surrendered resignedly to silent grief. She pressed a hand to her mouth to stifle her sobs and stared fixedly into the darkness, beside herself with suffering. 'How could I possibly forget?' she asked herself guiltily as if it were actually the first time she had failed to remember. Slowly she crept out of bed and went to the icon shrine.

'Holy Madonna!' she pleaded. 'Don't make me suffer this affliction! Mermaid Madonna, don't take this from me as well as my child!'

When day came, she waited till everyone had left the house. When she was certain she was alone, she opened a small chest of white poplar wood. Out of it she took some of Zena's shoes and stockings, a little bag with her dresses in it, two shells, and the stained cloths she had dipped in rose vinegar to cool the child's face on that terrible night. Sorrowfully she pressed them to her face to recapture the evaporated acidity. Then she set all these souvenirs in a row and gazed at them on her knees, beating her breast and trying, through them, to recall Zena's face. But it was no use. Zena continued to withhold her features. The mementoes were of no further assistance.

She scattered them wildly and gave herself up to loud lamentation. As she listened to her sobs, it seemed as if someone else were weeping beside her. Suddenly, in the midst of her lamentations came a sound, familiar, pitiful, and for ever indelible. It was Zena's death rattle, a soft moaning with little whistling breaths and wracking gasps which convulsed the little girl's breast until she finally ceased and grew cold, her torment ended.

Once more Nerandji listened to these echoes of Zena's death struggle and began to reproduce them as if they had been on a gramophone record. And then—O wild joy—with these sounds emerged, clearly and perfectly, Zena's features that had been missing in the nightmare.

A great sense of release came to Nerandji with the obliteration of the memory of the dream, a joy filled with elation. But this proved to be the little one's way of saying farewell, as if she wished to withdraw gradually to the company of the other shades on the vast plain of the dead where they drift vaguely like dry ears of grain. In the rustling speech of the dead, they whisper what they remember of their former lives and sometimes when they think of the love and longing of those they have left behind in the Upper World, they return fleetingly in dreams like mysterious, shadowy birds of passage from the nebulousness of death to brush briefly the eyelids of the living.

So it was in Zena's case. The vividness of her memory blurred and melted as if she were drifting away in a blue haze. Now that the new baby had come out of the sea, Zena's departure became more peaceful and endurable. Nerandji accepted her fading with affectionate resignation.

From the day the foundling was brought into the house, everything began to change. The shattered world of Varouhos and Nerandji revolved around a new axis. The clamorous personality of this blonde infant set everything in motion. She was an unsuspected dynamo of energy. Her strange eyes stared at the faces around her while she smiled and prattled unintelligibly with invisible beings whom no adult was privileged to see. She was fair and rosy and healthy and gay.

She came into this black-draped home like a shaft of sunlight piercing the darkness and plunging its golden bolt into the depths of suffocating gloom.

Nerandji removed all evidence of mourning. She propped the window blinds wide open and let the sunlight enter freely. The child turned her face to the large, rectangular piece of sky and jabbered incomprehensibly. Once more the glistening masts were seen through the blue square of the window, swaying and inscribing elaborate capital letters against the heavens, which the child followed as if she could read and understand them. At night when the vices and pounding of the workmen ceased, the wash of the surf was heard like a magic incantation from millions of tiny waves. Nerandji was a bit startled to hear this music, which had not reached her ears for so long a time. It was glorious. The sands hissed as they drank the water, and the hollows in the Mount of the Modonna gulped the waves with bursts of laughter.

Quickening life poured eagerly through the window and filled the house with radiance. One day another incredible incident occurred. While Nerandji was cradling the child in her arms, a little song rose shyly from her heart. She sang it, very softly at first, then with a note of triumph. The child cried out and clapped her hands. Rapturously Nerandji improvised the words:

On my lady's cheeks
Are scattered gold florins.
On my lady's feet
Are pearls by the handful.

15

A F T E R the completion of the two-year mourning period, the baptism took place on a Sunday at the chapel of the Mermaid Madonna. The baby was christened Smaragthi, as Fortis wished, in spite of the schoolmaster's objections. The ceremony was followed by a celebration under the mulberry tree at the coffee-house. The drinks were all on the godfather, and Tsalekos was sent up to the village to fetch the musicians of Mouria, the famous Canaries, whose real name was Kanarides but whom everyone called the Canaries because of their sweet music. They were: Lefteris, who played the fiddle, and Yourgaros, who accompanied him on the lute and sang the drawn-out refrain during the dances. With them was Nasis, the clarinetist. On exceptional occasions like a wedding or the Feast of the Assumption, the band would be supplemented by a zither and a trumpet from neighbouring villages.

In the old days this band was famous throughout the island. They were frequently called to distant villages, sometimes even to Hora. But now that sheet music, gramophones, radios and other inventions had taken over, work was becoming more and more scarce. By day they worked in the fields and gardens, but when calls like this came, they dropped their spades and seized their instruments. Their roughened fingers regained sensitivity as soon as they touched the strings and keys.

During the rest intervals, Yórgaros told about the European tunes they played for you in Hora. Cocking an eyebrow ironically, he explained:

'Convenience. Everything is convenience, and when it's a matter of conveniences, take yourself off, for you needn't expect anything good. Written music—can that ever be music? What would happen if you put sheets of music in front of God's nightingales? They'd foul them and fly away.'

'What do you mean by written music?' asked Yoryis Apoldelipos.

'Why, they make a picture of the strings, my boy, and then they write the sounds on them, the signs, you see. Here you put one finger, there you put another, do you understand? This way you're always sure! Convenience, my boy! These European conveniences have ruined music. And they put singers into a box like sardines! How can there ever be pickled songs? Impossible, my boy!'

Fortis listened to the tirade on European music and was reminded of American marvels. So he pushed back his spectacles and related one of his own curious experiences.

A friend once took him to Luna Park. This is a place where there is a festival every night. You can see all the electrical wonders of America, so mysterious that you're quite likely to lose your mind. They simply can't be described. People would think you were crazy. Well, his friend showed him a robot there. It's a kind of mechanical man which Americans manufacture and it acts like a real person. 'It looks almost as if it could talk,' Fortis said. 'Of course, it can,' replied his friend, 'and what's more, if you sing a song into its ear, it will learn it in a flash and sing it back to you. All you have to do is put a half dollar into its mouth.' 'I'll bet I can sing it a song it won't be able to sing back,' said Fortis. 'Want to bet?' said his friend. 'It's a bet!' So Fortis put in a half dollar and sang to it an island song in the dialect of his village. Fortis sang the song for his guests.

'Did the robot learn it?' asked Nasis, the clarinetist.

'Did it learn it, he asks! My boy, it sang it back to me better than I'd sung it, the rascal, and after hearing it only once!'

Fortis looked triumphantly at the astonishment on the fishermen's faces. He enjoyed amazing these yokels with such tales.

Yorgaros alone was able to believe it. He struck the neck of his lute with the flat of his hand. *Jang!* The strings produced a fearful discord.

'So,' he cried excitedly, 'here I am, a poor devil of a musician, a man of small worth. Yet I reject America and the robots and all such devices!'

Fortis regarded him sadly.

'Is that so?' he asked teasingly.

'Just so! I say the world is beautiful and right, as God made it. And God didn't make robots. Man, I say, must be whole, with his longings and his dreams, each with his own form of happiness. All these machines, hear me, are sins in the eyes of God. And what is the greatest sin of all?'

'Tell us, so that in our ignorance we may learn!'

'It is that in the end, living men, whom God created with flesh and souls, will fall to the level of these robots. Then will come the end of the world. That's what I say.'

Yoryis Apolelipos, the crippled dynamite fisherman, stroked his beard thoughtfully with the hook that replaced his hand. Then he lifted his glass and drained it in one gulp, sloshing the drink about in his huge mouth.

'Ha-a!' he said. 'That's right. I think Yorgaros is right. I wouldn't want to be in America and go around like a machine. . . .'

Fortis nodded. 'He who eats beans, bears witness to beans! What do you say, Avgustis? You're the best educated.'

Avgustis raised his grey head wearily and tried to muster a smile.

'Every land has its own customs,' he said. 'What do we care about America? What is good for America may be good for Americans. This is Greece and all men—the Americans, the English and the French—respect her. From here came the Holy Light. In ancient times God spoke Greek. And Christ, also. We must not let our fires go out. When we let our ways fall into disrepute, it means we have let our fires go out. The Holy Light came from Greece for the whole world. And Greece came from Asia Minor. . . .'

'But how poor we are!' said Lefteris.

'We've always been so,' said the schoolmaster with a sudden flame in his eyes. 'That doesn't matter.'

Lefteris wiped his moustache, smiled and began to tune his fiddle. In his small, childlike voice, he said, 'Poor and sentimental eh?'

He raised his bow and spoke with greater clarity on the strings of his fiddle. Its voice was the real voice of Lefteris. Yorgaros took the lute into his arms and murmured an accompaniment to his brother's tune. The clarinet was silent, awaiting its time. When the violin finished, Lefteris gently lowered it from his chin and nodded to Yorgaros, who intoned the drawn-out vocal section:

> *He who is without feeling might as well be dead*
> *For in this world of beauty he is out of place!*

The guests joined in the refrain:

> *Your lovely, teasing eyes*
> *Stop me in my tracks. . . .*

High spirits kindled and blazed. The fishermen drank the godfather's health.

'May you live a thousand years, Comninos! And may you see her well married!'

They also drank Varouhos's health.

'May Smaragthi live long with you, Uncle Antoni!'

The schoolmaster in fun proposed a toast according to his preference.

'May Aphrodite enjoy a long life! Our Anadyomene!'

Again he seized the opportunity to explain to the fishermen that she should have been christened Aphrodite and how Aphrodite was for the ancient Greeks the most beautuiful of the divinities. And the baby was like her, blonde as wheat and her eyes greenish-blue like the sea on white sand. The waves opened and out she came, and the beach gleamed and the whole world was full of light!

'Go and bring her so we can drink her health!' cried one of the guests. Varouhos looked inquiringly at Fortis.

'Bring her,' said the godfather.

Nerandji demurred at first until she learned it was the godfather's wish. Then she took the child in her arms and stood silent and austere in the midst of the guests under the mulberry tree. She held the child proudly in her silk christening dress that Fortis had brought from the city. On the baby's bonnet were a goldpiece and a bead of blue glass, and around her throat was a gold chain from which hung a cross.

The fishermen gazed at Smaragthi a long while without speaking, so strange was her beauty. She possessed a radiance of her own, a luminousness of rose and gold, blue and green. She stared back and smiled, waved her arms and smiled again. No one understood this miracle, but they all understood that she was of stock other than that of their own children. The scene was like the Christ Child in the manger in the icons with the shepherds and Magi standing open-mouthed around the Infant.

Yorganos improvised the following verses:

Helios is the bridegroom, Selene is the bride
And the godfather is renowned in all Mytilene.
Roses, roses
Are the cheeks of the bride!
I'll toss a ringing florin in the marketplace
And with it buy the bride a thousand years of life!

All Panayia echoed with the chorus:

'Eyah! A thousand years of life!'

Nerandji shivered. She remembered how at the time of Zena's death, Aunt Permahoula had keened for the little girl as if she had grown up into young womanhood, married and left orphaned children behind. Nerandji made the sign of the cross over Smaragthi and left the merry company as silently as she had come.

Twilight descended in purple and gold over trees and faces. It filled the glasses to the brim with glowing colours and made the copper trays shine. The sun sank towards the sea and tinged it with deep rose. The water between the listless boats was saturated with prismatic tints.

The schoolmaster drank without saying a word and stared far off at the Anatolian mountains, which were shining like burnished copper. A yellow cloud spread its soft wings like the Holy Spirit and hovered above the sunset until it took on the colour of cyclamen. Suddenly all around it blossomed great flowers of golden flame.

On these men who were enjoying themselves fell the bitter-sweet burden of life, life which is filled with sorrow and pleasure, to whose breast all men passionately cling.

16

C O N D I T I O N S in Athens were steadily improving. With the passing of time, political disputes subsided, passions cooled, and life gradually returned to the course from which the distractions of war had diverted it.

The exchange of populations between Greece and Turkey was ratified and racial hostility was correspondingly tempered. Politicians of all parties strove to establish, on a soil still stained with blood, the foundations of good neighbourliness, if not amity, between the two belligerent races.

Meanwhile, the new fishing village was completed. Houses were assigned by lot so that there should be no complaints. As each man accepted his dwelling, the shiny, new key which he put into his pocket gave him an unfamiliar sense of pride.

Lathios and his family were now separate from Varouhos and even from Maria. From now on, mother and daughter each would bring forth children in her own house, and at night the youngsters would no longer sleep in a tangled mass on a common pallet. Nevertheless, when mother or daughter had work to do, she still would hand over her infant to the other to be nursed. There was always a new baby in the house.

Varouhos received a house in the first row, only a few steps from the shore, a bit of good fortune he attributed to Smaragthi. On one side the house faced the Aegean and Anatolia, and on the other the olive groves and the mountain of Mouria with the church of Ai-Lias on its summit, whose pate wore clouds like tufts of fluffy white hair.

'What shall we do for our schoolmaster?' asked the Secretary General of the Province, who had come for the drawing of the lots (the Bishop had declined because of illness). He inquired half seriously, for he was acquainted with old Avgustis's flaming spirit.

'Don't do anything for me,' the latter replied coldly, still stubbornly aloof. 'I'm a dry husk, wife I have none, children have I none. A tile roof is sufficient to cover my head. Just give me a place where I can gather the children and teach them what little I know and their duty to the Race. . . .'

So for a school and living quarters they gave him the wretched hovel which Varouhos and Lathios had occupied. The loose floorboards sagged underfoot, one or two steps were missing from the stairs, and the window blinds were fastened with ship's cable. A few old desks, donated by the community of Mouria, were placed inside, as well as a table and a few lithographs of the heroes of 1821 and scenes from the Old Testament to decorate the mildewed walls.

The fishermen's children as much as possible avoided setting foot in the school. Only a few girls attended regularly with their books. The boys were quite irregular, since their fathers needed them to help with the fishing.

It was on a Saturday that the refugees moved into their new homes and became men of property.

On that day, Avgustis felt himself completely abandoned. Not a child was in school; the entire population had hurried to the inauguration of the village. He wandered among the empty desks. He paused in front of the blackboard whose sombreness seemed to spread and cover everything with a flood of tar. As if to throw a ray of light against that blackness, he took a piece of chalk and wrote in large, elaborate capital letters: 'Forgive them, Asia Minor, for they know not what they do.' He remained till afternoon shut up in the old house, pacing back and forth, smoking and sighing. The ancient floorboards creaked and a grievous desolation settled upon him as if he had lost his family a second time. Then he wiped his brimming eyes and went to Fortis's to begin drinking.

'You're early, schoolmaster,' scolded Fortis.

Avgustis raised his head, looked at Fortis a while without replying, and then let it drop again. He emptied a glass of raki slowly and silently. Each time he took the glass from the table he stared absently into it, as if he were seeking to discover some secret at the bottom as fortune-tellers do with coffee cups.

Off in the distance, where the red roofs of the houses emerged in straight lines through the grey tips of the olive grove, were heard the faint sounds of gay voices and happy singing. The refugees were celebrating the occupation of their new homes and the merrymaking took on the atmosphere of a folk festival.

The coffee-house was deserted. Tsalekos was away at the farm. With obvious distaste little Lambis was performing various small tasks for his father, such as bringing olives for the schoolmaster or a glowing ember to light his cigarette.

Fortis performed the complicated ritual of preparing his *narghileh*. Finally he crossed his legs and the bubbling commenced. Then Lambis came to him, his bright eyes fixed on his bare feet, one of which persistently rubbed the other.

'Now that there's nothing else to do, can I go and look at the fishing village?' he asked.

'Eh, if you've finished everything, go and see the new village!'

The lad had vanished in a cloud of dust before his father finished his sentence.

Fortis and the schoolmaster remained under the mulberry tree. Cicadas filled the afternoon with their metallic whine, as if suddenly all the inanimate objects in the region had become vocal—walls, stones, leaves, and wood—and were trying out their voices in a kind of wild ecstasy.

In the harbour someone was singing as he manoeuvred the sails of his boat. The pulley sang high up on the mast and from the interior of the olive warehouses came the incessant pounding of a mallet on an empty barrel. The only sign of work at this hour; the sound was like a huge drum deeply and solemnly beating the rhythm for the delirious concert of shouts and whistles that came from the new village.

Fortis listened to the bubbling of his *nargileh* and gave himself up to the pleasant lassitude of afternoon idleness that is so important in the life of the Greek seashore and takes its tone from the drowsy lapping of the surf. The sea, saturated with sunshine, breathed gently and remitted the weary gulls to rock blissfully on its smooth surface. A host of silver butterflies descended from the sun and danced above the motionless deep.

Suddenly Avgustis set down his glass and softly started to chant a poignant antiphon of the church, the psalm of nostalgia:

By the rivers of Babylon	*In memory of our Sion.*
we sat down and wept	*Alleluia!*

As he went on, his voice, feeble with old age but supported by its training, gathered strength. The ancient threnody of the exiled Israelites now became the lament of the persecuted Greek race. The schoolmaster's voice, austere and despairing, negotiated with incredible sureness the rapid, heartbreaking climaxes, and when it reached the 'alleluia' the music became a trumpet call to a people on the march, a rhythmic dirge accompanying the painful footsteps of a defeated, disheartened host. This new Israel was laboriously treading on thorns and burning flints which marked the road of exile and was bearing its household gods with it. Countless feet, naked and wounded, plodded with dull, muffled echoes in this antiphon, marking the Anatolian wilderness on and on with a red trail of bloodstained footprints.

Alleluia!

The exhausted ones fell by the wayside. The thirsty ones wept for only a drop of water. They licked their tears with their parched tongues. The women trailed behind. Children died in their arms, but for hours, until their knees gave way with fatigue, they carried the lifeless bodies.

Alleluia!

Then the sweep of the music was retarded. The people of exile lifted to the heavens a solemn oath of fealty to the land of their fathers.

Let my tongue cleave to my throat,   *If I forget thee.*
O Jerusalem.   *Alleluia. . . .*

This time the 'alleluia' was a wild march, an expedition of return for vengeance, a charge with battle cries and lances. A shout of 'Forward!'

The schoolmaster dropped his head on his folded arms and wept silently with sobs that shook his bony shoulders.

Fortis carefully laid down the mouthpiece of his *nargileh* and got up. Slapping the old man affectionately on the shoulder, he said softly: 'Come, get hold of yourself.'

Avgustis arose, wiped his moustache, paid his bill, and stumbled off. Then he hesitated, turned, and said stubbornly: 'But the General in Athens! Let's see what he says, eh?' He lingered, smiling faintly as if waiting for an answer.

Fortis nodded affirmatively and watched the schoolmaster until he turned a corner. From far off still came the clamour of the village, the gay tumult of the refugees who were enjoying themselves. From the sea silver glints penetrated the foliage of the mulberry tree and played among the green branches.

At dusk, while the colours were deepening, a fishing boat rounded the Mount of the Madonna. Fortis watched it with pleasure. Now there would be plenty of cheap fish. The poor would have enough to eat tonight and tomorrow, Sunday, they would gorge themselves. And there would be bait for the hooks of Skala fishermen. This crew were Tchesmeliotes, bronzed by the sun and dressed in white shirts and breeches. At the tiller was old Captain Doumanis, who was well liked in Skala. He was rotund and ruddy with sly, laughing eyes as blue as beads that are worn to ward off the evil eye. He was always in a jovial mood.

Fortis gathered up his *nargileh* and went inside to light the fire and prepare a kettle of bean soup for the fishermen. Doumanis never failed to come with his crew.

Lambis arrived on the run, as abruptly as he had departed.

'El, how was it in the new village?' asked Fortis as he worked.

The lad expressed his admiration with a whistle like the sound of a sky rocket.

'Whew! You should see the houses, Father! They're red! They're yellow! They're blue! They're all new and beautiful and clean!'

'Ha!' said Fortis. 'Good thing you saw them today. Tomorrow they won't be clean, my son.'

17

T H U S the refugees arrived and took root around the Mount of the Madonna. Year after year, their numbers increased until the harbour was filled with new voices and the sea was thronged with new boats. They battled the waves with their bare hands while the Mermaid Madonna stood above them as their protector. She held over them the nets that hung drying on the walls of her chapel and on the flag-staff as long ago Pallas Athene had defended them with her fleece of sheep and goats.

The refugees came to love the stretch of shoreline that Greece had given them for a dwelling place. They adapted themselves to the islanders and found security in their surroundings. They knew better than even the islanders the lairs and wanderings of the fish; none knew better the channels and the treacherous shoals under the blue expanse of the sea, the deceptive rocks, the hiding places of octopus and lobster, or the virgin grounds where they might profitably cast their nets.

In time they also learned to love the sacred olive tree which for the islander is both religion and sustenance. Now that the bitterness which had poisoned their minds had abated, they watched with respect the peasants laboriously lugging earth on their backs in wicker baskets up the steep, gravelly mountain slopes so that a new planting might be added to the thirteen million trees already on the island.

Now they were able to understand the horror of the villagers when the refugees felled these venerable trees for winter firewood. As they became better acquainted with the island people, they realized what an impressive monument to patience and labour was this forest of olive trees that extended in a majestic silver tide from one end of the island to the other. Generation after generation had worked this soil and watered it with their tears and sweat. They knelt before it as one kneels in church to speak with God or as a man kneels before a woman to plant seed in her womb.

As years passed, the fishermen improved their skill and the value of the fish increased. Old boats were completely refurbished; some even became sailing ships and made voyages. A few of them were equipped with engines, which filled the harbour with noise and the smell of petrol.

Panayia's reputation as a fishing ground reached as far as Hora and on moonless nights whole fleets of motor-ships arrived. Their lamps set the sea ablaze so that on summer nights the women would sit on their rooftops and enjoy the festiveness.

New coffee-houses and taverns were opened and the bake-shops were kept busy. Visitors came in throngs from Hora: mechanics, shipwrights, and fishmongers. The fishermen of Skala sold their catch to the motor-ships, which transported the cargo directly to Athens in refrigerated holds.

The older fishermen had no use at all for this new age of engines and motors. They worked with equipment and methods inherited from their fathers and grandfathers: lines, wooden spears, and nets that they set in the open sea and hauled in together as a joint enterprise. The glass was used in shallow water, a skill which required stealthy rowing and accurate spearing with the head 'in the glass' and a firm grip on the gunwale.

On occasion, when there was no one to spy on them from the capes, they used dynamite. Nor did they entirely forget Anatolia. When conditions were favourable, they crossed over under cover of darkness and cast their nets in the Turkish waters.

This required courage and luck. The wind must be just right so that a fisherman could work swiftly before being overtaken by daylight near forbidden Anatolia and thus be in danger of arrest by a Turkish patrol boat. This meant his nets would be confiscated and weeks would be lost in the courts between Pergamos and Aivali. In the end he would pay a fine and be allowed to return without his gear.

Lathios was one of those who trespassed stealthily in prohibited waters. He would take his older sons and leave the harbour without telling he was going. Frequently he would return with a splendid catch, which he sold for a good price. As long as the money lasted, he would go to Fortis's in the evening and drink silently by himself until his mother-in-law came late at night to fetch him home.

The Turks had caught him twice and confiscated his nets, five or ten settings each time, a fortune, but he obstinately refused to quit and continued to invade their territory at the risk of being captured.

He was unable to understand the reason for these 'restricted waters' where they arrested him. 'Look how men are dividing up the sea!' he would exclaim. It was all right with the land. That was understandable. The land you ploughed, sowed, watered, and tended so that, at last, wiping away the sweat, you staked out a piece of earth and said, 'Here is my line.' But the sea belongs to God. Like the sky. Who ploughs the sea and plants it with fish? God does it for all people. For the Turks and for the Greeks.

Yoryis, the former dynamite fisherman, earned enough to buy himself a new sailboat. When he felt his own deck under his feet, he gave up dynamiting and turned to smuggling. But now it was not the Anatolians he must outwit. He was dealing with Greek revenue boats and they caught him with a cargo of contraband cigarette paper. They towed him to Hora and brought him to trial. His ship was sold and he was put in jail until his fine, an enormous sum, was paid.

He remained behind bars only five or six months. It was a waste of time to hold him, the authorities concluded. Free, he could earn something to pay the State. Here they had to feed him.

So one day he was summoned to the office. They would release him, he was told, if first he would sign a note for the balance of his debt to the State.

'Of course,' said the smuggler. 'Where's the paper?'

'Sign here,' a sallow-skinned clerk ordered him.

He indicated the place on the document with the nail of his little finger. It was an unbelievably long nail. Yoryis stared in wonder at this extraordinary fingernail. He decided it must be some kind of professional instrument. No doubt the man needed it to show prisoners where to make their signatures.

Then with his good hand, Yoryis took the pen which the clerk offered him and regarded it with admiration. Finally he dipped it in the ink and set about writing his signature with illegible flourishes, protruding his tongue with the agreeable effort. When he finished, he sighed and cocked his head to one side while he complacently admired the scrawl. Finally he looked up and asked: 'How much does the note say I owe you?'

The clerk blotted the precious document with official impressiveness and replied curtly: 'One million, nine hundred eighty thousand, five hundred one drachmas and thirty-seven lepta.'

Yoryis gaped with astonishment. 'Oh, my!' he said, gripping the desk with his hook to keep from falling.

Then he made a mental calculation, frowned, and said ingenuously: 'So you must now pay me nineteen thousand, four hundred and ninety-eight drachmas and sixty-three lepta.'

'Why?' asked the sallow-skinned clerk in surprise.

'To make it exactly two million, you see, to round out my account with the State so that we have no misunderstanding.'

Yoryis returned to Skala on foot as penniless and destitute as when he first came from Anatolia. Now he must go back to dynamite fishing and start all over again. But he never lost his sense of humour nor was he discouraged.

The other fishermen had fun treating him to drinks and getting him to tell his story about the note. They gave him baskets of small fish on credit to peddle in Mouria so that he might earn enough for bread and raki. When some housewife was impatient for her change, Captain Yoryis would reach his hand into his pocket for the money, draw himself up with an air of wounded pride, and say as he waved his hook towards the sky:

'See how topsy-turvy the world is. Great Greece gives me credit for one million, nine hundred eighty thousand, five hundred one drachmas and thirty-seven lepta, but you bother me about the pittance I owe you!'

One thing he could not tolerate, however, was the motor-boat. One night when the fishermen were sipping drinks at Fortis's and the noise of fishing with lights came from the sea, Yoryis banged the table with his hook and unburdened his heart.

'That isn't fishing,' he said. 'It's cheating.'

'How so?' challenged Fortis. 'Man progresses with his inventions.'

'Man progresses and leaves God behind,' said Varouhos. 'Our fathers and our grandfathers didn't know about machines and new-fangled gadgets. They sifted the sea with the net and God filled the sea with abundance. Thus it was that Christ fished with the Twelve Apostles. Now they go out with motors and the water is polluted with petrol. Men become cunning and they put their cunning into machines. Then the sea is despoiled and God turns his wrath on us. .'

'That's true,' said Lathios, his nose in his glass.

'You lure the fish with lights,' Yoryis grumbled again, 'you stun them on the head, and you shovel them up like dung. That's not honourable work.'

Fortis took up the defence of science as a matter of course.

'How about baiting a hook, throwing pieces of bait as a lure, tying rags on hooks, in this honourable work? And how about dynamite?'

'That's not the same thing,' said Yoryis heatedly. 'We fish courageously. We go out and hunt for them. We throw the spear. They know how to dodge it. We lie in wait for them with the net. They can break through. We drop baited hooks and they come and nibble at them. They steal the bait and go away. We fling the torpedo at them. It's war. You eat me or I eat you. See, I've given my flesh fighting with the fish. I don't complain. Tit for tat. But lolling and sleeping in the stern and then getting up and scooping in the fish without so much as wetting the seat of your breeches? That? Varouhos is right. The machine puts a distance between man and

God. That's all I have to say.'

Fortis chuckled, turned his chair and touched Yoryis on the knee.

'It's not so,' he said with conviction. 'With the machine man comes constantly closer to God. Once when I went to Hora to testify in court, I went to the cathedral to pay my respects to the Bishop. He had just returned from Athens. He is always going there on behalf of his hospital and home for the aged.'

He saw the fishermen lean forward attentively.

'What's that go to do with it?' asked Varouhos.

'It has much to do with it,' said Fortis triumphantly, 'since the Bishop goes and comes by aeroplane.'

All of them, including Yoryis, exclaimed: 'By aeroplane!'

'Now listen,' Fortis went on. ' "Bishop," I said as a joke, "excuse me, but isn't it rather odd for a bishop to fly?" Then he stroked his beard and said with a sly look: "It shouldn't seem strange to you, my son, for a bishop to fly. Even the angels fly around the face of God. And I, a lowly worm of the earth, every time I find myself above the clouds, I cross myself and say: 'Thank you, God, for bringing me five miles nearer to you'!" '

'The godfather knows he is joking,' smiled Varouhos. 'Christ didn't fish at night with motor-boats, that's for sure.'

Fortis waved his hand impatiently.

'Of course, He didn't because electric lights hadn't been invented at that time.'

Varouhos stopped smiling and regarded Fortis reproachfully.

'Shame on you, godfather,' he said. 'You've been to America and you've seen a lot of the world. And yet you've missed one important thing! You see, there's nothing in the universe or on earth that God doesn't know before men do.'

Lathios, who seldom put in a word, stopped his glass at his moustache and said corroboratingly: 'Right. . . . How could it be otherwise!'

Fortis was nonplussed. He knew that the right was on his side but he had to admit that what Varouhos had said was true. In his soul, which worshipped America, he agreed that thousands of years before Edison, God had known about the electric light and the gramophone. He even knew how to make artificial teeth and vending machines that served you for a small coin. Then why had He let the world muddle along so many years with candlesticks and oil lamps that irritated your nostrils with their fumes? And when He did decide to reveal these mysteries, why did He choose the Americans, who are not members of the Orthodox Church? This was something to think about. It was God, he concluded, who was mixed up!

He lifted his eyes as if to find an answer in the sky. Night had fallen. The heavens were spread out, dark blue, cool like the sea, filled with stars, that twinkled above the masts of the boats and through the boughs of the mulberry tree. But no enlightenment was vouchsafed from that quarter.

Down below in the darkness, the figure of old Permahoula jutted from the trunk of the mulberry tree to which she seemed attached like a growth. Her voice, monotonous, humble and pleading, was directed towards Lathios's table, which was apart from the others.

'Come now, get up and come home. The little ones are hungry and want to eat.'

Lathios and his friends pretended not to hear. Accustomed to this game, they sipped their drinks in silence.

But the old woman had learned her role years ago. She waited a little and then repeated the plea in the same tone as the priest uses when he reads the Canon of the Liturgy with no one to hear him except God.

'Come, I say, get up now.'

She spoke thus, two, three, five times before Lathios got up and paid his bill. Then the old woman was like a cricket in the night when it has wearied of chirping under the stars. Only the soft padding of her bare feet was heard as she started to leave. At that moment Fortis called to her and treated her to a glass of strong brandy.

The aged tippler seized the glass eagerly, closed her eyes, and downed the drink in one gulp. Then she smacked her lips with gratification.

'My blessing on you, my son! My blessing from my twenty nails!'

The fishermen chuckled softly in the night.

18

V A R O U H O S' S house very quickly became the most attractive of all the homes in the fishing village. Nerandji planted vines around the doorway and soon their cool leafage spread above the lintel. She placed stools on each side so that she and Varouhos could sit there in the late afternoon while the sun was setting. She engaged Maestro-Yoryis, the blacksmith and machinist at the factory, to install iron supports outside the windows for flowerpots.

Smaragthi grew like a sturdy plant in the arms of this good woman, who devoted herself to the service of her adopted daughter with an almost religious zeal. During the day her care and attention surrounded the child with an atmosphere of loving tenderness, and even at night Nerandji would linger by the pillow of the sleeping infant to gaze at her in ecstasy under the dimmed lamp.

The little one formed the habit of sleeping on her back with her arms around her head, which was framed by her wavy golden hair. She breathed lightly and her rosy face was so lovely among her thick curls that often Nerandji was secretly afraid to look at her. She dreaded lest any moment the soft breathing might stop and this marvellous creation of God would be destroyed. She would make the sign of the cross over the child's breast and avert her eyes to prevent the intensity of her love from bringing some evil to the girl.

On winter nights she would take the child's arms carefully from the pillow and put them under the covers to keep them from being chilled, but almost immediately the sleeping infant would withdraw them and place them once more around her head.

Sometimes Smaragthi would wake up and see Nerandji's face looking down at her. It was thus that the woman's features were imprinted on her mind and imagination. It was a sweet, anxious vision which uninterruptedly sheltered her entire existence with the mantle of its protection. The face was thin and brooding, like that of the Madonna of the Sweet Kiss, with two great eyes filled with blazing light and a fine skin which on the forehead was etched with tiny wrinkles like silk cloth. The dark circles around the eyes made them seem incredibly large and luminous. But the child was never frightened by their brilliance, for at once the flame was transformed into a smile, the sweetest that ever illumined a mother's eyes.

'Mama!' she would say and squeeze with her little hands the care-worn fingers which were gently arranging her hair. Love unfolded her like warm sunshine. It was only when she started to walk and ventured beyond the safety of the house that she met her first enemy.

The enemy was Markos, an old brown dog that the factory watchman kept to guard the vegetables in the olive mill garden. The garden wall bordered Varouhos's house on the side facing the mountain. Above this wall, on which were stretched four rows of barbed wire, she saw Markos's head staring at her for the first time. She was frightened and took to her heels, for the dog's eyes were hostile and his lips were drawn back viciously, baring his sharp fangs, yellow with age.

Smaragthi had never known till then what it was to be afraid, but a curious reluctance kept her from saying anything about it to her mother. It was the same every time the dog and the little girl met. Markos was not considered a vicious dog, however ferocious he appeared with his powerful legs and huge head. Everyone found him gentle. It was only towards Smaragthi that he displayed this inexplicable hostility, growling, baring his teeth and trying to get at her.

Smaragthi tried to win Markos's friendship by throwing him pieces of dry bread or a bone from a safe distance. Then she would smile and wait for the dog to wag his tail. In vain. The dog became more furious than ever and barked as angrily as if she had thrown a stone at him. He even appeared in her dreams at night and terrorized her. Finally what she most feared happened.

One day Nerandji sent her to the boat with her father's lunch, since he had some work to finish and could not come home. Smaragthi set out with the food wrapped in a napkin. While she was walking along the shore, just before she reached the square of Skala, Markos rushed from a side street and leaped upon her.

The child screamed when she felt the dog's hairy muzzle on her face and the touch of his shaggy pelt. She fell face down on the ground, blood streaming from her cheeks. Some men came to her rescue and drove away the enraged animal with clubs. Then they picked up Smaragthi and carried her home. Her dress was ripped to tatters by the dog's teeth and she trembled from head to foot for a long while before they could calm her.

Only then did she reveal to her mother her previous encounters with Markos, his unaccountable antipathy for her and how she had tried to overcome his hostility. Nerandji, her eyes flaming with a vengeful light, soothed her. While she reassured and comforted the little girl, she thought of hundreds of ways to erase this terrible shock from the child's mind. At last she persuaded Smaragthi not to worry any more and promised her that Markos would never molest her again. As she spoke, the ominous flame again appeared in her eyes.

Nerandji took care that Smaragthi never left the house alone from then on. Either she or Varouhos accompanied her, or Aunt Permahoula or Manolis, Lathios's oldest boy. The latter told her that as long as he was with her neither Markos nor the fiercest monster in the world would dare to attack her.

'Are you so strong?' Smaragthi asked incredulously.

Manolis made no reply to this but told her about Panayis the Koutalian who, when he was attacked by a ravenous lion, seized one of the beast's jaws with each hand and tore him in two like a small fish.

Next day he showed Smaragthi a sling he had made out of a strip of sailcloth. They went to the beach and he put a stone in the sling.

'Now watch,' said Manolis.

He whirled the sling about his head with all his might and let the stone fly over the sea. It sped with a beautiful whistling sound until it dropped into the waves.

'This is for Markos,' the boy said. 'Some day I'm going to kill him because he bit you.'

A few days later, Markos was found dead.

'You killed him,' Smaragthi said indignantly to Manolis.

'No,' said Manolis. 'I didn't do it.' And he lowered his eyes guiltily.

The watchman said the dog had suffered terribly from cramps before he died. There was no doubt that someone had given him rat poison. The huge corpse was thrown into the sea. For three days it floated there, its belly bloated and its legs straight and stiff. Then the wind changed and the body disappeared.

The next time Smaragthi passed the wall with the barbed wire, she glanced instinctively towards the place where she had met the huge, shaggy head with brown eyes that were filled with unappeasable hatred. At first she felt a chill of fear and her heart pounded. Then gradually the chill passed and she felt a relief slightly touched with sadness.

Another day when she and Manolis were talking once more about Markos, he said to her: 'I wish I had killed him for biting you, but I kiss the cross that I didn't do it.'

Again he let fly a stone which sang even farther over the sea before it vanished. Then he turned to her and said: 'However, if a lion should ever happen to. . . .'

The baleful fire which had flamed in Nerandji's eyes when Markos was mentioned now was quenched.

There was general speculation about the peculiar animosity which the inoffensive animal had displayed towards the child. Old Permahoula alone nodded her head, looked at Smaragthi and remarked enigmatically: 'Eh, there are some things I could say. . . .'

'What things, Aunt Permahoula?'

'Oh, nothing, nothing.'

She refused to divulge what was in her mind.

19

T H E day arrived when Smaragthi also appeared among the fishermen's children who fitfully attended Avgustis' school. She carried an oilcloth schoolbag and wore sandals on her feet and a blue ribbon tied with a bow in her neatly combed hair. The other children crowded around her in amazement.

'Are you going to wear such things every day?' asked one little girl with a grubby face.

'Yes,' replied Smaragthi as if she had committed a fault and wished to be forgiven.

'Then what will you wear for Easter?' the girl asked, curiously, touching the ribbon with her finger.

'It's because she's an only daughter,' a boy explained.

Yanna Gadjalis flared up. Scowling with her black eyebrows, she said spitefully: 'An only daughter? I'm an only daughter. She's a bastard!'

At this Fortis's son Lambis flew at her and pulled her plaits until she howled in pain.

'What did you butt in for?' another girl asked Lambis.

'Smaragthi is my god-sister.'

Yanna was wailing loudly and Lambis was flaming with rage.

At this moment the teacher came out of the school and the disturbance subsided, but the word weighed like a stone in Smaragthi's mind. When school was over, she went straight home to ask her mother what it meant. Nerandji's dark eyes snapped as she glared in the direction of the Gadjalis house. Then she took the child passionately into her arms as is she were shielding her from a blow or from some filth about to be thrown at her.

Smaragthi immediately displayed an aptitude for learning. She was interested in everything Avgustis tried to explain to the children. Avgustis, charmed by the girl, confessed frankly to Fortis: 'I give my word, Comninos, that I labour only for your god-daughter. With the others I accomplish nothing.'

'Do you hear that?' Fortis asked his son.

Lambis was shamed in the presence of his teacher. He twisted a button of his shirt, blushed to his ears, hung his head and thought all the while about Smaragthi.

It was not merely that Lambis disliked school, but that he detested old Avgustis, the drunkard, who stank of raki in class. Besides, he kept talking about things that had nothing whatever to do with the sea and the trees. Sometimes, even, he sat at his desk and wept and blew his nose, incapable of teaching the lesson. Meanwhile the children caught flies, impaled them on slivers of wood, and sent them buzzing across the classroom. The result was a wasted half day which Lambis could have spent swimming, fishing and hunting birds. None of the boys liked school, but Lambis went further. He absolutely hated it.

Smaragthi, on the other hand, who listened to the teacher's stories with her sea-green eyes wide open and who smiled in a way that made your heart swell—how was it possible not to be in love with her?

Lambis, when he went to school at all, did it as much to win her approval as to please his father. He knew that the other boys went for the same reason, to see her on the old bench in her blue frock, her clean sandals among so many bare feet, and her blonde plaits tied up with a blue ribbon.

Lambis was thinking about all this while his ears burned and he twisted his shirt button.

'Don't you want to learn anything?' asked Fortis in a voice filled with disappointment.

The boy made no reply.

'Speak up! I asked you a question!' ordered his father.

The boy lifted his bright eyes which mirrored the leaves of the mulberry tree and the sun-glints on the water in the harbour.

'No, Father,' he said, 'I don't.'

He lowered his eyes again and his long lashes cast a shadow on his cheeks.

'And what will become of you? Will you go after garfish or will you spend your life herding goats?'

Without raising his eyes, Lambis replied: 'I'll stay with you, Father. When you grow old, I'll be here to run the shop and manage the farms.'

He spoke seriously and decisively as one who had thought things over and made up his mind.

Fortis tried to look stern but his heart melted with affection. He wanted to take his son into his arms, kiss his full red lips, and stroke his black hair, but he was ashamed of showing his feelings.

'Off with you,' he said, giving the lad a slap on his bottom. 'It seems your destiny is to go barefoot and be good for nothing all your life. Now go swimming! That's what your heart desires, you ragamuffin!'

Avgustis made a gesture of indifference.

'Who knows?' he said. 'Perhaps the boy is right. It is one thing to learn and another to be wise.'

'But how will he ever amount to anything?' Fortis sighed worriedly.

The schoolmaster replied quietly:

'Let me tell you something, Comninos. In life some go by the heart and others by the mind. One or the other rules him. From childhood I have loved books. Yet I have lived by my heart. My wretched heart! (He tapped his forehead with his finger.) I have sharpened this as well as I could. What use has it been to me? It has remained a whetted sword that has never been drawn from its scabbard. If it had ever been taken out, it would only have been plunged into my heart.'

'But still an ignorant man . . .' insisted Fortis.

Avgustis shook his head.

'Don't say it! You don't know the learned ones! From them have come the misfortunes of the Race! They speculate with property in the exchange of populations. They make false depositions. . . They even invented this infamous word "exchange"!'

His voice grew more excited and his hand trembled.

'What exchange, indeed? Do you exchange a Turk for a Greek, head for head, like goat for goat? Do you exchange souls for shares and money? My family whom they murdered, my house and trees, my annotated library, the church pew that was polished by the elbows of my dead father—what about them? Eh?'

He sighed and gulped down a glass of raki.

'Those are the learned men who barter the flesh and blood of Greece . . . and . . . listen to what I say and write it in your memory: If one bit of Greece remains uncorrupted, this will be due to the simple, uneducated folk, my dear Comninos!'

He drank immoderately to drown his grief until his hands shook and his knees failed to support him. He subsisted on the titbits that were served with the raki: olives, cucumbers in vinegar, and octopus slices roasted on hot coals. Drinking dulled his appetite and his meagre diet weakened him. Thick veins stood out on his gnarled hands and on his forehead near his temples.

He was consumed with relentless misery. His declaration of property abandoned in Anatolia had been rejected. In the column where he was expected to itemize his losses, he listed his wife and children, the old blue house with vines in the courtyard, and the fig tree in whose bark the children had carved their names. Everything that pertained to the ancient, beloved Greek homeland of Anatolia, which he had left over there near the Gulf of Adramytti, where the water gleamed in the sunlight and turned the colour of hyacinth in the evening.

At the end he wrote:

'In all, I left behind two thousand years of Greece and civilization.'

And he signed his name.

The members of the Committee on Reparations read it and laughed uproariously. The paper was circulated from hand to hand.

'He's an alcoholic,' explained a member of the local committee, smiling obsequiously at his colleagues from the city. 'A good, honest man, but a little light in the . . .'

Avgustis pinned his hopes on the General, the symbol for all who remained loyal to Anatolia. The election was approaching. There they would speak.

'He is the Moses of the Race. He will lead us back to the Promised Land which runs with milk and honey.'

'When?' asked Fortis.

'Very soon . . . very soon!'

On Saturday nights only did Avgustis go to bed sober, for every Sunday morning he put on his good clothes and went up to the church in Mouria. There he served as first chanter to supplement his slim income from teaching and to delight in the elaborate Byzantine melodies. He followed the ancient tradition that has been kept alive by simple chanters through direct oral transmission from the days of Orthodox Byzantium.

His voice, however, was deteriorating from drink and the church elders grumbled about its huskiness and lack of vigour when they gathered in the sacristy for coffee one Sunday after the Liturgy.

'Eh, it comes from old age. We all reach it sooner or later. What is there to do?' said Avgustis, smiling wanly and lowering his head to his cup.

'If it were only from old age!' observed one of the elders, nudging Avgustis significantly.

The others sounded their agreement with loud sips.

Avgustis was given nothing else to drink.

20

A S soon as Smaragthi grew big enough, Varouhos took her with him in the boat to lend him a hand when the need arose. They pushed the old boat with a punt pole until it lumbered sluggishly into open water. Then the girl seated herself at the oars, while Varouhos, leaning over the gunwale, thrust his head into the frame of the fishing glass. Now that it was turning grey, his hair looked shaggier than ever. The boat listed to one side with the weight of his gread body.

Smaragthi rowed forward or stopped, her young hands firmly gripping the oars and her ears straining to catch the terse commands which her father gave in a muffled voice from inside the tin cylinder that held the glass.

'A bit forward . . . now to starboard . . . there.'

'A bit astern. . . .'

'Easy. . . .'

'Forward . . . hold it! . . . Keep to starboard. . . .'

The sunlight penetrated to the floor fathoms below the surface. The red keel was reflected like an armful of scarlet ribbons that had been cast into the sea to writhe in confusion.

Often Smaragthi took the glass, buried her head in it, and told Varouhos to take her over the wondrous submarine landscapes. Across the glass pane slowly passed bright shallows strewn with blue pebbles and ornamented with shells and green sand. Gaily coloured fish swam back and forth in the streaming, liquid light, some indolently as if luxuriating in the golden, limpid radiance, others swiftly as if they were on some urgent business. Some swam alone, but there were also large schools which moved in military formation, obeying the command of an unidentifiable leader like small, well-drilled soldiers on parade.

Smaragthi learned from Varouhos the name of each kind, according to its shape and colouring. She was deeply impressed with the Christfish which bore the marks of his two fingers. But she liked the barbel best of all. These fish had filmy green, red, and orange ribbons which hung down from head to tail. Smaragthi liked especially the marvellous blue barbel, a creature of the sea but tinged with the most delicate azure of the sky.

Beyond the shallows the land fell away and revealed mysterious caverns beneath the rocks laden with marine plants. Obscure serpentine shapes slithered in and out of them, and men-of-war rose to the surface and spread their sails.

Varouhos pointed out the lairs where the octopus lurks with its tentacles extended in readiness for action. Among the mossy stones he showed Smaragthi the hermit crab, which crawls about with a growth of marine flowers on its back, not for decoration but for concealment from its enemies.

The mysteries that were explained to her day after day became a part of her life. At night she saw these landscapes again in her dreams. She wandered through luminous waters. Submerged in their shimmering silver, she pushed aside long festoons of blossoms from the entrances to nacreous caverns where rosy starfish gleamed inside and the terrible octopus lurked with its cold, evil eyes full of guile and hate. Everything about the sea and its mysteries attracted her.

The schoolmaster also nourished her lively mind. Fascinated, she would listen to him when he told stories from Homer or from mythology. He told, for example, about the Mermaid, the sister of Alexander the Great, who swims from place to place in the sea. She flicks her tail and rises up from the foam in front of Greek ships. Anxiously she inquires about her brother; and if the sailors speak to her in a friendly manner, she teaches them new songs.

'She is Greece,' said the schoolmaster, swept away by visions stimulated by the fumes of raki which befuddled his mind.

'This Mermaid is Greece. Half land, half sea. When you grow up and become captains, what will you reply when she asks you, "Does King Alexander still live?" '

Then the children, who had learned this story from their parents, without interrupting their sport of torturing flies or flicking paper pellets at the ceiling, would answer in unison: 'He lives and reigns, my Lady, and rules the world!'

Smaragthi imagined her rising from the waves in the form of the Mermaid of the Mount. Above the purple pallium she wore a heavenly crown and she stared gravely with her wide, green eyes as she stirred up the sea with her silver tail.

One day Nerandji took her to the chapel to burn incense. As Smaragthi crossed herself before the icon, she seemed to hear the Madonna put the traditional question to her. In alarm she broke off the prayer she was reeling off silently and promptly gave the answer:

'He lives and reigns, my Lady, and rules over the world.'

And the Madonna smiled at her in such a way that she was reassured and finished her prayer.

When Smaragthi's school days were finished in the course of time, Avgustis felt a pang in his heart as he faced the bench where every morning he had grown used to seeing the curly head with the golden plaits. No longer was there the green-blue flame of her eyes to transfigure the rickety blackboard, the warped window blinds, and the dilapidated chair. Other children must have felt the same, for Lambis, who was kept two or three years in each class, never returned to school after his godsister left.

Lambis liked to climb the highest cliff of the Mount, which was called the 'balcony', and watch Varouhos's boat as it moved towards Vigla with the old man at the oars and Smaragthi standing at the prow, her slim body with legs apart finally planted on the deck. She was like a gay banner when the breeze whipped her short blue skirt above her tanned thighs. When the boat disappeared, the boy would saunter home with lowered head. At the coffee-house he would whistle a soft tune, inspect the parting of his hair in the reflector of the lamp, and thrust his hand in his pockets like a man.

Varouhos himself was at times inordinately proud as he looked at his adopted daughter. He sensed something about her like a breeze from far-off places, and he was puzzled without knowing what it was he was trying to explain.

Smaragthi would remain silent for a long while and gaze beyond the sea and the rocks, the distant trees and the hills covered with yellow grain, where the colours of sky and sea meet and blend along the burnished coast of Anatolia.

'What are you gazing at so quietly?' the old man asked her one day.

Startled, Smaragthi shrugged her shoulders and laughed in embarrassment for want of anything to say. Then the question seemed funny and she laughed loudly and ran her fingers through her father's thick hair. He listened to her laughter bubbling like a spring of joy and health.

'Can I swim now?' she asked. She found her greatest happiness in swimming, so that when her mother wished to punish her, she would say sternly, 'There'll be no swimming for you this week.'

'Go ahead and swim, you goldfish,' the old man said.

After going to the cabin to undress, she shot like a javelin into the dark blue sea.

'The sea draws you to her,' muttered the old man through his moustache. He considered her the gift of the sea.

The first time she had swum into the open, leaving behind the other girls who were bathing behind the cliffs of Vigla, the mothers were scandalized and Nerandji was frightened.

'What's the meaning of this? Swimming in the open sea, a big girl! Don't let me catch you at it!'

The threat, however, had no effect; and finally both men and women came to accept it as natural that Smaragthi should bathe differently from other girls.

Fortis understood the purity and the independence that characterized everything she did. He wasn't surprised. 'In America girls . . .'

But Varouhos explained her by repeating: 'It's the sea, you understand, that draws the youngster. Wasn't it the sea that gave her birth?'

Smaragthi often teased her mother to tell her the way she arrived.

'But I've told you so many times, daughter!'

The girl would lay her head in her mother's lap and press to her face and caress the small, worn hand.

Then Nerandji, fondling the waves of golden hair, would turn her sad eyes once more to the past and tell the story.

'Well, then. It was summer, very early in the morning just when I had opened my eyes. I was still in bed when I heard the knocker strike. It was your father returning from Hora. He'd gone there to see the Bishop, our kinsman. "Get up, wife," he called. "See what I found in the boat whimpering in the tackle-basket under the prow. Oh, the rascal, the rascal!" I undid your wrappings and I said to him: "For your information, the rascal is a girl!" There, that's the way you came to us. God loved us and sent you.'

Smaraghti also asked Varouhos: 'Father, tell me how you found me.'

'I've told you. The sea sent you to us.'

'Mother says God sent me.'

'It's the same thing.'

'Oh, all right. Now tell me.'

'I've told you. I'd been drinking. I was coming from the city. I heard gurgling and whimpering in the prow. "Hey," I said. "How the devil is there a puppy in the boat at this hour?" I got up from the tiller, sleepy and befuddled from the raki and staying awake. I bent over the basket and it was you that was crying. There, that's the way it was. . . .'

21

A U N T Permahoula, for whom marvels and folklore were the warp and woof of her life, had a different explanation.

Smaragthi, more than any other of the other children, held the golden key which opened to her, whenever she wished, the old woman's enchanted world. In it was a magic garden, suffused with cool, rosy twilight and filled with dense, exotic plants. On the silver foliage and branches of pearl perched birds that carolled in a way only princesses and beggars could understand the hidden meaning. Among them were golden birds with bright ruby-red eyes like ripe pomegranate seeds.

Jewelled peacocks strutted under the trees that lined streams flowing with rose water. They opened their tails into fans which overspread the sky, the sea and the night with stars. Goldfish swam in the cisterns, each fish with its own name. Aunt Permahoula would call them and they would put their heads out of the water and reply in human speech: 'What do you want, my lady?'

One evening she found Smaragthi on the beach cleaning fishlines. Between her legs was the basket and she munched dried figs as she placed the washed hooks in a row around the rim.

Aunt Permahoula sat down beside her, drew from her bosom a small flask of raki, and took a deep swallow with her eyes closed blissfully. Then she wiped her lips with the palm of her hand and rubbed one against the other to dry them.

'Ah, the Lord be praised!' she sighed with the melancholy satisfaction of aged people who are still steady on their feet.

Without interrupting her work, Smaragthi begged her: 'Tell me a story, Granny, to pass the time.'

'What story shall I tell you, my sultana?'

'Tell me a fairy story.'

'My life is a fairy tale. What other can I tell?'

Pushing aside the basket of fishlines, the girl turned to her with a smile.

'Come, Granny, tell me. Father says the sea brought me. Mother says God sent me. Now tell me. . . . Were you there when I came?'

'Naturally I was, my lady. It was early in the morning and the sky was clear. There were loud voices and a great commotion and a crowd came running to the house. Who could explain how such a baby came to be found in the boat of a drunken fisherman? She lay like a star in the basket. They all stood around staring at her and touching her in astonishment. She had gold in her hair and emeralds in her eyes. She gazed back at the people around her and at once their hearts bloomed like roses. She smiled and the heavens opened. Such a strange child. Eh, what do these people know? They're simple folk, interested only in fishing and raki. They're short on brains and sight. What they don't know, they don't see. What they don't see, they don't know.'

She paused, touched Smaragthi's knee with her fingertip and continued confidentially.

'But when one happens to be a Saturday's child like me and when you've lived in this world for more than a hundred years, then you know many things that you don't talk about. You ask why? Eh, my dove. People nowadays have got far away from religion. They make fun of you if you say anything to them and treat you as if you were mad. When man loses faith, Smaragthi, he becomes sly and self-centred. God doesn't love such people. That's why the Lord forsook us and sent us the seven curses and the twelve plagues.'

She drew out the bottle, took another swallow, and carefully corked it again.

'People weren't like this in the olden days, my daughter! They hadn't learned yet how to be sly. . . . One told them how the Madonna conceived while she was smelling the lily which the angel brought her from heaven and it never occurred to them to disbelieve it. Look, the Mount of the Madonna is close by. Ask your godfather, who is an islander. He must have seen it when he was a boy. Before it was blown up with dynamite, the footprints of the Madonna were on a stone up there. It happened while she was wandering among towns and villages in search of her only Son. The Good Friday story tells about the tribulations of her who is full of grace. The angels brought her here on their wings. She perched on the Mount like an eagle and from that time it was known as the Mount of the Madonna. Where her golden feet came to rest, the stone became white and received the imprint as if it were soft as wax.

'The old ones knew this and came to kiss the stone and burn candles. I knew it, too, for when I was a young girl my parents brought me here in a boat and we celebrated the Assumption of the fifteenth of August. Go today and speak of it to those who no longer celebrate the feast. They'll say you're crazy. . . . Now they go up there only for their water, the outlaws!'

'Think how many of us there are here. She rescued us from the sword of the heathen and yet not a single person takes her a sprig of basil or an embroidered apron. If it weren't for your mother, her lamp would go out and become tarnished. It's because of such unbelief that God has withdrawn His hand from us. And so with many other things. Talk about them and people look at you askance. I remember things that happened in my childhood that these people would call nonsense. So I tell them only to my granchildren and great-grandchildren in the form of fairy tales. You see, it's only as fairy tales that men are willing to listen to God's truth. Well, there was a man named Daras. . . . He was from Moschonisi, the stepson of Nikolaras Mitoufis. . . . So I say that my life is a fairy tale. What other can I tell?'

She stopped, dreaming of the past and shaking her head as her mind wandered among distant memories.

'Who was this Daras?' asked Smaragthi eagerly.

'Daras, my lady, was the handsomest *pallikari* in Moschonisi and a famous smuggler. Tle Turkish police trembled at his name and the Aivaliotes were jealous of him. He transported tobacco through the city in broad daylight. His loaded horses passed the guards, Daras at the head with his musketoon under his fur coat and his *pallikaris* behind him. The police pretended not to recognize him and called out friendly greetings in Turkish. I was only a small child, but I remember my mother showing him to me. He had black eyes and heavy eyebrows. He was a handsome, debonair *pallikari*. One looked at him and said: "God give me two more eyes!" One day a lady saw him on the seashore and fell in love with him.'

'Who was this lady?' asked Smaragthi.

The old woman glanced right and left to be sure no one was looking, took another drink from the bottle, and resumed her tale with gusto.

'She must have been a fairy. A mermaid, you know. A creature of the water. A kind of nymph. Her hair was green like seaweed and her eyes . . . eh, like yours. She looked at Daras, fell in love with him, and inflamed the heart of the young *pallikari*. In return for her love, she took away his power of speech. That's the trade they make. The *pallikari* never spoke again, he who had sung so eloquently that he caused the hearts of maidens to quiver like aspen leaves. He hung his musket on the wall and removed his cartridge box. He gave up smuggling and grew thin and wan. He dragged his feet from stone to stone along the shore and from ship to ship. He would spend hours looking down into the water. He would shade his eyes with his hand and gaze far off over the surface of the sea. "What's the matter with you, Daras?" people would ask him, but he said nothing, just smiled sadly and sighed. He was looking for the lady, but she was never seen again. That's their way. When they fall in love with a *pallikari,* they get a child by him and then go back to their own kind. Well, one day my grandmother (God rest her where her bones, desecrated by the Turks, are bleaching) was walking along the shore with some other women, and there they found on the sand a newborn boy. They picked him up but he was dead. He wasn't like other human beings. His flesh was white, like snow, and his hair was as long as that of a two-year-old child and was red-gold, like fire. And on his neck above the shoulders were green scales like those of a fish. He had the smell of fish. They wrapped him in a cloth and took him to the priest for burial but he refused to read the prayers and wouldn't allow the body to be buried in the cemetery. So they buried it outside the churchyard after they read the prayers of exorcism over it, because they realized that it was a fairy, the offspring of Daras and the lady.'

'How did they know that?'

'Well, on the cheek under the eye was a black mole the size of a lentil. Daras had the same thing. It was a sign.'

Smaragthi sighed regretfully.

'The Mermaid never came back to Moschonisi?'

'Never, my lady.'

'She had green hair? How was she otherwise?'

'Who can say? Only Daras saw her and, you see, he never spoke again. But everybody knows that the ladies of the sea are so beautiful that they cause a man to lose his wits. . . .'

'And this Daras never spoke after that?' asked Smaragthi, quite disappointed.

'Never, my lady. He wasted away and died without a word. God have mercy on him!'

The old woman brought her face so close that Smaragthi could smell the unpleasant reek of raki on her breath. She touched the girl's knee and confided solemnly:

'Thus, my dove, I think was your own origin. As soon as I saw your father bring you in the fish basket that morning, and the house radiant as if a star had entered it, I understood. But how can one speak of it to these pagans who fish during Holy Week?'

Smaragthi was startled by this unexpected conclusion. She laughed, but her laughter was forced.

'Look at the back of my neck,' she said jokingly. 'Feel here with your hand, Aunt Permahoula. I don't have any fish scales!'

The old woman drew back the girl's headcloth and undid her hair. It fell gleaming around her, flowing over her shoulders and covering her cheeks. When the crone rubbed it between her long fingers, it rustled like silk.

'You don't have fish scales, but you have this hair. Do you think it's like other people's hair? Have you ever seen such hair on the head of any other person? Tell me, my lady, as a favour!'

'No!' laughed Smaragthi.

'And you never will. And your eyes? Have you ever seen any other eyes like yours?'

'No, Aunt Permahoula!'

'And you never will, my dear, except in a mirror. For only out of the depths of the sea do such marvels come.'

Old Permahoula pointed with her lean finger to the sea, which was scattering golden glints at their feet and blushing like a rose in the distance. She remained thus for a long time staring into the mysterious, transparent water as if she were seeing plaits of gold and faces with large emerald eyes in its depths.

Smaragthi raised her head and gazed at the sea without laughing, as if at this very moment she expected the head of Daras's beautiful mermaid to thrust itself above the surface, laughing with her greenish-blue eyes and her hair as golden as the evening sun undulating with the waves like strands of seaweed.

Without turning her eyes from the water, Aunt Permahoula spoke once more.

'Under the rocks in the deep place of the sea are the caverns of the mermaids. They are strewn with pearls and fine coral. There the mermaids dwell, combing their hair and talking pleasantly together. Their bodies are white as ivory and their hair is red, gold, or green. Their eyes are the same. Some of them have eyes as ruby-red as pomegranate seeds. Others have green eyes like yours. Still others have eyes the colour of moonlight. Your mother was one of these mermaids. She had emerald eyes and hair like spun honey.'

Smaragthi felt a pang in her heart.

'My mother! . . .' she whispered dreamily and her breath quickened.

'Your mother, my lady. She bore you, beautiful as you are, and laid you in Varouhos's boat that night. Their law, you see, doesn't let them keep a child they've conceived by a human being, however much they long to.'

'Truly, Granny?'

'Truly, my lady.'

Both were silent and looked at the fantastic shapes wandering over the waves in the distance. The only sounds were a small wave lapping the shore at their feet and the cool hiss of the sand as it drank the water.

'How much you know,' Smaragthi sighed in awe and admiration.

She sighed again and looked at the gaunt, aged creature crouching on the sand like a huge crab that was about to plunge into the sea.

'How much you know!'

The old woman nodded her head gravely and replied with calm, wistful certainty.

'I know many things, my child. Many things!'

Suddenly Smaragthi was distrubed by a mysterious terror. She picked up the basket and the fishing gear, left the old woman, and ran home. There she threw herself into her mother's arms in a way that alarmed Nerandji and caused her to look uneasily at the child.

'What's happened to make you act like this?'

'Nothing. Only I love you and I've come to you. You are my mother!'

She spoke rapidly as she nestled in her mother's embrace and closed her eyes.

'You are my mother!'

There she felt safe, as if she were protected by God's blessing. Nothing in the world could be sweeter to her or more precious. Here she was free from the spell of fairy tales which numbed the mind and weakened the heart. Here was Mother. She seized the brown hand and pressed it close to her cheek to feel the rough fingers against her flesh. She had no way of knowing that Fate had chosen this same beloved hand to give her the first cup of bitterness in her life.

One morning Smaragthi and her father were fishing out at sea. Suddenly they heard a loud outcry from Panayia. They looked and saw that the Mount was black with people. The men were waving their cloth belts and the women and children were screaming and motioning frantically. Someone was sounding monotonous blasts on a conch at regular intervals.

'What's going on up there?' said Varouhos. 'Are they holding a festival on the Mount or have they gone mad?'

Suddenly Smaragthi felt her heart turn to ice. She looked the Mount and then glanced right and left around them.

'They're making signals, Father,' she said. 'They're signalling to us. There's no other boat out here.'

'You're crazy, I say!'

Without further delay, Smaragthi threw herself at the oars, turned the boat about and rowed for the harbour.

'Oh, father, I can't go on.' Her knees were knocking together and her heart was quaking.

Varouhos stared at her. Then the child's inexplicable fright pierced him like a lance. He snatched the oars from her grasp and drove the boat forward with all his might. As they came within range, they heard voices from land shouting distractedly to them.

'Quick! Come quick! Aunt Nerandji! Nerandji!'

'Holy Madonna, they're calling about Mother,' the girl said and crossed herself.

They ran home as fast as they could. The crowd that up to this time had been shouting and gesturing now ran after them without speaking. Forever afterwards there lingered in Smaragthi's memory that sound of feet thudding dully behind her back, that multitude of bare feet pounding the earth.

They found Nerandji dying, unable to recognize anyone. She was dying without a cry, stretched out on the divan, opening and shutting her mouth like a strangling bird. Fortis was there with his bottles, unable to do a thing. Aunt Permahoula and Lathios's wife tried to revive Nerandji with vinegar and ether, without success. She died shortly thereafter, uttering only a soft, prolonged sigh.

22

S M A R A G T H I was unable to realize completely the enormity of
the disaster. It was more than her senses could register or her mind
accept. Without relating the facts to herself, she heard Lathios's wife
tell Varouhos how Nerandji had gone out that morning to gather
figs. In the fig tree she had missed her footing and fallen. A boy
found her sprawled on the ground at the point of death. He ran to
the village and reported the accident to some men, who brought her
home on a litter.

There was no wound or abrasion anywhere on her body, merely a
trickle of blood from her nose and a lump on the back of her head.
The injury must have been to her brain and her internal organs.

Lathios's wife took Smaragthi by the hand and led her into the
kitchen. The girl walked in a daze, like an automaton. For a long
time the good woman talked to her, stroked her hand, and tried to
comfort her. This was as meaningless as the other murmuring voices
in the house. At last Lathios's daughter came to the kitchen.

'Finished?' her mother asked.

'Yes, it's finished,' the daughter replied and wiped her eyes with
the hem of her headcloth.

Lathios's wife arose and guided Smaragthi gently back to the
room where Nerandji was lying. The house was empty now.
Smaragthi saw only her godfather standing in a corner as she crossed
the hallway. Fortis was on the point of holding his arms out to her,
but he checked himself and let her pass.

Aunt Permahoula, her hands clasped around her knees, was
sitting on a yellow cushion beside the dead woman's head. Nerandji
was laid out in her best clothes. She now appeared strangely
elongated, while the divan seemed to have shrunk correspondingly.
Her eyes were closed and in her hands was a small icon of the
Madonna. Two yellow candles were burning with flames that were
almost invisible in the noonday glare. They were fixed in earthen
cups, one at the head and the other at the feet.

Then all at once the girl was struck by the full meaning of her loss.
There was no more calling for the doctor, no more bustle, no
pounding feet, no clothes soaked in vinegar, no more small bottles.
That was over, for ever, and her mother was lying there in her best
dress, as decorous as if she were in church. Here was something that
removed all hope. The awful significance of annihilation dawned on
Smaragthi's young mind. She uttered a scream and threw herself on

the gaunt body of her mother who this time failed to open her arms. Only her head moved from side to side from the jolt. The girl heard the rustle of dry seaweed in the pillow. She felt her mind founder in dark waters. At first she made a feeble effort of resistance. Then, defeated, she let herself go and dissolved, slowly and quietly, into tranquil insensibility.

·   ·   ·   ·   ·

When she found herself alone in the house which now reminded her so intolerably of the absent Nerandji, Smaragthi was disconsolate. Her loneliness was bitter, poisonous, and menacing. The bitterness she felt with her senses. The menace she was unable to define, but she was aware of it lurking about her like a shadow clinging to the walls. Now in a flash she understood Nerandji's love in a thousand ways she had never noticed before.

While her mother was alive, Smaragthi's childhood had been filled with happiness as natural as the passing of spring over the earth or the flower-tinted evening clouds floating lightly above the sea. Now her days were starved for this love that had unceasingly nourished her soul. She longed for it in the morning when she awoke; she missed it when she came back from the sea and through the night.

The pattern of her daily life was inevitably altered. Smaragthi discovered the incredible amount of work her mother's thin hands had accomplished so that everything should be in order. The rooms cleaned, the dishes and kettles scoured, the bedding and clothes washed and ironed, holes mended and buttons sewn on. The problem of daily meals solved inconspicuously. And everything executed with a tender, indescribable smile on her melancholy face.

'How much you do for me!' Smaragthi had once said to her.

Her mother had put her hands on the girl's shoulders and said to her simply: 'What I do for you is very little. God sent you to me, and I thank Him for it.'

How was it possible that all this should be taken away in an instant? But so it was.

At nightfall, Smaragthi's loneliness would increase. When her father came home from the coffee-house, her uneasiness would abate, but later the fantasies and vague, indefinable fears would set her heart beating and keep her awake: a cupboard creaking in the dark, the sputtering wick of the vigil lamp, a casement window opening by itself. For a while, she asked Aunt Permahoula to come and sleep in the house until she got over her anxiety.

Varouhos accepted the situation in his own way. After the funeral when the women had left the house, he sat in a corner near the window and stared at the sea. He sighed and smoked, smoked and sighed. That was all. No one could get a word out of him.

Men in the villages are not in the habit of displaying their grief. They leave tears, words, and lamentations to the women. Actually they don't miss their wives very long. A wife is a kind of necessity, a companion who shares poverty and keeps house for her husband, taking on herself the burden of whatever befalls. When she dies, the husband has a hard time at first. Things are upside down, now that the hand that maintained order is lacking. Then life gradually forms a new pattern, and in the end the husband gets used to it and settles down to the routine of work, the coffee-house, and drinking. This goes on until he marries again.

Varouhos began to drink like the others. At first it was to take the edge off his loneliness. He had relied on Nerandji to make all the decisions. She possessed the kind of intelligence that forms sound judgements in matters of action. All these years, Varouhos had followed her directions. He turned the tiller over to her and was satisfied it was in good hands.

Now suddenly the house lacked the mind that had governed it and the hand that had kept it in order. There was no one to tell him when the house was to be cleaned or when he should sell the dried octopus and what price he should charge for it. He was a ship without a compass. He would come home at the usual time, as if he were expected. He would sit in a corner at a loss for something to say or do. He would look at Smaragthi, wrinkle his brow and say nothing.

Then little by little Varouhos became used to the new situation. He made a discovery at the same time. He realized how independent he was at last. He had grown up to manhood under the strict domination of his father, who was generous with cuffs and blows when he was in an ugly mood. After his father's death Varouhos married Nerandji and quite naturally accepted the authority of this stong-minded woman. And now Nerandji was dead.

Varouhos was like an old work horse that has spent its youth in harness and then one day is aware that the wagon has been unhitched and the harness removed. At first the horse is confused and unable to understand the change. At last it grasps the truth and trots off to the meadow to demonstrate its new freedom.

This was the way Varouhos behaved, especially when he was drinking. At such times he was carried away with the elation of using his own judgement, which meant that he must do the opposite of what Nerandji would have decided.

Fortis grumbled irritably when he stayed late.

'Come on, get up and go home,' he said. 'It's a shame for the girl to stay up so long waiting for you.'

One night he flatly refused to serve any more drinks to Varouhos.

'No more raki for you tonight.'

Varouhos opened his heavy eyelids.

'What do you mean? I pay you for them!'

Fortis patted him on the shoulder.

'It's not a quesion of money. I'm concerned about you and my goddaughter.'

'She may be your goddaughter, but she's my daughter. I'm responsible for her'.

'And I also. Am I not her spiritual father?'

'Will you bring me raki or not? Tell me!'

'No, I will not!'

'All right! Then I'll go somewhere else. Good night to you!'

He stumbled to his feet and went off towards the Gadjalis tavern at Ammouthelli. They had opened a new shop away from the houses and the other coffee-houses where they could easily carry on smuggling. There the younger fishermen gathered along with strangers from the motorboats when they stopped overnight at the harbour. One drink of their raki and you'd murder your own father. The charges increased according to the drunkenness of the customers.

Midnight came. Lathios long since had gone home but Varouhos was still away. Smaragthi feared something had happened to him. She went to Aunt Permahoula and asked her to investigate. Meanwhile she kept taking the kettle off the fire and putting it back on again so that the supper would be hot when her father returned.

The old woman found him at the tavern.

'Up, I say. Smaragthi is worried. . . .'

Guffaws of laughter broke out all around. Varouhos was stung with chagrin.

'What did she say?' he asked.

'She said Smaragthi wants you to come home.'

'Ah, so now Smaragthi is giving the orders?'

He treated the old woman to a glass, sent her packing and stubbornly remained to drink. He arrived home blind drunk. Smaragthi, faint with hunger, heard him at the door and rushed to set the table. Her face was haggard and her eyes red.

'Sit down and eat with me!' her father ordered without looking at her.

'I don't want to, Father. I'm not hungry.'

That did it.

Varouhos flew into a rage and raised his thick voice.

'What does that mean? . . . Are you being funny with me? I say you eat, and eat you must! Do you hear me?'

Never before had he spoken to her like this. She was shocked and deeply hurt.

'Sit down at the table!' he commanded.

She sat down trembling, her heart pounding. She bit her lips to keep from weeping.

'I told you to eat!'

'I can't, Father!'

Suddenly she burst into tears and sobbed chokingly. This infuriated Varouhos even more.

'Listen to me. I don't like this snivelling. And another time don't send anybody to look for me in the coffee-houses, because. . . . Don't tell me you have the notion I brought you into my house to give me orders!'

This thrust was so cruel that Smaragthi lifted her head and stared at him. Through her tears she saw his contorted face and it frightened her. His lower lip, bloated and red, hung nastily below his moustache. His eyes were bloodshot and ugly. He seemed so strange that she thought she was seeing him for the first time in her life. This savage mask terrified her.

'Eat, I said!' thundered Varouhos dementedly.

In spite of the grief in her heart and the lump in her throat, Smaragthi kept her eyes fixed on him. Firmly she replied: 'I will not eat.'

The drunkard seized the earthen platter of fried fish and hurled it at the window.

'There, since you won't eat!'

The crash of the shattered panes sounded loud in the quiet of the night.

In terror, the girl screamed, 'Mother!'

She threw open the door and ran to old Aunt Permahoula as if she were being pursued.

Those in Lathios's house had heard the uproar in their sleep and understood. The old woman was still awake. She took Smaragthi outside and they sat down together on the doorstep. The girl was shaking from head to foot and unable to control herself. The old crone caressed her back to soothe her.

'I'm afraid, Granny!'

'Don't take on like this, my lady. Come, don't act like this. It isn't anything. You've got to learn about men and get used to them. Look at me. Not a night went by that the captain didn't mistreat me. He was gentle, a man with a heart of gold. But he'd drink and then he'd come home like a raging tempest. He'd go for me for nothing at all and beat me. It was the drink, you see. It's this that drives them out of their minds. They're not to blame. They're tired at night and they drink to amuse themselves. My own man was like this. . . .'

She talked to Smaragthi quietly in the night, for the others were asleep. Then she took the girl's hand.

'Now you must sleep. I'll tell your father that you're staying with us tonight. Don't worry.'

She went to Varouhos's house and found the old man sprawled, fully dressed, on the divan. Without awakening him, she cleared the table, turned down the lamp, and banked the ashes in the fireplace so that the sparks would not fly out. Then she closed the door softly behind her and went home.

For a hundred years Aunt Permahoula had dealt with men enough to know how to care for them in every situation.

23

W H E N Varouhos went down to the harbour in the morning, he found Smaragthi in the boat washing the deck. Barefoot, her sleeves rolled back, she was pouring water from a wooden bucket. The old man was aware that the girl knew he was there, even though she hadn't looked up from her work.

Before going aboard, he stood uncertainly on the breakwater rubbing the edge of his moustache and watching the girl as she performed this daily task with her customary thoroughness. He followed her movements as she leaned over the gunwale to toss the bucket into the water for refilling and then neatly hauled it up without spilling it or letting it strike the side of the boat. After that, he saw the way she sluiced the water without getting a drop on her black dress.

All these things were transfigured with grace and beauty in the limpid morning light which, perfumed by the fresh, gleaming azure sea, suffused all things. Water splashed coolly from the bucket, ran between the girl's feet, brightened the paint of the timbers, and trickled melodiously back into the sea from the scuppers.

Varouhos was filled with tenderness by this sound, the colours, and the girl's movements. He had taken this tall girl under his wing and had brought her up. She was his own child. Seizing the rope, he pulled the boat closer to him and leaped lightly aboard.

Smaragthi turned and looked at him. She set the bucket down on the deck, wiped her hands, gathered her streaming hair and tied it up at the back with a black ribbon. When she lifted her elbows and stretched her slender body, her immature breasts were thrust forward like two small fists. Varouhos had not noticed before that his daughter was growing into young womanhood. He felt ashamed of his behaviour the night before. Suddenly he seemed to see in front of him the housewife whom he had always treated as his superior. Something of Nerandji's severe efficiency was present on this immaculate boat moored in the calm harbour. He rubbed his chin sheepishly.

'Good morning, Smaraghti.'

'Good morning, Father.'

She answered him, crouching at the tin stove, which she had lighted, in the stern. Shortly afterwards she stood up and brought him his coffee in a blue earthen cup. Her face, gilded by the morning sunlight, was gentle but aloof.

Varouhos took the cup in his fleshy hand and was at a loss how to go on. He turned his head towards the sea.

'Have you noticed how smooth the sea is today? We'll have calm weather all day, Smaragthi. . . .'

'That's right.'

'Unless . . . maybe, you know, a fresh wind might blow down through the straits. . . .'

'Eh. . . .'

He saw that he could get nowhere on that tack. He drank his coffee with loud sips, looking fixedly at his cup. Then he set it down beside him and said abruptly:

'You see, Smaragthi, a person isn't the same all the time. . . . That's the way it is. . . .'

Smaragthi said nothing.

'You slept away from home last night.'

'I slept at Lathios's house.'

'I know. I'm not speaking of that. . . . It was my fault, you know . . . do you think I don't know it? It was the drink, you see. . . .' He paused.

'But why do you fret about last night?' he went on. 'Just take for granted I don't remember anything I said or did.'

'You said you didn't take me in to dictate to you.'

'Ha! You see! Drunken words . . . don't hold them against me, Smaragthi.'

'I don't, Father.'

She picked up the cup, washed it and put it back in its place. Then she brought from the cabin an earthen plate of small fish. Taking the lines, she set about baiting hooks without saying anything except in connexion with her work.

That night Varouhos came home early from Fortis's, at Nerandji's hour. When he and Smaragthi had eaten, she turned down the lamp so that they could sleep. Varouhos remained at the window toying absently with his conversation beads. Suddenly he stopped and, turning towards Smaragthi's pallet, asked softly:

'Are you asleep, Smaragthi?'

'No, Father.'

'Ah . . . then listen and try to understand. . . . As we were saying . . . I know that every time I get drunk I'm a changed person. That's the way it is with this habit . . . it turns a man into a beast. . . .'

'Yes, Father.'

'Eh, and you, when you see me in such a state, don't hold it against me. . . . You mustn't hold it against me. . . . It's possible I may say too much. So what? It's the raki speaking, not a person. . . . Are you listening, Smaragthi?'

'I'm listening, Father.'

'When he's drunk, a person may do all sorts of things. He might even lift his hand. . . .'

From the pallet came the girl's voice through the night, even and gentle, but firm.

'If you lift your hand against me, Father, I will leave home and never come back.'

The old man was startled. The conversation beads dropped to the floor with a clatter.

'You say you'll go away?'

'If you lift your hand against me, I will go away.'

'And where will you go, may I ask?'

'Anywhere. I'll fish in the summer and find work harvesting olives in winter. I'll support myself somehow.'

The fisherman looked at the ceiling and laughed good naturedly. Then he lighted a cigarette, puffed at it vigorously, and said:

'Listen, Smaragthi. From the day God put you into my hands, life in this house was changed. We were two childless people, two dry husks. Everything was black. Honey in your mother's mouth turned to gall. We floundered about in our misery. Then you came, and all was changed. . . . And your mother changed. Think of your mother, Smaragthi. She was rather strict and fussy, but nobody was ever more thoughtful and clever. And she had the heart of a *pallikari*. Whatever she did, she knew what she was doing and she always did what was right. . . .'

He was silent for a while, lost in memories. He heard the girl sobbing in the darkness. It was not the first time she had wept during the night because of the loneliness. Varouhos sighed and expelled a cloud of smoke. He made a gesture of resignation.

'What can one do? It was God's will she was taken from us. When Death comes, you see, he doesn't ask why and how. . . . He reaches out and takes the person and leaves you. And so from the time you were still in baby clothes, your mother had one concern. That I provide you with a fishing boat. Your own boat, as strong and new and as beautiful as you are. So that you would have a dowry when the time came for you to get married, when the time came for us old ones to leave this wicked world. Your mother knew what she was doing. I turned over to her what money we made and every so often she would put aside a little into a fund for you. Now that you're growing up and I see you have intelligence and good sense, I'm telling you about it so that you'll know of it when the time comes. Over there near the fireplace is a yellow stone that is different from the other floor stones. If you lift it with a boat hook, you'll find underneath it a brass coffee tin. Take the cover off and there's the money. I imagine there'll be nine or ten thousand drachmas, whatever your mother and I have been able to scrape together all these years. . . . Are you listening to what I'm telling you, Smaragthi?'

'Yes, Father, I'm listening.'

'I've got to tell you this. I meant to tell you as soon as you became a young woman. Till now I've thought of you as a baby. Today I saw that you've shot up. You women are like that. You swell like dough in the breadpan from hour to hour and outgrow your clothes. And parents are caught by surprise because we're used to treating you like babies. . . . So it is. And now, thank God, I still hold up. If no misfortune overtakes me, I'll have bread to eat until my strength fails. . . . Eh, till then I mean to add a little also to your mother's coffee tin. . . .'

Smaragthi said nothing and again he asked:

'Eh, what do you say to that? Can't you say something?'

'What can I say, Father? May God keep you well.'

'Not that. Say something so that I can hear you. . . .'

'Well . . . don't drink, Father. Drinking will ruin you.'

'Ha, is that what's been sticking in your crop all this while? It's just as if my wife, bless her, were speaking to me this minute with her own mouth. And yet everybody drinks and nobody's the worse for it. Lathios! Is there anybody else who soaks up so much raki? Answer me that!'

'He's used to it, Father. It doesn't affect him. . . . Look, when you threw the platter at the window and I was frightened and ran to Aunt Permahoula, I heard Lathios say something from where he was sleeping. . . .'

'What did Lathios say?'

'He said: "You've got to down drink and not let it down you".'

There was a long silence. Then Varouhos said:

'All right. I'll stop it. . . . Now go to sleep. We've got work to do in the morning.'

Varouhos spoke with sincerity, but he was unable to keep his promise for more than a few days. While he went to Fortis's, all was well. But when suddenly he stopped visiting the coffee-house, Fortis knew that once more he had fallen under the spell of the Gadjales and was drinking.

Sometimes Varouhos was carried home drunk. Those nights were a martyrdom for Smaraghti. He was abusive and the more shame he felt in the girl's presence, the more furious he became. When this happened, Smaragthi left him and went to sleep at Aunt

Permahoula's. But not a word of complaint escaped from her mouth. Withdrawn into herself, she swallowed the poison and next morning showed herself bright and gay to the neighbour women and the fishermen.

But Fortis observed the girl's tragedy and one day when Varouhos was in a reasonable frame of mind, he took him into the shop and talked to him frnkly.

'The road you've taken,' he said, 'will bring you to a bad end. Give up the raki before it ruins you. Drinking isn't for you. You started very late, you see, and you can't take it. You used to be the most level-headed among the fishermen. They respected you as long as Aunt Nerandji was alive. Now they grin when they talk about you. The night before last I saw you brought home by your neighbours, the Gadjales, who get you drunk in order to rob you. They yelled— it was midnight—and pounded on your door for the girl to open it. "Come down, Smaragthi, and let the old man in!" All Skala was filled with their shouting and catcalls and you joined in with those louts: "Come down, girl!" I heard it and I was ashamed of you. I am this girl's godfather. In a few days she'll finish the fourteenth year from the time we christened her. Now tell me, is it proper that such riff-raff should have her name in their foul mouths?'

Varouhos hung his head as he listened. Fortis took off his spectacles and wiped them with a handkerchief. Then he carefully replaced them, threw his head back, and looked at Varouhos from under them.

'Think what a disgrace this is.'

The fisherman nodded in agreement. The simple-minded giant with a greying moustache and powerful neck resembled a shamefaced schoolboy who has been given a scolding. Lowering his voice, Fortis went on:

'I'm concerned mostly for the girl. She's growing up, and you've paid no attention to her. It just won't do for the drunken Gadjales to yell at her. In this world we must have respect and if we are unworthy of respect, we might as well tie a rock to our neck and jump off the Mount of the Madonna . . . am I right? Tell me. . . .'

Varouhos' eyes were filled with tears. He brushed them away with his finger and laid his hand on Fortis's knee.

'It's as you say . . . I must stop thinking. . . Well . . . you see my misfortune was to lose my wife. As long as she was with me. . . . Let it be. But don't think I haven't thought about the girl. Smaragthi has what she needs and some day when I become feeble like an old dog she'll have a house and a boat of her won. A new boat, as lovely as a young girl. . . .'

He told Fortis about the coffee tin and the money.

Fortis was pleased at this information and looked at Varouhos in a better light. He called to his son to bring them coffee as his treat.

Lambis brought the little cups on a shining brass tray. The fisherman regarded in amazement the tall, strong lad with the bright lively dark eyes.

'When did he shoot up like this?' he exclaimed. 'He's a real *pallikari.*'

'He's a big lad but not in his mind,' said Fortis, secretly admiring the boy. 'Books are his enemies. Old Avgustis has washed his hands of him. "Let him alone," he said. "He's not meant for schooling." I became discouraged and let him go his own way.'

Smiling behind his moustache, he measured his son from head to foot.

'I don't deny he's a good lad. But headstrong. Hard as flint. But his heart—pure gold. In four years or so, he'll be twenty and I'll turn the shop and fields over to him. "Ford and Son." And I'll climb up in the mulberry tree and lie in my stork's nest and smoke my *nargileh* until my hour comes. . . .'

His heart was moved with tenderness by his sentiments until he caught sight of the hens picking up crumbs at his feet.

'Shoo, Skoufati!' he shouted.

He had given each of them a name and they had learned them so well that they would take grain from his hand as he walked towards them and called them.

'Look, look, look! Off to your nest, Parthalo, Hioni! Come here Kanella!'

The first two went to the hen coop but Kanella ran to him clucking happily.

'Ts, ts, ts! They're droll creatures. They have a brain the size of a chick pea and yet they understand as if they had minds!'

'It's so,' Fortis explained. 'You've just got to know how to treat them. The only bad animal is man. No matter where you touch him, you soil yourself.'

The schoolmaster was approaching beyond the holm oaks. Since his dismissal as church chanter, he had grown bent and feeble, mere skin and bones. 'I wasn't singing for the pay,' he told the elders when one of them spoke to him tactfully about necessary retrenchments. 'I kept my place at the lectern so that the Byzantine chant wouldn't be lost.' 'Eh, never mind,' he was told. 'You can still help out whenever you like on the left-hand side. You've grown so weak that your feet have a hard time when you climb up to Mouria.'

The schoolmaster arrived, dragging his feet. The leather laces of the slippers he wore for shoes hung loose. His eyes squinted, dazzled by the sunlight. Seeing Varouhos get up to leave, he greeted him with a nod and sat down in the farthest corner. Fortis accompanied the fisherman to the door and watched his bowed figure depart. 'Remember what we talked about!' Varouhos looked back and nodded confirmation of their agreement.

Fortis remained a minute watching thoughtfully as the fisherman went on his way. Then he sat down beside old Avgustis.

'Well, what do you say, schoolmaster?'

Avgustis made no reply. He merely rubbed the table top with his finger in a manner that seemed to give this action great significance. His fingernail, stained orange with nicotine, was oddly curved. Fortis observed how the schoolmaster's hands had aged. The veins stood out like tangled cords. Then he noticed that the old man's face showed the same deterioration. Cheeks unshaven and hollow, and eyes receding behind dark circles.

'You don't look at all well today,' Fortis said. 'Are you ill?'

The old man still said nothing. He moistened his lips, but no sound came from his mouth. He kept his eyes lowered on the fingernail that was rubbing the table and when he interrupted this mechanical action, his hand shook ungovernably. Both were silent.

Then abruptly the schoolmaster took from his pocket a newspaper, unfolded it and gave it to Fortis. His movements were nervous and jerky and made the paper rustle.

Fortis took the sheet. It was a copy of the *Refugee World,* which had been brought by the rural mail carrier. He adjusted his spectacles and read the leading article.

It was a truly incredible piece of writing. The General had unreservedly capitulated to the views of the government officials who stood for friendly relations with Turkey. The Prime Minister, who controlled the majority of votes and had signed the exchange of populations, deemed that it was not in the government's interest to undergo the turbulence of election at a time of such great political unrest. Therefore he decided to form a coalition government. In order to silence the General, who had stirred up the refugees with his demagoguery about the 'great return,' he had offered him the vice-presidency and the Ministry of Military Affairs. The General had accepted with enthusiasm. He renounced forthwith the cause of Anatolia, abandoned his faithful partisans to the mercy of God, and appeased the more 'idealistic' of his refugee leaders with certain appointments. He confessed that till now he had seen the problem in the wrong light, and he appealed to all the refugees to accept his decision and bring themselves to unite with other brethren who had stayed behind after the exchange and to erase 'the vain fantasies which had proved to be illusory, like an attractive mirage on the desert.'

Fortis, although he supported the government party, was shocked by the General's shamelessness.

'What a scoundrel!' he said as he put the sheet down.

He looked at the schoolmaster, spat on the floor, and repeated: 'What a scoundrel! There's no honour or principle in people like that, curse them!'

The schoolmaster's head was bent to his chest and his hands clasped his knees. From his unbuttoned shirt, below his neck, appeared a tuft of grey hair rooted in his fleshless skin. He gave the impression of misery and decay.

'What a scoundrel!'

The schoolmaster picked up the paper, folded it slowly, replaced it in his pocket, and got up to leave.

'Sit down, my friend, and let me fix you a coffee,' suggested Fortis as he watched the schoolmaster drag his pitiful shoelace behind him. Avgustis paused at the door and turned his head.

'No, thank you,' he said in a whisper and departed.

Fortis watched him pass under the mulberry tree with dragging feet, doubled over as if he were carrying a heavy burden on his back. His brown trousers bagged at the knees so that he seemed to walk with bent legs.

It seemed to Fortis he was like a man going to a funeral, as indeed he was. Old Avgustis was on his way to bury his last dream, which was dead and putrefying in his jacket pocket wrapped up in the copy of the *Refugee World*.

Just as he was about to turn a corner and proceed to Ammouthelli, he seemed to feel Fortis's eyes still on him and he looked back. He saw the tall figure standing under the mulberry tree with his hands behind him and he felt ashamed. He pretended not to see and made haste to round the corner.

'And now the schoolmaster goes to the Gadjales!' sighed Fortis. He shook his head gloomily and spat in the direction of the tavern. Then his eyes brightened as he looked towards the path leading down from the hill of Vigla. Through the scrub oak and the gum trees he saw Lambis coming with the goats. His tall body was bent under a load of leafage, and he was singing a sentimental song.

He paused, put his fingers to his mouth and whistled a greeting. The sound curved through the air as gracefully as a sky-rocket at a festival.

'The rascal!' grinned Fortis behind his moustache.

He set about cleaning the copper milk pan; and when the boy arrived, he placed a low stool in front of one of the goats and with a handful of water rinsed off the teats of her distended udder. It was Ramona, the second or third of her line. He talked to her as he milked her.

'Are you listening, Ramona? "I'm listening," you say. Now pay attention and tell me if you make sense out of all this. Varouhos comes to drink raki and I drive him away from the shop. Then comes the schoolmaster and I send him to the Gadjales to be poisoned. And yet my business is to sell raki. Now you haven't a human brain, tell me how such a contradiction can be. And yet it is.'

Ramona turned her head in pleasure at the lightening of the udder. For a moment she stopped chewing her cud, fixed her yellow eyes on him and replied tersely:

'Be-ke-ke-ke!'

Fortis continued his milking and his discourse.

'Then let me tell you what the trouble is. Our self-interest is on top. Our humanity in underneath. When our self-interest is in the saddle, we behave like swine. When our humanity takes over, we become angels . . . right. So here is our great problem. What is our real interest? Where do we fail? Right?'

Ramona rubbed her ear against the bark of the mulberry tree, and Fortis plunged deeper into his analysis.

'You must understand that each person has another faith in addition to the Christian religion. A secret faith. He keeps it in his heart and this it is that steadies him and sustains him. If he loses this faith? It's all over with him! He collapses like an empty bag. Look here. Take Varouhos, for example. His faith was Nerandji. Nerandji is no more; Varouhos becomes empty. Then Avgustis, poor devil, his General deserts him, his "return of the nationals" is wiped out and the schoolmaster is lost. A tattered remnant. . . .'

'Be-ke-ke!' agreed Ramona.

'Now you'll say to me: "Comninos, tell us what your faith is. What is it, old man"?'

Lambis entered the house to wash his hands and clean up. At that moment the answer came. The lad stood in the doorway, a tall *pallikari,* towering above his father. He rested his arms against the door frames and gazed far off at the sea, where the sunlight was playing on the joyous water. The foliage of the tree sifted sunshine on the boy's dark red shirt, gilded his bare arms and cast shadows from his long eyelashes over his brown cheeks. Fortis could see the fine drops of moisture above his full, red lips.

'There's my faith,' he answered himself.

He admired the lad for a moment. Then he followed his son's gaze, which was fixed on a boat coming into the port. Aboard he made out the sombre dress and the golden head of his goddaughter. Smaragthi was standing up, rowing indolently at the oars, just enough to keep the boat moving.

'Well?' said Fortis, assuming great indifference.

The boy was startled.

'How was the swimming?'

Lambis blushed and laughed.

'Wonderful,' he said. 'We also went to the garden and picked watermelons. And I've brought you a basket of fresh figs.'

'I must make a sponge diver out of you, there's no doubt about it!'

24

A G A I N it was impossible for Varouhos to keep his promise. The demon of drink had lain in wait till Nerandji was out of the way to pounce on him. Now at last it had him in its power, and he was unable to master it. He would look at Fortis and hang his head. After a time he forsook the benches at the Mulberry Tree and went there no more, even for coffee. Instead, he would wander aimlessly until nightfall and then head for Ammouthelli and take refuge in the Gadjalis tavern.

His manner towards Smaragthi also changed. He no longer felt obliged to make excuses to her after his maudlin drunkenness. Nor did he receive encouragement from Smaragthi's proud, reproachful silence when he tried to explain.

Occasionally Varouhos came to his senses and was frightened at the downward course he saw himself taking. For a few days he would work with a kind of frenzy and wear himself out with night fishing. In the morning he would come home, his breeches wet from the sea and his eyes puffy and red. Smaragthi's heart ached for him, for she realized the old man's struggle with himself.

But this never lasted long. Varouhos would start drinking again in defeat and yield to the tyranny of his addiction without further resistance.

'I'm like old Anestis's mule!' he said to Smaragthi one night when he had been brought home drunk his clothes filthy with vomit. Smaragthi didn't understand what he meant. She thought he was out of his head.

The old man had said the same thing repeatedly that night while he was drinking at the tavern.

'I'm old Anestis's mule!'

The others had laughed and asked him to explain, but he only shook his head and replied with the saying of Captain Lias, the *dedes:* 'To each man his own mind.' Maudlin talk, the drivel of a sot, it might seem, but he knew what he was talking about.

One day at dawn when he was fishing for octopus with the glass, he had seen old Anestis, the market gardener from Mouria, painfully leading a mule along the path of Vigla.

The peasant was having a hard time. The mule was old, almost blind, and its knees were stiff and galled with sores. Varouhos called a greeting from the boat and Anestis told him what he was about to do. He was finished, he said, with this stupid beast that was good for nothing but eating hay. The slaver was dripping from its bloodless lips and its eyes were blinded with rheum.

'Where are you taking it now?' the fisherman asked.

'On a one-way journey,' replied Anestis. 'I'm taking it up on Vigla where I'll shove it into the sea and that will be the end of its worries and mine. . . .'

Later on, while Varouhos was fishing with his head in the glass, he heard shouting and curses and the rattle of falling stones. He looked up at the summit of Vigla and saw the mule fall from the cliff. It thrashed awkwardly in mid-air with its legs, its neck, and its whole body. Followed by a shower of stones, it splashed into the sea with the dull impact of a wineskin. Again the fisherman looked up and saw Anestis dusting off his hands. Then he lighted a cigarette and set off towards the village with the halter, which he had kept, thrown over his shoulder.

A few days afterwards, Varouhos approached the place where the carcass was floating with its legs stretched out. The waves washed in and out of its belly while thousands of crabs swarmed over its flesh and carrion birds quarrelled over its bones.

This was what had been running through Varouhos's mind. In that aged mule which the peasant led unresistingly to the brink of the cliff, he saw himself, led by his addiction to drink.

One day Smaragthi, at a time when she thought Varouhos was away in the boat, went barefoot to the room where the fireplace was. She stopped in confusion at the door and clasped her hands with a gasp of amazement at what she saw. Her father was on his knees in the corner, about to replace the yellow tile in the floor. At his side lay a boat hook and three hundred-drachma notes.

Varouhos heard her soft gasp of surprise. He turned and looked at her and then glanced at the money, abashed that the girl had caught him like a thief in the act. All at once his embarrassment gave way to fury. He glared at her truculently with his beady eyes and hurled abuse at her like stones.

'Hah! Now you come sneaking up on me from behind! Like a spy. Now you listen and get this straight—I'm not going to stand for it . . . and furthermore. . . .'

'I didn't mean to . . . I didn't know. . . .' stammered the girl.

The fisherman stuffed the money into his pocket. He got to his feet, his fury mounting.

'I tell you you're spying on me and meddling . . . as if I were stealing your savings and earnings. Did I earn what is down there with my own sweat or didn't I?'

After her first shock, Smaragthi recovered her cool composure. In a quiet, steady voice, she said:

'The money is yours, Father. I've never asked you for any of it. You are the master and you can take it and use it as you like.'

She crossed herself and added:

'By the soul of my mother, who is listening to us at this moment, I swear I came here by accident. . . .'

The oath, uttered so solemnly there in the shadow of the dead woman, shook the old man. He stood in the middle of the room and glanced at the hiding place. Then he took the three notes out of his pocket and showed them to her.

'No matter what you may think . . . I took three hundred-drachma notes that I needed. I want to replace that broken oar. Also I want to order an iron head for the spear with the rusted teeth . . . since you stick your nose into everything I do and I must give you an accounting of it! Ts! Tomorrow or next day after I sell the dried octopus, I'll put the money back, you needn't worry. Do you understand now or don't you?'

He spoke rapidly as if he were trying to excuse himself. Smaragthi had nothing more to say. She went to a shelf and took a spool of thread and a small wooden needle that she needed and left the room without haste. She seated herself under the vine at the door and proceeded to mend the torn meshes of a large net.

Another day Varouhos scolded her about swimming. Fishermen and mariners in general never swim from the time they begin their struggle with the sea. They associate the sea with toil and fatigue and do not play in it, just as tillers of the soil do not go for walks.

But Smaragthi was passionately fond of swimming. She was drawn to the immense cool water, so clean and bright, which gave her the feeling of buoyancy and stirred the great white wings she was aware of within her, folded and fluttering.

She enjoyed ardently and almost with intoxication the hours she spent in the sea when she had nothing else to do and could be alone as she liked. She would row behind the sheltering cliffs of Vigla, where she found coves and shady beaches strewn with porous cuttle-fish bones and fragrant seaweed. This was the bathing place of the women of Skala. They used the recesses for dressing-rooms, and no man ever came here.

At other times, when there were no boats about, Smaragthi rowed out in the open. There she felt endowed with absolute freedom throughout her entire body. She undressed in the presence of the sky and the sea and dived in head first with a voluptuous thrill. This almost savage joy she found only in the tingling refreshment which

107

the water gave her whole being. She felt the dullness of living then, as if she were only half-alive on land.

Her gleaming limbs flashed like swords in the water. Her flesh became firm and smooth like the rosy pebbles on the shore, which have been worked on for ages by the abrasive waves and the sun's fire until they are perfectly rounded and polished. This passion for swimming also kept her away from the trivial gossip and backbiting in which the other girls of the fishing village wasted their time.

One night Varouhos fancied he heard some equivocal allusions at the Gadjalis tavern. He was convinced that they were innuendoes about Smaragthi and were intended for his ears. He came home in a rage.

'What will it be next? Now it's your indecent behaviour!' he shouted and threw his cap on the divan.

'Indecent behaviour?'

Smaragthi listened open-mouthed to the accusation. Her eyes questioned him perplexedly. He saw them shining with frankness and innocense and shouted more loudly:

'Indecent and what else? I'm talking about your swimming. All Skala is gossiping about it. You've outgrown your clothes and still you think you're only a little girl!'

Smaragthi shrugged her shoulders. 'I don't trouble anyone. Nobody sees me when I go swimming.'

The old man went on, even more beside himself.

'I know! You get up at night and go diving. Never before have such things been said about any girl. Don't you have any fear? And have you no sense of shame?'

His lips trembled. Smaragthi went to him and looked him straight in the eyes.

'Tell me, Father,' she said. 'What improper thing have I done to be ashamed of and what have I done that I should be afraid?'

Varouhos stubbornly turned his head away.

'I don't know. They may not see you undress but to have it in their minds is the same thing. They are men and it stirs them up. . . .'

Again Smaragthi shrugged her shoulders, ripe and round under her black dress, and set the table. She understood nothing at all about these mysteries.

25

O N E night there was a gala entertainment at the Gadjalis tavern. The whole port of Skala rang with the tumult of voices and instruments till dawn.

A motor ship, one of those that transport fish and produce, tied up in the harbour and a small troupe of musicians came ashore. Among them was a young woman. At once word was circulated among the fishermen's wives that some 'prima donnas' had arrived at the Gadjalis'. By prima donnas they meant women of loose morals. Actually they were only a company of four miserable, hungry people who made a living by music. Hardpressed by lack of engagements in the cities, they had taken to the villages to eke out a pittance and tide themselves over the slack season.

The leader of the band was a young fiddler, thin, slender as a drumstick, sallow, with burning dark eyes and a comical snub nose. His ears were large, transparent and as flabby as the withered leaves of a plane tree, as if nature had attached them to him so that one could grasp him like an earthen jug. His trousers, for all his slenderness, reached only to his ankles and his sleeves also were short, particularly when he raised his arms to play his violin.

The second in rank was a kindly old man in a black suit. He was hard of hearing and was referred to as 'the deaf one'. He smiled vacantly and spoke so softly that those who heard him suspected themselves of being deaf.

The third was the star of the band. A tall man with a large chin and interminable arms, he was as scrawny and bony as an ill-fed mule. He played a tambourine with brass bells in its wooden frame, which performed miracles in his hands.

Under the vine trellis of the Gadjalis tavern, when the instruments had warmed up and the music began, the eyes of young and old were fixed on this tambourine. It was amazing how he invented games with this little sieve-like object. He tossed it high above his head and caught it upright on the tip of his thumb, where it spun as if possessed by a demon. He continually fretted it with the fingers of his right hand, with taps on his nose and sudden flicks and light blows that drew tiny sobs from the taut drumhead and soft, tinkling laughter from the bells. All the time he watched it with his narrowed eyes. He smiled at it, nodded to it, winked at it, and stuck his tongue out at it, as if there were an understanding between it and himself. As the crowd's enthusiasm took fire, he was treated to drinks each time he tossed the instrument up to the grapes on the trellis and caught it behind his back without missing a beat of the music and without its ceasing to jingle in a thousand ways. He sometimes played it on his knees, sometimes under them and, again, behind his neck, on every part of his body where the bones formed sharp angles. The guests applauded and shouted when at the climax he made it spin on his huge, prominent nose.

He was so absorbed in his playing that his large lips puckered and his eyebrows knit as if he were speaking to it and pleading with it, and the tambourine replied with metallic laughter almost like a human voice when he rubbed the drumhead in a certain way with his thumb.

The guests called him Maestro Apostolos, and he would have had no rival in popularity if Loulou had not been there. She was the so-called 'prima-donna'.

She let the musicians entertain the guests till nightfall. Then there was a silence. Gadjalis lighted the paraffin lamp that hung from the trellis. Then the tambourine jingled demoniacally and *baf!* a signal was given with a thump on the knee. Loulou came out of the tavern and stood like a dazzling star among the Pleiades. Brilliantly made up, she burst forth just as the merrymaking began to blaze. The musicians struck up the introduction and she launched herself into the first number, flinging one arm above her head and snapping her fingers while she rested her other hand brazenly on her hip.

> *Hey! Tralala!*
> *Laa—lalala!*
> *Hey! Tralala, la!*

From then on, everything else was forgotten. It was clear now that she was the star of the troupe, the flaming sun around whom the other members revolved as decorative, background figures.

A brunette, some thirty years old, she had dark eyes, arched eyebrows, and vibrant hair that hung in clusters and shone with soft tints. When she shook it, it gleamed like copper in the strong light which bathed her head. Her mouth was full-lipped and rouged. Her teeth were firm and white. She was not especially pretty. In fact she was rather short and dumpy. But she possessed the irresistible femininity of her type. Her flesh was firm and golden as breadcrust. She breathed sex from every pore.

It was the end of August. The hot night spread its languor on a sea of oil. The waves barely whispered on the pebbles of the shore in front of the tavern. The water was so transparent that under the glare of the lamp it became invisible and might have been mistaken for dry land. The bottom was visible as far as the light reached, as if the sea had withdrawn a couple of fathoms from the shore line. The young men and the fishermen who enjoyed this kind of entertainment were seated on benches and stone blocks under the trellis. Wine flasks were emptied and refilled as treating passed from table to table. From the moment the woman had burst among the men, everything took its cue from her rhythm and there was an excitable, hysterical tenseness in all things. The fishermen stroked their moustaches and puffed out their lips, each competing to appear the most dashing and gallant. This was all for her.

When Loulou finished her number, she took a chair at one side, among the musicians. She was reserved, statuesque, as colourful and resplendent as a barbaric goddess presiding at some mysterious, sacred rite. She wore a red silk blouse, open at the shoulders so that one's suspicions might be confirmed that her breasts were ripe and needed no support. Her skirt was of frayed black satin. When she raised her hand to her hair, the dark concavity of her armpit was revealed. When she crossed her legs, she exposed a plump knee above her shapely, stockingless calf.

The fishermen stared, even forgetting to eat the salty titbits which the Gadjales served to stimulate their thirst. All eyes sought her and enveloped her with a searing tide of frustrated passion, warped and unfulfilled, which found no way to escape the barren existence of the village where carnal love, in so far as it did not deviate from its natural course, was available only as a sacrament of the church accompanied by lugubrious parental lamentations and disputes over the dowry.

The staring eyes reddened under the hard light, and glances passed like soft tongues over the sweetness of this woman who smiled, half naked, among so many men. They were pitiful, like the eyes of starved butchers' dogs gazing at a sheep hung for slaughter.

Loulou's bright, amiable face encouraged the tables to send treats to her. Dainties that had been set aside for special occasions were brought from the village to please her: sun-dried lobster tails and honey-pale octopus broiled over hot coals, oozing juice on the plate and filling the air with their aroma as far as Vigla.

Loulou graciously raised her glass of raki and greeted each group of treaters. And they smiled happily, young lads without moustaches and even fathers with marriageable daughters, men who had never known love except from coarse-skinned, slovenly mates who even in bed reeked of fish and onions. This young woman could drink like a man and appear none the worse for it. It was astonishing to watch her down the drinks. She refused none, and yet her eyes remained unglazed.

Once more the tambourine jingled a signal that Loulou was about to sing. She arose and commenced another number.

All evening the fiddler had not taken his eyes off her. At first it seemed it was because he had to follow the tempo of her singing, which she varied with her mood. Then it was noticed that the little fellow kept his eyes glued on her during the intervals.

How those owlish eyes watched her pleadingly when she took a drink! They worshipped and adored her, they begged her, they scolded her when she smiled. At times they clouded with uneasiness as the fiddler's eyebrows drew together apprehensively.

His small face was shiny with sweat and his swarthy skin glistened unpleasantly. He was completely dominated by Loulou. From her he received breath and light. When she sang, her sultry voice was reflected in his features. He was tortured by the insipid sentiments of the lyrics and by the erotic innuendoes of the numbers from the Athenian revues, whose obvious nastiness the raki-drinking fishermen underlined for themselves.

The old man with the zither paid no attention to all this. His white head was bent over the metal strings. He smiled raptly and made the hammers dance to the notes. It was extraordinary how he was able to synchronize his playing so flawlessly with the other instruments.

Maestro Apostolos did not break his rapport with the tambourine. He continued to dance and wrestle with it, tickle it and make it laugh, caress it with his thumb, make it sob, shake it, and cause it to leap and spin on his back and head. Presently the carousers discovered another of his accomplishments.

Every time a fisherman enthusiastically took a silver two-drachma piece out of his purse and tossed it at the musicians, Maestro Apostolos, still absorbed with his instrument, would unexpectedly reach out his prodigious arm and with the tambourine catch the coin in mid-air, no matter from what direction it was thrown. *Hrap!* The piece would thump on the drumhead. He never lost the rhythm of the song or took his eyes off the tambourine. He merely smiled with his narrowed, ardent, mischievous eyes as if he had picked the money out of the air.

In this way the merrymaking continued. Bottles came and went, as well as plates of pickled peppers, salted sardines, and cucumber slices.

Suddenly the cicadas awoke among the olive trees of Vigla. Perhaps because of the powerful light, possibly because of the noise and the music, they began shrilling with all their might, as if it were broad daylight.

Then, above the treetops on the hill nearby, a silver gleam played like the light of dawn on the dark surface of the sea. Slowly, with majestic grandeur, the full moon of August rose above the olive groves. The azure night was wiped out, the steep cliffs cast gigantic shadows, and the water shimmered under a downpour of cold luminousness.

Women and children from the fishing village collected on the fringes of the tavern area. They had come to fetch their fathers and sons. Sitting in rows on the walls and on stone blocks, they watched and gossiped in whispers.

As time passed, the moon rose higher. Many of the guests got up and went home, sighing with regret and belching raki fumes in satisfaction. But others remained past midnight, resolved to drink till dawn. Among them at a table by themselves were Yoryis Apodelipos and Varouhos.

Yoryis struck the table with the hook attached to his mutilated arm to order treats and with this same iron device he assisted his right hand in rolling cigarettes. This he did ostentatiously and as he passed his tongue over the paper, he lifted his eyes and saw Loulou goggling at him in amazement at his dexterity. He offered the cigarette to Varouhos and proceeded to roll another, and then a third, which he put behind his ear. He performed still other feats with the hook. He picked up titbits with the point, put the edge into his mouth, and whistled like a steamship, all the while he kept one eye on the prima donna, who was admiring him.

Between Varouhos and Yoryis was a black papier mâché tobacco box. They smoked and drank. At first, Varouhos was inclined to be confused and taciturn, but as the evening went on, he got into the swing of things. When his spirits were fully aroused, he got up, pulled a handkerchief from his pocket and danced with one of the Gadjalis brothers, an island dance.

During the circular movement of this dance, the dancers are given an opportunity to catch their breath and may bestow 'stickers' on the musicians according to their whim or the state of their pocketbook. Varouhos took out his wallet and let it dangle from its cord as it unwound. Then he drew out a freshly printed fifty-drachma note. After folding his wallet, he went to the *prima donna.* He stopped in front of her, moistened the paper with his tongue and *fap!* he stuck it on the young woman's forehead.

She was startled and wrinkled her nose in distaste. Immediately, however, she recovered her poise and remained as patient as an icon

113

when a devotee sticks a silver coin on its face. But the paper failed to stick and the fisherman licked it and tried again. Suddenly the little fiddler interfered. He thrust out his hand and snatched the note. His dark eyes flashed and his oily moustache glistened with fury. His eyebrows twitched above his pale face and he quivered like a violin string. With a nervous, jerky movement he crumpled the paper in his fist and threw it away.

Maestro Apostolos, however, while his attention apparently was concentrated on his work, reached out the tambourine, caught the note in mid-flight, and stuffed it into his pocket.

All this happened in a split second without a break in the music or the loss of a beat; not for an instant did Maestro Apostolos cease to smile angelically at his tambourine. He merely wet his thumb and ran it in a circle over the drumhead, pirouetting at the same time on the heel and toe of shoe. The tambourine uttered a comical squeal, sharp and piercing, like little pigs when they are annoyed.

Everybody burst out laughing. Loulou, who was beginning to feel the effects of her drinking, threw back her head and guffawed. Her hair tossed and her breasts became taut. Varouhos was ready to fight the fiddler, but he, too, was seized with laughter and returned to the austere steps of the dance.

Then Loulou laid her plump elbow on the back of the chair that held the zither, rested her cheek on her hand, and during the intermezzo of the dance sang the usual *amané*. The instruments accompanied her with a soft, characteristic rhythm of two short and two long beats:

Tam-tam, taam-taam!

Looking through half-closed, velvety eyelids at the old man as he danced, she sang:

> *Aman,*
> *The world is the tree and we are its fruit,*
> *And death is the harvester,*
> *Aman,*
> *And gathers his crop.*

This grave song, its sinuous melody full of pain, and this philosophy of impermanence lent wings to the old man's feet during the quick tempo, which was picked up by each musician in turn. The mood took hold of all the guests and they accompanied the dancer with hand claps. Yoryis Apodelipos gave the nod for a treat to be taken to the dancers. Then he put the hook in his mouth and imitated the whistle of a steamship entering the harbour.

Booo! Booo! Booo!

The Mount of the Madonna and Vigla received the sound and sent it echoing farther and farther into the distance.

The revelry was resumed around this beautiful woman who in no way resembled the women of Skala, who was clad in a filmy silk dress that clung tightly to every inch of her plump body like the thin skin of purple figs waiting to be punctured by a fingernail to spurt their rosy sweetness.

All of them inhaled her presence and the music that hymned and caressed her, and from her there issued a subtle exhalation, rosy, tepid, and enervating, which enveloped the ungathered bunches of grapes on the trellis, the carousers, the glasses of milky raki, the shingle along the water's edge, and the gelatinous sea. The moon, round and hovering, transformed the olive grove into a black mass flecked with silver dust, and even the cicadas relapsed into silence in the transfigured night.

Around the lamp chimney, fascinated by the merciless light, a swarm of moths and beetles beat their wings. They were maddened by the white glare which drew them to it, drove them frantic, and caused them to wheel in a frenzy around the hot glass until they expired and fell like dead leaves.

26

A M O N G all the hot, hungry eyes was one deeply miserable pair full of agony, dread, and humble entreaty. It was a dog-like pair of eyes, large and round, belonging to the little fiddler with the snub nose who rose on tiptoe to reach a high note with his bow on the chaterelle string and to make glissandos on it. His strong arm fluttered in the tremolos like the wing of a wounded bird. His eyes were those of a watch-dog, of a devotee suffering continual martyrdom. The bow he drew was no longer a bow; it was a sword tormenting his heart which lay quivering in his hand. At such times his sleeve would climb to his elbow and disclose a soiled undershirt and a thin, fleshless arm covered with coarse black hairs.

It was obvious that the little fiddler was offended by all that was going on—the jokes they told Loulou, the treats they sent her, the gross innuendoes, the double *entendres,* and the erotic gestures that were exchanged among the tables. The fiddler shifted his round eyes from one to another in alarm, trying to sense the source of danger which was everywhere in the alcohol-impregnated atmosphere.

It was from Loulou herself that the evil came. Loulou now was drunk from the liquor and from the male exhalations which enveloped her. She stood up, reached out her plump arm, and with her polished fingernail plucked the shirt of Dinos Gadjalis, who was famous as a gallant and dancer. He sported a luxuriant blond moustache, which he stroked while he made ironical remarks.

The fiddler was horrified, and his whole body registered a convulsion of protest.

'No, Loulou!'

Paying no attention to him, Loulou stood erect and proud, her breasts arched and her hips firm. With her eyes half closed she looked down upon the fiddler from her high heels, not as a colleague, not as a lover, but only as a musician. Haughtily she commanded:

'The "Coachman"!'

The deaf man with the zither read the command on her lips, bent over the strings and, smiling indifferently, caressed them with the little hammers.

Apostolos shook his tambourine and a cool cascade of metallic laughter poured from the bells. The fiddler bit his lips and knotted his scanty eyebrows. Submissively he tucked a damp handkerchief under his chin to support his violin and complied with an air of helpless despair.

> *Coachman, coachman,*
> *With your whip in your hand!*
> *On, coachman,*
> *On to Cockayne!*

'Faster! Faster!' ordered Loulou, waving the rose-coloured scarf she held in her hand. She tossed her head and her hair fanned over her shoulders like the mane of an aroused animal. She felt she had to tame through motion and physical exhaustion the demon of desire which was furiously awake and clamorous in her vigorous body.

> *On, coachman!*

'Faster! Still faster!'

The fiddler exerted all his strength to keep pace with the young woman's feet, which had gone mad in the whirlwind of rhythm. His narrow chest panted, his pointed chin contracted above the violin and his Adam's apple rose and fell as if moved by uncontrollable sobbing. He rocked his whole body back and forth, he beat out the rhythm with his foot, and a drop of sweat dripped from the end of his greasy snub nose.

Maestro Apostolos alone enjoyed his work devoting body and soul to make the tambourine dance fantastically to the 'Coachman's Song'. He smiled ecstatically at his instrument, gave it tiny, sharp taps, tickled it and punished it with a thousand devices; and it answered him with soft moans and shrieks of laughter. One heard the coachman's whip-lash and the hoof-beats of the speeding horses.

> *On, coachman!*

'On!' shouted the fishermen in unison, clapping their hands and pounding the table with their glasses.

> *On to Cockayne!*

'On!'

> *Where the pretty girls are!*

'On!'

Loulou laughed wildly, completely drunk.

Suddenly, in the middle of the dance, Gadjalis seized the woman in his strong arms. He lifted her as lightly as one does a sick child. Then he buried his tousled head and thick moustache in her bosom.

'Ooooh!'

At the same instant the fiddler dropped his violin, drew a thin dagger from his waist, and rushed at Gadjalis. Before anyone could intervene, Gadjalis had frustrated the attack. Letting the woman drop to her feet, he intercepted the little fellow's blow in mid-air. He caught his arm and twisted it so that the knife, still in the man's grasp, penetrated the top of one of the tables. There he bent it from side to side until the blade snapped. Then, leaving the haft in the numb fingers of the fiddler, he gave him such a slap with the palm of his hand that the fellow was stunned and reeled unsteadily, his teeth covered with blood. He stumbled over some of the revellers, who caught him with a 'Youha!' and threw him like a ball to those on the other side, who in turn tossed him back.

During this fracas, Varouhos got up and left the tavern. He knew he was drunk. He could barely stay on his feet. Nevertheless, he set his course for the fishing village, inching himself forward, wall by wall, tree by tree. He was in a state of high excitement and his blood was boiling in his veins. In the bones of his great body he felt his pulse surge and pound like the surf during a tempest. He was outraged at what had happened.

'Phtou! on your shamelessness, you vermin!'

In the centre of the square the only fountain in Skala was singing alone in the night under the plane tree. It was an ancient Turkish fountain with horse blocks and a carved stone basin. Varouhos sat down on a horse block to rest and let the cold water pour into his burning bowels.

'Phtou! on your filthiness, you vermin!'

He leaned against the wall and closed his eyes. Inside his head something was turning and grinding like millstones. . . . It must be a watermill, for along with the droning was mingled the splashing of the water into the basin. With it came the vison of the woman who had laughed shamelessly and madly, who had laughed and danced with half-closed eyes while the tambourine rattled, *rou-rou-rou,* and the bells jingled. And that Gadjalis, the scoundrel, nuzzling his face and blond moustache between the woman's quivering breasts. He swelled with rage until he almost suffocated.

'Phtou! on you, you cursed slut!'

Then he sighed deeply and bent his head under the fountain. He felt the water run refreshingly through his tangled mop of hair, behind his ears, and down his thick neck. It dribbled over his inflamed eyes, through his moustache, under his shirt and wet his hairy torso deliciously.

For a long while he let the water flow over him and drench him. When he was quite refreshed, he felt as if the fountain had quenched the flames in his bowels and had expelled the hot fumes that were stifling him.

He arose and set out once more for home, where he could lie on his pallet and relax. Under the damp soles of his feet the ground was still warm from its all-day scorching. A dog, wandering about under the full moon, unable to sleep, approached the basin as soon as Varouhos had gone a short distance and commenced to drink. He heard the dog's tongue lapping up the water with eager delight.

The fisherman unlatched the door of his house and went inside. Usually Smaragthi would hear him and call out: 'Is that you, Father?' He waited in vain for the voice.

'Ha, the girl is angry because I stayed away so late tonight,' the old man thought. 'I really am a donkey.'

He felt guilty and ashamed. He wanted to weep. The water was seeping from his soaked trousers and leaving a trail behind him. He intended to go directly to his bedroom, fall on his pallet, and go to sleep without any talk.

He closed the door softly and walked down the hall. The cement was cool under his feet. In the kitchen the wick of the turned-down lamp burned feebly. His supper was laid out for him on the table. He looked at it with the grimace of a man who has no desire for food. Withdrawing, he opened the door of the big chamber without making a sound. There he stopped in stupefaction.

Exhausted from work, Smaragthi had given up waiting for her father. She had opened the window to cool the room a little, but there was no coolness that night. The sea seemed to have coagulated in the heat. The chamber was flooded with moonlight. Smaragthi had partially undressed and had bathed herself and sprinkled her neck with water from the jar on the wooden ledge outside where the air would cool it. Then she had dragged her pallet to the open window and lain down to wait for her father. Thus she had fallen asleep, and so she was when Varouhos entered the room.

The moonlight illuminated her face and produced shadows around her fresh mouth, so that her lips seemed parted like a half-opened flower. It also illuminated her breasts, which were naked and erect in their virginal bloom, rising and falling with the rhythm of her tranquil breathing. She was sleeping on her back with both arms above her head, as she had done from babyhood, and with her naked legs spread apart as children do during the great heat.

Stunned and shocked, Varouhos leaned against the wall. He stared, bereft of reason and sense. He was at a loss whether to go backward or forward, whether to wake her up or go away. He stood with his mouth open, his moustache drooping over his sagging jaw, looking with goggling red eyes like two inflamed sores. His hands trembled as they dug into the plaster behind him, his thick fingers shook and his legs shivered as if he had a fever.

All at once he broke away from the wall and without a sound, leaped on the body of the sleeping girl like a ravenous beast, his hands clawing and his face contorted by an ugly spasm.

Smaragthi awoke with a horrible feeling of terror, suffocation, pain, and loathing. She saw bending over her the bestial old man who was trying to violate her body, his fat, slobbering lips seeking to nuzzle her flesh wherever they met it. She felt her breath leaving her under his intolerable, loathsome weight, under his panting breath that stank of raki and tobacco. In this nightmare she saw his eyes close to her face, lighted by the moon—two red, swollen eyes filled with madness and lust.

Beside herself with horror and nausea, she screamed for help and tore with her nails at the monstrous, hairy face slavering with water and saliva. Her hand touched a tumbler. She seized it and struck the enormous, panting, shaggy head that was suffocating her. Then everything blacked out and she lost consciousness.

The room was rapidly crowded with neighbours who had been awakened by the screams and had run to see what the trouble was. Lathios was there with his wife, his three older boys, and old Permahoula, as well as two or three other fishermen and a number of women. Their loud voices created pandemonium and brought in still others. Old Permahoula and Maria lifted the girl and took her away to attend to her. The men seized Varouhos, dragged him on the floor, kicked him, and beat him with iron tongs, the broom, anything they could lay their hands on. The women tore out his hair and moustache and ripped his clothes off in frenzy. At last they left him unconscious, moaning on the floor like an ox, covered with blood which clotted his hair and, mixed with mucus, ran down from his nose.

Lathios was the last to leave. Before he went away, he took the water jar from the window, emptied it over the old man's head and chest, and spat in his bloody face. Then he closed the door behind him and went home.

27

W H E N God brought daylight back again, the fishing village buzzed with gossip. The family men and the women discussed Varouhos's scandalous act grimly and were in no hurry to go about their work. A crowd collected outside the fisherman's house. They shouted angry, obscene words, hurled stones at the dwelling of the evil-doer and cursed it with the maledictive gesture of arms extended, palms out and fingers separated.

The women congratulated Aunt Nerandji whom God had loved and taken away before she was forced to drink the cup of this disgrace. The men proposed cruel, shameful punishment for the culprit, such as emasculation with red-hot pincers. Boys brought petrol tins filled with rotten vegetables. They waited for the old man to appear so that they could greet him with abuse and make a public-example of him. The old women came with stinking offal and broken pottery to throw at him.

The erotic torment that subconsciously troubled these people through out their lives, the unspoken resentments and the unresolved frustration now found a violent outlet. Under the banner of morality they avenged themselves on the old man who had dared to break the law that inhibited all of them, men and women, and which without exception held them under its common yoke.

The emotions of the women had already been aroused the night before by the immodesty of the *prima donna.* She had challenged the little community where only permanent marriage bought what she offered with song and laughter as if it were a mere glass of undiluted raki.

The whole story of the goings-on at the Gadjalis tavern gradually came to light. Several old women who had hidden behind a nearby wall and some boys who had crawled under the bushes were able to give an account of everything and did. The details circulated from person to person and each in turn spiced them with his own elaborations.

They told how the Gadjales had made off with the dancer in a boat and her screams and laughing had been heard from outside the port till daylight. How the little fiddler had moped by the shore, weeping and beating his breast until the sinner returned. And how Gadjalis had sailed with the troupe to another port some two and a half hours away to the north.

When the fishermen returned to their homes from the revelry, they found their wives boiling with fury and many were the beatings that were administered that night throughout the village. One young girl who learned that her betrothed had been at the carousal broke off the engagement and sent back her ring. The women were vexed now that it had been impossible to hold the *prima donna* so that they could set her backwards on a lame donkey, put its tail into her hands and lead her about through Skala and the fishing village. She became the scapegoat for the shame they would suffer from Varouhos's crime in the contempt of the islanders, who were disdainful of the fishermen and their infamies and now had a story to tell.

So, instead they turned their wrath on old Varouhos. He was to pay for the scorn they had endured; he was to expiate the burden of their shame. All these years they had not even suspected what a lecherous goat he was, and they had entrusted him with their interests and taken pride in him. Now this man, a kinsman of the Bishop indeed, had betrayed the most sacred of things, the dignity of fatherhood, the innocence of an immature girl, and the obligation to an orphan placed in his care. Never before had such an outrage occurred in the annals of the village as an old man assaulting his daughter, and an unripe girl, at that.

'The antichrist should be burned alive!'

Each word fell like a drop of oil on the fiery passions these people had kindled within themselves. A woman went to Varouhos's door and rattled the handle so that he could be dragged out into the street, but the door and also the windows were locked.

Then the woman cried: 'Let's set fire to straw and smoke the dirty beast out of his hole!'

The children were delighted and began fetching thornbrush from the hedges and straw. Not a word was said about calling the police.

The fishermen immemorially had regarded the police as enemies and the same feeling existed among the islanders. They might be devouring each other but no one would report it to the police.

At this moment, Fortis appeared. He thrust aside the women and children and kicked away the fuel that had been piled in front of the door. A few tried to interfere, but Fortis, tall and austere, calmly shook them off and took a stand on the threshold. He adjusted his spectacles, touched his bald spot, cleared his throat solemnly and spread his arms out towards the crowd. As he waved them like the moulted wings of some large, gaunt bird, there was instantaneous silence.

'Listen,' he said. 'You are quite right to be so upset, as we all are, by this unheard-of scandal which has brought disgrace to Skala. Also, I myself have a personal reason for being concerned about the girl. It was I who anointed her with oil at her christening. I am her spiritual father. She is now at Lathios's house. She is in good hands, and I will take charge of her from now on.'

Someone interrupted him: 'Let's make a public example of the dirty scoundrel!'

Fortis motioned with his hand for silence.

'In your lives,' he said, 'you have known more than I have. We know life and death and we must not allow ourselves to be trapped by the devil. Let us not lose our humanity. Look. This man, I must tell you, has been lying on the floor in there since last night. He has been severely handled. He is covered with blood. He may even be dead. How do I know?'

'A bad dog doesn't die!'

'Let the cursed one suffer! May his soul go to the devil!'

'If he is dead, how could he lock himself in?'

'Right!' shouted angry voices.

Fortis silenced them. From his trousers pocket he took a key and showed it to them.

'That he's locked in means nothing,' he said. 'I came and locked him in at dawn after the disturbance. I tell you the man is in a bad way. He is beaten up and is in a dangerous condition. Now make certain of one thing. This is no land of outlaws, nor is it Anatolia, where you put a piece of silver into a policeman's hand so that he will look the other way. This is Greek territory. The law exists to judge. And when it is learned that you have maltreated Varouhos, you will be handcuffed and taken to prison. You may be sure that if Varouhos dies, none of you will escape. You will all suffer for it.'

There was silence. Then a man who was standing with an oar over his shoulder moved off towards the harbour, saying 'I didn't hit him. I only cursed him with my open hand. . . .'

Fortis now realized that this was the time.

'Somebody clubbed him on the head with an iron bar!' he said.

The fishermen were frightened and began to argue among themselves as to who had struck Varouhos and who had not. The women led their husbands away so that they would not be involved in case of trouble.

Fortis unlocked the door of the house, went in and locked the door again on the inside.

He found Varouhos moaning on the pallet. His face was swollen and disfigured by the blows, his lips were puffy and one eye was closed. On his head was a deep gash that reached to the skull. The sufferer had managed to treat it with a handful of tobacco held in place by a handkerchief for a bandage. He had difficulty in speaking, and it hurt him to change his position on the pallet. His entire body was a mass of sores and bruises.

From the bottomless pockets of his trousers Fortis took a small bottle of iodine, some cotton, and strips of cloth for bandages. He cleaned and disinfected the wounds, bound them up, and examined the huge, scourged body.

'They didn't break anything' he said. 'You got off cheap. In a few days you'll be on your feet again. But I must tell you that, considering what you did, they handled you very gently. . . .

Antonaros sighed and said nothing. He merely groaned and nodded his head in assent. Fortis wrapped up his medical supplies with great care and stuffed them back into his pocket.

'When you're better,' he said, 'I'll come again and we'll have a serious talk about the girl. You're in no condition now.'

The old man's eyes lighted up.

'Yes, yes,' he nodded eagerly, and this attempt to communicate caused his mouth to writhe with pain.

'I'm going now. I'll lock you in, for they're waiting outside to make an example of you. But, don't worry, I won't desert you.'

It was impossible for him to abandon a man in this state.

In two or three days Antonaros was able to get about in the house. He hobbled around and waited on himself. Then one night Fortis paid him another visit.

The two of them sat by the lamp, rolling cigarettes, and talked for a long time. It was very late when Fortis arose to leave. Varouhos followed him with the lamp as far as the door. There Fortis took a solemn farewell. He gripped Varouhos's hand firmly and said, 'Well, God be with you. . . .' In his other hand he held a tin box tied crosswise with a sandal lacing. It was Nerandji's coffee tin.

In the morning when the fishermen came down to the harbour, they found Varouhos's boat missing from her mooring. Yoryis said he had seen the old man making for the open sea in the dark of the night, and the others thought he had recovered and gone quietly back to his work.

But evening came and Antonaros's boat did not return. Everybody was waiting to see how he would face them after his disgrace. But he failed to put in an appearance that night, nor did his boat show up next day.

Fortis, who retained possesion of the key to the house, listened to the noisy speculations of the fishermen under the mulberry tree. He bit his tongue to keep from giving so much as a hint of what he knew.

He merely shook his head to indicate he knew nothing, shrugged his shoulders, and said noncommittally:

'Hm, who knows what's become of him. . . .'

'Hm, what is there to say?'

A few days later, however, Fortis unlocked the house and called Smaragthi. When they were inside, he told her everything. He turned the house and the key over to her and informed her about the box of money he was keeping for her new boat. Tomorrow he would go to Perahora and look for Manos Alimonos at the shipyard. He would make arrangements with the shipwright so that her mother's dream and that of her ill-fated father might come true.

The girl recoiled in horror when Varouhos's name was mentioned. Fortis observed her reaction.

'Listen, Smaragthi,' he said. 'In America, in the boarding-house where I lived while I worked in the factory, there also lived a lad who was very agreeable but very unfortunate. His name was Telemahos Stefanithes and he came from the Dodecanese. He could find no work, so he collected used bottle corks to sell and washed dishes in the basements of large restaurants. I felt sorry for him because he was so skinny and coughed all the time. I helped him with whatever I could spare, and he was very fond of me. He was an educated boy and wrote poems. His dream was to become a famous writer and publish stories and poems. Everybody liked him. They called him MacStephen in the boarding-house and at night, when he was well enough, four or five of us Greeks would listen to him read to us from his manuscripts. One day I was talking with him about the wickedness of men and I said that all of us have more or less dark souls. Mac looked at me with his childlike eyes and said something as profound as the words of the Gospel. He said: "In the soul of every evildoer a saint is imprisoned, weeping and waiting for his release." This remark has given me comfort many times. When I went that night to talk with your father and learn what restitution he had made for what he had done, I found him weeping like a baby, an old man like him. Then I remembered MacStephen and the saint. He gave me the box of money and promised me that you need have no fear of ever seeing him again alive, for he would die of shame to meet you. Now he has left our community. He went in his boat to Mount Athos. There he said he would seek salvation for his soul. Then I said to myself: "Here speaks Mac's saint, weeping inside this sinful soul, and already it has found release"!'

The girl said nothing. She bit her lips and wept softly. Fortis blew his nose loudly on his large handkerchief and continued:

'You see, Smaragthi . . . I've never heard what became of the lad,

MacStephen. He went away one day and we lost track of him. But in the years that have passed over me I remember him every time I think of what he said. If I could talk to him or write to him now, if he is still alive somewhere, I would like to tell him something myself. "MacStephen," I would say, "isn't there something else? Think, doesn't there exist in the heart of every holy man an evildoer who is biding his time?" I would say that to him. For Varouhos was a good man, Smaragthi. Believe me. But there is a thrice-cursed devil who comes with a thousand wiles to awaken the waiting evildoer, sometimes in the form of a woman, sometimes in the form of drink. . . . It's like the temptations of St. Anthony. . . .'

28

F R O M that day, Smaragthi established herself in the house where from then on she was to be its sole mistress. At night, Aunt Permahoula would come there to sleep. She invariably brought with her one or two of her grandchildren or great-grandchildren, who argued as to who would be chosen to stay with the 'little aunt'.

On days when she had finished her housework, Smaragthi would fish with Lathios. She was an eager worker and each day became more expert with the spear and net, since till then she had done only octopus and line fishing. Lathios watched her with astonishment, delighted with her progress.

'I swear,' he said to Fortis, 'she's no mere housewife, only fit to knead dough in the kitchen. She's a real fisherman and holds the sea in her hand. There are some fishermen we know, Comninos, who could learn from her now how to hold the spear.'

As Lambis heard this, his heart leaped and he bit his lips. Fortis, the mouthpiece of his *nargileh* between his teeth, swelled with pride and rewarded Lathios generously with treats.

One day Lathios took Smaragthi and his older boys over towards Anatolia, to his old fishing ground near some barren islands off Aivali. There they happened upon a huge school of fish, a fortune, moving in to feed on the muddy shoals at Dalyani.

Lathios drew some torpedoes from his belt. He tied three of them together and showed them to Smaragthi.

'Look here,' he said. 'What do you say to these?'

A curious excitement shone in her green eyes. She looked at the fishermen and waited. He saw her excitement, watched her breath quicken, and smiled with satisfaction.

He took the charge in his right hand and held a lighted cigarette in the left. Taking a puff, he flicked the ash away with a finger, ignited the fuse, held the charge a moment, and then threw it.

'*Boom!*'

The charge exploded in the sea, and the land nearby echoed the detonation. The water boiled with large white bubbles. For a moment the green bottom was revealed and then obscured. After the disturbance subsided, a host of fish rose to the surface from the depths.

Some swam about stunned; others trembled and expired with their silver bellies upward. Nets were hauled in again and again and still it was impossible to diminish the wealth which kept rising from below.

It was the first time Smaragthi had witnessed a spectacle of this kind. A prickling sensation thrilled her from head to foot during this outlawed kind of fishing that is so easy and yet so appalling.

Lathios noticed her agitation, her burning eyes and her trembling fingers.

'Not like that,' he said brusquely. 'We get nowhere that way. This work takes cold blood, as cold as fish blood.'

They returned to the port loaded to the gunwales, and since there was no cargo ship from Hora that day, the fishmongers of Mouria and nearby villages came down and bought the entire haul. There was fish for all at bargain prices.

The customs inspector was a newly married man, elderly, with dyed moustaches. He played backgammon all day opposite his house so that he could keep an eye on his young wife. He was so jealous of her that he kept her behind closed doors even in summer. He was unaware that the fish had been taken with dynamite. The tax collector, who recognized the illegal nature of the business at first glance, did not bother to tell him. Since he had a family of his own to support, he was satisfied with imposing a tax large enough to give him a good percentage.

Smaragthi went home glowing with excitement and enriched by a new sensation, tangy and heroic. She now understood fully the delightful risk which Yoryis Apodelipos had paid for by contributing portions of his body one after the other to the sea.

While they were returning to the harbour, she had touched the crippled hand of Manolis, Lathios's eldest son, as he was making fast the sail's taut rope. The two middle fingers were missing, sheared off at the roots.

He trembled, looked at , and blushed.

'Was it from that?' the girl asked.

At first Manolis failed to understand. Then he looked at the mutilated hand and smiled bashfully.

'Yes,' he said. 'They went for bait.'

Smaragthi learned with surprise that the fishermen considered such things as the commonplaces of everyday work, not worth talking about.

Later came the memorable day when Lathios let her throw the torpedo for the first time. The three older boys were aboard, and she felt their eyes fixed on her.

'As we said,' Lathios admonished her. 'Good blood, like fish blood.'

When she had thrown the torpedo and recovered from the exquisite thrill, she felt a great joy deep inside her. Those broad wings, which slept folded up, were again aroused and were beating as mightily as the water that had opened and closed in front of her. The torpedo had set free something fettered in her soul. Now it seemed to her that she could meet people with confidence.

During the return trip, she leaned against the gunwale, thinking of many things as she watched Stratos and Vatis at the oars.

Lathios was sitting in the prow with his eldest son, silent as usual. Manolis noticed her looking at his brothers. Indicating them with a motion of his chin, he said with a laugh: 'The twins are jealous of you. Father has never entrusted the torpedo to them, you know.'

Smaragthi was awakened from her reverie. She had given herself to the blissful tingling which still quickened her soul.

'We're not jealous of Smaragthi,' said Stratos.

Vatis, who had been born a half hour later than Stratos and regarded him as his elder brother, smiled at Smaragthi with his full, red lips.

The twins were as like as two drops of sea water, but they had different characters. Stratos, stronger and more tanned, tried in every way to be like Manolis, who was a *pallikari* of nineteen years and accounted himself an adult. Stratos tried to be serious and sparing of words like his big brother. He parted his hair as Manolis did, walked with his head thrown back, barefoot, legs apart, his hands in his breeches pockets or clasped behind him. He dreamed of the day when he also would go to the barber on Saturday and to the tavern, when he would be allowed to own a tobacco box of yellow brass and would not have to smoke on the sly, huddled with his companions behind the cliffs. He even envied his brother the two missing fingers. He considered their absence a sign of manhood.

Vatis, however, was more delicate and slender with wide-open, misty eyes, An unbaked body, Lathios said. No good for work.

The old man was right. Vatis liked to spend hours gazing at the sea and at the white clouds leisurely drifting or massed overhead with bright colours. He idled about and let his mind go wool-gathering. He had a red mouth and hands as fine and soft as a girl's. All this caused the male members of the family to treat him as something of an oddity. Nevertheless, his mother and old Permahoula—she above all—loved him dearly. For Vatis was a lad who needed and responded to affection.

At home, after Smaragthi had gone to her own house, Manolis told of the girl's expertness. He had watched her throw the spear as she stood erect on the prow and he had marvelled at her. He praised her courage and the sureness of her hand.

'Her eyes see fathoms down in the water. This girl is a mystery....'

Stratos half closed his eyes as Manolis did. With raised eyebrows he repeated gravely:

'Truly, she is a mystery-girl.'

The old woman had the same things to say. She wagged her head knowingly and said to the men:

'Now you're beginning to understand. From the day when Antonaros found her in his boat, I've been telling you. This girl is different. . . .'

Lathios, who was smoking silently in a corner, laughed.

'A sea nymph foundling. Say it!'

The twins burst into laughter, but the old woman nodded her head patronizingly.

'We've discussed it before,' she said. 'You men can't understand these things. You just toss words into the air. "This girl is a mystery," you say. That has its meaning, my son! And when I (may God give you my years) begin to tell you what this mystery is which your dull wits have stumbled on, you laugh and jeer at me, because you don't understand the things that I do!'

Vatis raised his head. 'I don't make fun of you, Granny.'

The old woman looked at him fondly.

'The blessing of my twenty nails on you. You don't belong to a race of unbelievers!'

'Maybe you're a nymph foundling, too,' Manolis teased him. 'Haven't you noticed how your mind is wool-gathering all the time?'

When evening came, the old woman gave Vatis a skein of yarn to hold for her while she wound it up. They were alone outside the house and Vatis felt free to renew the subject.

'Tell it to me, Granny.'

'What should I tell you, my son?'

'Why, the secret about Smaragthi. I believe you, Granny.'

The old woman wagged her head thoughtfully.

'You must understand,' she explained, 'the nymphs are of two kinds. The ones that dwell on land and the others, the sea nymphs. The first kind are those that inhabit valleys and streams, that go abroad at night under the moon and lie in wait at crossroads as naked as on the day they were born. They are beautiful demonesses and easily ensnare wayfarers who know nothing about fairy folk. They sit in the middle of the road, set up their distaffs, and spin their thread. They draw their wool from the moon when it's full, and that's why it wanes. They crisscross the paths with threads, and whoever comes along gets tangled in their moonskeins, falls under a spell, and either loses the power of speech or wastes away.'

'And the others?' Vatis asked.

'The others are the nereids. They're called mermaids. Like the one painted on the Mount of the Madonna. down to the waist they are women, the most beautiful of all. From there on, they're fish. They sit on lonely islands and comb their hair and they sing on the rocks and dunes. When they see a human being, they take fright, slap the water with their tails, and plunge to the bottom. If a fisherman or a sailor pleases them, they rise to the surface, seize the stern of the ship, and steer it according to their whim, just for fun. The steersman leans over to see what the trouble is, glimpses their beauty and their gleaming breasts, hears their seductive speech and is bewitched. As he reaches out to touch them, they slip away and slowly sink, looking the man in the eye and smiling. They smile so alluringly that the man leans farther and farther until he falls into the sea, and they take him with them.'

'With them?'

'Yes. To the invisible world. There they take out his eyes and string them on a necklace.'

'Why do they take out his eyes?'

The old woman knotted a broken thread. Then she wet her finger and shrugged her shoulders.

'That's what they say. They seem to like the eyes of *pallakaris*. Ask and find out. Every time a drowned *pallikari* is taken from the sea, his eyes are always missing. But don't think the mermaids don't suffer sometimes. As they seduce the seamen, so they themselves fall into their own trap. They fall in love with men, sleep with them, and conceive a child. If this child resembles human kind, they place it on the seashore in some spot where a passerby will find it and adopt it. If it resembles the mermaids, they keep it with them.'

'And when the child is saved?' the boy asked, entranced.

'When it is saved and lives, it is different from all others in character and appearance. It grows to be very beautiful. It has the marks of the numphs, you see. It becomes very clever, but all its life it is drawn to the sea. If you take a nymph foundling and bring it up on land far from the sea, it wastes away and dies. The salt air nourishes it and gives it strength like wheat bread. And it is said that while it lives among men, it brings either great good fortune or great misfortune.'

The boy stared at the old woman, fascinated by what she had told him.

'It's true, Granny, just as you said!'

'So it is, my son, and not otherwise.'

29

S O M E months later, Fortis drew Lathios aside, treated him to a coffee, and drew up a chair beside him.

'I want to talk to you about something, Panayis,' he said in his
Lathios nodded that he was ready to listen.

'It's about the girl. How is she doing? You have had her with you for a long time. Has she got the knack of the work or not?'

'The knack of fishing is never full mastered,' replied Lathios sententiously. 'I who have grown old at the oars, even now I'm just beginning. . . .'

'I mean, is Smaragthi fit to work by herself and manage her own boat?'

The fisherman sipped his coffee unhurriedly to the last drop, set the cup down, and replied with conviction:

'As for that, I can assure you that there are not many young fishermen in the port of Panayia like this girl.'

Visibly satisfied, Fortis touched his bald spot lightly with his fingers.

'I heard from Perahora today that her boat is ready,' he said. 'Painted and fitted out to the last detail. Can we turn it over to her to manage by herself?'

Lathios looked at him gravely and said:

'Why not? People will be rather surprised, but what of that? Smaragthi has more good sense and judgement than five men. Besides, I'll always be nearby to guide her and lend a hand. For a long time now, we've thought of her as our own daughter. . . .'

So they agreed to go secretly to Perahora in Lathios's boat and bring back the new one. They would wait till the fifteenth of August when there would be a great festival for the Madonna on the Mount. They chuckled as they made the arrangements. Nobody else would know of the plan. On the day of the festival, Lathios's women folk would persuade Smaragthi to lay aside her mourning, and while she was enjoying the festivities after the liturgy, they would arrive with the new boat and tie it up in the harbour before her eyes.

And so it was done.

The eve of the festival arrived. Merrymakers poured down from Mouria and neighbouring villages in their holiday finery on mules gaily decked-out with bright saddle cloths and with red tassels on their bridles.

Even the fishermen were drawn into this mingling of feasting and piety; not, as at other times, to dry their nets or to seek the Madonna's protection when the police descended on them in Skala in search of contraband merchandise. They would hide under the altar whatever smuggled goods they possessed— tobacco or cigarette papers—and the Madonna would graciously guard them until the officers departed.

On this eve of the festival there had already arrived lottery operators and pastry vendors who hawked round confections coated with minute, coloured confetti sugar. Also there came toy peddlers with paper whistles and small clay water-pipes that warbled like nightingales when the children filled them with water and blew through the mouthpieces.

At daybreak more villagers and young women came down carrying wicker baskets of offerings on their arms for the Madonna. Glass bracelets tinkled on their wrists and the air rang with their laughter.

There were loaves, baked to perfection and stamped with the double eagle from wooden moulds made on Mount Athos, flasks of oil for the lamp, candles of yellow wax, and embroidered aprons for the icons on the altar screen. There were garlands of jasmine blossoms and wreaths of pinks, camomile, basil and marjoram. All these were brought by the women who went up on the Mount to dress the Madonna, polish the chandelier, scrub the floor, clean the walls and throw lime on the filth that had been left by the fishermen during the previous year.

The chapel shone after its cleansing and was filled with the perfume of flowers. The aprons dedicated to the Madonna hung unfolded on the icon screen, some of silk, others of calico. Especially fine were those brought by the brides of the year, on which in the centre were embroidered with silk and gold thread the words: 'Hail, Mary, Full of Grace'.

Smaragthi was one of the few women of Skala who went up on the Mount. She had discarded her mourning and her beauty outshone all the others.

The village girls who saw her the first time were astonished at her charm. They touched her hair and smiled or stood troubled before her stange eyes. A golden light streamed from her whole presence, a mysterious radiance of health and vitality that surrounded the girl like an aureole. The extraordinary events of her short life endeared her to everybody.

Old Permahoula went up on the Mount with her and when Smaragthi asked her for a bit of thread to tie on the Madonna the wreath she had woven from her own flowers, the old woman made the sign of the cross over her, spat three times, and said:

'You, my lady, are the loveliest flower we've brought Her Grace this year.'

Smaragthi made a playful face at her, wrinkling her nose and sticking out her lips as children do.

At this moment two boats rounded the point of Cape Korakas and made for the harbour.

'Visitors from Perahora!' the woman cried and stared from the cliffs.

Presently the Skaliotes recognized one of the boats. They identified her as Lathios's by the broad beam and the two patches on the sail. But the other one in front? This was her first appearance in the waters of Panayia, and she aroused everyone's curiosity. For this boat, red and white, was rigged out as elegantly as a bride and gleamed with fresh paint. A new flag fluttered from the mast and the lateen sail was like a scarlet blossom on the violet waves.

When the boat came nearer, all her ropes and cables were seen decorated with red, blue and gold paper streamers. From the mast hung dancing Japanese paper lanterns of various colours.

When at last the boats were moored in the harbour, it was discovered that the men were Lathios and Fortis in the new one and Manolis in the other, and when the name *Nerandji* was read on the sides of the prow, everyone at once understood and shouted:

'It's Smaragthi's! It's Smaragthi's boat!'

Smaragthi heard the shouting of the crowd, saw her mother's name in black letters within a yellow border, and gripped Permahoula's hand.

'It's ours,' she said and felt her heart tremble.

30

A F O U N T A I N of emotion arose within her and filled her eyes. She fled from the crowd and ran home, where she locked herself in her room and in solitude surrendered to weeping, laughing, and delighting in the pain of this happiness.

Then she wandered restlessly about the house, through all the rooms and the hallway until at last she stopped at a window from which she could see the Mount. It was covered with people in their gay holiday costumes, and the breakwater was black with staring figures.

She knew that they were all talking about her and her mother. She was embarrassed and blamed Fortis and Lathios for having made such a fuss over the boat. Again she wandered about the room and looked at each object as if she were seeing it for the first time. Everywhere there were reminders of Nerandji, whose love never ceased radiating around her and over her like a heavenly light.

She stood before the crude little mirror with its wooden frame like that of a child's school slate. Here her mother used to look at herself and arrange her hair before she tied her headcloth over her black tresses when she was getting ready to go up and burn incense to the Madonna.

Now Smaragthi saw in it her own youthful, rosy face and her own golden hair catching the sunlight which swept in through the window. She drew back angrily and snatched from her head the red ribbon which she had been persuaded to wear for the first time since her mother's death.

She was ashamed of being so young, so glowing, and so golden and melancholy. It seemed that her flower-like face was brazenly replacing another face in the glass, a small, thin face wrapped in a sombre headcloth. In it two eyes flamed like coals with sleepless, fanatical love and seemed to consume the slender, waxen body as a candle consumes itself.

This face with its sad smile was always near her and she sensed it watching over her even while she slept. Frequently before she opened her eyes in the morning, she had the impression that she had only to open them to see that gentle, austere face with the heavy brows and the wistful mouth.

And when she had recognized Lathios and Manolis far off in the boat and her godfather scanning the girls with his American field-glasses in search of her, she thought she glimpsed, at the prow of the brightly decorated boat, another form, sitting with hands firmly grasping the gunwale and enormous, burning eyes staring at the calm water of the harbour.

It was thus that her mother had stood on the Mount of the Madonna when she went up to pray and burn incense. She would lean over the cliff and look down at the dark green water. Then she would sigh softly and cross herself before beginning the descent and say, 'Glory be to thee, O Lord!'

If God had only spared her mother, she would have asked Him for nothing else!

A knock on the door brought her back to herself. She went and opened it. There stood her godfather, his bald pate shining in the sun like a halo. Freshly shaved and formally dressed, he entered and held his hands out to Smaragthi.

'You saw it, eh? My dear this is no boat. It's a young girl, an angel, and it flies over the water. So, good luck . . . Captain Smaragthi!'

The girl took his hands and kissed them with trembling lips.

'Come! Put on your best clothes and let's go to the coffee-house.'

'To the coffee-house?'

'Yes, of course! The Lathios family is there, and everybody else. We're going to have the boat blessed and drink a health to the good faring of the *Nerandji*. This blessing will be her christening, you see. In America, you know. . . .'

How her godfather enjoyed all this commotion. She realized it would spoil all his fun if she let him down. So she silently capitulated.

Fortis withdrew to the kitchen to give her time to get ready. From there he told her in a sustained monologue how in America they christen a ship the moment they release her to the sea. Smaragthi listened to his chatter as he became involved in his memories, even though she could find no meaning in it. Every now and then he would ask:

'Are you listening, Smaragthi?'

Startled, she would reply: 'I'm listening, Godfather!'

At last she was ready and went to the kitchen, where she found Fortis examining curiously an unused tobacco pouch suspended by a silk cord. The design, in white, yellow and blue beads, was a wreath of roses encircling two doves, which were kissing each other. It had been Aunt Nerandji's betrothal gift to Antonaros.

Fortis was on the point of asking her jokingly what this bauble was, but he saw her look at the piece of handiwork with such pain in her eyes that he hastily changed his mind and said:

'Well, well, well, what a beautiful lass you've become, and we've never noticed it! Come along now, let's go quickly. The priest is waiting for us.'

With the girl at his side, Fortis strutted through the fishing village like a turkey cock. He was wearing the indestructible suit which dated back to his years in America and which he used only on solemn occasions. They were greeted by the women from doorways and windows:

'Best wishes, dear Smaraghti!'

Smaragthi blushed and looked from side to side in confusion and felt like weeping.

'Thank you! Thank you!'

She was wearing a light blue dress with white polka dots which fell full about her slim legs. A band of the same material held up her hair but had difficulty in controlling its wavy abundance. Sun and salt air had given it the lustre of old gold with occasional strands of the deeper shade of strained honey.

In his pride, Fortis altered his usual pace. His progress through the centre of Skala's public square and arrival at the coffee-house with his godchild at his side was a real triumph. The priest and guests were waiting for them under the mulberry tree. From there, led by the priest, they all trooped to the boat, which was moored near the mouth of the harbour. The priest went aboard with the cross and basil in his hand, accompanied by Lambis with a white bowl of water. They were followed by Lathios and Fortis and, last of all, Smaragthi. The rest stood in a line on the breakwater. The priest read the prayers and Fortis assisted by chanting the responses in a nasal voice. Then the priest sprinkled the boat fore and aft with holy water and likewise the four points of the horizon and the sea so that the latter would be kind and gentle for the new craft and would be compassionate to all the poor folk who earned their living on the water. He also sprinkled the people, touching them on the forehead with the basil as they came up one by one to kiss the cross and his hand. Fortis took his godchild's face between his hands and kissed her on both cheeks. Two teardrops sparkled behind his spectacles.

'May you live for me as long as the mountains, my daughter!'

Lambis was still holding the bowl of holy water. He watched with his large eyes without saying anything.

'Come here and kiss your godsister,' Fortis said to him. 'This is a day of great happiness for her.'

The boy suddenly went red. He tried to smile, but his lips trembled. With a light leap to the gunwale, he went ashore without replying.

137

'Don't mind him,' laughed Fortis. 'This yokel of mine isn't quite civilized.'

The company now returned to the coffee-house and the treating began. Raising their glasses, they drank to the health of the boat and Smaragthi. Everyone said: 'God rest blessed Aunt Nerandji,' but not a word was said in reference to Antonaros.

Smaragthi kept thinking about this. She found it natural and yet there was a pang in her heart. Then Fortis raised his glass and said: 'Eh, good luck to those who are not with us,' and in one voice the company responded: 'Amen!' Smaragthi looked pleadingly at her godfather. Then she saw his eyes smiling cannily at her through his spectacles and smiled back at him. She felt that this also was as it should be, and her heart was healed.

Then, since it was not proper for her to remain among the men, she arose and left them to continue their celebration of the festival. Taking old Permahoula, Vatis, and several others of Lathios' brood, she went aboard her boat. Vatis hoisted the anchor, untied the mooring, and with a pole punted the boat out of the harbour. Then Smaragthi made the pulleys sing as she took the new rope and raised the sail.

The paper pennons rustled in the breeze. Everything was bright and there was a fragrance of new wood and fresh paint. The Lathios youngsters screamed with joy and jabbered gaily as they leaned over the gunwales and trailed their hands in the water. Vatis sat at the tiller, which he gripped with both hands. He looked at the breakwater, which was black with people, and then at the girl.

Smaragthi was sitting beside the old woman in the shade of the sail. She heard Permahoula talking softly but paid no attention to what she was saying. She looked around at the boat, fingered the wood here and there, the shiny iron books and the beautifully-shaped oars which were resting beside their locks like folded wings. She was glad that from now on she would be alone in her own boat to caress it and come to know its features as she would those of a beloved face. This was her boat and it was named *Nerandji*. It was rocking her in its arms as if she were in a cradle. It was all like a pleasant dream, yet sad and incredible. She remembered what her godfather had said to Lambis. Was happiness like this, then? She wondered and was puzzled.

Suddenly she became aware of the words the old woman was muttering in her ear like the meaningless sound of running water. She was saying:

'. . . This, you see, is extraordinary, my daughter. For you, a young girl, to be so unwomanly as to captain your own boat! And to do the work of the sea which needs a man's mind and a man's hand. . . .'

'That's true,' said Smaragthi and she felt the heavy responsibility on her young shoulders.

But she had no qualms. With lively curiosity and secret joy, she sensed the new life that was beginning for her. This boat was going to liberate the mysterious wings that were folded-up within her.

'To Vigla or to Koufovouno?' asked Vatis from the stern. These were two hills which guarded the entrance to the harbour.

'Make straight for the open sea,' replied Smaragthi.

This was the first time the lad had seen Smaragthi in blue and so grave. She seemed much older and more remote. The red sail wrapped her in its shadow and when in the rocking rhythm the sun passed across her face, a lock of hair on her right cheek caught fire with a red-gold flame.

'Oh, how beautiful our Smaragthi is!' the boy's heart sang in his breast. He reflected on their good luck in having her going in and out of the house as if she were their sister, a sister whom they worshipped.

Smaragthi stood up to manoeuvre the sail for the return. Her supple body stretched and relaxed near him and her dress touched his knee and fanned his face with a cool, sweet breeze as if it had passed through a grove of pomegranates loaded with bursting fruit.

Vatis looked at her waist, her firm breasts and her rounded hips; and his mind was dazzled. His heart told him that, alas, this girl could not continue to remain near them as a sister. But what was there to do?

He understood many things. Other things, which were beyond him, were revealed by his quick imagination and his almost feminine intuition. He knew thus that the same disturbance he felt was experienced by all others, children and adults, when Smaragthi was present.

31

S M A R A G T H I was aware of all this herself as she grew up and the lines of her body matured. That dreadful night with Varouhos had been the awakening. After Antonaros fled the house and she was left alone in the world, she realized with a shock the masculine urgency that surrounded her. Now she understood it. While she worked and conversed with other fishermen, she frequently caught in their eyes the familiar glitter of the hungry male.

Another horror, similar to this, haunted her like a sleeping memory, a chill deep in her bones and in the roots of her hair. Try as she might, she could not track it down. Then one day a ship guarded by a fierce, red dog tied up in the harbour. As she passed the ship, she was shaken to the core with a fit of trembling. She realized that she still had not outgrown the terror of the dog which in her childhood had pursued her with inexplicable and unappeasable hostility. It was the same resentment that she noticed from time to time in the eyes of men as they looked at her. It was the gleam that had been in the eyes of Varouhos. At once she would turn to ice. An alert sounded within her, to beware. Her fear revived, and she was as angry as if they had abused her with foul words. It was especially disconcerting to detect these vicious glances from fathers of families whom she respected.

On the other hand, she occasionally accused herself of becoming suspicious. They all could not be like that. Otherwise she would have to be prepared to meet at every moment the inflamed eyes, the bloated lips and the clutching hands of Varouhos which, even though he had departed, would now be those of the very men who had wanted to kill him that night. They would be like the herd of swine, in the Gospel, into which Christ drove the demons from the madman. . . .

One evening Vatis asked old Permahoula.

'Granny, did you ever see the mermaids?'

'No, my son, not with my own eyes. But my mother once saw a man bewitched by them abandoned on the shore, and your grandfather saw them in the flesh when he sailed between Malta and Egypt on Hadjidiamandis's two-master. I've only heard a mermaid.'

'You heard her, Granny?'

'Yes, my son. I was about your age; and it was a stormy night, and the wind whistled in the chimney and made the curtains billow like banners. Our house was by the sea. In winter the waves would beat against the doorsill. The brass knocker on the door would rattle as if someone wanted to come in. The lamp in front of the icon had gone out, and the room was dark. Father was away on a voyage, and I was sleeping on the same pallet with my mother. We tried to deceive each other by pretending to be asleep, but both of us were twisting like snakes. Suddenly in the wind and the fury I heard her voice. The voice of the mermaid. . . .'

Vatis went to the old woman, seized her hand and drank in her words.

'What was it like?' he asked.

'It was a thin, soft voice, like the sound made by a reed. But it was a woman's voice and it could be heard above the storm. It seemed to come from far out at sea. It was slow and sad. There were no words, only the crooning that mothers make when they rock their babies to sleep. It would stop and then start again, so sweet and sad that it made one heartsick to hear it. . . .'

'Were you afraid?'

'What do you think? I held my breath. I pulled the covers over my head and heard my heart pounding like a hammer. I gripped my mother's hand. "Do you hear it?" I asked her in a very soft voice. "Yes," my mother said. "What is it, Mother?" I said and pressed close to her. "Be still and go to sleep," she said. "It's the mermaid singing a lullaby to her baby. The storm woke it up and she's singing it to sleep. Now go to sleep yourself and don't talk any more, for it doesn't do any good. . . ." '

'And then?' asked Vatis, his heart a-tremble.

'Nothing more. The singing drifted farther and farther out to sea into the night. The roar of the surf and the howling of the wind swallowed it up. The mermaid went away in the storm. . . .'

'Maybe she went down to her chamber at the bottom of the sea,' Vatis suggested gravely.

'Maybe, my son. Who can tell?'

'Maybe she was the same one who bore the boy with the scales on his back, eh?'

'Maybe, my son.'

Vatis turned this story over in his mind for a while. Suddenly he asked: 'Tell me, Granny. When a mermaid dies, does one say, "She is dead," or do we day, "She is carrion"?'

'Well, I think we should say: "She is dead." For, you see, she has a human form and mind and speech. And also she can have children by human beings.'

'And they're very beautiful, aren't they, Granny?'

'Beautiful enough to make you lose your mind. Their flesh is white as milk and their eyes are green as the sea. They sparkle like diamonds. And their hair. . . .'

'You're thinking of Smaragthi, Granny, when you talk like that.'

It was true. And he also had Smaragthi in mind when he thought about the mermaids.

'Granny, when I become a captain, I'm going to build me a big ship with three masts. I'll load it with ship's biscuit and water and I'll sail and sail until I find the mermaid.'

The old woman stroked his hair which fell down over his forehead.

'I wish you health, my son, and may you be a man and the captain of a great ship and may you travel, but may you never find her. Those who have found her have never had good fortune.'

Vatis said nothing. He smiled and shrugged his shoulders. Then he bent down, picked up a piece of flat tile and threw it out over the smooth sea. He remained bent with his face turned towards the sea, watching the feathery object skim like a red butterfly above the surface. Silently he counted the skips until the last one. Twelve. Then he straightened up and, looking the old woman in the eye, said to her in a low voice:

'Only to have the luck to see her—isn't that enough, Granny?'

32

T H E Lathios family was Smaragthi's sole support and comfort now that she had undertaken to live and work among the fishermen. She trailed in her own boat behind Lathios' and went in and out of his house as if it were her own. The women loved her and she helped them with their household tasks.

People marvelled at the girl's ability and charm. They talked about her in all the nearby villages and ports. Passing fishermen and crewmen on the motorboats had seen the new boat rocking on the waves and Smaragthi, her head at the glass, fishing for octopus in the shallows. Generally, one of Lathios's boys worked the oars as she gave the orders:

'More to starboard . . . a bit forward . . . there!'

This was the jargon of the art, which she had heard from childhood and which seasoned octopus fishermen had learned from their fathers and grandfathers. And now it was Smaragthi's turn to repeat the same, monotonous words that had been spoken for centuries, with her head inside the tin frame of the glass as if she were speaking to the sea and alone heard and understood the answer that came back to her from the deep.

Varouhos had taught her to distinguish at first glance the slightest movement of a tentacle among the mossy stones. Instinctively she picked out every lair and hiding place. She knew how to attract the octopus with a piece of white cloth, how to entice it with a bit of octopus meat and, as a last resort, how to drive it forth with a handful of lime. As soon as she got the creature into the open, it was as good as caught. She aimed her spear, cast it deftly, and drew it up. The octopus would writhe its tentacles frantically, attach its suckers to the haft until one of the Lathios boys hit it on the head. Then the octopus would loosen its hold in the lad's arms and go limp.

'Health and joy Captain Smaro!' the men would greet her from passing boats. She would turn her head to see who they were and then with a laugh, she would call back: 'Health to you!' If they were people she knew, she would raise her hand in greeting. Her arm, bare to the shoulder, would gleam in the sunlight with the colour of bronze.

Nevertheless, even with the passing of time and her own maturing, Smaragthi still felt herself beset on all sides by the covetous stares of the men. Wherever she went, on land or on water, they followed her with their hungry eyes, searching and exploring her inside and out.

Peasants are accustomed to regard a woman as a helpless quarry who by nature has no way of defending herself against the passions of men. Protection is the duty of the father, the brother, or the husband. If these ordained champions are lacking, the woman is considered fair game for any predatory male. Smaragthi's situation was further complicated by the Varouhos incident, the spicy details of which awoke fantasies and whetted tongues.

From the time that she began to work independently in her own boat, she was suffocated by the sultry atmosphere that enveloped her, but she thought of it as a sentence imposed by life which she must endure. She discovered how difficult it was for the fishermen to accept her as a fellow-worker, no matter how strictly she attended to her business. The revulsion that had rooted itself in her soul on that night of horror spread throughout her entire being as soon as she felt the amorous look of a man aroused by desire or the slightest physical contact with him.

Little by little, however, she became accustomed to what could not be helped, and her lot took a turn for the better. She lost the panic of a hen cowering with ruffled plumage in terror of the shadows of hawks circling overhead. She noticed that the fishermen became more relaxed and gradually accepted her as a matter of course, as if with the passing of time, they had to a man concluded that 'she is for no one'. But how she had laboured to earn this respect!

Even so, there was no settled peace, only a truce that would be automatically nullified if once the girl should deviate from her total repudiation of men—unless, of course, she should put on the wedding crown. Then everybody would regard as final the conventional status of a married woman.

But for the present, Smaragthi had won her peace of mind without relinquishing any of the freedom that her nature demanded as its right. Now that people were convinced of her unassailable chasteness, they slowly adjusted themselves to the girl's way of life, which in the beginning had upset them. On moonless nights Smaragthi would go out alone in her boat and by torchlight. If no other boats happened to be nearby, she would row to the sandy cove beyond the hill of Vigla. There she would extinguish the torch and dive into the sea.

33

O N E afternoon Smaragthi was sitting in the stern of her boat inside the harbour, putting her fishing gear in order. Vatis, who was with her, suddenly said: 'What do you say? Are there or aren't there mermaids in the sea?'

Smaragthi smiled.

'Since your grandmother knows I'm a mermaid's child, how can it be that there aren't any?'

'Don't you know who your mother was?'

'Of course. She was Nerandji.'

'Not her . . . the other one. Your real mother, the one who bore you.'

Smaragthi shook her head gravely and said with finality: 'There wasn't any other. And if any woman or mermaid came and said to me, "I bore you," I would refuse to recognize her, even if she were a queen.'

'All right. But what do you say? Are there mermaids in the sea or aren't there?'

'I say there are. All voyagers say there are. So did Avgustis in the school. Don't you remember? Why are you always asking?'

'Because I want to marry a mermaid.'

'My poor Vatis, you're only a child yet!'

'What's that got to do with it? I'll grow up. When I'm twenty-five, I'm going to find a mermaid and marry her.'

'Why do you have to be twenty-five?'

'This is why. Yesterday our Manolis told our father that he wants to get married and father shut him up. "Marriage," he said, "requires a settled mind. When you're twenty-five you can get married".'

'Ah! And who'll be his bride?'

Vatis did not reply immediately. He baited one of the hooks. He held the minnow dangling in front of his eyes and regarded it from all sides. Then he shrugged his shoulders.

'I don't know,' he said.

'Ah, you don't know. Well, it's no matter. When the right time comes, he'll choose someone worthy of him.'

The boy lowered his eyes.

'I do know,' he said.

'Then tell me. I'm like one of your sisters.'

Vatis looked at her challengingly through his half-closed, twinkling eyes.

'You know her yourself. You couldn't help knowing her.'

The girl shrugged her shoulders with annoyance.

'Since I told you I don't know. . . .'

The boy wagged his head vigorously, his face flaming red. At last he managed to speak.

'It's you he wants to marry. There! He hasn't breathed it to anybody. He hasn't mentioned your name. But I understand. And so does Stratos. Even Grandmother. Nobody else. . . .'

'Indeed! So the three of you understand it and discuss it among yourselves?'

The boy looked up at her in alarm.

'Ts! We haven't said a word to each other. None of us knows that the others understand it. And it's never entered Manolis's head that the three of us know.'

Smaragthi fixed her eyes on him sternly.

'And you? How did you come to understand all this that you've told me?'

Vatis dropped his eyes and picked at the basket of fishing tackle. Smaragthi removed his hand.

'You'll pick the basket to pieces if you aren't careful. Just tell me how you found out all these things. Are you a fortune-teller and read what's in people's minds?'

'I'm not a fortune-teller,' the boy said defiantly, 'but I understand things. I . . . it's something else.'

'What else? Explain yourself.'

Vatis summoned all his coursage, raised his eyes beseechingly to her, blushed, and looked down again. Then he blurted out, 'Well, I . . It's that I want to marry you myself. That's why.'

Smaragthi stared at him for a moment with her mouth wide open. She wanted to reply sharply. She tried to be severe but suddenly she burst out laughing in the childlike manner which at times overcame her and made her hold her sides.

'You? You? What do you know about such things, a young rogue like you, not even fifteen years old?'

With an effort she stopped laughing when she saw the lad's eyes fill with tears and his lips tremble at her amusement. Then the tears ran down his cheeks and he sniffed them back miserably.

'Now listen,' Smaragthi said to him seriously. 'In the first place, you're only a child compared with me.'

'I'll grow up.'

146

'It's still the same thing. But that's not what I want to say. Since you brought the matter up, I've got something to tell you.'

The boy looked questioningly at her eyes and mouth.

'I'm never going to get married, Vatis.'

'Never?'

'Never.'

'Not even to our Manolis?'

'Not even to your Manolis or anybody else.'

The boy's face lighted up. Then he shook his head incredulously.

'Impossible. You say this. But all girls get married. And so will you, too.'

'No, my boy. If that's what's worrying you, set your mind at rest. I'm not going to marry anyone.'

'Will you kiss the cross on it?'

The lad held out his crossed fingers to her.

Smaragthi solemnly bent down and kissed the two grimy fingers which smelled of fish.

He insisted further and made her swear the most fearful oath he knew:

'Say: "May I swim in God's blood.'

The girl repeated evenly: 'May I swim in God's blood.'

Vatis remained sunk in thought. Then he arrived at a plausible solution.

'I understand. It's because you're a mermaid's child. Isn't that it?'

Smaragthi looked far off, shrugged and sighed.

'It seems so, Vatis. Come now, all hands to work. With all your jabbering the bait will begin to spoil.'

Later, when the job was finished and they were talking about various things, Vatis suddenly said:

'And, you know, Lambis is in love with you, too. He's a year older than me and he's in love with you.'

'Again the same story? And how do you know? Do you two talk such nonsense together?'

'No. I noticed it by myself. I notice at once when anyone is in love with you. Lambis . . . he's a stubborn dog. He never says what's on his mind. But he loves you. How he loves you, Smaragthi!'

She checked his gossip with an impatient gesture.

'So, Vatis. Over and done with. I won't listen to any more of your nonsense. Now be a good boy so that I can love you in my own way.'

'All right,' said Vatis conclusively. 'Now that I know. . . . But I'll say it to you once more so there'll be no mistake. You aren't ever going to get married.'

Smaragthi laughed. 'All right . . . all right.'

147

'Don't laugh,' said the boy earnestly. 'But I want you to know that I'm ready to do anything for you. Even to die. . . .'

'Christ and the Madonna have mercy on us! Just don't forget to ask your father to let you give me a hand tomorrow morning if he doesn't need you himself.'

Vatis nodded his head, his face glowing.

Smaragthi watched the lad leap nimbly from the stern to the breakwater. His breeches of blue ticking, his thin, brown arms flapping in his wide shirt sleeves, which opened and folded like the wings of a bird. She saw the curls wave on his boyish head and the sprig of basil over his left ear, an indication of how eager this amiable youngster was to pass for a man.

She smiled at his agile, bare feet. She would so much have liked to play with him as her brother, to ruffle his hair, ride on his back, and take him swimming with her. But all this was forbidden, all these yearnings of her childish heart.

Once she was alone, she pondered deeply on what the boy confided to her. Bitterness fell drop by drop into her disquieted mind.

The Lathios family were people among whom she had enjoyed the warmth of homelike love whenever she was lonely. With them she felt pure, unsullied friendship, the hospitality of relatives. She had lavished on the children all the tender affection of her feminine heart. They were all she had now that God had taken her mother and the demon of drink had driven her father away.

In the company of Lathios's sons she had felt the security of sister among strong, loyal brothers. Now Vatis had destroyed this sense of security. If the other brothers should be in love with her without showing it, this would be one more misfortune. She would be obliged to erase from her life those fine youths with whom she had eaten from the same dish, drunk from the same glass, and learned to work in the same boat.

It was as if all her people were being taken from her, one by one, just as death had taken her mother. Even in the house of her godfather she now must be on guard because of Lambis. No, she shouldn't take this childish babbling seriously. Vatis was a fanciful youngster who liked to exaggerate. Cut herself off from the Lathios family? That would be a third orphanhood.

Aunt Permahoula, of course, remained, as always, a great comfort. At night, after the children had eaten, she would come to sleep at Smaragthi's house. With her she would bring two or three of the urchins who continued to multiply and overrun the shore. But otherwise, on the sea, in the struggle to make a living, who would be near her if she cut loose from Lathios?

And she loved those fine, strong, *pallikaris* as if they were of her own blood. Manolis, with his proud look; and Stratos, the big brother whom she worshipped like a god. And Vatis, Vatis the dreamer, with his girlish face and ecstatic eyes. She would do anything for them, as she would for Lathios or his wife. As she would for their grown-up daughter, who waited every year for her sailor husband on his annual month's leave to present him with his latest child and let him beget the next one.

She tried to recapture their behaviour, their words, their glances—especially Manolis's; to detect the truth in some revealing detail. She could find nothing to confirm Vatis's fantasies. Even Manolis had never shown her anything other than the same protective concern of his father.

Frequently while they were resting on the sandy beach when their boats were anchored in the shallows, she was aware of his eyes on her as they sat side by side near the sea without talking. This had never made her feel self-conscious. She would look at him with casual friendliness as if to say: 'Well, what shall we do now?'

And Manolis would smile back at her and smoke without lowering his gaze, for he had nothing to hide. Thus they had looked on each other as brother and sister, comrade with comrade. There were times when, in the heat of work, he had spoken to her sharply as men do to each other, but she had never resented this any more than did Stratos and Vatis from their elder brother or Manolis from his father. This was the language of work, rough at times, but brief and to the point. A command must be like that.

Smaragthi sighed deeply, wearied by all these reflections which suddenly pressed down upon her like a heavy burden.

34

AS Smaragthi, now that she was a young woman, tried to make sense out of the prattling of a fanciful boy, she reached a decision. She would leave everything to the resolution of time. Meanwhile, she would pay more attention to people around her and what they did. She sounded out Aunt Permahoula. Was it true that Manolis had asked permission to marry? The old woman laughed and nudged Smaragthi's knee, glad of the opprortunity to indulge her garrulity.

'That's the way men are, my child. They go out of their way to find trouble. God, you see, has arranged things like that so the world will increase and multiply. And now our Manolis, young as he is . . . it's God's way, you see. His father says "No. Wait till you're twenty-five!" If you want my opinion, daughter, I say Lathios is wrong.'

'But is Manolis ready to burden himself with a family?'

The old woman wagged her head and smiled slyly with her wrinkled lips.

'Eh, my lady,' she said. 'Time offers wood for sale and winter buys it. When the nursling cries for the breast, give it the breast. When a young man wants a wife, let him marry. It's for this that mothers bear and raise their daughters. They ought to let Manolis get married while his heart is set on it. Love is folly in my opinion and so is marriage, but, you see, without folly there's no flavour in this world. A man should commit all his follies while he is young, in order to have a proper old age. "Woe to the young man who acts old and to the old man who acts young,' says the proverb. In Anatolia we call young men the "ones with madness in their blood" and when we let the time for madness pass, how can we expect a man to undergo the folly of marriage? Everything goes according to God's ordinance, daughter, and I say we ought to leave it as the Lord wants it.'

'Your concern is about something else, Aunt Permahoula,' teased Smaragthi, 'and I know what is it.'

'Eh, then tell me, so that I, poor, ignorant wretch that I am, may learn!'

'I'll tell you, Aunt Permahoula. What you want is a new generation to begin at Lathios's house. You think you can't wait for the younger girls to get settled, so give the boys a push and let them have their turn and give you something to do. . . .'

The old woman was delighted with the teasing. She laughed heartily and took a long pull at the bottle which she drew from her bosom.

'How you talk! Health to your mouth! It's true, my dove. When I make the sign of the cross over my pillow before I go to bed, I close my eyes and say: "I'm old, Lord Jesus Christ. I've eaten my bread. I've seen many things and passed through many tribulations. For all, God be praised. Today I number my years at a hundred and six or a hundred and ten. That's a lot and may God give twice as many to those who have grown up in my arms. Not that I want to die, Lord. No. Let the black archangel come in his hour when it is Thy will and welcome to him." So I speak, my Smaragthi, every night when I go to bed. There are nights when my mind is restless and sleep won't come. Then I start to count my grandchildren and my great-grandchildren. I say their names, one by one, and I go over them again and again from the beginning till I fall asleep. But in the daytime I think of them all as married. There are fifteen right now, not counting the one in the womb. Eh! Let the fifteen get married. Let Skala, the quays and the beaches be filled. Let the sea be crowded with boats and sails, masts and oars. . . . Eh, Mermaid Madonna, Lady of the Sea, let your Mount be filled and may your Grace bless them! Like the small fry that swim in shoals in the foam, let me see them swimming, Madonna, along your beautiful shore. And may the Saracen who slays them burst. Let me hear them chatter, sing, quarrel, and play. And may I watch over them, nurse their fevers, gather them in at night, Lord Jesus Christ, and count their little heads and listen to their breathing while they sleep—an endless line of them—and let my heart be glad. At night when I close my eyes and try to remember their names, let me forget them and mix them up and let me complain and not be able to sleep and weep foolishly, I, the dotard, weighed down by the years, who no longer know what I am saying. . . .'

She drew out the bottle and took another swallow. Smaragthi saw that she was weeping. Then she put the bottle back in her bosom, shook her head from side to side and gazed at the sea. Her eyes were streaming and tears were dripping from the tip of her chin.

The girl smiled and patted her aged hands.

'Don't worry, Aunt Permahoula. You'll live to enjoy all of them to your heart's desire!'

She stroked a wisp of white hair which had strayed from under the old woman's headcloth. A whiff of her breath hit the girl in the face.

Presently Aunt Permahoula said: 'And you, my lady, why are you wasting your time? Your hour has come also!'

151

She passed her hand lightly over the girl's swelling breasts and rounded flanks.

'You see? The fruit is ripe. May the harvester not be slow in coming. Choose a *pallikari*. Let him be strong, let him be handsome and a good provider. And may he not have my husband's nature. May he not lift a hand against you. I couldn't stand seeing you suffer, my sultana. But remember, he must not be a landsman, one of those who spread manure on the fields and stink of earth and sweat! Yours must be a man of the sea. Not that I love the sea, which has brought so much pain to my people. But you're a child of the sea and she doesn't permit her offspring to be carried off.'

'Don't vex yourself about that,' laughed Smaragthi. 'My husband won't be a landsman or a man of the sea. And he won't beat me. I'm not for beating or for marriage.'

'That's what all pretty young things say in their cool moments, but later when the fig begins to warm. . . . Listen to me, my lady, who knows more than you do. Women and honey are best enjoyed while they're fresh.'

Was this an intercession in Manolis's behalf? Had the old woman noticed his inclination, as Vatis had said?

Smaragthi had not been able to learn a thing from this conversation, but she was more at peace that day when she left the old woman.

On her way home she heard the pleasing echo of the bell of Aya-Fotini coming down the mountain from Mouria. It was sounding for vespers. She crossed herself, took oil and incense, and went up to light the lamp of the Madonna. Since her mother's death she had not failed to perform this task every Saturday evening. On the Mount she found old Avgustis.

The schoolmaster had gone from bad to worse. He was a mere bag of bones. Now that he was too feeble from age and drink to work, he lived only on a small pension which he received as a retired civil servant. Withdrawn and morose, he ate little and dragged himself from tavern to tavern, broken and pathetic, to drink up his pension.

Smaragthi had not seen him for some time, and as she came upon him in his threadbare clothes, huddled on the rock and gazing across at Anatolia, she felt heartsick over his deterioration. She went to him and greeted him. His white moustache and two fingers of his hand were stained from excessive smoking. Ashamed of his condition, he extended his hand to her in embarrassment. It trembled uncontrollably.

'I can't see very well any more,' he complained. 'That's bad. Soon I shall be blind like old Vastagos. Look there!'

Smaragthi looked where the old man pointed.

'Can you see? Where some houses shine white on the shore?'

'I see them.'

'Eh, now look to the right. There's a mosque. It's minaret towers above the red water. A path runs past it. It winds like a ribbon up the low hill. Then it disappears. Do you see it? In the sunset it shows clearly.'

'I see it.'

The old man let his arm fall on his knee. He sighed.

'Eh! But I can't see it any more. . . . This is the worst thing. The path you see goes down the other side of the hill to a plain. There is . . our village. My house. . . . There the land doesn't lie fallow. Water flows everywhere. The gardens are full of cantaloupes. The pear trees and the pomegranates bend down with fruit. We prop them up with cleft poles so that the branches won't break. Beyond is the meadow. All grain. All this used to be a part of Greece. From the time of Byzantium . . . before Byzantium . . . from the time when this island sent out colonists as far as Sigeum! And we have betrayed it all. We have sold it. So many centuries of history . . . so much labour . . . so much bloodshed. . . .'

His voice cracked and he stopped. For a while he was racked by a fit of coughing. When he recovered his breath, he turned to the girl, who was standing beside him. His head was shaking like his hands.

'Eh, my child . . . this is the worst thing. Till now I could come here and see them. But lately even my eyes have begun to fail me. I look and look, I shade my eyes with my hand but I can't see a thing. It's all blurred, the sea, the sky and Anatolia, confused, mixed up. . . . Now I've lost everything . . . everything except what I've got locked up in here. . . .'

He laid his hand on his breast. Smaragthi saw that his vest had only one button and his shirt was soiled.

As Smaragthi descended the stone stairs of the Mount, she promised herself that she would attend to the old man's clothes. She would see to it that he wore cleaner things and she would mend the holes and sew on the loose buttons.

35

B E L O W, sitting on the breakwater with their feet dangling in the water, she found the inseparable gang which consisted of the Lathios twins and their friends. They were seated beside the mooring rope of her boat and talking in subdued but animated voices. As soon as they saw her, they fell silent. Vatis was the first to leap to his feet.

'Want anything, Smaragthi?'

They were waiting for her to give them the joy of doing some errand or some small task. They were in the habit of watching her from a distance out of the corners of their eyes, and as soon as she needed help, they would spring to her like footmen. The adults observed them and called them humorously 'Smaragthi's crew'.

The 'crew' included four boys: Stratos, Vatis, Lambis and a sturdy, ill-favoured fisherman's son, Thymios Thodoras. He had the small brown eyes of a faithful dog that has just been whipped by its master. His broad face was without expression when he stood and stared at the sea, not a thought in his mind. His wide lips never managed to cover his strong teeth which gleamed, large and square, and lighted up his face when he smiled. He was treated as a stupid lad, good only for unskilled work. He never refused to do anything he was asked and was called Thymios the Bulldog.

'Look at him!' Vatis said to Smaragthi. 'Did you know that Bulldog eats raw fish? Yes, by the Madonna, raw fish!'

'Is that so?' asked Smaragthi, a little astonished.

'It's true,' said Stratos. 'I've seen him do it!'

Vatis added: 'He eats the small fry that he picks up from the ground after the fishing boats have unloaded their catch. He goes off by himself and eats them raw! Phtou!'

Thymios's stupid smile faded. He hung his head and blushed down to his neck.

It was obvious he didn't want this mentioned before Smaragthi. She observed his burning ears and said promptly:

'What's wrong with that? If he likes them raw, let him eat them that way. We eat uncooked sea urchins and mussels, don't we? And if I liked to eat raw sardines, I'd eat them!'

Thymios glanced up and saw that she was serious. He bubbled over with gratitude like a dog when one rubs it under the chin. He was so moved tht all he could say was 'Eh.'

He looked right and left. A little way off lay a rusty anchor, half buried in the sand. He made two steps and stood in front of it. He looked at the other boys, spat on his hands, bent over, and grasped the anchor. Slowly he lifted it and held it above his head. All the muscles of his sturdy body bulged with the great effort. The veins in his neck stood out like cords, and his face turned dark red with the rush of blood. His friends bit their lips and said nothing.

Then Bulldog threw the anchor to the ground, took a deep breath, and sauntered away with his hands in his pockets. The others understood the reason for this exploit.

'Bulldog is very strong,' said Smaragthi with a smile.

The boys looked vexedly at the piece of iron on the ground and shrugged their shoulders grudgingly.

'Bulldog can lift even a donkey,' said Vatis.

Stratos pitched a piece of tile into the sea. Lambis looked at the girl with his shining eyes and pointed out to sea. 'So what?' he boasted. 'I can swim to Cape Korakas and back. Can Bulldog do that?'

Then he pointed to the topmost ledge of the Mount, about fifty feet above the sea.

'I dive head first from the "balcony". Can he do it?' Looking at the other two, he sneered: 'You can't do it, either!'

Smaragthi left them to their bragging and wrangling. They had it in for Thymios.

'He was trying to show us up,' said Stratos and threw a heavy stone with all his might so that it clanked against the piece of old metal.

Vatis sat down on the ground, rested his elbows on his knees, and cradled his delicate face between his hands. Looking at the sea, he growled:

'And you all do the same thing. You do it every day when you're with her. All these stunts are silly and she laughs at them. Bulldog with his anchor and Lambis with his swimming. Yesterday in Ammouthelli I even saw Stratos walking on his hands. Shame on you!'

'I did it because I felt like it,' Stratos protested. 'You can't do even that!'

Without turning his head, Vatis answered calmly:

'You did it because Smaragthi was on the breakwater looking at you. Not one of you has a speck of dignity, I tell you. Phtou!'

He spat contemptuously to one side.

'You have dignity,' said Lambis. 'But who respects you for it? And you consider yourself a man!'

155

'Why shouldn't he consider himself a man?' intervened Stratos angrily. He stood in front of Lambis with his hands behind his back. Lambis shrugged.

'Huh! I can throw him any time!'

'So! Showing off again!' replied Vatis. Still looking away, he flung a hand with fingers extended at Lambis.

'You throw him! Just let me see you do it!' challenged Stratos. 'I'll break your head like a flowerpot!'

They commenced to abuse each other with stupid, insulting language.

Of the three, Vatis was the most restrained, perhaps because he was the weakest and therefore a pacifist. Stratos called Lambis a dolt. They went into a clinch and wrestled on the sand. Panting, they pummelled each other and yelled. At first, Lambis held his own, but suddenly Vatis tripped him and Fortis's son fell on his back. Then Stratos leaped on his belly, gripped Lambis's legs between his knees, and pounded him with his fists to make him beg for mercy. Lambis refused, and Strato pressed his eyes. Still Lambis was silent. At last they got to their feet, scratched and dusty.

'I'd have had both of you if I hadn't been tripped from behind,' said Lambis, rubbing his eyes. He turned his back on them and refused to speak to them. Stratos gave him a friendly poke with his elbow.

'Come on, it wasn't anything. Only next time don't bite!'

When the quarrel was patched up, Vatis said:

'I think we were fighting over nothing. The best thing for all of us is to stay away from Smaragthi.'

'What's Smaragthi got to do with it?' said Lambis, stamping his feet, his eyes blazing. The twins looked at each other and said nothing.

After a while, Stratos asked: 'Shall we stay away from her?'

Vatis proposed that they should stop hanging around Smaragthi while she was working. The 'crew' would disband. Then there would be an end to further brawling and churlish words among them.

'Well, what do you say?' he asked finally.

Lambis wanted to object, but he scowled and agreed.

'All right,' he conceded.

'All right,' echoed Stratos. 'Only we've got to tell Bulldog.'

They called to him where he was sitting on the breakwater, staring vacantly at the sea and spitting into the water. He ran to them, eagerly as ever, as soon as he heard their summons.

When they told him what they had agreed to do, he fell in with it promptly. It was the first time he had been made to realize that he did these things to please the girl. Till then he had never realized that he did anything for any particular reason. Now he saw that he did have a reason, and he was dismayed about it.

'And if she needs something,' asked Stratos, 'and calls one of us herself?'

Vatis had foreseen this possibility, which was of special concern to him.

'If she calls any of us herself, we'll help her, of course. We'd do the same for anybody else. But the point is that we are not to hang around the girl's skirts all day long. That's disgraceful, I say, and people are laughing at us behind our backs.'

Lambis drew tobacco and cigarette papers from his trousers pocket. They rolled cigarettes and went up on the Mount to smoke in secret.

36

T H U S the matter was settled and the gang recovered its cordiality, which for a time had been dangerously near collapse. It was not the first time their solidarity had been tested by blows.

'Let's play smugglers,' proposed Bulldog.

This was a good suggestion. It served as a diversion and a strengthening of the peace. They went home to get their tin boats. Suddenly Lambis raised his hand and they stopped.

'What if one of us breaks his word?' he asked.

'What will happen then?' asked Bulldog in dismay.

Vatis came forward with a heroic solution.

'The rest of us will fall on him and give him a beating.'

This was found to be fitting and proper. It gave them a way of dealing with Bulldog if he should go near the girl.

'Agreed?'

'Agreed.'

'On our manhood?'

'On our manhood.'

'Kiss the cross?'

Each one raised his crossed index fingers and kissed them, swearing at the same time the grim oath:

'May I swim in God's blood!'

'All right,' said Lambis. 'Now go and call everybody you can find to come with their ships.'

Soon all the available 'shipowners' arrived. They were fishermen's sons from twelve to seventeen years old. One of them was Thanassis Verzeves, a tall, lean lad, tanned to the colour of a copper skillet. He was called 'Shark' because in his upper jaw he had a double row of teeth. Under his arm he clutched a large ship. From his shoulder hung a wide tin funnel on a stout cord.

'What's that?' asked the others in astonishment. Never before had he brought to the game a piece of equipment like this.

'It's a megaphone,' Shark replied proudly. He passed it round and then replaced it over his shoulder.

There was a veritable mobilization of all the youngsters, each with his tin sailboat, and their noise awakened the whole village. Most of them wore only breeches, but the youngest ran naked on the sand, their skins burnished by the sun.

The 'shipmasters' lined up with their sailboats, which were beautifully decorated by their captains, some of them coloured with oil paint, the keels red and the gunwales yellow or black.

The ancestors of these boys, more than a hundred years before, had been pirates who prowled about these waters, hiding by day in coves and bayous, by night pillaging the coastal towns of the peaceful islanders and Anatolians. After piracy was broken up, they turned to smuggling into Turkey the contraband tobacco, gunpowder and arms which they obtained in Greece and sold secretly to their fellow Greeks under the Turkish yoke who were preparing for the great hour of their liberation. The smugglers, whose trade gave them the status of national heroes in the eyes of the enslaved Greeks, fell to the level of common criminals as soon as they took up residence on Greek territory.

They handled cigarette paper and tobacco, coarsely ground in a mortar, but the enemy was the same: the Greek Royal Revenue Service, whose police motor-boat, a powerful, swift, lead-grey two-master, patrolled the waters between Turkey and the islands day and night. There was a shiny machine gun in the prow and she was manned with a contingent of revenue men.

The boys had turned into a game this adventurous profession of their forefathers. First they selected the police ship, which had to be the largest and strongest. They hung a red banner on its mast for identification. Shark's boat was the undisputed choice. She was half a metre long, red and blue and fully equipped. From her stern she towed a felucca, exquisitely carved from a single piece of wood.

The game was quickly organized. First they posted sentries on the heights so that they would not be caught off guard by the revenue ship. Then they rolled up their breeches to their thighs, put pebbles in their ships for ballast, and waded into the sea up to their knees, pulling their ships behind them on long strings. In this way, encouraged by loud cheers, the fleet set sail for high adventure.

Thanassis was the first to break formation. He rounded the point where the cookshop was located and hid with his ship behind a stone on the breakwater.

At the outset, the smuggling ships went in a line along the shore towards Ammouthelli. The boys who remained ashore gave orders with their hands cupped to their mouths.

'Captain Nikolas! Ahoy, Captain Nikolas!'

'Ahoy!' replied the captain from the sea.

'Tonight we'll bring ten bales of tobacco!'

'Bring it!'

'And three cases of cigarette paper!'

'And 150 packs of playing cards!'

'Right!' replied the captain. 'To the Three Rocks! To the Cave of Tsikouthia!'

'How's that?'

'I said the cave! Bring mules and some experienced lads. Watch out for the agents!'

The Cave of Tsikouthia consisted of two joined sea rocks not far away, barely knee high, near a turpentine tree which overshadowed the shore. Here was the secret anchorage.

Orders were given with a loud confusion of voices. The cargo was unloaded after a thousand precautions. It was buried in the sand and the spot was marked with white stones or dry cuttlefish bones. The boys shaded their eyes with their hands and looked warily from side to side.

'Look out for spies! Ahoy, sentinel, keep your eyes peeled!'

They were all serious, keyed-up and quick-tempered as they strutted legs apart and their hands behind their backs, drunk with heroism and eager for great exploits. Suddenly a shout came from a sentry on the highest cliff.

'Ahoy! You on the ships! Police boat approaching! To the west! Quick, lads, she's making for the harbour!'

It was true. At the mouth of the harbour appeared Thanassis's police ship advancing majestically with all her sails spread and the red battle-flag flying from the masthead. Thanassis put his megaphone to his mouth and challenged the smugglers.

'Ahoy, you on the ships! Furl your sails! Raise your oars or I'll blast the lot of you!'

'At him!' screamed the mob of youngsters. 'Quick, all of you! At him, everybody, and we'll sink the scoundrel!'

'Hurrah! Hurrah!'

'Up with your oars, you riff-raff!' the megaphone sounded again.

At this the battle began. The police ship had the privilege of bombarding the smugglers with handfuls of pebbles while the smugglers tried to capsize the revenue ship by entangling her in their towing strings. This was a rule of the game.

The crowd of boys on land cheered on the captains, jumping up and down with frantic gestures.

'Sink her! Down with the scoundrel! Slacken your rope, Lambis! Slacken your rope!'

Their eyes flashed and their faces were red with excitement.

Finally the battle ended, as it invariably did, with the sinking of the police ship after she had wrought havoc with pebbles on a large number of the smugglers' boats. The victory raised a shout of triumph from land and sea. The boys went wild with joy and their screams filled the air and echoed from the Mount of the Madonna.

'Hurrah for Captain Lambis!'

'Down with the dog! Down with him!'

The dog was Thanassis the Shark with his double row of teeth.

While this pandemonium was going on, Smaragthi appeared on the breakwater with a wicker basket under her skirt between her knees, and waded up to her ankles to rinse the seaweed off the basket. The older boys looked at her rounded thighs and her strong hips which protruded as she bent over. Lambis cast a mistrustful glance at his friends. They were silent, whistling softly and pretending not to see anything, but each was furtively eyeing the others. Shark looked off into the distance and sighed without knowing why.

'Who sank the police ship?' the girl asked brightly as she kept on working.

'Lambis!' the boys shouted with one voice.

He flushed with pride.

Smaragthi shook the water off her basket and straightened up.

'Oh, shame on you! All you seamen let a landsman get ahead of you!'

'I'm not a landsman!' Lambis protested indignantly, throwing his ship to the ground. 'My father runs a coffee-house but *I'm* going to enter the Royal Navy.'

'Eh, what of that? Till then, you count as a landsman,' the girl teased as she went away.

Lambis felt an impulse to box her ears and then crawl at her feet and snap at her legs like a dog. Let her trample him with her lovely feet. Let her walk all over him. Let him feel her bare soles crushing his chest.

Next day Smaragthi took a couple of the smaller Lathios children with her early in the morning to fish for octopus in the boat along the shore. The children stood at the gunwales watching the many-coloured fish swim in the clear water under the keel. Every time the girl brought up an octopus on the point of her spear, they hurried enthusiastically to take it off. They knew how to kill it by biting its head.

When the sun grew hot, Smaragthi guided the boat into the shade between the high, cool cliffs of Vigla. She leaped out nimbly with her basket of octopus and helped the children ashore. Then they began to maul the octopuses on the stones.

Presently a familiar whistle was heard and a curly head popped out from behind the rocks. It was Fortis's son pretending he had come upon them by accident.

'Lambis!' cried the children.

Blushing, he came around the rocks, his breeches rolled up on his thighs, and walked to the shore. Smaragthi looked at him inquiringly. The boy lowered his eyes and made a vague gesture seawards.

'I was looking for limpets. . . .'

'The stones are swarming with them. Did you find any?'

'Of course,' he said with embarrassment.

He opened his hand. Clinging together it were two, small miserable limpets. He felt the girl's eyes on his motionless palm. With a flick he tossed the creatures into the water.

Just then Bulldog's ugly head popped out from the other side, his hair bristling like the quills of a hedgehog.

'The Lathios twins are here, too,' he said, pointing with both hands, and laughing foolishly with his eyes closed. 'See them sliding down over there!'

Immediately the twins were heard rolling down the steep slope, tearing through holly-oak and brambles. Soil and gravel rattled into the sea from under their bare feet which tried vainly to find a hold on the roots and ledges of the cliff. The air smelled of broken stems and bruised lichen.

'Eh! Everybody is here!' said Smaragthi, nonplussed. 'How did you two happen to be perched up there?'

'We were after figs,' said Stratos. 'We saw you fishing for octopus and we came in case you needed help pounding them.'

'And Thymios?'

Bulldog blushed and shrugged his shoulders, the only one who told the truth.

'I . . . I saw the others and came along, too.'

Smaragthi bit her lips to keep from laughing at the sheepish way they looked at each other. Suddenly Thymios went to her. Then they noticed that in his hand he held a handkerchief knotted together at the four corners.

'I brought you this,' he said.

He laid the handkerchief at her feet and the children gathered around it. Something alive was squirming inside.

'Open it,' said Smaragthi.

Thymios undid the handkerchief and out rushed a grey creature. The children scattered in fright. The reptile scuttled to the sea, then turned and disappeared among the stones.

'It's a lizard!'

'It's not a lizard,' said Thymios seriously. 'Lizards are green. That was a crocodile. A dark crocodile with scales.'

'You scared us with your crocodile,' said one of the little girls.

'They're nothing to be afraid of,' said Thymios. 'I catch them with my hands. I even put them against my bare chest.'

'Don't worry. Nobody's afraid of them,' said Lambis. 'Yesterday I killed a viper with a stick, but I didn't tell about it. A real viper!'

They all laughed at this retort. Smaragthi called a halt to the talking.

'Now that you're all here by accident, give a hand and we'll finish this job right away.'

The situation was eased all around. They went to work furiously. The cliffs rang with their blows and happy voices. Not one of the four boys gave a thought to the solemn oaths they had sworn the previous day.

37

T H E Gadjalis family were beginning to think of Manolis as a suitable husband for their daughter. One afternoon Yana's mother took her distaff and called on Lathios's wife, whom she saw knitting stockings on the doorstep. At first, the fisherman's wife had no intimation of a hidden motive, although the visit seemed odd to her. A little later, Yana passed by on the other side with a water jar on her hip. The Gadjalis woman pointed to her proudly with her distaff.

'See what a woman I have on my hands there. That's the way it goes with these girls. They go to bed one night as flat as bread-boards and wake up in the morning with their bodies filled out.'

'It's the result of good yeast,' said Lathios' wife. 'The dough rises and overflows while your back is turned.'

'That's why they should go to the oven as soon as possible. . . .'

The conversation followed this line pleasantly until the fisherman's wife soon was aware of its goal when the other woman confided to her that for some months Yana had been sewing on her trousseau like the well-reared daughter that she was and that, an only daughter adored by her three brothers, she would have a sizeable dowry.

It was obvious that an offer of marriage was in the offing, but Lathios's wife cagily maintained to the end the pretence that she entertained no such suspicion.

The campaign was soon renewed, this time by Yana herself. Returning from the olive groves one evening, she found Aunt Permahoula resting on the beach under the shade of a plane tree with a basket of chicory at her side. The girl sat down with her and began a friendly coversation. The old woman was puzzled by her cordiality. When she got up to go home, Yana arose and walked beside her. In the basket she placed a bouquet of cyclamen that she had been holding.

'Take them, Auntie, and put them in water. You'll like their fragrance.'

'But, my lady,' the old woman said, 'I can't smell very well any more and I can't see well. For us old folks there are only cemetery flowers. Hyacinths and cyclamen are for girls and young lads.'

'Eh . . . take them for the young lads,' said Yana, blushing like a poppy.

Aunt Permahoula related all this to Smaragthi and waited to see what she would say about it.

'It wouldn't be at all bad for our Manolis,' the girl said, going directly to the kernel of the matter. 'Yana is a good girl at heart.'

The old woman interrupted her irritably.

'All the Gadjales are rotten, root and branch,' she said. 'Parents, sons, daughter, they're all alike, a nest of vipers that should be wiped out with petrol and gunpowder!'

Smaragthi smiled at this outburst.

'And Manolis?' she asked. 'What does he say?'

'Manolis!' snorted the old woman still more indignantly. 'No fear of him saying anything. He's a plugged fountain. You try to talk with him and he looks off into the distance at the ships and whistles. He lets you chatter by yourself like a fool! He! How can a body know what's in his mind?'

This conversation took place one morning. Just then they saw one of Lathios's youngsters come on the run from the harbour.

He brought bad news. His father and the older boys had returned in the boat with their nets ripped to tatters.

'A shark tore them, Father says!' the lad reported scowling like a grown-up.

Lathios, who was accustomed to accept everything, good or bad, patiently and without useless grumbling, left the boys to carry the nets up to the Mount of the Madonna and sent this lad home to tell everybody to get busy with their twine and needles while he himself went to Fortis's. He sat down in his favourite corner and called for a small carafe. He would drink until the nets were mended. It would take several days.

Smaragthi also went up with her needle and pocket-knife to help. She found the entire Lathios family deployed around the nets.

They ate their noonday meal up on the Mount and worked till twilight. When the air grew chilly at dusk, they stowed the nets in the chapel overnight and went down. The women went first to get supper. Last to leave was Manolis, who lingered to roll a cigarette, and Smaragthi, who was putting the wooden needles, the twine, and the knives into a basket.

The sun was sinking slowly between Mount Athos and Cape Babas. The hill of Vigla glowed rosy red among the trees and a deeper red tinted the tall cliffs along the shore. Finally, there remained on the water only a little island of fire, which burned briefly and then vanished.

Smaragthi pointed with her outstretched arm.

'If one could only go there,' she said.

Manolis smoked without replying. He contemplated her face, which was blooming like a wondrous flower of rose-coloured flame. In the depth of her eyes, which were opened wide enough to contain the whole sunset, he watched the splendour reflected from the waves blaze and go out.

When she turned her eyes on him, he lowered his gaze in confusion, drew deeply on his cigarette and tossed the butt into the sea, which had begun its nightly murmur at the foot of the Mount. As if waiting to hear the cigarette hiss in the water below, he listened for a moment and then said evenly:

'You know, Smaragthi, I'm thinking of leaving my father. I wanted to tell you so you'd know it, too.'

'Leave him?' the girl asked in surprise.

'Yes. It's time I was thinking about it and now I've made up my mind. I intend to work for myself in my own boat. I've put some money aside. If God wills, I'll make a go of it.'

They began to descend the Mount. As always when her opinion was sought, Smaragthi thought carefully before she replied. Then she said without hesitation:

'As far as I can see, I don't think it's a bad idea. You're a *pallikari* and you can manage better than anyone else; once you've saved enough, do it. It will have to happen some day, sooner or later.'

Manolis smiled with satisfaction.

'I'm glad you think so. I haven't spoken about it to anyone else. I know they'll be upset about it at home. . . . '

'Yes. You're your father's right hand man, but the question is what is best for you. If you ask me, I think it's better to be the head than the right hand.'

'Right!'

She felt him smiling at her, obviously surprised that such an idea should come from the mouth of a young girl. She proceeded to set him right.

'Don't look at me like that, Manolis. Ever since I was a little girl, I've been different from others, and now that I'm older, I understand myself better. I don't think I could take orders from anybody for all the world.'

She looked him straight in the face. The *pallikari* smiled bashfully.

'Eh! That isn't what I meant. But you'll change your mind as you grow older and then you'll want other things like all women.'

He faltered. Smaragthi stopped in her tracks. She realized that the time had arrived for certain explanations. She asked boldly:

'What things?'

'Well . . . like . . . more domestic things,' said the *pallikari* with a vague gesture.

He turned, looked at her frankly and asked:

'Well?'

With an anxious smile he waited for a reply. Smaragthi,

166

unperturbed by the intensity of his look, replied: 'That will never happen, Manolis.' There was a note of sadness in her voice, as she spoke softly and tenderly in the twilight.

'Never?'

Almost harshly she repeated, 'Never!'

His desire to talk was abruptly checked. Both were silent as they walked the length of the breakwater. Absent-mindedly Manolis touched in turn with his finger each of the mooring bitts of the caïques. Suddenly a fierce barking came from a ship that had just arrived from Chios. A black ship's dog bared his teeth viciously.

Smaragthi's knees grew weak with fright. Involuntarily she drew towards Manolis. Then, as if ashamed, she moved away from him and laughed nervously.

'Did you see?' she said. 'It's been so many years since Kanellos bit me and I'm still afraid. Every time I hear a dog bark at me, my hair stands on end and my heart skips a beat.'

'How long ago it was!' chuckled Manolis softly, relieved that the silence which had separated them now was broken. 'You were only a little girl then with a blue bow in your hair. . . .'

'That's right,' the girl said gravely. 'You were always my big brother. Now we've grown up. Before long you'll have your own ship and your own home. You'll build your own house. I . . . I'm not like that . . . I only pray to the Madonna that, whatever you are, whatever I am, you'll always go on being my big brother.'

Manolis was about to say something, but Smaragthi checked him with a movement of her head.

'That's it. Don't ever stop being my big brother, Manolis.'

They paused where the road divided. One way led to the fishing village, the other to the coffee-houses. Neither spoke. Then Manolis sighed.

'Well, good-night,' he said.

Each took a different way.

At home Smaragthi sat by her window, listening to the sea and trying to bring order to the thoughts which evoked in her mind confused questionings and tender, wistful sadness.

She was glad she had found the occasion to set Manolis straight about herself. It was going to be more difficult to set herself straight about life, which she saw as a marvellous composition of colours, fragrances, stars and also of mire, an ambiguous, fluid design for which there was no one to provide her with an interpretation or explain its form, so sweet and yet so terrible.

From the street came a voice.

'Do you want Father to give you some smelts he has left over, for bait, Smaragthi?'

She saw Vatis's slender form in the deep shadows. She was unable to distinguish his features but even without his voice she would have recognized him by the way he stood with his chin lifted, his hand in his trousers pocket and his head gracefully inclined towards his shoulder.

She replied that she did not intend to fish the next day. Immediately she saw the boy's figure disappear around the corner of the house and heard his whistling fade in the distance.

She recalled the heedless things he had said to her and was amazed how accurately he had sensed the dreams that his older brother was weaving around her. It was written that before long she was to discover how far from mistaken he had been concerning other matters about which he had gossiped to her.

38

T H E autumn nights wrap the Aegean islands in blue darkness. The land masses drift on a sea filled with stars. The soil, the rocks, and the timbers of the boats are still warm. The water breathes slowly and deeply.

When the sounds of day are stilled, the liquid tongues of the sea are heard lapping the sands and hollow places. Then the moon rises above the olive trees, the expanse of the sea, the boats and the high cliffs. The motor-boats depart and the fishermen are left to enjoy the beauty of the night.

Smaragthi had anchored her boat in the shallows near the fishing village early one evening. She intended, once all was quiet and deserted, to wade out, go aboard, and push off with the pole until she could use the oars.

As she moved out past the boats with sleeping fishermen on the decks, the moonlight flooded the harbour and trickled in rivulets down the cliffs. It made the exposed faces of the slumbering fishermen look like the dead kings of Mycenae overlaid with masks of gold leaf.

She rounded the threatening cliffs of Vigla and made for the beach of Kaya, between Vigla and Cape Korakas. Here there was a small, shallow elbow among the rocks, sheltered by dense undergrowth which came down to the shore. Smaragthi anchored in the shadow of the rocks, stripped off her clothes, and dived into the water.

The cool water stung her flesh with a pang of keen delight. It was a vivid feeling of bliss and release, which refreshed her very soul, as if she were clothed by the whole sea, a nebulous, fluid garment like those long, filmy gowns with soft pastel tints which those ladies with bodies as buoyant as clouds wore in Fortis's American magazines. She seemed to possess a tail, streaming so endlessly behind her that it touched distant shores washed by tiny, multitudinous waves of foam.

For an instant her body gleamed under the moon like a large gold-fish. Then it vanished. On the spot where she had dived, the moon threw a handful of silver coins. She surfaced some fifty feet away. Her head appeared first and then her throat and shoulders. She tossed back her heavy mane of hair like a filly snorting with the joy of life. Then at once she began swimming farther and farther out.

Soon she found herself swimming in a beam of moonlight, a broad, empty path of liquid light which reached to the horizon, rising and falling.

Once when she was still a schoolgirl, she was sitting at night in Lathios's boat with old Permahoula. It was the first time she had ever seen the moonpath.

'What's that, Granny?' she asked in wonder.

The old woman partially closed her eyes as she did when she was visualizing the marvels she described in her fairy tales.

'It's the road of Christ,' she said. 'It's the road Christ took when He walked over the sea to find the fishermen and bless their nets. Christ loved the fishermen and associated only with them. He walked on the waves into the open sea to find them. His silver footprints remained behind him on the water. Now when the night is radiant, they show again and the sea rejoices. This shining path is made up of them. See, it goes clear to where the sky lies on the water.'

'Will Christ walk on it again, Granny?'

'No. It won't happen again till the fishermen become good people. Nowadays the fishermen have deserted Christ, and He has abandoned them. Nowadays the fishermen get drunk and beat their wives, and they don't go to church even for the Sacrament.'

'Doesn't anyone walk on the path of Christ, Granny?'

'Of course. The sea sprites do. Some have fish tails like Her Grace. They swim. Others have legs like ours. They come out and walk on the path of Christ. They put on silver sandals, open their little parasols of gold silk and go for a stroll. Only nobody can see them unless he's a Saturday's child. Other people see only their hair and when they comb it out to braid it. There, do you see it?'

She pointed to the yellow stream of reflected moonlight which undulated and twisted like serpents and wove into braids among the rocks.

'Do you see them?'

Smaragthi, full of simple faith and wonder like all children, replied softly: 'Yes, I see them, Granny.'

She was filled with a thrill of delightful awe, for she had actually seen the golden braids. Once or twice she even glimpsed a naked arm and a silver head rise above the surface and then vanish.

She knew not that the sea sprites do not come out for a stroll on the silver path of Christ, but every time she swam in the moonlight, she never failed to enter this enchanted path.

As she swam farther out, her body seemed to have no weight, as if she were soaring in the air. Sometimes she stopped, turned on her back, and let the breathing sea support and rock her gently. She gave the water a slap to see the moon lilies unfold. When she swam with her face to the water, the sea kissed her on the cheek and toyed with her ear. A host of enormous golden eyes shone everywhere. They were the broken reflections of the moon, or possibly they were the eyes of the sea which open only at night. She wanted to shout with joy.

At the peak of her happiness in the night which filled her whole being with peace, something happened that she had not foreseen. While she was watching the play of light on the water, she caught sight of a huge, dark shadow dart swiftly hardly more than a fathom below her.

Her heart froze. Immediately she thought of the shark that had ruined Lathios's net. Terror crept over her like a cold adder. She turned back towards land, but her strength ebbed from her and her limbs refused to obey. Her throat constricted so that she could not scream. She fought the water blindly and desperately, flailing it with her arms and legs, without co-ordination. Something hard and icy scraped her belly as it slipped past her.

Convulsively she summoned all her strength and managed to utter a shriek of pure frenzy.

'Help! Save me!'

After this effort she felt that she was about to lose consciousness.

At that moment a human form sprang from the bushes on the cliff and dived with a splash into the sea. When it surfaced, it was swimming to her with powerful strokes. It reached her as she was threshing about aimlessly and taking in water. It seized her by the hair and swimming with feet and one arm, dragged her to the shallows where her boat was anchored. Panting from the effort, it took the naked girl in its arms and placed her in the boat. It was wearing only breeches secured with a belt.

This touch of flesh against her nakedness brought Smaragthi brutally to her senses. There was something repulsive in it, like the awakening that other night in the arms of Varouhos. In an instant she relived that whole night of horror.

Immediately her strength returned. She drew back and struck as hard as she could the face of the person who had saved her. Then she seized the boat's rope, leaped into the water, and tried to conceal herself behind the rudder. She picked up a round stone for a weapon.

'Go away!' she ordered the person who was standing there, not knowing what to do. 'Go away or I'll kill you.'

The moon illuminated his shoulders and arms from behind. His chest was heaving powerfully. When she turned, the light shone on his face. Then Smaragthi recognized him, and her terror slowly dissolved. It was Lambis.

'You?' she said in surprise.

He nodded affirmatively and remained uncertain whether to go backward or forward. He was naked to the waist, tall and strong, his hair lying wet on his forehead. Unable to lift his eyes, he stood smiling foolishly.

'Go into the boat and get me my dress!' she commanded, her chin trembling with anger.

The boy took hold of the gunwale and leaped aboard. He picked up Smaragthi's dress in the stern and handed it to her with averted eyes. She seized it, quickly slipped it on and went to the shore. Lambis started to go away, hanging his head in shame.

'Can I do anything for you?' he asked with his eyes still lowered. 'Shall I lift the anchor?'

Smaragthi was sitting on the sand, her hands clasped about her knees and her toes in the water. She was breathing deeply and rapidly. Tears streamed from her eyes, but she was not sobbing.

'Get out of my sight!' she said. 'Aren't you ashamed to have done this, you disgusting boy?'

Lambis tried to justify himself.

'You were drowning, Smaragthi!'

She seized a handful of pebbles and flung them into the water with unreasonable rage.

'Suppose I was! What business is that of yours? I'm not your sister. I'm not even related to you!'

Choking with emotion she continued after a short silence:

'Better to drown than be saved by your vileness! Better that than what you were doing up there. Aren't you ashamed? What would my poor godfather say?'

Lambis jerked his head up in alarm.

'Nobody knows,' he said quickly. 'Father thinks I'm in bed. If he learns of it, I'll . . . '

'What will *you* do!' She glared scornfully at him.

In a cool, determined voice, Lambis said: 'I'll kill myself.'

This statement impressed her. She smoothed her hair and said coldly:

'A good thing for you and all your kind. How you have lowered yourself!'

The boy started to leave.

Smaragthi heard the pebbles grind under his feet. She turned and watched him depart with bowed head and arms hanging loose. On his right arm above the elbow she saw a dark trickle running down to his wrist.

'What's that?' she asked.

Lambis halted. 'What?' he said.

'There on your arm. Your right arm. Above.'

He touched it with his finger. It was blood. It was dripping off his hand and making dark stains on the pebbles.

'It's nothing,' he said. 'I just scratched myself when I dived from the cliff.'

172

Smaragthi went to him.

'Wait,' she said. 'You can't go home like this.'

From the locker in the cabin of her boat, she fetched a clean handkerchief, red with white dots. She pushed Lambis like a child to the sea, made him kneel down and washed away the blood. Then she bound the wound tightly with the handkerchief.

'Now go,' she said. 'And remember if I find that you've been spying on me again, I'll break your head with a stone. I'll tell my godfather so that he'll know what kind of person you are. . . . '

Lambis vanished agilely among the shadows.

Smaragthi went aboard her boat. She hoisted the anchor and fitted the oars into the rowlocks. Then she rowed out towards the open sea. She was lost in thought and paused from time to time, trying to understand this mystery of herself.

Presently she was aware that once more she was in the enchanted moonpath, the road of Christ, which was glittering with silver butterflies. All around was peace!

She drew the oars into the boat, made the sign of the cross at the sky and stretched out in the stern, alone, at peace, secure from evil. She felt as if she were in the hand of God, like a gold medallion, a small medallion held above the abyss in the hand of God.

The moonpath extended in front of her, broad and radiant, sparkling with millions of little, trembling lights.

'Where does the road lead, Granny?' a little girl had asked a long time ago.

'This road, my lady, leads to God.'

Now on this night the girl at last understood. The highway of the moon does lead to God, a bridge, the colour of golden wheatstraw, spanning the sea between earth and heaven. To God.

This is why it was so deserted, so empty. The loneliest road in the world, a road from which there is no turning. . . .

39

T H E cool Aegean autumn was fragrant with the heavy odours of fruit and broken boughs. In the public square the produce that the peasants had brought down for shipment was piled on carpets of freshly gathered bracken. There were hummocks of pomegranates, late pears, quinces, and dried figs. The Mouriotes unloaded their harvest, checked the weight, took their money and tucked it into the black pouches that hung from their necks. From the caïques came the scent of laurel and osiers which had been strewn in the holds. All these odours made the air languorous with the lassitude of the earth, lying like a mother breathing happily beside her offspring.

A crowd of women and children sat on the ground or squatted on their heels and sorted out the piles of fruit. They put to one side the ripe ones that would not last out the voyage. With them they put the bruised fruit which would spoil in the hold and cause the rest of the cargo to rot.

The sun stood at midday when Smaragthi rowed her boat into the harbour. As she approached the breakwater, she saw Lathios waiting for her at the marble mooring post. She tossed him the coiled rope and dropped anchor.

'Get anything?' he asked her.

She nodded cheerfully and leaped lightly ashore. Pointing to the wooden bucket, she said:

'Three octopuses, one with three tentacles gone!'

Lathios looked at her and then lowered his eyes. 'Listen,' he said. 'The old woman isn't well. Her mind is wandering and she says things that make no sense. I think she's burned up her oil. She keeps calling your name. Go to her right away.'

He took the bucket from the girl's hand and watched her run to the fishing village. Then he sat down and commenced to maul the octopuses on the stones of the breakwater.

Smaragthi found the old woman sitting on a pallet. She appeared to be unaware of the girl. Apparently she was in another world and saw nothing around her. Smaragthi knelt beside her and tried to interrupt the flow of her delirious words.

'Granny!' she wailed brokenly.

The old woman made no reply, but merely rocked her head from side to side like a pendulum. Her words were jumbled and without beginning or end. Interspersed was Smaragthi's name.

'And Smari, too, she also . . . so many jewels, so many birds and a basket of green almonds . . . take the feather duster, take the censer, cense the icons . . . '

She made strange movements with her hands as she spoke, as if she were catching butterflies or dragonflies with fragile wings before her face. She caught them neatly with two fingers and placed them beside her. She was absorbed in this occupation and darted her eyes here and there lest any of these imaginary insects should escape. Smaragthi laid her hand on the old woman's knee.

'Granny, I'm here beside you. I'm Smari.'

The old woman did not hear her. She continued to ramble until her voice became fainter and fainter and only her lips moved. Then, suddenly, her voice recovered its strength. She spoke distinctly and more calmly, but still without order or sense.

Besides Smaragthi, only Lathios's wife and daughter were present. The others were away at work or took no interest. Smaragthi was heartsick. She put an arm tenderly around the old woman and took hold of her hand.

'What's the matter, Granny? Are you sick?'

The old woman gave a puzzled look at the hand which the girl was holding. Then she spoke in a monotonous, colourless voice. As if she were reading from a book.

'Now I. . . . It was coming from far out. It was a fishing boat. Red with black stripes. And the fishermen all in black. On their heads they wore black handkerchiefs. Welcome, I say. You're from Tchesmeli, aren't you? Lord Jesus Christ, not a word from the fishermen. They looked at me without saying a word. Just pulled at the oars. But the Other One sat at the tiller and steered. Who is the Other One? I ask. He isn't like the rest of you. They enter the harbour, pulling at their oars and saying nothing. Dear me, I say, can it be that the eight of them are coming to port? They say nothing. It's their way. And the Other One at the tiller. They make straight for the breakwater. You're going to crash, I say. You're going to break up on the rocks. They keep at their work. The boat crosses the breakwater onto the land! The eight at the oars and the Other One at the tiller, straight on. The Other One says nothing; he just stares. Christ and the Madonna, a boat sailing on land! What things can happen in this world! The boat travels on land with oars and the Other One sits at the tiller. Let him not speak, I say, let his lips not break into a bit of a smile! On and on and behold! the boat comes to a stop in front of our doorstep! Oh, Lord Jesus Christ, the Other One opens his mouth and speaks. "Up, we've come for you, Auntie! Come out. We're in haste to be off!" Well, since you've come for me, my son, since you've come for this sinner, what else is there to do. . . . '

Smaragthi listened in dismay. She dropped the old woman's hand and got to her feet.

'We must send for the doctor,' she said to the women.

Lathios's wife was silently knitting a stocking. She looked at the girl doubtfully and said calmly:

'What do you want him to do? Mother's hour has come. Nobody can do anything for her. Didn't you hear her say they've come to take her?'

Smaragthi turned to Lathios's daughter, who was standing at the window with her arms folded. She nodded in agreement with her mother. Smaragthi could not understand how they could leave the old woman unattended. She refused to believe that she was going to lose her. With the loss of the kindly Aunt Permahoula, she would lose the fairy tales, the love and the countless thoughtful services the old woman performed for all of them—all these things would go out of her life for ever. And these two women sat there and saw her about to take leave without so much as reaching out to detain her by the sleeve.

'Oh, Aunt, let me do it!' she implored Lathios's wife, clutching her arm.

The fisherman's wife shrugged her shoulders indifferently. To her it was all foolishness.

Smaragthi ran out and hailed a muleteer who had sold his produce and was about to return to Mouria. He agreed to make the trip both ways with the doctor. Smaragthi promised him a glass of raki if he acted promptly.

Platanas arrived in less than two hours with his old medicine bag, now battered by the years. He himself was still fit in spite of hearty eating and drinking. His thick hair was whiter and white tufts now showed in his shaggy eyebrows and sprouted from his ears and nostrils. As always, he was stout and agile, his cheeks ruddy from drink and good living. Folds of flesh hung around his neck as is the case with fat people when they grow flabby.

As he entered the fishing village, he was followed by a crowd of noisy women who were indignant at the wanton extravagance of bringing the doctor down from the village so that a decrepit alcoholic like Aunt Permahoula, a hundred and ten years old, might die with the luxury of Platanas's services. Yana said it was pure ostentation and the other women concurred. Even the men in the coffee-houses treated it as a joke and ridiculed it. Furious over the gossip, Lathios got up and went home.

'What's the meaning of all this?' he demanded of Smaragthi. 'Everybody is making fun of us!'

The girl did not answer but he saw the tears well up into her eyes. He patted her affectionately on the back.

'Come, I didn't mean to hurt your feelings. Do what you think is right.'

No one understood, except Vatis, who stood by in case they needed to send him on some errand. He was closer to her than any of the others, for he, more than all of them, had lived in the old woman's enchanted world. She herself had chosen him out of the whole throng of children as her favourite. Now he heard them say that she was going to die and he discovered that his father had sent a boy to the village to order a coffin and other things needed for the funeral.

Vatis realized most of all that it was not only his grandmother who was about to leave, but also her marvellous retinue, which would follow her and never return. The house would be empty—the nooks, the divans, the hearth, all the places she had peopled with creatures of enchantment. The princes would go; their shining palaces would melt away. Snow White would gather up her three costumes, the sky with its stars, the sea with its fish, the earth with its flowers, and depart with the forty ogres and their mother, the ogress. Little Cinderella with her slippers of pearl and the princes with their steeds, the winged horses that fly on the wind, their manes and tails streaming among the clouds. The Hairless Ones and the Moor with the magic flute would trudge at the old woman's heels. The magic basket and the stags, each with a star in the centre of its forehead, all of which were enchanted princes, whose ways the old woman knew because she had lived with them. And the mermaids who were beautiful like Smaragthi, they too would go with the others, an endless escort, silently, without even the sound of the hoofbeats of their steeds or the tinkle of the silver bells on their bridles or the fanfare of trumpets or the marching tread of the ogres and monsters.

Vatis looked at Smaragthi and understood how unspeakable was her despair. He felt that she also was watching the great, magic company making preparations for vacating the house and was unable to stop them. All at once he realized that of all the fairy world, she alone would remain behind, their Smaragthi, who was lovelier than Snow White, more charming than Cinderella, and fairer than the nymphs, with eyes more emerald-green than those of any of the mermaids. She would remain with them! Vatis wished he could tell her how wonderful this was, how splendid and how comforting.

While he was sitting by the hearth thinking these things, Smaragthi said to him: 'Run, Vatis, and see if the doctor is in sight!'

She had said this three times already and each time he had rushed out to do her bidding as if he were performing some great exploit to win her favour. This time he saw the doctor approaching and acknowledging the greetings of the women at their doors. He returned with the joyful news.

'He's coming, Smaragthi!'

Smaragthi hastily put herself in order, gathering her hair under a blue kerchief, and the women who were present did the same and

177

arranged the cushions and blew off the dust that had gathered on them.

Platanas made an impressive entrance with his hearty voice, his bustling hands and feet and his leather bag. He wheezed a greeting and set his bag and hat on the divan. He unwound from his short neck a red and yellow muffler and rubbed his hands cheerily.

'Aha! Let's see what old Aunt Permahoula's been up to that you had to drag me away from my garden this evening. I planted Arabian pistachios, my lady, and they grew! Do you understand? Arabian pistachios! What a holy soil this is, eh? Some day I'll stick my walnut cane into the ground while I'm making a call and by the time I leave, I'll find it has sprouted branches and green leaves. Like the staff of Ayi-Vasilli, eh? Ha, ha! "And the staff was dry and it put forth green shoots!" '

He opened his round, puffy eyes in surprise that Lathios and the women did not appear amazed.

'Arabian pistachios!'

'Shall I bring the lamp closer, doctor?' asked Smaragthi, impatient with anxiety.

Platanas patted her paternally on the cheek.

'Bravo, my child! You must be Antonaros's Smaragthi! I've heard about your beauty, but I didn't believe it. My child, what are you doing among these sooty pots? You're a goddess from Olympus, not a fisherman's girl from Skala! Are you Athena or Aphrodite or Artemis? Come, hold the lamp so that we can see what the trouble is with Aunt Permahoula and why she has us worried. Come, don't act like that. It isn't anything.'

Smaragthi drank in his last words and her heart felt eased and grateful. She held the lamp so that the doctor could find his way to the patient, and her eyes smiled triumphantly at Lathios's wife. If for no other reason than what the doctor had said, she knew that she had done the right thing.

Platanas pushed a chair near the old woman's pallet and examined her. He drew from his pocket a heavy, silver watch, took hold of her hand and counted her pulse. Then he snapped the watch case shut as if it were a tobacco box and smiled. Very gently he let the old woman's hand fall. With a finger he opened her eyelid. Then he nodded for Smaragthi to take away the lamp and sat down on the divan. His ruddy face was imperturbably cheerful.

'It's nothing,' he repeated.

'Will she recover, doctor?' Smaragthi asked joyfully.

The doctor turned to her, laid his pudgy hand on her knee and smiled. He nodded affirmatively.

'The end will come tonight,' he said. 'About midnight or maybe a little after. Nothing's wrong with Aunt Permahoula. It's old age, nothing else. She is departing full of days, as the Scriptures say. You mustn't be alarmed by her delirium. It's senile delirium. But her pulse! Her heart! There we are! This poor heart had done its work and wants to stop. How many years has it been beating, eh?'

'More than a hundred, doctor,' said Lathios's wife.

'You see? A female Methuselah. Even if this heart were of iron, it would have to stop beating after so many years. . . .'

Smaragthi bit her trembling lips and asked:

'No medicine? Aren't you going to give her any medicine?'

Platanas smiled indulgently.

'You are poor folk,' he said. 'Why should I take money from you unnecessarily? If she were in pain, I would give her something to relieve it. But she's not suffering. She's going out like a lamp that has burned up its oil. This is natural death.'

'For her delirium, doctor?'

He lifted a fat, sausage-like finger, pleased with his comparison.

'You see? It's like a lamp going out. Haven't you sometimes heard the wick sputtering at night? Eh? That is the old woman's delirium. The wick, which had drunk its oil to the last drop, is sputtering. Later it will go puff! The flame will detach itself and ascend to heaven to join God's light. Here only the burned-out ashes will be left to smell. That's the way it is with us, my child.'

He rubbed his hands together jovially.

Smaragthi brought him a small glass of brandy and some salted almonds on a tray. Her hands were shaking. The doctor smiled. 'To a good end for the old woman and for all of us, and may we all reach her years,' he said as a toast. He drank the brandy, smacked his lips and added, pointing to the empty glass:

'There. If you were to ask me and I were to speak frankly, I would say give the old woman a full glass of brandy. I know she loves it. There is the sedative, the "comforter" as we call it. Well then? I'd do this if I were a real doctor and not a physician with a lot of scientific prejudices. That would give her a complete euthanasia. One brandy. Her last glass. In any event, her organism has become used to it and craves it. She would be grateful for it, she would feast on it and . . . she would stop. She's going to stop anyway. You ask why I don't prescribe it, eh? Why don't we give a person the last happiness that he can take with him out of this world? Because we are mixed up about good and evil. You know what is good but you're unable to do it. You know evil and you can't escape it.'

He arose, wrapped the muffler around his neck and picked up his hat and bag.

'So, good night to you. I—er—I won't fail to say a few words in church when you take her up there. Don't worry. I'll find a few good verses for Aunt Permahoula. She deserves it, for she's a rare phenomenon, a female Methuselah.'

Stratos accompanied the doctor with a lantern as far as the square, where the muleteer was waiting for him. Lathios went to the coffee-house for his customary drink.

At midnight Lathios's wife, who was knitting stockings for her husband, began to yawn. Lathios came home earlier than usual. This night Aunt Permahoula had not emerged from the darkness to repeat in her patient voice: 'Come now, Panayis! The children are hungry!'

He stood at the door. All was quiet. No one spoke except occasionally. Suddenly the old woman began to talk more distinctly and they all listened in silence.

'How is she doing?' asked Lathios.

His wife shrugged her shoulders.

'How could she be doing?'

She put away her knitting and stood up.

'I'll get something to eat,' she said to Smaragthi and Maria. 'Then I'll put the children to bed. Call me if you need me.'

Vatis also got up, although he had no appetite, but however late Lathios might come home, he always insisted on seeing his brood together, dipping their spoons in the earthenware porringers as fishermen dip their oars.

Meanwhile, the old woman reverted to her former incoherence, although her voice was as strong as ever. She was still going on about the fishing boat and the Other One who sat at the tiller.

'Who are you there? Maybe you're Stamatis Tchemellis. Why don't you open your mouth and say something? Could you be Captain Yoryis from Aivali? No, you're not Captain Yoryis. Where have I known you before, all black that you are? I'm old and my eyes are dim. I don't remember well any more. Where did you say we're going? I'll come, my son, if you're headed for Aivali. Just let me think a bit and get my shawl and my new slippers.'

'She's getting ready for the voyage,' said Maria. 'The doctor was right. She won't last till dawn.'

The old woman began again:

'What time did you say we'd set out? Dawn is fine. The sun will be warm. Eh, that will be a good hour. Let it be just as you wish. . . .'

A small boy, one of Maria's, appeared at the door.

'The baby is awake and crying,' he said softly to his mother and vanished. Maria got up and left slowly and quietly.

Smaragthi was left alone to listen to the old woman's rambling. Presently the door opened and Vatis came in to watch with her. He sat down in a corner and said nothing.

The old woman's talk became more confused. Suddenly in the midst of her delirium she pleaded:

'Oh, my daughter, if I only had a drop to drink, to cool my lips! My throat is dry from talking. I'm choking and . . . only a drop, a tiny drop!'

Smaragthi tried to get her to drink some camomile tea from a glass which she had ready beside her. The dying woman turned her face away in disgust.

'She asks for it but when I put it to her mouth, she won't drink,' said the girl in distress.

The old woman pleaded again;

'Just a drop, I say, to cool my parched lips!'

Vatis got up and left the room. He returned shortly with a large earthen cup from which Aunt Permahoula used to drink her coffee. His face was the colour of sulphur, his expression was tense. He went to the old woman and held the cup under her nose.

'Here, Granny, I've brought you something to drink. . . . It's me . . . Vatis. . . .'

The old woman seized the cup, with both hands helped the boy to hold it. His hands were as shaky as hers. She drank greedily with long swallows which interrupted her breathing. She drank to the last drop, threw her head back and gave an 'aaah!' of delight. Her face brightened with relief. She said:

'My blessing on you! . . . My blessing from my twenty nails!'

Vatis stared worriedly at this radiant face.

Smaragthi looked on in amazement. Suddenly she snatched the cup from the boy's hands and put it to her nose. Her eyes widened. The boy was frightened. Then the girl patted his head.

'You did well,' she said. 'I . . . I couldn't have made my hands do it . . . Now go to bed.'

Vatis left at once, still shaken. Smaragthi heard him sobbing in the hallway.

Aunt Permahoula died as a bird puts its head under its wing and goes to sleep. The Other One took her at the appointed hour. She departed at daybreak, at the moment the sun burst forth. She was singing a lullaby: 'Sleep, my morning star, sleep, O Pleiades.' She died with a smile on her face like a child falling asleep during a very long fairy tale.

The tale had lasted so long that the child had grown to be a hundred and ten years old, yet, even so, it was broken off unfinished.

Lathios's wife closed the old woman's eyes and tied a new headcloth around her chin. Then she placed beside the body a white bowl of clean water and a clean, white towel, according to the rite, so that St. Michael, the black angel, who comes for the souls of Christians on the island, might wash his sword and dry it.

40

I N the island villages life flows monotonously like water in the irrigation ditches. It is only on the great annual festivals like the New Year and at weddings, christenings, and fairs that the villagers meet at homes and churches for general reunion and sociability. There is also one other occasion that brings people together—a funeral. When the death-bell tolls, they all go to the chapel in the old cemetery.

So it was that a large crowd gathered at Aunt Permahoula's funeral. The weather was cool and the children were shouting joyously as if it were a fair. Even the adults were having a noisy good time, making jokes about the old woman's age, her mannerisms and her character.

The doctor came down in his black suit, starched cuffs, a frayed, detachable collar which chafed his jowls, and his heavy gold watch chain stretched across his waistcoat. He raised his hand, adjusted the cuff which kept slipping down, coughed impressively, and in his rumbling voice declaimed the following verses for Aunt Permahoula:

O-o-h! Thou hast measured out thy life, ancient one!
Thou hast entered Paradise to find Zenovia!

Then he turned towards the living and in his normal voice explained:

'Zenovia was the little daughter of the late Nerandji, wife of Varouhos of Moschonisi, who died years ago and whom the old woman loved very deeply.'

Then he turned back to the deceased, rolled his eyes and continued in the same grandiloquent manner:

Many things didst thou see and suffer, venerable Permahoula,
May you bequeath to all of us the years you lived!

'Amen!' said the villagers in unison and after the priest had put the customary piece of tile and the cross on the dead woman's mouth and had thrown a handful of earth on the bier, they all briskly filed past, each person throwing his handful of earth on the lowered coffin. Then they pressed around the baskets which Lathios's children were holding and consumed the funeral meats with lusty appetites, and each drank a glass of wine for the repose of the old woman's soul.

Soon the cemetery was deserted except for Smaragthi and Lathios's wife. Smaragthi wanted to burn incense at her mother's grave.

The weather was calm, but from time to time sudden gusts of wind rose from the valleys, making the olive trees bristle and setting the yellow-leaved poplars a quiver. A few bluish clouds drifted across the tranquil sky. Their shadows sped swiftly over the graves and swept up the slopes. Beyond, towards Anatolia, an indigo haze hugged the horizon. It was especially dense in the vicinity of Cape Babas.

Smaragthi tightened her black headcloth under her chin and watched the clouds fleeing like hunted creatures across an apparently windless sky. The evergreen oaks that wooded the cemetery cast sombre shadows on a soft, spongy carpet of leaves which had lain decaying there for years. Mushrooms absorbed the putrefaction through their roots and exhaled a sweetish odour. From outside the walled enclosure came the faint murmur of the fountain, a runnel tinkling into the stone cavity it had carved for itself during the course of centuries. This liquid voice, gentle and soothing, went straight to Smaragthi's heart like a kindly, soft-spoken message. She surrendered herself to its music.

The graves were scattered about the area, each with a black wooden cross at its head. Along the upright was crudely inscribed the name of the deceased in white oil paint. At the base was the blackened box that held the vigil lamp.

The two women found Aunt Nerandji's grave. The earth had settled and the cross, rotted by the rains, leaned to one side. One of these days the bones would have to be exhumed. Smaragthi tried to straighten the cross and saw a rose-coloured snail with a shell as fragile as tissue paper laboriously making its way up the deteriorating wood. A trail of glistening slime behind it marked its path. It was impossible to guess how long it had taken to reach its present point. All around, the vegetation was luxuriant and aromatic. There were clumps of wild mallows and spiny thistles. The women put incense in a burner, crossed themselves and censed the grave. Then they set the censer on the ground, where it smoked pungently, and seated themselves on a stone with their knees clasped and wept in memory of Aunt Nerandji.

Smaragthi grieved as if her mother had died only this day and had just been buried and she was lonely in her complete orphanhood. She wept for both women simultaneously, as if they were one person, her mother having lived to be a hundred and ten and now resting in the new grave.

Overcome with grief, she abandoned her pride and complained to Lathios's wife of the uneasiness she felt when she was with other people. Even when she was among women, she suspected that they gossiped behind her back. Why? She watched her very shadow lest it offend anyone.

'Tell me what to do. I feel like taking my boat and going away as my father did.'

'No, don't do that. You'll find the same thing wherever you go, and other things, even worse. Only one thing will save you, my dear.'

'Tell me.'

'Get married. That's what you must do. Have a husband who will tell you what to do and who will protect you. You're alone. That's why the men act the way they do. You're with men all day. You're attractive. But you resent their way of looking at you. How else can they act but in the way that is natural for them?'

She paused, hesitated, and then continued:

'And while we're on the subject, my dear, I might as well say that I don't understand you, either. You've become a young woman, everything about you is—how shall I say?—exactly as it should be, and yet nobody has ever seen or heard of you being with the *pallikaris* as other girls are.'

She became more specific;

'And I know some *pallikaris* like cypress trees. I know one of them who would set fire to his father's house to win you!'

Smaragthi interrupted her in embarrassment.

'I know. You mean Manolis.'

She reflected a moment and then said gravely:

'Listen, Aunt. You know that in the whole world I have only your home and the godfather. I think of your children as my brothers and sisters. I've grown up with them. I love all of you. I'd give my heart's blood for you.'

'And we also, Smaragthi.'

'I know it. I appreciate how much you've all stood by me. But look. It's Manolis, isn't it? If I were to choose a husband, I would be honoured and proud if Manolis would marry me. I know our Manolis's place in my heart. But . . . how can I tell you?'

'Tell me, my dear. I'm your mother today.'

'Well, I'm so made that I can't bear intimacy with any man. Every time I think of a man, even the best, touching me with his hand, I'm seized with nausea and disgust. I shudder, my heart turns to ice and I feel like vomiting. . . . There . . . now I've told you. So how could I ever get married?'

Lathios's wife stared at her, dumbfounded, and crossed herself.

'How awful! This again? It makes my ears ring to hear it. I could almost believe the slanderous things the Gadjales say about you.'

'I don't know why they slander me. I've never bothered them.'

'You disturb them, too, Smaragthi. Don't you know they're fishing to catch our Manolis for their Yana?'

'Yana is all right.'

'Let her take herself out of my sight! They are evil witches, mother and daughter. But if Manolis wants her, I'd say nothing. He'd be marrying her, not I. So here's the snarl. Yana wants Manolis, Manolis wants you, and you . . . you don't want anybody! It's all a mix-up.'

'What do the Gadjales say about me?'

'It's impossible to imagine. That you're not the child of a woman. That's why you don't act like a woman. That it's written you'll never see a husband on your pillow. That it's your nature to resist men. . . . '

Smaragthi listened in frank astonishment. Till now she had not realized how far the gossip had gone, the gossip that was closing in on her like a net day by day with its stout meshes. Suddenly she recalled a bad dream that had upset her one night. She had awakened from it in great distress, yet, try as she might, she had been unable to remember what it had been about. Now it came back to her in a flash. A net was closing around her on all sides. She was struggling in it, naked, but it drew tighter and tighter and seemed to smother her. Standing about' was a crowd of people laughing, jeering, and slapping their knees in derision. This hideous nightmare was now a reality.

'What else do they say?' she asked indignantly. 'You must tell me everything.'

'Oh, a lot of crazy things. That it's your destiny to bring misfortune wherever you go.'

'Whom have I injured?' Smaragthi asked feebly.

Lathios's wife wanted to end this conversation which had begun well but was taking a bad turn, but Smaragthi insisted on knowing everything. With considerable reluctance Lathios's wife told her that people attributed to her non-human origin most of the mishaps that had befallen Skala from the time she had come among them. Concerning Aunt Nerandji's death, they said that she had fallen and been killed because of the mermaid's curse. About old Varouhos, they said that Smaragthi was the cause of his being driven away in disgrace. There were a thousand other similar instances, equally childish. But Smaragthi must not take them seriously. They were only the malicious fabrications of envious people. No sensible person could believe them. Speaking for herself, she, Lathios's wife, would consider it an honour if Smaragthi should enter her home as the bride of Manolis, her finest son.

The girl felt her heart grow numb. She was stunned by the hostility that surrounded her and the extent to which she was alienated from the life of the village. Perhaps she really was an abominable being rejected by mankind, a weird, fantastic creature of a different race, incapable of enduring the touch of a man! She squeezed her eyelids together to restrain the scalding tears that collected behind them. Then she surrendered and wept piteously.

'What shall I do?' she sobbed. 'What shall I do?'

Lathios's wife regarded her with benevolent detachment. She shrugged her shoulders. She had said all she could. She knew no other advice to give this odd girl.

'Have patience,' she said. 'This is the lot of us women. Be patient.'

A prolonged peal of thunder rolled across the sky like a heavy wagon drawn by runaway horses over sheet-iron roads into the distance.

It came from Anatolia near Cape Babas. The clouds which had gathered there had darkened into a black, molten mass, spreading its gloom across the sky like a curtain and obscuring the sun. As soon as she heard the thunder, Lathios's wife glanced at the sky and crossed herself.

'May God send rain,' she exclaimed devoutly. 'May God send rain!'

As if in response, a second roll of thunder shook the air like the boom of a cannon, echoed ominously, and finally died away at the horizon.

Immediately a wind swept through the trees and extinguished the vigil candles at the grave, leaving the wicks to smoke acridly. Two tall, slender poplars outside the cemetery wall bent in alarm to let the intruder pass over them. Golden-yellow and russet leaves were detached from the frail branches and fluttered through the air like a swarm of startled butterflies. The rustling of the foliage and the murmuring of the trees fell refreshingly on the ears of the women, as if repeating the prayer of Lathios's wife.

'May God send rain! Rain for the thirsty trees and for men whose lives are threatened with famine. May it rain so that roots and beasts may slake their thirst!'

And the rain even now was racing through the sky on the moist wings of the south wind, sweeping over the sea, blotting out the daylight and filling the air with the pungent odours of dead leaves, parched, cracked soil and crackling discharges of lightning.

The first drops, heavy and violent, splashed with a cool hiss, pelting the plants on the graves, the sombre evergreen oaks with their spiny metallic leaves and the hot stones. The glowing coals in the censer sputtered and went out.

The women withdrew under the tiled portico of the church. They sat on a whitewashed bench awaiting the end of the shower. Suddenly they threw their arms around each other in a terrified embrace.

A blazing flash of lightning struck directly in front of them, followed by a crash of thunder that caused the venerable church to quake. The murky curtain across the sky was ripped from end to end like a veil. The women blanched and crossed themselves.

'Christ protect the mountains and the valleys!'

The squall increased in violence. It punished the soil unmercifully and whipped the dying leaves from the trees. The zinc roof sounded a tattoo like a thousand tambourines. As if its time were limited, the shower emptied in the space of a few minutes the remaining contents of its dark wineskin and expended its mighty wrath, its din and flames.

And that was all. Wherever you looked, it was finished. The sky cleared and was more spotlessly blue than ever. The sun reappeared and flooded the earth with its light. The evergreen oaks dripped gleaming, iridescent threads of jewels from their glittering spines. The down-spout of the church alone was singing a hasty epilogue. Then it, too, was silent save for a trickle of drops like final notes.

Lathios's wife was the first to get to her feet.

'Let's take our time going down, my dear.'

They followed the path that led down to the sea. Neither of them spoke. When they came to the level gardens, Smaragthi stopped in amazement to watch Lathios's wife linger to dig greens. She put them into the wicker basket that had held the wine bottle and tumblers at the funeral. Apparently she had thought of gathering greens at the very time she was preparing the old woman's funeral! Her foresightedness was proved when the kitchen knife she always used for digging greens appeared in her hands. Smaragthi was unable to understand how this woman's mind could deal with two such different tasks at the same time and she gave up trying. Instead, she picked for the Mermaid Madonna a large bouquet of cyclamen, which, after the rain, were unfolding their embroidered leaves and dainty chalices everywhere. There were so many of them that they covered the stone boundaries of the fields and their delicate blossoms poured a mild fragrance on the earth from their inverted petals.

As they reached the first houses of the fishing village, Lathios' wife paused and said:

'You know, Smaragthi, I think that inside you're still only an unripe child, even though on the outside you look like a grown woman. Any other explanation would be impossible.'

Smaragthi said nothing. Lathios's wife went on:

187

'As soon as you've ripened inside, you'll mate like all other creatures of God, and you won't say any more the silly things you said this afternoon.'

Then Smaragthi realized that all the while Lathios's wife had been digging greens, she had been concerned only with anxiety for the love-smitten Manolis.

41

T H A T night, Smaragthi, exhausted with thoughts and memories and unable to relieve her depression, sought diversion at Lathios's house from the loneliness that was suffocating her.

She found the family talking about the old woman in subdued, melancholy voices. On a low table in the corner where Aunt Permahoula had died burned the three-day vigil lamp for the dead, a small, yellow frame which at times was motionless and at other times came alive and flickered impatiently on its wick. The family occasionally stopped talking, looked at the frame and thought of the dead woman. Then they spoke of her again, but always as if she had merely gone away on a journey. Nothing more.

Lathios was away sipping his customary drink at Fortis's. The two older boys also were at the coffee-house. Stratos had found companions at the Gadjalis place, where the young men gathered. Manolis went there, and Stratos copied whatever his big brother did.

Vatis, however, was at home with the women and children. He said nothing and did not join in the laughter when little Garoufallia, Aunt Permahoula's great-granddaughter, unexpectedly asked Lathios's wife:

'Grandma, now that my great-grandmother is dead, doesn't she feel anything any more?'

'No, my child.'

'And if you twist her finger? Still no?'

'No, not even then.'

'Our Diamandis twisted my finger and I cried.'

A bit later she asked again:

'Granny?'

'What is it?'

'Why did they put her in the ground?'

'That's what they do with dead people.'

She thought that over, hesitated and then asked in her piping voice:

'Now that they've put her in the ground, is she deader than ever?'

Everybody burst into laughter and a somewhat older brother of Garoufallia's was so overcome with mirth that the tears ran down from his eyes.

But the little girl had still further difficulties about the mystery of death.

'Grandma, if anybody tickles her now on the soles of her feet, won't she laugh at all?'

Vatis turned on her angrily and shouted:

'Oh, shut up!'

His outburst was so brusque and violent that Smaragthi stared at him in surprise. He felt her eyes on him like a searing, emerald flame. His grieving for Aunt Permahoula melted into tears and he began to weep uncontrollably.

Garoufallia, seeing Vatis in tears, also commenced to wail. Smaragthi took her on her lap, kissed her wet eyes, and promised to take her with the children who were going to sleep at her house that night. She was going to tell them a marvellous story.

'One of Granny's fair tales?' the little girl asked.

'Yes, if you stop crying.'

Still sobbing, the child asked further:

'Will you tell the one about the fairless elves who stole the millstone?'

She was promised this and stopped crying.

The older boys came home, said good evening, and sat down on the divan. With a gloomy smile Manolis said:

'Well, it seems we've lost the old woman. . . .'

'God rest her soul,' they all said in unison.

'Father not home yet?'

'Not yet.'

Stratos made a bitter joke.

'He's at Fortis's waiting for her to come for him.'

Manolis rolled a cigarette. His mother took a glowing coal from the hearth and gave it to him for a light.

'Where have you two been?' she asked, for something to say.

Manolis explained that he also had started going to the Gadjales's even though he knew they were scoundrels, father and sons. But you had to admit they knew their business. They got the crowd and made money, you see. They were ruining the other coffee-houses. Only Fortis held on to a few at his Mulberry Tree and most of them were Mouriotes.

'The respectable men all go there,' said Smaragthi.

Manolis smiled.

'What of it? The respectable men, except our father, don't spend money. What can you make selling coffee and camomile tea? Not to mention those stories about America that everybody knows backwards and forwards.'

'The godfather is an honest man,' said Smaragthi somewhat piqued.

'I agree. The Gadjales are hoodlums, but they know how to take a fellow out of himself. They've got a wonderful gramophone and all kinds of dance records and popular songs. The dancing begins, the treating goes around and the wine flows like a fountain. They have a paraffin lamp that lights up the whole beach so you could sew by it. . . . The Gadjales have already ruined Fortis. And yet they hate him. What they have against him, they don't say. They had a row with him the other night. On account of the boy, Lambis.'

Smaragthi pricked up her ears. Stratos and Vatis became interested.

'What's Lambis been doing?'

Manolis shrugged his shoulders and laughed.

'Ha! It's being said that the lad is in love with their daughter.'

'With Yana?'

'Exactly. Seems they caught him hanging around at night under her window. Something like that. The old man warned Fortis to keep his son away or they'd take care of him themselves.'

'It's the end of the world!' said Lathios's wife, slapping her knee. 'Truly it's the end of the world. Lambis! A lad of good family. Why, yesterday he was only a baby!'

'If it's true,' said Maria indifferently.

'I don't know,' said Manolis. 'But if it is, he needs a stiff laying on of Fortis's American razor-strop!'

Manolis said teasingly to Smaragthi:

'The drums are beating in your neighbourhood, Smaragthi, and you don't hear a thing!'

It was true.

The Gadjalis house was behind hers in the direction of the olive grove. The windows of both their bedrooms faced each other. Fortunately between the two courtyards was a large fig tree with stout branches and dense foliage so that, even in winter, it was impossible to look from one window into the other.

In summer this huge tree was loaded with fruit and since it belonged to nobody, anyone who wished had the right to climb and pick the figs. Under the tree was a hen coop that was never occupied, since the foxes allowed no fowls to remain alive inside.

It was here that Lambis was reported to have been seen loitering at night, under the Gadjales's window, while the men were at their tavern.

Fortis had asked his son sternly what he had to say for himself. Lambis replied that it was true he sometimes passed the house on his way home from the olive grove. The road was shorter that way. He added that he also often climbed the tree to pick a few figs. Was he supposed to ask the Gadjales for permission to do these things?

It was agreed by all that Lambis was quite within his rights and that the Gadjales were being too officious lately because of the money that jingled in their pockets from their clandestine smuggling activities. Besides, nobody had a bad word for Fortis's boy. He was as responsible as an adult and helped the old man in every way. A sensible, dependable lad. When he was spoken to, he blushed like a girl.

Smaragthi said nothing. She was thinking how much better than they she knew this youth whose appearance so belied him with its chaste beauty and shy boyishness. The Gadjales without doubt were right. Lambis was a perverse lad and apparently was in the habit of spying on young girls at night while they undressed.

When Lathios came home and they had eaten supper, Smaragthi took three of the children, including Garoufallia, home with her.

She put them to bed in the kitchen, all on the same pallet, after they had gabbled their prayers in sing-song voices, impatient to hear the story she had promised to tell them.

They fell asleep before the end of the story. Smaragthi took the lamp and went to her bedroom. On one side was the window that looked out towards the mountain and the olive grove. Facing it was the great fig tree that concealed the Gadjalis house. The other window looked out over the sea. Aunt Permahoula had called it the summer window, because in winter when the north wind and the gales rode the waves, this window and its shutter were kept closed. The other window, which was sunny and sheltered, she named the winter window.

Smaragthi stood at the summer window and became absorbed in watching the movements of the motor-boats at their fishing. The night was an expanse of deep violet filled with the lapping of the surf and the noises from the sea.

42

S M A R A G T H I threw herself passionately into her work. Physical weariness brought an easement she was unable to find otherwise. The tempest in her soul would sometimes swell and lift its waves and sometimes there was peace and tranquillity. Then she felt a harmony with all around her, which filled her with ineffable happiness without form or name. She would guide her boat among the hidden recesses between the steep cliffs and swim and listen to the rustling of the mysterious wings within her. She would pick a bouquet of wild cyclamen and take it to the Mermaid Madonna, who would look down on her with her enormous oblique eyes, the fin of her coiled tail reaching up to her waist.

Manolis made no more hints to her. Smaragthi, in turn, visited the Lathios family less and less frequently, especially when the boys were there. Nevertheless, she preceived that Manolis was convinced that sooner or later her better judgement would prevail on her to marry him. In his reserved manner she saw on optimistic patience. His earnest, tender glances were those of one dealing with a child.

'Don't worry,' he seemed to say. 'You're still a little girl and you don't understand. When the right time comes, I'll be at hand!'

As for Lambis, there was no need for further wariness. After what had happened that night, Fortis's son had avoided crossing her path. If they did chance to meet, he was visibly ashamed. He would drop his eyes and nervously flutter his eyelids when he greeted her. After Manolis's bit of gossip, she regarded Lambis as a worthless lad whose moral degeneration she deplored.

Yet for all the precautions she took to avoid the boys, who were as crafty as their elders, she was not desined to be finished with them for the present.

Towards noon one day she had anchored in the shallows outside the entrance to the harbour and was tidying up her boat when she heard the splash of the lads as they dived from the Mount of the Madonna. The whole gang was there: Lambis, Stratos, Vatis, Thymios the Bulldog, and their comrades.

They surfaced and swam for the open sea. She thought no more about them until she heard them return. Lambis came first. His handsome head and muscular body moved ahead of the others with every stroke. By the time he reached the mouth of the harbour, he had left his companions far behind.

He turned and gave a look of satisfaction. Then he slowed down and merely glided over the water with easy, graceful strokes. Each time he thrust his right arm forward, his body arched above the surface, firm and polished like bronze. From his self-conscious behaviour, it was clear that he knew the girl was watching him, although he never once glanced towards her boat. He tossed his head lightly with the beautiful grace of an animal, his wet hair flying and a blissful smile on his face.

Far behind came the others, Vatis the last of all. He swam erratically and out of line, so that he came nearer than the rest to Smaragthi's boat. As he drew alongside and passed, panting hard, he called out gamely:

'See what real diving is like!'

Smaragthi made no reply. She merely smiled amicably at the infatuated lad and went on with her work.

The boys stretched out on the flagstones of the breakwater to rest in the sun. Then they got up and began to play sponge divers. In this game, each one took a large stone from the breakwater, clasped it to his chest, and walked into the deep water until he was completely submerged. Their bodies could be seen moving forward with slow steps on the blue-green sand of the bottom. Each tried to carry his stone further than the others. Through the water their limbs glimmered like cold green marble. On the other side of the breakwater a few fishmongers and idlers watched the contest with keen interest.

Thymios was the winner.

The ugly lad carried his stone from the harbour to Smaragthi's boat. She saw his great head of coarse black hair like the bristles of a brush suddenly surface at the prow. He shivered, gulped deep breaths of air, and spat into the sea. He was pale yellow from his strenuous exertion, and uglier that ever. He opened his beady eyes, reddened by the salt, darted a complacent glance at the girl, and grinned broadly. The white line of his huge teeth divided his face horizontally from ear to ear. Then he walked smugly to the breakwater to rest.

'Bravo, Bulldog!' cried the men who had been watching. The other boys, except Vatis, joined in. Thymios looked towards the boat to see if Smaragthi had heard the 'Bravo, Bulldog!'

Vatis regarded him sulkily. Up to his waist in the water, he stood pale and tense beside his brother. Of all of them he was the least robust and the least tanned.

'I'll dive again by myself!' he cried and picked his rock up in his arms once more.

The boys laughed. They thought he was fooling. But the lad moved slowly and determinedly forward and sank deeper and deeper until at last he submerged. When the sea covered him, he proceeded stubbornly into the deeper water towards the mouth of the harbour.

Everyone watched him with admiration and then with astonishment. It was inconceivable that such a frail physique could hold out so long. Thymios arose from where he had been preening himself under his laurels of victory and watched uneasily the unforeseen challenger steadily approaching his record. Suddenly Stratos, also worried, leaped up and cried: 'He's drowning!'

Immediately he swam with swift strokes to his brother. Lambis caught up with him, and Thymios dived from the rock where he had been sunning himself.

They had seen Vatis drop his rock and flounder about aimlessly. Air bubbles were rising from him. He lost his balance and his pale green body lunged this way and that on the sandy bottom.

The boys' cries set Smaragthi's heart pounding. She dropped her work, quickly hauled in her anchor and punted her boat to the breakwater where they were bringing Vatis.

When he was stretched out on the rocks, they raised him by his legs and held him head down to get rid of the water he had swallowed. He was pale as death and his body looked pathetically lifeless. Lambis gave him two stinging slaps and his eyelids fluttered. After another slap he sighed and regained consciousness.

He rubbed his forehead with the back of his hand. Then he spat several times, opened his eyes and looked around, exhausted.

Smaragthi ordered them all to stand aside to give him air and sunlight. Through his daze Vatis heard her voice. He looked up and met her face. Her large straw hat hung from her back and her hair flamed in the sunlight like a golden cloud. Modestly he drew his drawers up around his waist. Then he braced himself against the breakwater and sat up.

'Do you feel better now?' the girl asked. There were still vestiges of anxiety in her green eyes. Vatis noticed this and a faint smile of happiness appeared on his wan face, which was gradually regaining colour. He nodded his head pluckily.

'If this dizziness hadn't come over me,' he said, 'you'd have seen!'

Smaragthi went home shaken.

What was the meaning of this in connexion with Vatis? Her mind was running on the vicious gossip that was being circulated about her. Was this one more example of the misfortune she was supposed to bring with her? Did her shadow fall like a curse on everyone who came to her with love? What if Vatis had not opened his eyes? What if his young body had remained limp and inert as she had seen it when they brought it from the sea with the arms dangling lifelessly?

The Madonna had taken pity on her and come to her rescue, for it was certain that Vatis had performed this foolhardy exploit to please her. She had read the truth in the lad's blinking eyes when they opened from his swoon and filled themselves with her presence.

From now on, she must be more careful than ever. No one could foresee what violence might break out among such hot-headed people. She must stay away from the Lathios family and from her godfather's house.

Besides, there was another reason for visiting the Mulberry Tree less often, and the godfather himself was thoroughly in accord with it.

43

HITHERTO, the company which leased from the government the contract for collecting the taxes on fish was represented by Mr. Apostolides, an elderly man with dyed moustaches. He was referred to as 'Mister' because he wore a collar even on workdays, shaved every morning so that his white whiskers would not show, and invariably carried a black walking stick with an ivory knob.

Mr. Apostolides was a peaceful man, scrupulous to excess in all matters, and a backgammon addict. He had, however, commited one folly ill-suited to his advanced age. He had fallen in love with a very poor, young refugee girl from the vicinity of Smyrna. He was not long in discovering that gratitude is not enough to extinguish the flame of youth in a young woman's heart, so he devoted his full time to keeping watch over his youthful spouse. At night he went home as early as possible to the two rooms he rented opposite Fortis's coffee-house, after spending the whole day playing backgammon with one eye on the windows lest the girl should stick her nose out and be seen by some masculine passer-by. In the year and a half since he had arrived in Skala, nobody had seen his wife after she came off the ship.

From the first day the blue curtains with white flowers had been kept drawn in the street windows, even when the cicadas were bursting with protest at the heat. As a result, the sun had faded the blue so that the white flowers no longer could be seen. These curtains were raised only briefly at night and then within the window frame was discernble a figure silently gazing at the harbour and the lamps of the fishing boats out at sea. But as soon as the room was lighted the curtains fell again and on them appeared the faint shadow of a young woman moving about. People who had been present at the girl's disembarkation said she was quite beautiful. Although actually she was not unattractive, the secluded life which Mr. Apostolides compelled her to lead surrounded her with mystery and gave her the reputation of being almost supernaturally beautiful.

It was incredible that this wretched imprisonment should have continued without murmuring or outright rebelliousness on her part. But it was rumoured in Skala that the bird had fouled her nest, that during the very first months of his marriage the tax collector had intercepted a love note from her to a captain and from that time she had not dared to speak up against her husband.

Since his secluded wife was not allowed on the streets, Mr. Apostolides himself had to undertake the tasks customarily reserved for women. Thus he was in the habit of filling the water jar at the fountain in the square. He was an odd sight as he held the jar in one hand and his black walking stick with the ivory knob in the other.

This situation, however, at last became a matter that concerned others besides the belatedly married man. The tax company was suffering the consequences of this incompatible union. The fishermen were declaring only a small portion of their catches. Whole boatloads went untaxed while Mr. Apostolides, at his observation post, kept watch on his wife.

One morning a motor-boat arrived from Hora with a new tax collector aboard with a letter instructing Mr. Apostolides to surrender his duties and records and return to Hora on the same boat. The Skaliotes ran to the breakwater to bid him farewell and get a glimpse at last of the beauty whom the ogre with the dyed moustache had guarded so successfully for a year and a half.

Disillusionment spread over every face. Was that she? A young woman, of course, but in no way exceptional save for her long, black hair in two enormous plaits that hung down her back to her hips.

The new tax collector had hardly stepped ashore before he became the most fascinating personage in Skala. Everyone discussed him—the fishermen in the coffee-houses, the women at the fountain and the boys in swimming. They realized at once that they had to deal with a man who knew his business and did not tolerate half measures. This was made clear in his first conversations with the fishermen.

He looked round for a room where he could observe the harbour at all times and found what he wanted on the upper floor of Fortis's coffee-house. He paid a month's rent in advance and had some branches of the mulberry tree cut off because they interferred with his view of the harbour.

But he made an impression in another way, which amused everybody. He was a vain young fellow who was convinced that all women sighed for him. He was short. His hair was plastered down with brilliantine and carefully smoothed with a brush. He had a droll little moustache like two tiny lines painted with the point of a water-colour brush.

Never till then had the Skaliotes seen such a curious moustache. They stared at it in fascination and thus nourished the vanity of this newly arrived cockerel. Even the little tots pointed at it when he appeared on the breakwater.

Since such a thing had never been seen or heard of in Skala, each person had his own theory about it. Lambis and his gang concluded that he had the mange. Fortis said that in America Charlie Chaplin stuck a moustache similar to this on his lip to make people laugh.

But young and old found him intriguing. The Lambis gang even admired him because he dressed so elegantly—striped tie, straw hat, silk handkerchief hanging from his jacket pocket and fluttering in the wind, creases in his trousers, and shoes half black and half white. One thought one was dreaming when he walked among the barefoot fishermen with their black breeches and hairy ears.

It was his name, however, that was most astonishing.

'Will you oblige me by telling me your name, sir?' Fortis asked him with his usual courtesy as he treated him to a coffee by way of welcome.

The young man smiled and replied:

'Kokos.'

'How's that? Kokos?' asked Fortis, who did not understand.

The tax collector shrugged his shoulders condescendingly.

'My name is Kokos. Kokos Achtarides.'

Fortis threw his head back to examine him better from under his spectacles.

'It's impossible he could have been so baptized,' he thought.

But man of the world that he was, he concluded after brief reflection that perhaps there were Orthodox Christians bearing a name which little children used to designate an egg.

Lambis, who served the coffee, watched the lodger take a round mirror out of his pocket and fussily make certain the knot of his cravat was correct. Later Lambis asked his father perplexedly when they were alone:

'Are we going to address this grown man like that, Father?'

Fortis replied in embarrassment: 'Since that's the way he wishes, how does it concern you? A good thing he isn't called Pipi!'

One night when the coffee-house was empty and Fortis was taking in the chairs, Kokos called him aside, slapped him chummily on the shoulder, and asked him with a wink:

'Tell me, Uncle, how does the other business go here?'

Fortis did not understand.

'What other business?' he asked naïvely.

The tax collector nudged him slyly with his elbow.

'The other business? I mean the clandestine business!'

The old man's eyes brightened. He thought he now understood what the other was getting at.

'Oh, don't fret yourself about that,' he reassured Kokos. 'Everybody does it here on the sly. Nothing to worry about. Otherwise, the poor would go without a cigarette. You see, a day's wages here is barely enough to buy a day's cigarette with the tax stamp on them. The boxes you see stacked on the shelves are only for show. For the benefit of the police. Sometimes they make an unexpected raid and tan the hides of the poor. They have their commissions, too, you see. . . . '

Kokos listened impatiently to the old man's gossip. He coughed, giggled, and slapped Fortis mischievously on the knee.

'I don't mean that, Uncle Comninos,' he explained. 'I'm talking about women. What do you do about them here?'

Fortis was shocked. His smile froze on his face. He seized the white hairs of his moustache with the edge of his lower lip.

'Oh! You . . . mean that!'

'Of course! What does a young fellow who is a bachelor do here?'

Fortis, at a loss, raised his arms, and replied sharply:

'He gets married, my boy. That's what he does!'

He drew himself up and continued:

'As for the other "clandestine" business, as you call it, so it is, thank God! You do as you can!'

From that day, Kokos took his *apéritif* at the Gadjalis tavern. At Fortis's he took only his breakfast of coffee with goat's milk and a piece of well crusted bread. At Ammouthelli he found the company with whom he could talk about women as he liked. The young fishermen craned their necks to hear his tales about Hora. And as for the mysteries of Athens—heh-heh-heh!

Kokos told them things so unbelievable that their simple minds would never otherwise have imagined them. At last he brought the conversation around to Smaragthi. How was it, he asked, that with such a pistachio in their grasp they did nothing but sit and drool behind her back? And what a wench. . . . !

'You don't know what Smaragthi is like,' he was told.

'What is she? A bastard, that's all. She has no father to be feared, no brother, no relatives. What has she?'

One youth sighed and said:

'She's got something that nails you to your place, that's what she's got!'

Kokos winked, put his fingers in his braces and leaned back. 'Just watch me,' he said. 'I'm the man for a girl like that.' He whistled as if the difficulties already were in the past. 'Leave the mermaid of Skala to me. One of these days I'll have news for you.'

This day, as a matter of fact, was not far off.

The fishmongers were in the habit of coming to Fortis's small square under the spreading mulberry tree to bid informally on the fish which the anglers and the net fishermen brought in. The tax collector also was present to record the final bids for the fish. It was one such day that Kokos chose for his great undertaking.

Smaragthi was seated on the ground with a large basket of fish beside her. She had a considerable number of choice fish, among them two or three flounders. Kokos assumed a jaunty position in front of her with his hands in his pockets. He cleared his throat ostentatiously and said in a syrupy voice:

'Do me the favour, my dear, of selecting for me about a kilo of fish for broiling. I'll send someone to your boat to fetch them.'

'Gladly,' said Smaragthi, pre-occupied with her work.

If she had paid attention to Kokos, she would have noticed that this day he was groomed with particular care. He glistened with pomade and reeked with perfume from head to foot and the crease in his trousers was razor sharp.

Vainly he posed on one foot and the other, and under the remains of his moustache flashed a smile which he considered irresistible. He cleared his throat nonchalantly and accented the knot of his cravat with an aristocratic flourish of his hand, his little finger elegantly extended.

Smaragthi settled her account with the fishmonger who bought her catch, took her money, and set off for her boat, followed by three of Lathios's urchins, two carrying the empty basket and the third a wooden bucket of choice fish.

After they cleaned the boat, Smaragthi sent the children home to light the fire for cooking. It was about noon and the late October weather was still hot at this hour. Smaragthi let down the sail to form an awning and sat in its shade to clean some red mullet for the tax collector and a large flounder for Fortis.

It was then that Kokos put in an appearance. He pretended to be strolling along the breakwater. With his hands in his pockets, he stepped gingerly over the stones, softly whistling an Athenian popular song. When he reached Smaragthi's mooring, he drew the boat closer by its rope and leaped aboard. Smaragthi, under the awning, thought it was the children.

'What have you come back for?' she asked.

Kokos ducked under the awning and presented himself before her like a trump card.

'Heh-heh-heh!' he tittered. 'It's me. I've come for the fish.'

Smaragthi pointed to the string she had kept for him. She was just getting to them. He would have to wait a bit. A bit? Oh, please, he was in no hurry at all. He would wait. It would be a pleasure to wait. There was no reason for haste. There was plenty of time, heh-heh!

'How so?' said the girl. 'It's noon and you've got to have them broiled, isn't that so?'

She hurried so that she could give them the fish.

Begging her not to be uneasy, he sat on the gunwale, leaning forward swaying so that the awning would not disarrange his hair. Smiling and swaying from side to side, he began to flatter her. His mind could not grasp—and she must pardon him—how such a creature as herself, a little angel, could live among such uncouth people. What did these brutes find to appreciate in such a marvel? She must pardon him, but the saying fits in this case: 'What does the shepherd see in a soufflè?' Heh-heh-heh! isn't that so, eh?'

The girl made no response, and he took courage.

'Tell me, have you ever happened to go to Athens? Ah, no? Too bad! Every time I accompany a cargo of fish to the capital, I travel first class, no less. There you see a fine city and the world. The streets are scrubbed so clean you can see your face in them. And there are the fashionable shops with tall windows and everybody, men and women, dressed in the latest style. The girls—they're perfect dolls!'

'But aren't there any poor people?' asked Smaragthi.

'Inevitably, but they're well dressed, too. Besides, the police don't allow ragamuffins to loiter about on the marble pavements of the main streets. And flowers. Ah! Flowers! They hang everywhere, from lamp-posts and from the terraces of the mansions. And from the balconies. And what girls! They stroll about with silky-haired dogs on silver leashes. They're always strolling about.'

'Don't they get tired of that?' asked Smaragthi. 'They must sit down and rest sometimes.'

'Hee-hee-hee! That's excellent. They do sit down, of course—in the parks in the centre of the city, where there are fountains that sound like music. The girls sit on wicker chairs and sip coloured ices through long, thin straws. It's charming to see them. . . .'

'Eh, they're city girls and have their own ways,' said Smaragthi. 'Our ways are all right for us here. Now take the fish. Here they are all ready!'

She hung the string of mullet on the rowlock beside Kokos. The tax collector was carried away by his eloquence. His face was red, his nose was shiny and his beady eyes gleamed.

'No,' he said fervently as he fumbled in his pocket for his leather wallet from which, with trembling hands, he extracted a fifty-drachma note. 'If you were there, Smaragthi, everybody would stop and look at you.'

'Of course they would,' laughed Smaragthi. 'A carnival figure like me in the public square of Athens! But wait, I must give you your change.'

She took the note and bent down to unlock a green cupboard in the cabin where she kept her change.

'Please, please!' said Kokos in an unsteady voice. 'No change. It's not necessary. I don't want your money. I ... I ... I only want you. ...'

With knees and hands shaking, he seized her from behind as she was bent over in front of him, his mouth nuzzling the back of her neck and his hands groping about her body.

Once more Smaragthi was assailed by the loathing which she had experienced so violently years before. It was as if her violated virginity had been quiescent within her all this time and now this buffoon had awakened it to rear itself over him like a wild beast bristling and snarling with fury.

With a wrench of her entire body, the girl tried to throw off Kokos as if he were a loathsome monster. Pride forced her to stifle an outcry, for it would only bring a crowd on the run to laugh at her predicament. The tax collector loosened his grasp, bumped against the sailyard, but refused to let her go. He clung to her with his legs hooked around her. Then the awning fell on them and they struggled among the folds of the sail. Suddenly Smaragthi's eyes caught sight of an old dress on the deck. She had been patching it, and a darning needle and thread was sticking in it. She seized the needle and stabbed her assailant with it wherever she could reach him.

The tax collector screamed and fled precipitately. Howling with pain and impeded by the folds of the sail, he tumbled from the gunwale up to his armpits in the water.

By this time the fishermen had heard the fracas. A crowd gathered from boats and coffee-houses to watch the fun. They saw Kokos in his unfortunate plight and cheered him mockingly as he floundered out of the sea and scrambled on to the breakwater. The men on the boats sounded blasts on their conchs until the place was a tumult of laughter, whistling, and jeering.

After Kokos, with difficulty, reached land, he took to his heels to hide in his room and change his clothes. He ran doubled up, moaning with pain and keeping one hand on his hip. His dripping trousers left a trail of water behind him. The fishermen's children pursued him, yelling 'Youha-a!'

Fortis, who was eating his dinner, heard the hubbub and came out of the shop with his mouth full; he saw his lodger running towards him, drenched to the skin, with the crowd booing him. Fortis stood under the mulberry tree with his hands behind his back and shook his head. As Kokos drew near, he pushed back his spectacles and stared at the tax collector. Then he inquired politely: 'You're a bit damp, aren't you, Mr. Achtarides?'

This, however, was not the end of the affair. Shortly after the disturbance had subsided, one of Maria's little girls came to Smaragthi's boat, jumped aboard, and said:

'Mammy says have you got a darning needle to lend her since she wants to sew something and hasn't got one handy?'

She spoke this sentence in one breath exactly as her mother had said it; she had repeated it over and over to herself on the way so she wouldn't forget a single word.

Smaragthi was still recovering from her recent ordeal. Panting for breath, she pulled herself together and set up the fallen awning. When she saw the child, she picked up the fifty-drachma note by one corner and gave it to her.

'Take this money to Uncle Comninos's and give it to that nincompoop who dropped it in the boat.'

The child took the money, but before leaving she reeled off her message once more in the same way, like a record:

'Mammy says have you got a darning needle to lend her since she wants to sew something and hasn't got one handy?'

Folding and unfolding the money, she waited for a reply.

Smaragthi looked at her, disraught, and then shrugged her shoulders.

'The needle?' she said. 'That nincompoop took it with him. Ask him for it.'

The little girl set off for the coffee-house with the money and gave it to Fortis. Again in one breath she recited the revised message:

'Smaragthi says to give this money to that nincompoop who dropped it in the boat and for him to give me the darning needle he took away with him and which my mammy wants because she hasn't got one handy.'

Several customers under the mulberry tree were laughing about the recent affair and waiting for the tax collector to come out of his room to see what kind of face he would put on. Now when they heard what the child said, they understood why Kokos was screaming and held his hand on his hip while he ran. So they began to call out under his window:

'Kokos, the needle! The needle, Kokos!'

The phrase was made a byword and a taunt. The tax collector was tormented by a sustained, uninterrupted outcry whenever he showed himself. It accompanied him on his walks and at his work, it sounded from the Mount, it came from the boats, from the thickets of osiers, from the fig tree and the hedges. It was flung at him like a stone at the most unexpected times when he thought himself quite alone. The transient fishermen heard the story and bedevilled him from their motor-boats. The Mouriotes also learned of it when they came down to the harbour on business. Even the women of the fishing village joined in. It became intolerable. At last, in desperation, he packed up and fled one morning.

But as the motor-boat rounded Cape Korakas and he believed that at last he had put his cursed tormenters behind him, suddenly from far off, above the tall cliffs of the empty shore, again was heard the merciless jibe:

'Kokos, the needle!'

It came in unison from four boys at his final farewell from Skala.

Smaragthi's handling of the affair won her the admiration of the fishermen. This girl of the fishing village had given that foreign cockscomb to understand what stuff she was made of. They looked upon her with increased respect. She had the heart of a *pallikari*. She was no weakling!

44

T H E night was calm and heavy with heat. Many of the men were sleeping on the terraces or half naked on the boats. The moon, above the motionless water, played with the shadows of the cables.. The crickets in the crannies fretted the silence with their chirping and the flowering jujube trees drenched the air with their oppresive fragrance, sticky and sweet, so tyhat one could even taste it.

Stratos crept stealthily from the shadows of the breakwater. He looked around cautiously to make sure that no one saw him. Then he drew the rope of Smaragthi's boat and leaped soundlessly aboard. Preserving the same caution, he untied the mooring, hoisted the anchor, and slipped the oars into their locks. Quietly and slowly he rowed out of the harbour into the open sea. He was wearing only his breeches, and his body gleamed in the moonlight. When he was far enough out, he stopped, removed the oard, and laid them on the deck. For a while he remained motionless. Then he knelt down, drew out an axe he had stuck in his leather belt, and raised it to strike the bottom of the boat.

Suddenly someone sprang from the cabin and grasped his arm.

'Don't,' he implored from behind.

The boy let the axe drop in fright. He turned and recognized Vatis.

'You!' he said and his voice trembled with anger and frustration.

'Don't do it, my brother!' Vatis pleaded. 'What you have in your mind is wicked. Wicked and unjust!'

Stratos's anger drained away. He sank to the floor in grief, his eyes flooded with tears.

'You have no pity for our Manolis,' he said. 'You don't know what misery is devouring him. Tonight he's drinking at the Gadjales's again and where he'll wind up in the state of mind he's in. . . ?'

'I know,' said Vatis calmly. 'I know. But how is the boat to blame and how is our Smaragthi to blame? Do you think it's because she's conceited over her boat that she doesn't accept him? Nonsense! She doesn't want anybody. She won't have any man. Never in her life.'

'Who says so?'

'She did, my brother.'

'Has she talked to you about our Manolis?' Stratos asked in astonishment.

'We've talked together about it. She gave me her oath and kissed the cross. She won't marry anyone. Not our Manolis or anyone.'

'How is that possible?' said Stratos.

Vatis shrugged his shoulders.

'It's true just the same. It's . . . her nature.'

Stratos stared at him and tried to understand.

'Her nature!' he said, as if he had been enlightened by this absurd explanation. He sighed deeply.

'It will be the death of our Manolis,' he said and bit his lips to keep from weeping.

'He won't die. Our Manolis is a *pallikari* and he'll get over his sorrow in time. Don't fear for our Manolis. He's a man, not a cry-baby.'

With these words he put the oars back in the locks and they rowed towards the harbour. Then it occurred to Stratos to ask his brother how he happened to be in the boat at such an hour.

Vatis explained that he'd had him under observation since the day he heard him tell their mother that it was Smaragthi's boat kept her from accepting his older brother. It wasn't the first time Vatis had hidden in the cabin to forestall some mischance, and that very day he had seen Stratos take the axe from the cellar and later conceal it under a pile of dirty clothes.

They returned home together. As they walked slowly, Vatis tried to explain to his brother his views on the strange destiny of girls who are born of mermaids and cannot mate with any man. He told him all the lore on the subject that he had been told by their grandmother.

Stratos was not one to take such fairy tales seriously. But everything around them was transfigured under the enormous moon which spread over all objects and figures the vagueness of a dream and made the wildest visions and thoughts appear as realities.

They found Manolis sitting on the ground in front of the house, humming a song. He looked at the twins under his heavy eyelids. His eyes were bleary from drink and his face had an ugly grimace in the moonlight. Stratos gripped Vatis's arm in anguish.

45

T H E strained relations between the two coffee-houses continued. With the coming of winter and the resumption of work at the olive press, the villagers descended on Fortis in crowds, both landholders and workers. The harvest was bountiful and people were in high spirits because their security for the coming year was assured and their indebtedness to the banks would be eased. Not for years had Fortis been so busy.

The big stone provided comfortable warmth in the shop. There was the aroma of camomile tea, the tang of betony, and the fragrance of good tobacco. Lambis was in a thousand places at once, waiting on the customers. Everybody congratulated Fortis because God had given him such a capable helper in his old age. Fortis listened to them and said: 'Bah! the rascal!' But he smiled behind his white moustache and glanced proudly at the boy as he hustled among the tables like a grown man.

The Gadjales alone gave him no peace. One day they sent him another message:

'Keep your son away from the courtyards of the fishing village or we'll attend to him ourselves in our own way.'

They sent the message by a drunken muleteer. The sot came to the coffee-house at a time when it was full of customers, and the message was heard by all. Conversation stopped, and the men turned and stared at the boy and then put their heads together and spoke in an undertone.

Fortis was furious with chagrin and vented his rage in an ill-considered reply:

'Go back to that riffraff,' he said to the drunkard, 'and tell them that one who has a garden keeps watch over it!'

He regretted his words as soon as he spoke them. It was not his nature to speak without thinking. He was angry with himself for letting his temper get the better of him.

He was sullen all evening, seething over the unfortunate incident. Later, at night, when he was alone with his son, he said to him irritably:

'Listen to me. I'll not stand for your passing their house again or so much as looking at it. What are you? A hoodlum like them?'

Lambis replied: 'It's a lie. I've never looked at their house!'

Fortis, more and more furious, shouted:

'Truth or not, I tell you this and you write it well in your mind. I didn't father a son to make me ridiculous in front of respectable people!'

Lambis looked at him with flaming eyes. His lips trembled, but he said nothing. He merely shook his head. This enraged Fortis still more. He gave the boy his ultimatum:

'From today on you will not go through the fishing village. Do you hear? And don't shake your head at me!'

Lambis looked him straight in the eye.

'I have to go through it,' he said, 'and I will.'

Fortis lost his self-control. He raised is hand and struck the boy on the face.

The tray fell from Lambis's hand and his teeth were bloody from a cut on his lips made by his father's ring. At first he was stupefied. He did not cry out or say a word. He merely spat blood on the floor. Then he laid his waiter's napkin on a marble table, opened the door, and disappeared into the night.

He did not return. One night, two nights, three nights passed; and still he did not return. He wandered about the olive groves and slept in cabins; but he did not go up to the village, nor did he appear in Skala. Then one day he presented himself at the factory. He went to Uncle Yoryis's workshop and asked him for work.

The machinist saw that he was determined and took him on. Uncle Yoryis was a good, hard-working man who had spent his life round this machinery. He had become its soul, the demon that moved its belts and wheels. All day he and his helper worked, making repairs at the forge and the anvil. At night he laid aside his hammer and tongs and drank his glass of raki. He had no child of his own, but he understood young people.

'Since the lad's mind is made up,' he said to Fortis, 'let him stay with me, things being what they are. He's a strong, ambitious *pallikari*. His mind is sharp and his hands learn quickly. Let him learn the trade from me and be grateful to me some day. Every misfortune brings some good.'

'Very well,' said Fortis, who was contrite and ready to make amends. 'But he must come and sleep in his own bed. It's a disgrace to me for my only son to live away from my house. Everybody is gossiping about it and the Gadjalis family is overjoyed. . . .'

Lambis agreed to sleep at home, but he could not yet bring himself to meet his father. With a heavy heart Fortis listened to him come home late at night and leave at daybreak with the first blast of the factory whistle. Every night he lay awake in bed to hear the grating of the door, then the footsteps carefully ascending the creaking stairs, and finally the springs of the bed as he sat down on it. He heard him take off one shoe and then the other. Then the light under the door disappeared and he knew that the lamp had been put out. With a sigh he surrendered himself to sleep.

'I've got myself a son with no sense of honour,' he grumbled fretfully.

Uncle Yoryis, who understood Lambis much better, said to Fortis one night while he was sipping his glass:

'It's not as you think. It's just because of his great sense of honour that he still can't look you in the eye. If he had no self-respect, he wouldn't act as he does. Let things ripen. He'll get his balance in time. The lad is suffering from too much pride. I watch him and study him while he works.'

'Then I'm the one who's to blame?' asked Fortis, who deep in his heart was convinced he was very much at fault.

Uncle Yoryis, perhaps because he was hard of hearing, perhaps because he wished to avoid replying, said with a conciliatory gesture:

'He's young and hot-blooded. That's his only fault.'

That was the truth.

Lambis became taciturn and scowled when anyone began to talk to him about the matter. He broke with his companions and shut himself up in the melancholy of fierce, voluntary isolation. A host of obstinacies, grudges, and shames wrestled inside him and there was no one to help him. He threw himself headlong into his work so that by sheer physical exhaustion he might subdue the turbulence in his soul.

The machinist observed with concern how he drove himself beyond the strength of his years.

'That's enough,' he would say. 'There's still tomorrow.'

Lambis would smile and wipe the sweat from his grimy face with his apron.

'Let's finish this bit, master,' he would say. 'There'll be other things to do tomorrow.'

Time and again Fortis felt swept by a strange tenderness for this untamed creature. Frequently he had the impulse to get out of bed, go to his son's room, throw his arms around him, and kiss him and kiss him . . . a thing he had never been able to do when the boy was a small, motherless child.

But he thought better of it end devised another way of expressing his affection. In the evening he would leave a glass pitcher of warm milk with a clean napkin and a tumbler at Lambis's bedside.

At first the boy left the milk untouched. Fortis would go to his room as soon as he left and when he saw the milk, his heart tightened. But each night the pitcher of fresh milk was in its place. One morning Fortis found it empty. And again the next day. And then every day. The old man smiled and his eyes filled with tears.

'Rascal,' he said. 'Shameless rogue!' He laid a piece of scented soap beside the clean towel.

He found a new, peculiar kind of happiness in his grief. In the morning he would watch the boy as he left for work. He concealed himself, like a lover, behind the partly opened casement window, so that Lambis would not catch sight of him.

One day he saw the lad pause outside the door. There on a high bracket was a whitewashed flower-pot with basil in it. Lambis thrust his face into the fragrant plant and inhaled its pleasant odour. Then he broke off a sprig and took it with him.

The same day, Fortis removed the flower-pot and put it in the boy's room by his window.

Thus every day he tried to think up some new token of affection, some new service, that would bring his unseen presence closer to the boy's wounded heart.

46

O N E night in the dead of winter a wild gale was rattling the windows and whining among the ships' cables without abatement. In the midst of this icy tempest was heard an outburst of screams and curses. Immediately the fishing village resounded with the uproar, which had started outside the Gadjalis house. It was very late and the coffee-houses had closed for the night.

Through the thick darkness came the shrieks of women. The disturbance grew louder near the fig tree. Then torches were lighted, revealing faces distorted with fury. The whole Gadjalis family, men and women, were throwing stones and cursing.

A shrill female voice yelled:

'The scoundrel jumped over here. . . . Head him off!'

Lighted lamps moved behind the window panes in neighbouring houses and illuminated frightened, anxious faces that were trying to see what was going on outside. But their eyes were blinded by the light and they could see nothing.

Smaragthi was undressing for bed when she heard the rumpus under her window. She slipped on a dress and opened the window. The uproar was on the other side of the fig tree which stood between her courtyard and that of the Gadjales. She recognized the voice of the oldest son, who was keeping up a continuous stream of obscenities. In the light from the torches she saw the old man and the mother and daughter. The man was holding a torch in the air and the old woman was waving a ship's lantern and screaming:

'The rascal is hiding over here! In the hen coop! Inside the coop! Pound it!'

All the Gadjales ran to the empty hen coop and began to whack it with boat hooks and broken oars.

'Here he is!' cried the old man. He had felt his club strike something soft.

'Oh!' came a muffled cry from within. 'Oh!'

There were stifled groans but no words.

The men dragged out the person who had taken refuge in the coop. They lowered their torches and under the flickering light they recognized Lambis. They pulled him over the ground, scratched muddy, with blood and filth on his face and hands. They shoved him under the light, spat in his face, and clouted him. Even Yana threw herself at him like an infuriated wildcat and clawed his face with her nails. Both mother and daughter tore out bunches of his hair, shrieked like maniacs and shook their fists contemptuously in his face.

The neighbours, after the first alarm had passed, saw that trouble was brewing. They knew the Gadjales. So they put out their lamps and watched the fracas unseen. This way they would not become involved as witnesses in the event of a lawsuit.

But from Lathios's house came the old man, Manolis and Vatis with lighted torches. Smaragthi took courage when she saw them and came along too.

She saw Lambis on his knees in the mud while they were kicking him, tearing his hair and clubbing him on the back; she could hear the dull thwacks on his flesh. She saw him, alone against so many, fighting back with tooth and nail, so young and so cruelly beaten. She heard the muffled groans he uttered to keep from weeping, and her heart was sick.

'You're going to kill him!' she cried desperately and approached the men to intervene.

Lambis heard her voice and lifted his eyes to her face which was illuminated by the torches. Then he gave a lugubrious cry like that of a wild animal in distress. Reeling like a drunkard, he picked himself up, sprang with lowered head and vanished into the darkness.

'We caught him up in the tree watching our daughter undress!' explained Gadjalis, panting and foaming at the outrage. 'It isn't once or twice he's done it. The hoodlum comes every night and peeps.'

That night Fortis waited in vain to hear the boy's footsteps. He heard nothing, but the blustering wind wailing through the boughs of the mulberry tree. While he waited, he fell into a light sleep. Suddenly from the street below he heard a savage, derisive voice:

'Eh, Uncle Fortis! We set a watch in our garden as you advised us to do!'

Startled, Fortis opened his eyes. 'I seem to have gone to sleep,' he thought. He listened but he heard nothing more. The gale subsided a bit. 'Someone was calling under my window, or maybe I heard it in my sleep,' he said to himself.

He tried to ease his restlessness. 'You see?' he said. 'I fell asleep and didn't hear the boy pass my door.'

He closed his eyes to prove that was how it was and that nothing unusual had happened, but still he was unconvinced. 'Is the boy in bed now?' he kept asking. At last he got up, lighted a candle from the vigil lamp in front of the icon and went softly to Lambis' bedroom.

It was quiet inside, the stillness that results only from the total absence of an occupant. Again he said: 'Now I'll just push the door open and I'll find him asleep in bed. Maybe he'll be startled and will open his eyes. The rascal will catch me red-handed! Let him!' He pushed the door open and went in.

The room was empty; the milk pitcher was full and the bed undisturbed. Dawn was breaking outside the window. The movements of men and animals sounded far and near in the streets.

'It's daybreak already,' he said numbly.

He went down to the shop and lighted a fire under the tea kettle. Soon afterwards he heard the deep voice of the factory whistle. Clear and strong it rose in the darkness that was still resisting the soft light of dawn. It spread over all the sounds of awakening life and echoed on the Mount like a wave breaking and receding. Then it drifted up through the mountain defiles to the village to arouse the householders, the muleteers, and the olive workers. It blew again and a third time, prolonged and final. Gradually it died away into silence as if after making a flight it had come to rest its broad wings on its perch.

The voice of the factory seemed to Fortis to bring a doleful message. It always seemed mournful to him, but today it sounded especially heart-rending and hopeless.

The jeering cry he had heard in his deep kept recurring: 'Uncle Fortis . . . we set a watch in our garden as you advised us to do . . . Uncle Fortis!'

'He must have slept at Yoryis's workshop,' he concluded. 'The rogue!'

Fortis went to the workshop. The machinist had just got up.

'My son?' Fortis asked.

Yoryis, although he pretended to hear well, had not heard a thing of the previous night's disturbance.

'It's still early,' he said. 'Don't look at it as we old ones do. We don't need much sleep.'

After leaving the workshop, Fortis met Lathios. They went to the coffee-house, where the fishermen told what had happened during the night. Fortis mentioned the early morning messenger. It must have been one of the Gadjales on his way to Ammouthelli.

Fortis felt shame pouring over him like filth. This was intolerable, that in his old age he should become the laughing-stock of everybody, particularly of a tribe of riffraff. He who had lived abroad, who for so many years had seen all the nations of the earth, and to whom nobody, no, not anybody, could say: 'Get out of my way!' So he would wait for his son to return and then he would straighten him out, once and for all, so that he would not forget it, the shameless clown!

47

T H R E E days passed and Lambis had not appeared at the machinist's shop or at his father's house. No one came to Fortis to say: 'We saw him here, we heard of him there.' Fortis inquired everywhere. No one had anything to tell him.

'He's ashamed of his beating,' said Yoryis by way of comfort. 'He's hiding somewhere. He may even have gone to Hora. Let's wait and see.'

They waited. Days and nights passed. Nothing happened.

One morning Fortis arose very early and went to Lathios's house. It was an ugly, sullen day with a sharp north wind which ripped the leaves off the trees and drove the sea thundering against the cliffs. The waves drenched the street along the shore and fell in dark masses that threatened momentarily to invade the houses.

He found the fisherman huddled on the divan beside the hearth. The wind howled in the chimney. The thunder of the sea, even in here, depressed the mind with sombre incessant rhythm. The women and boys were away at work, some at the olive harvest and some at the factory. Lathios told one of his granddaughters to make coffee for Fortis. He indicated a cushion. Fortis sat down, clasped his knees and stared dejectedly at the flames dancing on the burning chunks in the fireplace.

'Well?' the fishermen asked laconically when he saw that his visitor was not disposed to speak. 'Nothing about the lad?'

Fortis shook his head gloomily.

'Nothing,' he said. 'Except . . . a nightmare that I had last night.'

'Too bad my mother-in-law isn't alive,' said Lathios jokingly. 'She'd explain it to you in no time.'

Fortis continued in a weak, troubled voice, as if he had not heard, staring all the while at the fire from under his spectacles.

'Last night, just like every night, I lay tossing in bed. I was waiting for his footsteps. I stayed awake until cockcrow. Then I fell asleep in spite of myself and had this dream. The lad came into my room. His teeth were bloody, as they were the night I struck him. He stood in front of me with his hands behind his back, as he always does. His head was bent as if he were ashamed. His eyelids were lowered and his eyes were fixed on the floor. His bloody mouth was smiling as it is when he's worried about something. "Eh," I said to him. "What do you want standing there in front of me like a church candlestick? Do you want me to admire your handsome figure?" He heard me and lifted his glance from the floor. He was smiling all the while, and I saw where my ring had cut his upper lip. I saw his lowered eyelids and his twitching eyebrows. Then he spoke and said: "Father, don't you know why I've come?" "What do you want?" I asked him. "My eyes," he replied. "I've come for you to give me my eyes." "Your eyes?" I said. I was about to say, "Come, my son, have you completely lost your mind?" But before I could get the words out, he raised his eyelids. And the sockets were empty. Two gaps. Two hollow holes... But I felt that, even so, he could see me. He looked as if it amused him to frighten me, and all the while his bloody mouth kept smiling. My hair stood on end. I cried out in my sleep and woke up in a cold sweat.... Well, that's the story....'

He broke off, bit his moustache, and coughed to stifle a sob that rose in his throat. Two large teardrops trickled down from under his spectacles. He let them run over his moustache and drop on his overcoat without wiping them away.

The little girl, who was kneeling at the hearth preparing the coffee, looked at him curiously. She placed the little earthen cup before him on a small tray and withdrew noiselessly. Again nothing was heard but the thunder of the sea.

'Come, forget it,' said Lathios calmly.

He raised himself on his elbow and stirred a chunk with the poker to make it blaze up.

' "Dream and bubbles," as the saying goes. Now drink your coffee....'

Fortis reached over and tapped Lathios on the knee.

'My friend,' he said, 'I'm being consumed with a burning agony. My mind suggests fearful things to me... frightful things. I've come to you for help.... Take your boat and let's go out... and search....'

The fisherman looked at him in alarm.

'Hey!' he said. 'What's on you're mind! Ts! Ts!'

Fortis nodded affirmatively and continued: 'The other time he stayed away from home only a few nights. This is another matter! Something inside me says that the murderers have drowned the lad. It was saying this to me all night and I pretended not to hear it. How do you think such an evil thought got into my mind? Anyhow, I'm being eaten up with anguish. We've got to go and see.'

They tried that day but without success. The sea was as purple as wine lees and was rolling so high that no boat dared to go out. Nevertheless, they rowed to the end of the harbour and got themselves thoroughly drenched as they fought against the waves. But the water was too murky to see through and they were unable to hold the glass in the boiling surf.

Next day the weather was somewhat calmer, but the sky was so overcast that nothing could be seen on the bottom. They rowed about for a long time in vain. Everybody watched the two old men probing the storm-tossed waters. They said nothing, but they all suspected the truth and were excited.

On the third day, when the storm had subsided, other fishermen joined in the search, even Smaragthi. They poured oil here and there to settle the turbulent water.

It was the rainy season. A mist of fine, chill drops was falling. All was gloom in Skala. It spread to the village of Mouria, where there was whispering everywhere, in the coffee-houses, among the olive harvesters, in the fields, and in the shops. What was the news of Lambis, Fortis's son? What was being said in Skala? They watched the boats propelled by oars and poles, move slowly from place to place along the shore. 'They're looking for the lad,' the word went around. 'The Gadjales killed him.'

Finally one day the sky cleared, the wind fell, and the water recovered its transparency. The bottom could be seen as clearly as if it were summer. Lathios was at the oars of his boat while Manolis leaned over the gunwale working the glass. The twins were rowing Smaragthi's boat as she also searched the depths. All at once, behind the Mount of the Madonna where the water was very deep and the bottom was dark brown with seaweed, Manolis raised his arm.

'Stop!' he called without removing his hand from the frame of the glass. The old man braked with his oars and the boat came to a halt.

The same thing had happened many times when Manolis saw a shadow on the bottom, so Lathios attached no special meaning to the order as he held the boat steady. The young man took another careful look and then drew his head from the glass. His face was pale and his eyes were haggard.

'Here he is, Father! He's jammed to the bottom!'

'What's that?'

The old man seized the glass and leaned over to look. When he straightened up, his eyes were appalled at what he had seen. He crossed himself.

'Yes, by God!'

He took the conch and blew a signal to Smaragthi's boat. The girl came quickly alongside.

The other boats also heard the signal and collected near the cliffs. Through their glasses the fishermen could make out the corpse, white against the shadow of the Mount of the Madonna.

It slanted head down, as if it had taken a dive and had been caught in the rocks. Hooks were tied to ropes but it was impossible to raise the body. It waved its arms as if it were trying to free itself, but just as it seemed about to come loose, it would slip back, hesitate and then resume its slanting position.

'Something's holding him to the bottom,' said Lathios. 'There's a weight tied to him. It isn't a rock.'

Then Thymios, who was in one of the boats, stripped to his underdrawers. He told them to lower a rope with a noose at the end, over the corpse. When this was done, he crossed himself and dived head first. The others held their breath with beating hearts. Leaning over, they followed with their glasses the boy's efforts under the water. They saw the rope tighten.

Thymios was greenish-yellow when he surfaced. He caught hold of a boat and reported gasping, his large teeth chattering.

'There's a piece of iron tied to his neck,' he said. 'A small anchor.... I passed the noose around its points. Pull...and it will come up....'

'Go ahead!' ordered Lathios.

In the harbour a raft made of six pieces of poplar wood nailed to some timbers was weathering. It was used for hauling stones and wood and in summer the children rode out on it when they went swimming. The customs inspector, as the only official in the place, ordered it to be brought and the corpse laid on it as soon as it was raised. No one was to disturb it until he could telephone the authorities to come and make an inspection.

The body was raised. Lambis was fully clothed and around his neck was a red handkerchief. Smaragthi's knees grew weak and she bit her lips when she saw it. It was the same one she had used to bandage his bleeding arm that moonlight night. They laid the body on the raft, which was secured with two anchors so that it would not drift away. The rope was left around Lambis's neck and the small anchor was placed beside his head.

The body was not much damaged, but on the right cheek was a dark bruise, starting from the eyebrow and running down to the chin. One shoe was missing. As they were laying him on the raft with his face up, Lathios, who was helping arrange the arms and legs, noticed that the eye sockets were empty. Fish had eaten the eyeballs. The fisherman remembered Fortis's dream and shuddered.

The sea was rising and falling without waves. The raft rocked like a large cradle. A crowd from the fishing village and from Mouria had gathered on the Mount to stare at Lambis as he lay stretched out on his back, his hair wet by the sea, his vacant eye sockets turned to the cloudy sky.

Fortis was sitting in the coffee-house resting from his work. When the news came that his son had been found, he wiped the steam from the window pane and watched the boats returning to the harbour. 'Eh? Is that so?' he said, as if he was unable to grasp what he had waited so long to hear. He tried to stand up, but his legs were too weak to support him and he collapsed on the chair. He seemed to have lost his ability to understand. He could not weep while they were talking to him. He merely removed his spectacles so that he might see more clearly, but his sight was as blurred as ever. Then he saw Lathios approaching.

'You see?' Fortis said to him. 'I knew it. They've killed him ' He rubbed his hands together as if to dust them off. Then he added:

'So now it's all over, eh?' He stared at Lathios, waiting for an answer.

A crowd had gathered at the door. Fortis turned and looked at them. He cleared his throat and said tonelessly to Lathios:

'He came in the night and asked me for his eyes.'

With those words he broke down and wept, the tears running down his face in streams. Then he threw his grey head on the table and sobbed for hours.

48

TOWARDS dusk, Lathios took his wife and Smaragthi and went in his boat to place a vigil light by the corpse. The customs officer also went along to see that no one tampered with the body. At the last moment Vatis jumped into the boat. They set a ship's lantern beside the head of the dead youth and lashed it stoutly with wire so that the waves would not upset it. The women bound the lad's hands with a strip of calico and between them they placed a small iron of the Madonna.

When they had finished and were returning in the boat, Lathios' wife began a slow, drawn-out lament. Vatis looked over the gunwale and wept and gazed at the glimmer of the lamp as it fell on the boy's hair.

Smaragthi was unable to weep, but she felt an inner disquiet that was .heightened by the soft keening of Lathios's wife. She was impatient to get ashore so that she would hear it no more. Before her eyes constantly hovered the vision of the red handkerchief with white dots that was knotted around Lambis's neck.

At home she sat at her window for a long time gazing at the vigil light. She had wrapped herself in a thick woollen shawl, and she remained behind the closed window until daybreak, watching the little lamp rise and fall in the tranquil sea. She felt she could not leave the dead youth forsaken without a living soul nearby to watch over him.

During the night a fine, cold rain set in, and it continued next day. About noon, two police officers and a doctor in grey raincoats and leather gloves arrived and went out to the raft to make the necessary medical report.

They concluded that death had come from drowning, but Fortis passionately maintained no, that the Gadjales had killed the boy and thrown him into the sea to mislead investigation and escape punishment. Hadn't they seen the bruises on his face and body? Moreover, they had found no water in his lungs. How could this be if the lad had fallen alive into the sea?

The little doctor listened patiently, smoked expensive cigarettes, and quietly explained that the absence of water in the lungs could be accounted for: the anchor rope had strangled him before the sea could drown him. One must take into consideration that the skin around the throat showed a dark abrasion from the stricture of the rope.

The old man refused to listen and the case dragged on through the courts. The principals spent half the winter going back and forth between the harbour and Hora. Witnesses had to be transported, and the laywers reaped a fortune. The village and Skala were divided into two factions, one saving this and the other that.

Fortis suddenly aged ten years. He became stooped and went about glum and unshaven. His bald spot was paler than ever and his scalp looked like oilskin. When he served coffee, his fingers shook.

The Gadjales finally were acquitted of murder. They were convicted of molesting the boy and were sentenced to a few days in jail. They returned to Skala more arrogant and odious than ever. Fortis appealed against the verdict, and the case went to the court in Syra. Again there were expensive, fatiguing, time-consuming voyages from Skala to Hora, Hora by steamship to Piraeus, from there by another ship to Syra, and back. All this was an inconvenience to the subpoenaed witnesses and a burden on the principals, who had to pay for it.

Early one morning Yana passed Fortis's house and sang a jeering song. Fortis flew into a rage. He went to the door and accused her of being vulgar and wanton. A crowd gathered to watch and listen. Green with fury, Fortis screamed that he would pluck her head a hair at a time if she dared to come there again.

For this the Gadjales brought an action against Fortis and haled him once more to Hora. He was sentenced to ten days in jail. When he heard the sentence, he was dumbfounded, but the judge told him not to worry. He could pay a fine and costs and go home. Unfortunately Fortis had no ready money with him. He gave the judge a note to a friend through his lawyer, asking him to lend him the amount. In the meantime, the police took him to the prison while the formalities were being completed and a writ executed. There he was not confined but was allowed to walk about the coutyard within the huge fortress until he was informed that he was free to return home.

49

S P R I N G comes to the Aegean shores by way of the sea. One morning the sky seems more blue and the waves lap the sand with a brisker rhythm. The sea smells fresh, and everywhere its surface is flecked with fleeting glints. Silver circles, iridescent as peacocks' breasts, open out on the shimmering water, numberless, one inside the other, each pursuing the other clear to the horizon. Out of the heart of this unfolding sea blossom steps the Aegean spring, like Aphrodite. On all sides there is a fluttering of white and blue wings. The air is festive, as well as the earth, the fleecy clouds, and the silken sky. The ships in the harbour all hoist their sails to dry them, and this is itself is a sight to behold. In the shallows, long, slender stalks of marine plants attached to hairy stones way with the waves. Indolently they put forth soft, pearly filaments from which hang skeins of tiny fruit the colour of unripe cherries.

Wherever you look, nature celebrates renewed youth immersed once more in the eternal joy of God.

When spring comes out of the Aegean, she steps ashore and advances leisurely up the slopes to the villages and gardens. From her dainty ears hang cherry-bud ear-rings. In the wake of her moist feet throng gorgeous insects and young lambs with their new red bells. From the sunny cloud of her hair swarm myriads of small butterflies. In her closed hands she tenderly guards a swallow's nest. She visits the vineyards, the olive groves, and the fields. She enters the cemeteries, spreading flaming poppies over the bleak graves and entwining the weathered crosses with blue trumpet flowers.

If early in the morning you walk on the beach of Kaya, you will see on the sand close to the water's edge small imprints made by the naked feet of spring—dainty, slender footprints like the bone of a cuttlefish. The tide fills these little hollows with water and when you bend over them, you see the sky looking up at you with its blue eyes.

Men and beasts inhale the intoxicating air, which is tangy with camomile and pennyroyal. Their hearts are filled with a gentle restlessness. The women sigh and gaze far out to sea, some because they are no longer young and others because they still are.

The harbour of Panayia is loud with a gay bustling. Lined up at a double cables, the men pull caïques into the water. Boats are being caulked and repaired. There is the smell of fresh paint and boiling tar, to which the sea adds an acrid fragrance.

The fishermen's wives take boats and go to gather branches. They load the boats to the gunwales with wild holly and thorn bushes for the oven and tender shoots for the goats. From the crevices on the cliffs hang thick clumps of broom with golden blossoms. The sea is like a blue flower-bowl filled with broken twigs and leaves.

And with the first pleasant days, boats from other ports begin to appear in the harbour.

One morning Smaragthi found a pair of sponge-fishing boats tied up next to her mooring bitt. Massive and sturdily built, they looked even less attractive as compared with the elegant lines and bright colours of the *Nerandji*. Their dull grey was almost funereal. They were broad in the beam to make room for the air pumps and winches. Their decks were irremediably stained with the foul slime of fresh sponges. Some of the crew were oiling the two engines, and some were squeezing sponges on the wide deck. The milky fluid dripped from the scuppers and polluted the harbour water.

The girl and two of Maria's moppets leaped into the boat and wrinkled their noses with distaste. The crew dropped their work and stared at Smaragthi.

One of the men was short, middle-aged, and as muscular as a wrestler. His grey hair curled close to his round head. His moustache was white but his eyes were dark and kindly. Serenely he measured Smaragthi from head to foot as if he were looking at a child. The girl returned his gaze frankly. Then the man smiled broadly and revealed two rows of even, white teeth.

'Are you Smaragthi, the fisher lass?' he asked with his hands in his belt.

'I am,' replied the girl. 'And who are you?'

'My lads and I are from Kalymnos. Trampados is my name. Uncle Trampados. You will call me that, too, since we're going to be neighbours. These are my machines and we're fishing in your waters for the first time.'

His voice was steady and gentle and Smaragthi immediately felt at ease with him. She smiled.

'Welcome,' she said, 'and good fishing. Only I don't think you'll find anything around here.'

'Of course I will,' said the captain. 'We already have. I've made a note of two bars where there are no net fishermen. Today we'll see....'

Smaragthi liked this old man with his firm jaw and bronzed skin.

'I have a daughter like you,' he said. 'She's beautiful, too, only she's dark. Her name is Angela, good luck to her. And I have a son. They are as like as twins.'

Smaragthi's eyes searched among the men of the crew. The captain answered her glance.

'Achilles isn't here. He went up to the village to buy something. He's a citified sponge fisher.'

The girl laughed with him.

'A citified sponge fisher?'

'Absolutely! As educated as a schoolmaster. But don't get the idea that book learning has turned his head. On the job he's like the rest of us, even better. You'll see when you come to know him.'

Smaragthi came to know him in an unexpected way.

She had gone out alone to fish for octopus between the cliffs of Vigla. They come to feed there in the shallows, attracted by the oil that the wind drives in from the presses. Great rocks jut out of the sea and form hiding places and passages like canals.

As she tried certainly to identify a tentacle waving among the rocks, she saw a great shadow emerge and she started back in alarm. The shadow advanced and stopped under her keel, four or five fathoms below. Then she saw it was a man in a diving suit. His arms and legs moved weightlessly with slow, fluid undulations. As he stepped from stone to stone, he seemed like a strange, unsubstantial dancer executing incredibly graceful leaps. His bluish shadow followed him, curving over the bright rocks and stretching out over the sandy flats. From under the boat he stared up at Smaragthi through the window of his iron helmet, meeting the girl's green eyes, which were filled with amazement and consternation. Then Smaragthi noticed that he was laughing. He leaned back against a rock, pushed aside the air hose, crossed his legs and devoted himself to smiling and making funny, friendly faces. His teeth and eyes were like those of Uncle Trampados. She was fascinated as he sat so oddly on the floor of the sea, and was unable to take her head from the glass. Then he saluted her with a sinuous gesture, pretending to remove his helmet like a hat, and bowed to her with his hand on his chest. He laughed boyishly behind his window. This caused a silver bubble to explode under her glass and she saw his form distorted and broken into thousands of greenish-yellow globules. She straightened up, put aside the glass, and rowed back to the harbour. As she emerged from the labyrinth of rocks, she saw one of the sponge boats lying a little farther off.

The man at the air pump was turning the wheel. A few of the crewmen were attending to the engine or sorting and handling some blackish sponges. The girl passed close by and greeted them gaily.

'Good luck to you!'

'And to you!' they replied in unison without interrupting their work.

Smaragthi felt someone looking at her. Lifting her head, sne saw Stratos on the top of a cliff.

'Hi!' she called to him in a loud, friendly voice. He did not reply but merely nodded sourly.

The day was like wine. Yellow blossoms covered the shore and the stones glowed red, green, and gold like lighted Chinese lanterns. When Smaragthi rounded Vigla, the Mount of the Madonna suddenly appeared, rosy against the blue, water.

A song came to her mind. She hummed it softly to the languid rhythm of the oars. She had not sung for a long, long time. It was the silver music of youth which she heard within herself.

50

I N the evening Smaragthi went to see Fortis at the Mulberry Tree. Since his tragic misfortune, she often visited him and tried in as many ways as she knew to bolster his morale, which was very low, and to distract his mind from its obsession for justice, which now was his sole purpose in life and was slowly eating up all his resources. Already he had sold his best olive plantation and the money from that had evaporated in a few months in travel expenses and lawyers' fees. The legal actions against the Gadjales were not yet ended; and his desk drawers were full of documents, transcripts and receipts on coloured papers covered with stamps. He sorted out the papers, filed them in green folders, and studied them at night by lamp-light, pawing them over and writing letters about them.

One day Smaragthi had succeeded in taking him with her in her boat to divert him. She entertained him as she would a child.

'Look through the glass, Godfather. It's a wonderful view!'

She handed him the glass and Fortis leaned over the gunwale and looked at the floor of the sea. She thought he was watching her play an octopus, as she sought to lure it from its lair with a bit of white cloth which she dangled in front of it on the point of her spear. Then she noticed that his shoulders were shaking.

She bent over him and saw that he was silently weeping into the sea. She realized how thoughtless it had been of her to make him look down there. She did not take him with her again.

When Smaragthi arrived at the coffee-house that evening, the great ceiling-lamp was lit. Along one whole side at three joined tables were sitting the sponge fishing crew, drinking and nibbling snacks of fried sardines.

The girl bade them good evening and they returned the greeting cordially. She did not see Uncle Trampados among them, but she did pick out Achilles, whom she recognized at once from his lean, tanned face with the handsome dark eyes. They tended to slant towards his ears and thus possessed an ironical quality. His mouth was bright red and his teeth flashed merrily, as they had behind the window of the diving helmet. In a corner on the other side of the room she saw Stratos observing her. The lad's face was glowering, almost hostile.

Smaragthi went directly to the counter behind which Fortis was sitting, aloof from the company, hunched up in his chair smoking his *nargileh*. She drew up a chair beside him and they talked together isolated from the noise.

'Wait for me tonight at home,' Fortis said to her when she was about to say good night. 'I've got something to say to you.'

He accompanied Smaragthi to the door and watched her slim figure fade into the darkness. He was aware that every eye had followed her. The eyes of Achilles, and the eyes of Stratos.

When Smaragthi had gone, Trampados's son called out to Fortis:

'May you have joy in your goddaughter, Uncle Comninos. She's a ray of sunshine!'

If his father had been present, Achilles would have refrained from speaking thus, but now he gave full expression to his feelings.

Fortis paused, looked at him benevolently, and said:

'She's all sunshine.'

Without saying a word, Stratos arose and left.

Later, when the work of the coffee-house was finished, Fortis locked up and went to the fishing village. Smaragthi was waiting for him. They sat down facing each other.

'You see,' said Fortis, 'once I was a father. Now it's all over. I'm childless. In Mouria I have some cousins. Except for them I have no one else in the world, and they are a tiresome lot, full of envy and spite. They don't care a thing about me. It's as if they didn't exist. Now in my old age, I bow my head and thank God for sending you to me, Smaragthi. I say to myself: What good are you, you burned-out fellow? And I find two things that prevent me from jumping off the cliff. One is the God in whom I believe and whom I honour as an Orthodox Christian. A long time ago, Barba-Lias, the *dedes*, said to us: "Don't get far away from God. One day you'll need his help." The other thing is you, Smaragthi. So I'm comforted and say: You dunce, you're not childless. This girl depends on you as parent and protector. That is why God sent her your way.'

Smaragthi laid her hand affectionately on the old man's bony hand.

'Don't worry, Godfather,' she said.

Fortis was silent for a while. Then he resumed:

'So I used to tell myself sometimes that God sent me to be your spiritual father for your own good. Now I understand more than ever that you are my support, the staff of my disheartened soul. I'm not your support. You don't need one. God has given you good sense and a pure heart. And he has given you strength to ride the tempests of life. That is a great thing, my daughter.'

'It's a matter of luck, Godfather. Does anybody know how things are going to turn out? We just make the best of them. We sail with the wind, Godfather.'

'No,' said Fortis quietly. 'You have defied the weather many times.

You've sailed against the wind and you've come through without losing your course. Only an exceptional person could do it with such gallantry.'

'Oh!'

'Yes, I know what I'm talking about. But this isn't what I wanted to say. For several days I've been thinking about something else.'

He sighed, polished his spectacles with his handkerchief, and carefully replaced them.

'Smaragthi,' he said, 'I've failed a great deal since my misfortune. My faculties are growing weaker day by day. I know it won't be long before I'll be making the climb to the cemetery.'

'Oh, Godfather!'

'Yes, it's true, and you ought to know it. I don't want to leave you until I've got you settled. I must render an accounting to God, I who held you over the baptismal font in His great name.'

Smaragthi started to speak.

'Let me finish. I know that Manolis wants you. He's the worthiest, the most praiseworthy in Skala. Marry him, Smaragthi. You'll be happy with him. You have the *Nerandji*. You have your house. And I have a few things to add to them. The coffee-house, some small pieces of land and various other things. The last time I went to Hora I went to the notary and recorded them for you in a will. All that is left after my death will be yours. There, that's what I wanted to tell you. . . Now you. . . .'

Smaragthi took his shaking hand and kissed it. Her hot tears ran over his dry fingers. Fortis laid his other hand on her cool hair as if he were blessing her youthful head.

'Good,' he said. 'So that's settled. You have my blessing.'

Smaragthi raised her head and lowered her eyes.

'No, Godfather.'

Fortis stared at her in astonishment.

'What do you mean, "no?" '

Smaragthi wanted to explain but she feared she would talk nonsense, because she did not know how to go about it. What she wanted to say, it was impossible for her to say to a man. So she merely tried to make him understand that she had no intention of ever getting married. Her godfather was not to regard this as silly, girlish talk. He must know that her freedom was her most precious possession.

This was her essential truth. Locked inside her was a passionate happiness which was bound up with her independence; with not being subjected to a husband and with the liberty to manage her life as she wished, just as she managed her boat. Yes, that was it. To hoist her red sail whenever she wished and head for the open sea over the laughing waves which splashed cool water over her face and hair. To have around her only the gulls and the blue above and below. To rule with the tiller and the halyards as the boat leaped over the waves.

How could she explain these things to other people when she did not have the words to express them and it was impossible for another person to get inside her and feel her longings? How could she speak of those folded wings, powerful but useless, which sometimes stirred in her soul? Oh, if only old Aunt Permahoula were alive to interpret these things to her! Whence blew the wind of which these slumbering wings dreamed?

Fortis departed discouragedly with bowed head. He could not understand her. He concluded that, for all her intelligence, her mind was still immature. Besides, it was not easy, it seemed, to reach an understanding with young people any more these days. It had been different in his time. Then they had respected a parent's judgement. He was thinking particularly of Lambis.

'To love them, to worship them, but not to know their language and for them not to understand yours. This was the greatest bitterness of all. This alone.'

Smaragthi lingered at her window a long time. She put out the lamp and gazed at the transfigured spring night. The sky had unfolded its glorious fan like a peacock's tail. The trees of Vigla outlined their slender forms against the velvet darkness. Multitudes of stars winked among the leaves on the upper branches like wondrous jasmine blossoms.

From her head Smaragthi took the net which held her hair in place and let the cool tresses fall around her neck. She felt silky moonbeams touch her hands and face.

'How much pain I gave Godfather tonight,' she thought, but without a trace of sorrow. Then she recalled Stratos' glowering face and wondered what she had done to offend him. For no reason at all, she felt weary.

Out in the fields she heard a turtle dove disturb the tranquillity of the night with its four notes. She listened to it with her eyes closed. The bird's call did not seem so desolate as usual but blended with the unearthly softness of spring like a nostalgic cry from the heart of the night.

Her hand chanced to touch the leaves of a musky plant in a flower-pot. Unconsciously she rubbed a leaf between her fingers. At once the whole night, the sky and the sea, the stars and her thoughts were perfumed with the fragrance. Gazing at the Mount, she breathed a deep sigh and murmured:

'Mermaid Madonna, make them all leave me to my peace and my poverty. I ask nothing more.'

51

S M A R A G T H I got used to the sponge boats anchoring beside hers, going off for as long as a day and a night and reappearing at the mouth of the harbour slowly and ponderously. She enjoyed the musical voices of men and the tales they told her of their strange life, which were like fairy stories.

One of the men was a giant for these parts. He was huge, with coal-black eyebrows that met above his nose. When he neglected to shave, nis beard sprouted as far up as his eyes. One looked at him, silent and ferocious as he was, and said: 'Holy Madonna, what a villain!' Actually he was awkward and shy. He said nothing because it was difficult for him to express himself. His name was Yakimis and his job was to turn the wheel of the air pump. He used one hand, for the other had only one finger, which pointed like a skewer.

'Dynamite?' Smaragthi asked him.

'Oh, no. That isn't our kind of work.'

He said this with such dignity that Smaragthi felt ashamed of her people, of Lathios and Manolis. She had not realized before that among the toilers of the sea methods of fishing are evaluated according to various standards.

'Then how did it happen?'

'A moray,' he replied tersely. He blushed with happiness because here was something he could talk about with her.

'A shameless fish. Or is it a serpent? It lurks in crevices and lies quietly in ambush. When a diver reaches out his hand to take hold of a rock, *crunch!* it cuts off the hand with one snap. It has fine, sharp teeth and jaws as hard as pincers.'

He hid his mutilated hand in his pocket. 'It's a rough life,' he remarked and could think of nothing more to say.

Uncle Trampados chatted for hours with Smaragthi. He also could joke about the most grim details in the work of sponge divers in African waters, under cruel captains who exploit them and treat them like slaves. Underfed from stinginess and the nature of the work, which permits little food and drink for divers, they drift about like vagabonds only to end up paralysed with the bends or devoured by sharks. 'What a man won't do to make a living. . . .'

Every time the divers came back from work, they brought Smaragthi some small keepsake. An unusual shell, a piece of coral or a petrified shrub, all gathered from the bottom of the sea for her favour.

'Beauty and the forty ogres!' said Uncle Trampados.

Achilles sometimes treated her as if she were a child. At other times he became confused in her presence and broke off in the middle of what he was saying, seized with such a fit of laughter that he could not finish. Smaragthi thoroughly enjoyed his laugh, which bubbled clear and spontaneous and made his strong teeth gleam like blanched almonds.

'Listen,' she said to him one day when they were talking together. 'You're educated like Uncle Avgustis. Will you tell me the meaning of this story? Once there was a little girl. Nobody knew who her father or mother were. She was brought up as a foundling by a fisherman. There was a dog named Kanellos. He was as big as a small donkey but was strong and gentle. He never bothered anyone. He belonged to a gardener and the children used to harness him to a box with pulleys for wheels. They would get into it and he would draw them about and never became angry when they tormented him. He would just wag his tail and whine and lick the hands that struck him. But when this Kanellos first saw the little girl, he became wild and fierce and tried to bite her. He leaped against the wire of the fence and tried to break through. The little girl did all she could to tame him. She threw him bones and crusts of bread without success. Each time, he became more and more enraged at the girl. One day he found her alone. He sprang on her and would have torn her to pieces if people hadn't managed to free her from his jaws. So it was until at last someone poisoned him and he died.'

'Didn't anyone ever find the reason for his hostility?' Achilles asked interestedly.

'No. But an old woman, more than a hundred years old, who had learned many things in her lifetime, said that this little girl was a mermaid and no child of woman. The dog sensed it and that was why he couldn't endure the sight of her and tried to kill her.'

After a brief silence, she said:

'You have read so many books, do you believe in sea nymphs?'

Achilles gazed out at the sea and smiled. Then he turned and looked at her tenderly.

'I've believed in them,' he replied, 'for three weeks now. . . .'

One day Uncle Trampados saw Achilles come up from diving empty-handed, except for a rosy shell with silver glints.

'I understand,' he said. 'You, my *pallikari,* will bring up such gewgaws from down there until you come up with . . . a marriage licence!'

Stratos, who was nearby, heard the remark.

Achilles blushed, for the whole crew was standing around taking it all in. He looked at his father in embarrassment. Then he saw a mocking smile behind his father's moustache. At once he burst into boyish laughter. This saved him in many tight situations.

When the divers were working in the shallows and Smaragthi had nothing to do, she would take some of Lathios's children with her in the boat and follow them from above. Stratos affected disdain for this kind of entertainment. His words frankly indicated a smouldering hatred for the Kalymniotes. Vatis, on the other hand, followed the divers' work with keen interest. He cultivated the divers to hear their bizarre tales.

He had grown taller, and his face had lengthened and become paler. His dreamy eyes seemed even larger under the mop of hair that shaded them.

'When I become a captain,' he said to Smaragthi one day, 'I'll have a sponge divers' outfit on my ship and a pump to send air down to me. I'll go deep, not like these men who drag themselves about along the shallows off Kaya. A thousand fathoms down. Two thousand fathoms. Where no one had ever set foot. You'll see.'

'And what will you do so deep down there?' the girl asked.

'Nothing,' he said defiantly. 'I'll walk about and enjoy whatever I find. I'll sit down under the trees of the sea and think. And if I bring anything up from there, it won't be little shells.'

'I know,' Smaragthi joked. 'You'll fetch us that mermaid of yours so we can dry her in the sun. . . .'

She repented when she saw the boy's soft eyes turned on her full of wounded pride. A flush spread over his face as if he had been slapped.

'Oh, come on,' she said. 'I was only teasing you. I'm sure you'll be a fine captain, even better than Odysseus or Sindbad the Sailor. But if you've set your heart on prowling under the sea, you'll do well to protect yourself. There are morays down there, you know. You've listened to Yakimis. . . .'

Vatis replied, his face tense:

'If you want to know, I'll wander about under the sea like Achilles Trampados, and even better.'

Smaragthi gave him a sharp look and said, without irony:

'Just grow up and become a *pallikari* yourself, even a better one, I hope, than Achilles Trampados.'

They were sitting on the breakwater as they talked.

'Do you ever think of grandmother?' asked Vatis. 'I think of her all the time.'

'Yes, I think of her all the time, too,' Smaragthi murmured. 'Why did you ask me?'

232 .

The boy shrugged his shoulders.

'It just came to me.'

She noticed that the boy's eyes were gazing at her bare legs. She drew them under her skirt.

'Grandmother loved you,' said Vatis.

Then after a silenced he added:

'And she loved me, too.'

'That's true,' said Smaragthi. 'We grew up under her eyes. We're like brother and sister, Vatis.'

Vatis picked up a bit of pumice and ground it to powder on the breakwater.

'But Stratos,' he said, 'doesn't love you any more.'

'I know it. But I don't know why.'

'Because he sees our Manolis so sad. He sighs and won't say what's the matter. I know what it is. And Stratos knows. And he offers himself as a sacrifice for our Manolis. That's why Stratos doesn't love you any more. He says your boat had made you conceited and that's why you won't get married. Stratos also talks about that sponge diver.'

Smaragthi interrupted him.

'Again? We agreed you'd never talk to me about such things again. You don't know anything. You're a child who has filled his head with a lot of things you've imagined and that aren't true!'

Her voice shook with indignation.

'No,' the lad said obstinately and ground the pumice emphatically. 'I understand what I'm saying. Everything. I know that Achilles Trampados is in love with you, and our Stratos heard his father say he will marry him to you and he came home and cried.'

Smaragthi started to get up.

'Again you're annoying me with this nonsense,' she said. 'It's my fault for sitting here listening to a stupid idiot like you!'

'I'm not a stupid idiot,' said the lad. 'And what I told you the other time was true. And . . . if anybody knew what I know about that Lambis affair . . .'

'Lambis?' asked Smaragthi in surprise.

'Yes, Lambis,' Vatis repeated hotly. 'What do the judges know or the Gadjales or Uncle Fortis or even you? You're all right off the track.'

He looked at Smaragthi challengingly and nodded his head with enigmatic significance.

'But if I wanted to . . .'

Smaragthi sat down again.

'What are you trying to say?' she demanded, at the end of her patience. 'It's the duty of any honourable person to lay his hand on the

Gospel and tell the judge what he knows.'

Vatis opened his mouth to speak but changed his mind. He threw what was left of the pumice into the sea in the direction of the Mount. When he heard it splash, he said:

'They found Lambis there. I think I see him falling from the Mount.'

'All imagination. Maybe the godfather is right. Maybe the Gadjales did kill him. They're capable of doing anything.'

Vatis replied vehemently:

'Smaragthi, if I wanted to, I could make you sit here with your mouth open this very moment, you who think I've made up the things I say!'

'Go ahead! Why don't you speak up like a man?'

Vatis regarded her proudly with a melancholy smile.

'Because I don't want to upset you, Smaragthi.'

'Me?'

'Yes,' he nodded and shifted his glance because he could not endure the green flame in her eyes.

Smaragthi laughed scornfully.

'You sit here and prattle to me like a little girl . . . and I take you seriously. . . .'

These thoughtless words wounded the lad deeply.

'Is that so?' he said. 'Well then . . . Lambis drowned himself on account of his self-respect and his love.'

'That's the limit!' Smaragthi taunted him. 'It was because the Gadjales beat him up for spying on Yana. As for you, my child, your mother's milk is not dry on your lips yet!'

Vatis looked at her through his half-closed eyes, nodding his head with the rhythm of her words. When she finished, he replied cuttingly:

'No, my lady, Lambis did not die because of Yana. Lambis never so much as glanced at Yana or any other girl. Because Lambis loved only you. And only on account of you he drowned himself.'

'Lies!' screamed the girl, shaking with terror. 'What you say are lies. Shameless lies. They come from your imagination. I know you. You're conceited, and you want to infuriate me because I refuse to listen to your nonsense. Isn't that so? Tell me, you insolent boy!'

She seized his sleeve and shook his arm. Her voice failed, and her whole body was trembling.

Vatis was filled with remorse. Confused, deeply contrite, he said tenderly:

'No, it isn't true. Forgive me, Smaragthi for . . . Well, you see. . . . Oh, I should have held my tongue . . . But I've kept to myself for so long what I know. And now . . .'

'But what *do* you know? Tell me what you know!'

'Listen, Smaragthi. What I know and what nobody else knows is that the Gadjales were mistaken to worry about Yana. Lambis came at night to lie in wait to see you. He climbed into the fig tree and waited up there for hours to see you. He didn't want you to see him. He did this every night. And every day he hid himself wherever you might go and he could see you. He hid among the cliffs of Vigla. He crawled through the thickets to watch you go by in your boat. He followed your footsteps, always hidden from your eyes. He loved you, Smaragthi. Oh, how Lambis loved you!'

The girl listened in bewilderment until the end. Then she burst out: 'Where did you learn all this? Did he tell you?'

Vatis looked at her obliquely and shook his head.

'Who? Lambis? You didn't know Lambis. He say anything? He was a man, Smaragthi! I know these things because I suspected them and trailed him without his knowing it. If he'd found out, he might have killed me. He was like that. . . . And that's the way it was the night the Gadjales beat him up. The great disgrace was that he was punished before your eyes. When he looked up and saw you . . . you didn't notice it. But I was there and I knew. . . .'

Smaragthi shuddered as she listened.

'Then he broke away and ran off through the night. I ran after him. At first he sat down on the shore and cried like a baby. Then he saw that broken anchor near him that had been thrown away. He unfastened it, put it on his shoulder and went up on the Mount of the Madonna. I didn't understand. I wondered why he wanted the anchor. I crept behind the chapel and waited for him to show himself again. He took a long time to come round the rock. Then all of a sudden I saw him standing on the edge, on the "balcony." Then I understood. I called out: "Lambis!" And he jumped. . . . Well, that's how it happened . . . and I'm the only one who knows it. But now you know it, too. . . .'

'You . . . why did you follow him?' the girl asked.

Vatis remained silent.

'I asked you why,' she repeated. 'Why didn't you tell?'

Vatis whispered:

'Because you told me never again to speak to you about those things. . . .'

Smaragthi got up and left, crushed. Her mind seemed about to crack. She shut herself up alone and tried to get hold of herself. The night passed in torment. She knew she could never lift her head again after this blow. She was moving towards some end without knowing yet what it was going to be. It was like walking barefoot through a stone passage cold and full of mist. She heard her naked feet strike the chilled stones, and she staggered as if she were drunk. The passage was endless, and the mist was never dispelled. She did not know what would be at the end, but she knew one thing with certainty. The end would be there. The *end*.

Early in the morning she went to Fortis's. He was astonished at her swollen eyes and distraught appearance.

'Haven't you slept well?' he asked her. 'Are you sick? Have you been crying?'

He led her inside and they sat down in the dining-room.

'What's the matter?' he asked. 'Tell me what it is, my daughter.'

Smaragthi sighed.

'I've come to stay with you, Godfather. I've been thinking how you have no one in the world. Nor have I. I'm alone. I shall come and take care of you. I shall never leave you, Godfather.'

Fortis grasped her hands.

'Bravo,' he said with emotion. 'Bravo, my daughter. I see you've reconsidered what I said to you. . . .'

'That . . . and the other things, Godfather. Many other things. I've left my house for ever. Starting today, I shall live here. And my boat . . . I'm giving up my boat, too. . . .'

'Your boat, too, Smaragthi?'

'Yes. I can never fish again. I intend to give our *Nerandji* to Manolis. He's a fine *pallikari* and deserves it. And the house will go to Maria's daughter.'

The old man listen in amazement. He could make no sense out of what he heard.

'What's going on?' he asked uneasily. 'Has something happened?'

Smaragthi patted his bony hand and attempted a smile to reassure him.

'Nothing, Godfather. I've just decided that fishing is not for a woman. I want to be a housewife like other women.'

In order to conceal her emotion, she stood up and began to put the rooms in order, chattering nervously about various matters.

The old man, dumbfounded, followed after her. They entered the little room that looked out on the square.

It contained a neatly-made iron bed, a small table with a lamp, a large heap of magazines, books, and copybooks. Above the pillow hung a small icon of the Madonna with a dried laurel branch from Palm Sunday. Near the window was an enamelled washstand covered with a clean, embroidered towel.

Smaragthi stood with the broom in her hand and looked around. Then she turned inquiringly to the old man.

'Yes,' said Fortis. 'This is his room. It's just as he left it that night when he never came back. . . .'

'Godfather,' said the girl, 'would you like it to be my room? From now on, I shall be your child and you will be my father. And I'll love you twofold. . . .'

She fell into his arms and they wept together.

52

N I G H T fell. Smaragthi lighted the lamp and gave herself up to her thoughts. She ransacked the books. As she leafed through a pile of American picture magazines to divert her mind, she came once more upon those pretty girls who flew like dancers through the air with their bare arms stretched out like wings and their hair streaming in the wake of their flight. Behind them were tall trees and fountains of water leaping to the sky. The girls appeared happy; their faces were smiling and they had spread their wings.

Long ago these pictures had filled her childish imagination with beautiful dreams. Now this was all so far away. Her own wings were for ever mutilated and paralysed.

She remembered watching, one day, some fishermen's children playing with a seagull. These half-naked, cruel youngsters had broken the gull's wings. They were screaming at it and prodding it to make it walk. The bird uttered no cry, although it must have been in frightful pain. It merely stopped in the midst of its torture, exhausted, looked at the sea, and then moved on, dragging its broken wings which scratched trails on the sand. . . .

Smaragthi put aside the magazines and rummaged through Lambis' books. Their old school books. Once she and Lambis had pored together over these smudged, maltreated pages. Lambis had soiled them with fingerprints and had defaced the angels with moustaches in the Sacred History text. His copybooks were in even worse condition. Between the lines of badly written words he had drawn caïques, rowingboats and all kinds of ships in full sail.

Then came blank leaves interspersed with two or three pages with writing on them. Here the letters were better formed, but the words, as always, were mis-spelled. This apparently had been written later, much later, after Lambis had grown up. A few sentences were left unfinished. One or two leaves had been ripped out.

She read:

'She was going to drown. I rescued her. I took her in my arms and rescued her. I wish I had died at once then. She scolded me. But she left me her red handkerchief. Now every night I shall spread it on my pillow and sleep on it.'

'Today I saw her again. She looked sad and I watched her from behind a tree. If I only could have gone to her.'

'Yesterday I dreamed of her all night.'

'The fig tree has begun to turn yellow. In a few weeks the leaves will fall. . . .'

'They say it isn't right for one to marry his god-sister.'

'. . . There is the handkerchief. There is also the blue hair ribbon I stole from her at school.'

'How beautiful you are! How beautiful you are! How beautiful you are!'

'Poor father, if you only know how much I love you!'

Smaragthi burst into tears. She laid her arms on the copybook, rested her face on her hands and sobbed. She wept for a long time, until she fell asleep face down on the table. Even in her sleep she wept.

Was this, then, the end?

At first a confused tempest of thoughts and emotions assailed her in violent waves. In this whirlwind her weak, defenceless, overwrought mind tottered on its foundations. Then, little by little, each day brought tranquillity. Out of the confusion emerged certain contours which finally received definite shape.

It was the figure of Lambis, now completely altered from the memory she had preserved. It was not a soothing light that relieved her torment. It came like a flash of lightning and instantly rent the sombre clouds. It was the flame that illuminates and sears.

There was no remorse, no nagging sense of involuntary guilt, no weakness or contrition. It was love, a mighty, genuine love that possessed her, violent and triumphant, to be henceforth the unswerving purpose of her life. Each day its roots pushed deeper within her, and it grew to an immense height, thrusting its branches into the silence and the darkness.

She alone would know it. She was proud that she would never have to share this love with anyone.

From now on, there would be only herself and her dead lover. Never would he disillusion her, because he would never touch her. Nevertheless, she felt him all around her; everything was saturated with him. In the little room, in his childhood copybooks, in the schoolbooks where his grimy fingers had left inky smudges. With bitter pleasure she collected, one by one, all her recollections of his life, the brief, ardent life which he was not destined to bring to maturity. She garnered them, arranged them in order, and saw them again in the terrible brightness of the passion that gave them meaning.

She now felt an insurmountable aversion for the sea. She no longer dared to look down into the clear water where the algae on the deep rocks spread out their filaments like the golden brown hair of drowned *pallikaris* and where certain plants are white like the ears of submerged corpses.

She dressed herself in black once more, never again to be laid aside.

'What's come over you?' asked Fortis. 'You're still a young girl and you're behaving like a widow!'

She liked this remark. She did not reply at once but treasured it within her like a precious discovery.

Then she said: 'It's because I've dedicated myself to the Madonna, Godfather.'

Her voice was grave, calm, and resolute.

Fortis knew her and said no more about it. Soon everybody in Skala and the fishing village and Mouria heard of it, discussed it, and finally accepted the fact of the girl's dedication.

Every day Smaragthi went up on the Mount and put the chapel in order, tended the lamp, and prayed before the strange icon.

And the Mermaid Madonna regarded her with her large, green eyes, motionless, wrapped in her mystery and her silence.

Always she held in one hand the ship and in the other the trident of Poseidon, and her fish's tail coiled itself, full of restless energy.

And from the caverns below, the voice of the sea rose, deep and sombre.